Weaver looked ~~sensor~~ data and tried not to flinch.

The good news was that given Dreen known accelerations, it was going to be at least eighteen hours before the main body of the unit arrived.

The bad news was, he now knew what a Dreen *fleet* looked like in sensor data.

One mega*grapper* ship. Six uberdreadnoughts. Nine Dreen production dreadnoughts. Three capital ships, emission type unknown, probably converts. *Seven grapping* carriers. Seven. That meant upwards of *four hundred* Dreen fighters. The rest were what were identified by humans and Hexosehr as cruisers, destroyers and frigates. Of course, a half dozen destroyers were considered a fair match for the *Blade II*.

Useful information, but there was no way in hell they were going to be able to show it to anyone. Not with over *sixty* Dreen warships in the system. Seven of the emissions were higher than any previously recorded, one of them was so immense he had to wonder if the Dreen used planetoids. It was a huge *grapping* emission for a ship. And it was definitely moving, albeit slowly.

Change that estimate to about an Earth day. But about thirty minutes after they arrived, every human on the space station would be dead.

CLAWS THAT CATCH

JOHN RINGO
TRAVIS S. TAYLOR

CLAWS THAT CATCH

Copyright © 2008 by John Ringo & Travis S. Taylor

A Baen Books Original

Baen Publishing Enterprises
P.O. Box 1403
Riverdale, NY 10471
www.baen.com

ISBN 13: 978-1-4391-3313-2

Cover art by Kurt Miller

First Baen paperback printing, December 2009

Distributed by Simon & Schuster
1230 Avenue of the Americas
New York, NY 10020

Library of Congress Cataloging-in-Publication Data:
    2008027066

Printed in the United States of America

10 9 8 7 6 5 4 3 2 1

DEDICATION

Dedicated to E.E. "Doc" Smith
and (cue music) **The Solar Beam**!

And as always:
For Captain Tamara Long, USAF
Born: 12 May 1979
Died: 23 March 2003, Afghanistan
You fly with the angels now.

JABBERWOCKY

Lewis Carroll

(from *Through the Looking-Glass and
What Alice Found There*, 1872)

'Twas brillig, and the slithy toves
    Did gyre and gimble in the wabe:
All mimsy were the borogoves,
    And the mome raths outgrabe.

Beware the Jabberwock, my son!
    The Jaws that bite, the claws that catch!
Beware the Jubjub bird, and shun
    The frumious Bandersnatch

He took his vorpal sword in hand:
    Long time the manxome foe he sought—
So rested he by the Tumtum tree,
    And stood awhile in thought.

And, as in uffish thought he stood,
    The Jabberwock, with eyes of flame,
Came whiffling through the tulgey wood,
    And burbled as it came!

One, two! One, two! And through and through
    The vorpal blade went snicker-snack!
He left it dead, and with its head
    He went galumphing back.

"And, has thou slain the Jabberwock?
    Come to my arms, my beamish boy!
O frabjous day! Callooh! Callay!"
    He chortled in his joy.

'Twas brillig, and the slithy toves
    Did gyre and gimble in the wabe:
All mimsy were the borogoves,
    And the mome raths outgrabe.

1

"So . . . what's with the different uniform?" Josh asked. "The Marines got a special one for making the worst mistake of your life?"

Second Lieutenant Eric Bergstresser fiddled with his tight collar and looked in the mirror over his shoulder at his brother.

"I'm an officer, now, you moron. Officers don't wear enlisted uniforms."

"Shiny," Josh said, tugging at the unaccustomed tuxedo jacket. "But you get to, like, rent them, right? Because, don't get me wrong, they look expensive."

Eric had once upon a time been promoted directly from private first class to sergeant. Winning the Navy Cross might have had something to do with it. Assuming that his next promotion, to staff sergeant, would be a long time coming, he'd invested in a set of the Marine Dress Uniform, just about the prettiest uniform the U.S. military services had to offer. And assuredly the most expensive that were made for junior enlisted.

He'd subsequently been promoted to staff sergeant rather quicker than he'd expected and then more or less ordered, by the President no less, to attend Officer's Candidate School. So the Enlisted Dress Uniform now resided in his closet until he could figure out what to do with it and he was fiddling with the collar of his new *officer's* dress blues while trying to ignore the fact that he was about to get married.

"No, you don't rent them," Eric replied. "And, yes, they're expensive. But with the visitors that we've got, I couldn't just turn up in greens."

Eric winced when he reminded himself of the guest list. Brooke's dad, thank God, was prior service. So when a few people made it known that they'd like to attend, and he'd seen who they were, he'd made it plain to Brooke's mom that, no, they could not be turned away.

Eric had been up to his hips in alligators when the additional guests were invited and hadn't found out for a couple of weeks. In a way he was glad. And even more glad that his tactical officer hadn't found out.

OCS had been a pain in the ass. It wasn't the chickenshit that had gotten him. He understood that. Marines were expected to maintain a high state of readiness at all times. Inspections were a part of daily life. Attention to detail was important in combat and to an extent even more so in space. Whether the Marine Officer candidates knew it or not, and while it was still Top Secret, the rumors were starting to go around, the Navy, and thus the Marine Corps, was about to transition from a "wet" service to a "space" service. Learning to fold your socks perfectly, first time, every time, was a way to develop the habit of doing the job right, first time, every time. Whether your socks were folded, in the end, really didn't matter. Whether you'd sealed your space suit did.

So Eric could handle the chickenshit and had. He'd been neat as a kid; Marine Corps boot camp had just put polish on. He knew the drills, which was why he rapidly made platoon guide. He could fire his weapon already, so he acted as a mentor to some of the candidates who, alas, could not hit the broad side of a Dreen dreadnought. He didn't even find the coursework hard. Most of the candidates were college graduates whereas he only had a high school education. But sometimes it seemed like college had made them stupider or something. And the new stuff, on particles and planetary environments, well, that was meat and drink to the job he'd been doing for two years.

What had been a pain in the ass was the instructors. He'd entered OCS with the absolute personal commitment to stand out as little as possible, glide through as easily as he could, get his bar and get back to work. The OCS instructors, however, had of course read his file. And while it didn't say *where* he got the Navy Cross, they weren't handed out in boxes of Cracker Jacks. And his file did note that he had two years in Force Recon.

The instructors did have a certain gate-keeper duty. Their job was to ensure that everyone passing through their course graduated as the finest example of Marine Officers possible. So whether it was that sense of duty, a dislike of "mustangs"—officers who had come up from the enlisted ranks—or just bloody-mindedness, the instructors seemed to pick him out from day one as one of the candidates they were going to *make* quit.

So it had been a pain. Not as much of a pain as Force Recon qual or Operator Combat Training, but a pain nonetheless. And in his opinion, an unnecessary one. He'd proven from day one that he was as good as any of the other candidates, better really. But nothing he did seemed to be good enough.

On the other hand, maybe it was time to quit mentally bitching. He'd been Distinguished Honor Grad so maybe the riding had a purpose.

But to suddenly get a message from home, right after the Crucible, that several guests had been added to what he'd hoped was going to be a very small and unnoticed wedding . . .

"Okay, try to explain this to me in terms I can understand," Josh said. "Who are these guys?"

Eric winced internally, again, and shrugged, again.

"Who's the biggest bigshot you can think of short of the President or Marilyn Manson?"

"I dunno," Josh said.

"That's who these people are," Eric replied. "One of the lower ranking ones is one of the very few guys alive to have gotten the Medal of Honor. Then there's the rest . . ."

"Okay, that one I get," Josh said, his eyes widening. "So why's he coming to *your* wedding?"

"Because God hates me," Eric replied.

God hates me, Captain William Weaver thought. *I should go back to being an astrogator. Hell, I should go back to being a scientist.*

Once upon a time, that is exactly what William Weaver,

Ph.D., had been. With doctorates in everything from engineering to astronomy, he'd been one of the corps of specialists, often referred to as Beltway Bandits, who solved problems for the military and other branches of the U.S. government, generally having acronyms that had an "A" on the end. NSA, CIA, DIA . . .

Which was why he'd been shanghaied one Saturday afternoon to explain physics to the National Security Council when an experiment in same had gone wrong.

Subsequent to the explosion in Orlando that had created the Chen Anomaly, he'd been blown up, shot, travelled to other planets, gotten stuck between universes and ended up saving the world. The Chen Anomaly, a black sphere that sat precisely where the University of Central Florida High-Energy Physics lab used to reside, had spawned a host of magical particles. The particles, at first referred to, incorrectly, as Higgs bosons, had the ability to link two particles and create a gate, one that looked very much like a mirror, between any two points. Some TV reporter had called them Looking Glasses and the name stuck. Since there were inactive bosons, apparently left over from some predecessor race, on other planets, the vast horde of particles spun out by the Chen Anomaly had created multiple gates to other worlds.

Some of those worlds were inhabited. Notably, some of them were inhabited by a species humans called the Dreen. The Dreen used biological forms for most of the processes humans used machines for and were apparently ravenously consuming Earth's corner of the galaxy. They'd linked to some of Earth's bosons and were intent on conquering the planet.

One of the bosons, however, had linked to a more friendly race called the Adar. About a hundred years ahead of humans in most sciences, the Adar had a weapon that could close the gates. The only problem being, it had to be shoved through one and if it went off on the wrong side it was going to destroy the sending planet. Though they had had a run-in with the Dreen as well, they'd chosen to go for stopgap measures rather than risk losing their planet.

Humans, with multiple attacks coming through and the Dreen seemingly unstoppable, had taken the chance. Weaver, with the help of a SEAL team and nearly a division of troops, had managed to get the device through the Looking Glass and saved the world.

The Adar also had a strange little device they'd picked up on one of the previously inhabited planets. The most they'd gotten it to do was explode on a very large scale. Weaver had figured out that rather than the suicide box it appeared to be, it was probably a drive system of some sort. After seven years, the humans and Adar had managed to create a warp ship with the little black box at the heart of it.

Along the way, Weaver quit being a Beltway Bandit and joined the side of light, taking a direct commission and, after lots of schools and several normal cruises, became the astrogator of that warp ship. Just before its first mission the Adar, who while technically and even philosophically advanced over humans still didn't quite get marketing, had named it the Alliance Space Ship *Vorpal Blade*.

Weaver had spent two tours as the *Vorpal Blade*'s astrogator and while both had been hair-raising and life threatening, he'd enjoyed the challenge. And, of course, he got to run around in space and see and do some really neat stuff.

But after the second cruise, when they'd finally located the Dreen, found another even more advanced race that was fleeing from them and generally gotten the *chither* shot out of themselves by a Dreen task force, he'd been offered a promotion to executive officer of the *Vorpal Blade II*. The latter had been entirely built by the new race, the Hexosehr, and was superior in every way to the original. So how bad could it be? Especially since the Navy threw in a wholly unlooked for promotion to captain. Hell, he could be looking at *commanding* the *Vorpal Blade* if he did a good enough job in the XO's slot.

But at the moment, that didn't look likely. If he couldn't get a few hundred rolls of . . .

"We're leaving in a week," Weaver said, as patiently as he could, to the woman on the other side of the counter. "If we don't have these supplies, experience tells me that our mission is going to go from possible to difficult if not impossible."

"Well, you're not getting them," the distribution clerk said, clicking her tongue. "For one thing, you're over budget on this class of item. For another, you're asking for our entire stock. I need to ensure that there's some for others, you know."

If she clicked her tongue one more time, Weaver was going to go all postal on her fat ass. She used that annoying tongue click as a grammatical mark. At the end of each sentence, "*click*," each comma point, "*click*." He'd been dealing with her for the last two months and he was going to strangle her if she didn't stop . . .

"This material is very *expensive* you know (*click*). And the last *two* times that your boat went out (*click*) you used up nearly your entire stock (*click*). *You* need to learn some *supply* discipline, Captain (*click*)."

Weaver tried to stop, but he was beginning to flinch in *anticipation* of her finishing a sentence. He felt like a hound dog that had been beat too much, no good for sniffin' *nor* treein'.

"And that is your final answer?" Bill asked, flinching at the fact that he'd actually asked for a reply. He'd *encouraged her* to . . .

"That is my final answer (*click!*). Unless you get a budget variance *and* authorization to entirely deplete the stock (*click*) the amount you've already drawn is the maximum you will be allowed. (*Click!*)."

Bill felt beaten. It wasn't that he couldn't find a way to get the variances and even the authorizations. The missions of the *Blade* were almost always of such high priority that variances were more or less automatic. But even if he got them, he'd have to deal with the click. That bloody, revolting, monstrous, infernal click! The horrid, wretched, ghastly, hideous, disgusting, VILE CLICK! THAT BLASPHEMOUS MONSTROSITY THAT ROSE FROM THE NETHER DEPTHS OF . . .

"Thank you very much," Bill said, nodding to her politely. "Have a nice day."

"I will (*click*)."

"You don't look so good, XO," Captain Prael said.

Captain Charles Prael was a submariner, and a good one. The previous skipper of the *Vorpal Blade* had been an aviator, a compromise reached among the admirals when it became obvious the navy was going to space. While the *Blade I* was built around a submarine, the former USS *Nebraska*, SSBN 739, there were aspects of both underwater and aerial maneuver to its actions. At least, that was the argument the carrier admirals had used. The argument had carried weight for several reasons, among which were that the carrier admirals were all former fighter jocks whereas the sub admirals were bubblehead geeks. In a way, it was right back to high school.

But Spectre had turned out to be a great CO for the mission. Each of the branches had their own priorities, cultural issues that seemed built right into the steel of their ships. And whereas with submariners, the boat *always* came first, fighter jocks were always willing to go to the mat. It was vastly unlikely that any submariner would have kept fighting the *Blade* after the pounding she took at the planet designated HD 37355. Their tendency would have been to back off and get fixed. Submariner tradition, due to the conditions under which they fought and especially since the days of Rickover, was that the boat came first.

Spectre, Captain Steven Blankemeier, though, was from the fighter tradition. No carrier ever shut down flight ops because they lost a bird. Hell, they wouldn't shut down unless they took so much damage they couldn't get planes on and off the deck.

On the other hand, at one point in the first mission, when they weren't all that far from Earth and had taken some damage, he was ready to turn around. That was what carriers did if they got dinged. They headed into port to get the dings hammered out. They'd finish the mission, if at all possible, but they'd head for home just as soon as it was done.

Submariners, though, just kept going until they had to return to port. They'd keep the boat running with spit and duct tape if that was what was necessary.

Spectre, in many ways, had set the tone of the culture of the Space Navy, a combination of submariner and carrier. The mission came first, damn the platform, came from the carrier side. Sink the carrier if you have to to take out the enemy. Damn the damage or equipment failures, keep going until your cruise was done or you were actively sinking came from the submarine side. The chief of the boat had coined the new motto: "We don't go home until we're out of food or bodies."

Prael wasn't an entirely unknown item. He'd taken over the helm almost three months ago. But how he'd deal in deep space was going to be interesting to find out. In the meantime, though, Weaver was going to have to confess to failure.

"I can't get supply to cough up any more 413, sir," Bill admitted. "I tried but the clerk wants variances on budget *and* authorization to release her full supply. The latter is stupid, frankly, because we're the only ship *authorized* to draw on that item."

"Ran afoul of Clerk Click, did you, XO?" the skipper said, grinning. Prael was a large man with an easy manner that belied years spent on the nuke side. Nuke officers tended to be OCD to an annoying extent, but when you're in charge of a nuclear reactor that is right on the edge of being a nuclear bomb, attention to detail is a survival trait. Prael had that in spades, but not the constant tension and didacticism that normally accompanied it.

"You know her, sir," Bill said. It was not a question.

"Oh, yes," Prael replied. "I can see you're already developing the twitch. Captain, you may be a fine astrogator and experienced in space combat. But you have much to learn about how the Navy *really* operates. I will admit, though, that it is part of my duty to teach you. Very well, XO, as part of your professional development, I will instruct you in the proper method for wheedling Clerk Click. First, you compliment her on her hair—"

"But her hair is thinning and that style is—"

"God awful," the skipper said, nodding. "Revolting. Disgusting. Compliment it. Then you ask how her dogs are getting on."

"Dogs?"

"Pomeranians. Fat, hairy piranha with teeth. She had eight last time I dealt with her," the CO replied. "Then you ask her if she's lost weight. She will then fill you in on the details of her newest diet. You have to agree to try it since it's amazing its effect."

"She's *lost* weight?"

"Never in my experience. Then and only then do you compliment her outfit. Since she appears to only have three such outfits, all equally revolting, in eye-searing colors that even the Adar would never wear, you have to lie through your teeth on that one. When you are done with complimenting her, listening to the latest medical horror story about her dogs or herself or both, when she is finished telling you to drink your own urine—"

"Surely not!"

"Then and only then do you bring up the particular item that you need her to authorize," the CO said.

"But . . . the . . ."

"Click. That God-awful, revolting, disgusting . . . annoying doesn't begin to cover it, click?"

"Yes, sir!"

"Captain," Prael said sternly. "You are a United States Naval Officer. Did John Paul Jones flinch in the face of English gunnery? Did Spruance back off at Midway? Did Dewey flee from the Spanish? No. Nor shall you flee that God-awful click, Captain! If it makes you feel any better, we're reasonably sure that the admirals, may their souls rot in hell, keep her in her position as a test of all XOs. To make CO, you have to be able to stand . . . The Click! If you can stand the Click, no lesser torture will do. But that is for tomorrow. Have you noticed the time?"

"Oh, Christ," Bill replied, accessing his plant. "I must have muted the alarm!"

"Or never noticed it in the face of The Click," Prael said, nodding. "It can do that. It's a most amazing sound. But we have other places to be. Right. Now. Dress fast."

"How's it going, son?" Steve Bergstresser asked.

"I'm ready to go," Eric replied, still fiddling with his collar button. It was that or stand around twitching.

"Come 'ere," his dad said, turning him around. He touched his son's cummerbund into place and pulled a probably imaginary bit of lint off the spotless uniform. "It's going to be fine. Admittedly, the chapel is packed . . ."

"Oh God," Eric groaned. "Dr. Pierson is going to have a heart attack! He can't afford a wedding this big."

"Dr. Pierson is a former submariner," Mr. Bergstresser said. "He's practically bubbling over. He's got three admirals and the commandant attending. It's the first time I've ever seen a father of the bride *happy* about paying for a wedding."

"I just wish it was over," Eric replied.

"A common problem," Steve said. "Weddings are for brides."

"And honeymoons are for grooms," Josh added with a grin.

"Watch your tongue, young man," Mr. Bergstresser snapped. "All that the groom is required to do is show up on time."

"And reasonably sober," Josh added, apparently unrepentant. "That's your problem, Eric. You're sober. I've got some moonshine . . ."

"Quit playing the West Virginia hick, Josh," Eric said. "It doesn't go with the earring and the Goth look."

"It's time," Second Lieutenant Burt Tomlinson said, sticking his head in the room. The newly minted lieutenant was one of Eric's fellow candidates, a group of whom were attending the wedding and acting as ushers.

"Don't lock your knees," Eric's dad said as they headed for the door. "You'll pass out."

"They teach us that in Basic, Dad," Eric replied. "And again in OCS."

"Yeah, and this is one time you'll forget. And try not to stand rigidly at attention. It makes you look nervous."

"I've got two ways to stand when I'm wearing a uniform,

Dad," Eric said. "Attention or parade rest. Take your pick."

"You know," SEAL Chief Warrant Officer Third Miller whispered as Weaver slid in next to him, "arriving after the bride could have permanently killed your career."

Miller had first met Dr. Weaver when the latter was sent to examine the then-new Chen Anomaly and figure out what was going on. He'd been caught in most of the resulting mess and suffered most of the resulting experiences. Along the way he'd developed a degree of admiration for the academic who was caught up in normal SEAL derring-do. Weaver hadn't quit, hadn't laid down, and just kept coming, no matter what the universe, gates and the Dreen threw at him. It also helped to have some-one as smart as Dr. Weaver around when the problem wasn't something you could shoot or blow up.

More or less shanghaied for the first mission of the *Vorpal Blade*, Miller had been less thrilled about *Commander* Weaver. Weaver's commission and advance-ment didn't just smell of special privilege, it absolutely *reeked* of it. But, again, Weaver had been a good choice for the position of astrogator. The *Blade* ran into a lot of strange stuff between the stars and Weaver, with some assistance, had managed to figure out a way through over and over again.

Captain Weaver was getting to be a bit much, though. Captains were supposed hoary old salts with eyes wrinkled from decades spent squinting into the sun. Admittedly, neither he nor Weaver was a spring-chicken, but Weaver had somehow managed to keep a boyish look, and boyishness, despite all the stuff they'd both seen and done. Looking at him in uniform, people sometimes wondered if he'd stolen his dad's for dress-up.

"What did Two-Gun do to deserve all this brass?" Weaver replied.

From what Weaver had gathered, both Berg and his bride-to-be were popular in their hometown but since the wedding was relatively far from home, neither had the sort of universal showing you would expect. Despite that, the small chapel was packed out.

On the bride's side were her family and the parents of her three maids of honor. They fit in the two front rows. On the groom's side, his family and a couple of friends from home also filled the two front rows.

But immediately behind them was the sort of brass you'd expect at a major military wedding. Three admirals, ranging from the Chief of Astronautic Operations, Admiral Greg Townsend, to a newly minted two-star named Blankemeier, the Commandant of the Marine Corps, and the brigadier in charge of Force Recon. Each was accompanied by his wife. Behind them was a row of aides, including the Navy captain who was the aide to the CAO. Behind them was a row of ladies, presumably the wives of the newly minted lieutenants doing usher duty. Then more Marines, with a sprinkling of sailors, spilling over to the bride's side.

"The way I got it, Spectre asked for the day off to attend a wedding. He's working for Greg Townsend now so Greg asked who was getting married. When the CAO said he was going to the wedding, the rest figured it was mandatory. Well, except Spectre. And the commandant."

Since the end of the Dreen War—and the more or less simultaneous end of the War on Terror as the mujahideen fed themselves to the Dreen in profligate numbers—there hadn't been many opportunities for the military to excel. At least known opportunities. The still Top Secret *Vorpal Blade* project was the exception. The Marines and sailors of the *Vorpal Blade* had faced more threats than any five divisions of regular troops over the last two years. And the casualty rates had been on the same order.

In other times and other wars it might have been unusual to see the space version of the Chief of Naval Operations and the Commandant of the Marine Corps turn up for the wedding of a Marine second lieutenant, no matter how decorated. But Two-Gun Berg was, by far and away, the best known of the Marine security contingent of the *Blade*. As such he was something of a celebrity within a very small and very black community. It didn't hurt that he was a damned nice kid.

"I mean, let's just do the list, shall we?" Miller whispered. "Stopped the crabpus attack on Runner's World while it was eating up the rest of the Marines like so much popcorn. Saved the conn of the *Blade*, more or less single-handed. Did the drop on Cheerick. Point man into the Dragon Room. Just about the last man standing in same. The guy who found the sole survivor of the HD 36951 colony. Point man in multiple EVAs on same mission. The guy who figured out how to survive the entry of the Dreen dreadnought. Killed a rhino-tank at short range, more or less single-handed. Last but not least, the guy who *captured* the aforementioned dreadnought, again single-handed."

"Hey, I was there for most of that!" Weaver whispered

back. "So were you, and closer. And it wasn't exactly single-handed."

"Quit mucking with my narrative," Miller said. "Alvin York wasn't exactly by himself. The point is the story that's become Two-Gun Berg, the guy who keeps going into the fire and emerging unscathed. That is why the CAO, the commandant and ComLinSpac are here. Partially, it's in homage to a fine Marine, partially, I think, that they're hoping some of his luck, and a lot of what he did came down to luck, wears off on them. The brass that have seen the intel estimates must be shitting a brick."

"Which just makes the next mission that much more important," Weaver said. "Speaking of which, you haven't been in the meetings."

"Meetings of my own," Miller said disgustedly. "There's much black discussion of what to do about SEALs these days. I'm not on the next mission. I'm going to have to attend a four-day Conceptualizing Event called 'Whither SEALs.' The upside is, it's in Maui. So you're on your own this time."

"Shhhh," Weaver whispered as the organist, who had been doodling along with various light music, suddenly shifted to the "Wedding March."

"Let's hope this goes off without a hitch," Miller nonetheless whispered back as a tall, blond girl entered the room holding the arm of her father. "I know people are going to take it as an omen, one way or the other."

Eric, frankly, didn't remember much of the ceremony. He remembered seeing Brooke and thinking that she was just about the most beautiful thing he'd ever seen in his life and then he was kissing her. All the bits in the middle were missing. He'd experienced the condition in combat before. One of the dozens of psychologists everyone on the missions had to talk to in after-action reviews had used the term "lack of ego awareness." Things happened and then it was over. He apparently got his bits right.

Normally, the bride was the first person out of the chapel. In this case, after the twosome paraded down the altar at the direction of the chaplain who ran the small facility, everyone else filed out first. When the chapel was clear, he and Brooke were directed to leave.

He took Brooke's arm and they walked down the aisle. He tried like hell to ignore the fact that the commandant was watching them. He also realized that he was walking so stiffly his legs were barely moving.

When they exited the chapel the reason for the change became obvious. His fellow OCS cadets had formed a sword-arch outside the doors. He and Brooke walked through the aisle to cheers and a bit of boozy breath; the cadets had clearly started partying early.

He helped Brooke into the limousine, then more or less tumbled in behind her.

"Was this shiny?" he asked quietly. Brooke was looking a little frozen.

"It was great," she replied, her face breaking into a smile. Then she threw her arms around his neck and kissed him, hard. "Perfect. I love you."

"I love you, too," Eric said, finally able to breathe.

"I was just surprised at some of the people," Brooke said. "I didn't want to get anything wrong in front of your bosses."

"Those people are my bosses the way that Bill Gates is the boss of a lowly Micro-Vac programmer," Eric said. "I'm not even going to *try* to figure out why they asked to attend. All we have to do is survive the reception and we're *out* of here."

"You just want to do more than what my mother refers to as 'spooning,'" Brooke said, grinning.

"I just want to get out from under the gaze of the commandant," Eric said, smiling back. "Not to say that I'm not looking forward to tonight."

"And no alcohol for *you* at the reception," Brooke said, crawling onto his lap. "At least that's what Mom suggested."

"'Wine giveth the desire but taketh the ability,'" Eric quoted.

"Is that from the Bible?" Brooke asked.

"Close," Eric replied with a grin. "Shakespeare."

"Captain," Admiral Townsend said, nodding at Weaver.

"Admiral," Weaver replied.

The reception had turned into an odd affair. Held at the Quantico Officers' Club, it was buffet style with tables and chairs but no defined places. It had started off rather aggressively split between the civilian attendees and the military. That slowly changed as it became evident that many of the civilians, the male ones at least, were former military. The town Eric and Brooke derived from had more than its share of veterans and while they tended to avoid the "brass," they had been more than willing to seek out the more junior officers, and the few enlisted permitted for this occasion on hallowed ground, for conversation.

The ladies, on the other hand, had completely ignored the civilian/military divide. Which had Brooke's grandmother, who, with only few exceptions had never left the confines of a small West Virginia town, in deep conversation with Mrs. Admiral Townsend, both of whose children had been born outside the contiguous United States, one in Hawaii and one in Japan.

"I'm waiting for someone to ask why we're all here," the CAO said.

"You're looking at the wrong captain, sir," Weaver replied. "I've spent more than half my total career in black operations. I don't ask questions unless they're germane."

"Touché," Townsend said, chuckling. "I'd forgotten you were in the black community before you got shanghaied."

"I wouldn't call it shanghaied, sir," Weaver replied, shrugging. "I volunteered."

"I talked to Jim Bennett, who in case you didn't know it was the guy who greased your skids," the admiral said, referring to a former Chief of Naval Operations. "He said he knew from the beginning that there wasn't a Naval officer who was going to be right for the *Blade*, one who really understood space. One choice was pulling back one of the Navy officers with NASA. But most of them were more expert at near-space, which wasn't going to get us anywhere. Then there were some officers associated with the Observatory, but they were a bit . . ."

"Geekish?" Weaver asked.

"Probably the best way to put it," Townsend admitted. "But the SEAL after-action reports from the Dreen War indicated that you were anything *but* geekish. Bennett quietly arranged, without either you or

Columbia realizing it, to pull you off the project over and over again, figuring you'd get fed up and try another tack. When you volunteered, it fit his plans exactly."

"So I was *manipulated* into becoming an officer?" Weaver asked, aghast. "He could have just *asked*."

"Probably what I would have done," Townsend admitted. "But Jim was a bit more Machiavellian than I. Anyway, just thought you should know."

"Shiny," Bill said. "Somehow that gives me the courage to ask. Are you all here because Berg is a really nice kid or for some other reason?"

"Oh, Berg is a nice kid," Townsend admitted. "But the President wanted to come and couldn't. So he ordered me and the commandant to attend. Spectre was coming, anyway. Everybody else? I think they just assumed if we were attending . . ."

"It must be mandatory," Weaver added with a chuckle. "More or less what Chief Miller said, except for the first bit."

"What the President doesn't realize is that this could have been a disaster," the CAO continued. "On many levels. One of them being curiosity. So far the press hasn't asked why we're all here. They still may. They're getting closer and closer to the truth."

"I saw the article in the *Washington Times*, sir," Bill said. The "Inside the Ring" column speculated, based on a number of data items, that the U.S. either had a space drive or was approaching having one. An earlier article had reported from "an anonymous source" that the Dreen had been located in real space and were somewhere near the Orion stars. That had probably come from the destruction of the HD 36951 colony. But with all the money that was going towards planning the Space Navy, the appointment of the CAO, the changes in training for every branch of the Navy . . . The reality was bound to break sooner or later. "I think the President's playing a very dangerous game in not releasing the information."

"He's the Commander-In-Chief," the CAO responded. "It's up to him, not us."

"Understood, sir," Bill replied. "Just my opinion as a citizen, not an officer."

"And one thing to learn as an officer is that that is a very fine line," the CAO said. "That was not a reaming, just pointing it out. You skipped a bunch of steps in your professional development and that might not have gotten through to you. We may have private political opinions, especially those based on our proprietary knowledge. We may voice them with close friends and peers. But we don't act on them except in the privacy of the ballot box. Among other things, even when we think we have the knowledge necessary to make a decision, often we're not privy to everything."

"Yes, sir," Bill said, trying not to smile. "And the officers who clearly have too many friends in the press corps?"

"If I find them, I will quietly move them out of any position of proprietary knowledge at all," the CAO said. "I'd, frankly, prefer to move them to Davy Jones's Locker, but there is so much paperwork involved in something like that. Diego Garcia will have to do. But so far the details are holding. So far. I should leave."

"Excuse me, sir?" Bill said.

"Young Bergstresser appears to want to introduce his bride to you," the CAO said, gesturing with his chin.

The bride and groom were circulating and being congratulated. Weaver had been watching one of the bridesmaids, a particularly pulchritudinous example of womanflesh, and hadn't noticed Berg and his bride getting closer and closer. As he glanced over, though, he caught a flash of Two-Gun looking their way and it was obvious he was unwilling to approach with the CAO there.

The next time Berg looked up, Weaver caught his eye and gestured with his head for him to come over. Berg's glance at the CAO was clear so Weaver repeated the gesture.

"Sir, Two-Gun has faced some of the worst monsters in the Galaxy," Weaver said as the bride and groom approached. "He can face the Chief of Astronautic Operations."

"Admiral Townsend," Berg said, nodding formally at the CAO, "may I present my bride, Mrs. Eric Bergstresser."

"Of course, Lieutenant," the CAO said, taking Brooke's hand and bowing to kiss it formally. "Mrs. Bergstresser, you are a vision. It is said that every bride is beautiful but you exceed all expectations."

"Thank you, sir," Brooke said, blushing.

"I know that you feel you've picked the finest man on earth to marry," the admiral continued. "And I agree. Sometime, sometime quite soon, you will be finding out just how extraordinary this young man is."

"Does that mean that his missions won't be . . ." Brooke's forehead furrowed for a moment then she shrugged. "I think the term is 'black'? Eric won't really talk about what he does."

"He can't," the CAO said, nodding. "I'm sorry for that but that's the rule and I'm glad to hear that he's following it. But, yes, pretty soon the operation will go white. How soon, I'm not at liberty to divulge."

Weaver's ears perked up at that. One bit of information that the CAO clearly had, and Bill did *not*, was that the decision to go white *had* been made and there *was* timing on it.

"But when it does, all will become clear," the admiral continued. "Including what an extraordinary man you've married."

"I already know he's extraordinary, sir," Brooke said. "But thank you."

"Two-Gun," the admiral said, "you've got a week. Use it well."

"Yes, sir," the lieutenant said, nodding. "Can I get a hint?"

"We're becoming archaeologists," Weaver replied. "I think that's indirect enough, isn't it, sir?"

"Just fine," the CAO said. "Archaeological mission, Lieutenant. Should be routine."

"Our normal routine, sir?" Berg asked, trying not to grin. "Or 'routine' routine?"

"Routine routine," the CAO answered. "But we never know, do we?"

"No, sir, we don't," Eric admitted. "And, Brooke, this is Commander Weaver. I told you about him."

"It's a pleasure to finally meet you, sir," Brooke said, looking him up and down. "You don't look like . . . what I expected."

The CAO barked a laugh at that and shook his head.

"People tend to say that," Bill replied. "They generally expect someone older and with less hair. And, please, call me Bill."

"Actually, I was wondering that you're not ten feet tall and breathing fire," Brooke corrected, grinning. "Bill."

"In that case, Eric has been exaggerating," Weaver said. "I have to add my compliments to the admiral's. You are truly stunning. Eric is a very lucky guy."

"That I am, sir," Berg said.

"What are your plans?" the CAO asked. "And to be clear, I'm referring to *after* the honeymoon."

"I've secured off-post quarters, sir," Eric replied. "Brooke will be occupying those and intends to apply for college."

"Well, it'll be easier to survive on lieutenant's pay, that's for sure," Townsend said. His aide whispered in his ear for a moment, then handed over a message form. The admiral read it, his expression unchanging, then looked up and smiled. "I hope you both do well. The captain and I, however, have a previous appointment."

"Yes, sir, I understand," Berg said, tugging at Brooke's arm. "Thank you for coming."

"Get Admiral Blankemeier and General Holberg," Townsend said to his aide. "I'll take Captain Weaver in lieu of Captain Prael. Is transportation laid on?"

"Yes, sir," the Navy captain said.

"Let's do this."

"May I ask what my previously scheduled event is, sir?" Bill asked quietly.

"We have to go to Camp David," the CAO said. "There's a meeting there in the morning. It seems the Russians *and* the Chinese are aware of the *Blade*."

❊ ❊ ❊

"Who is the girl with the blue hair?" Brooke asked, gesturing with her chin to a girl in a skimpy black dress dancing with a tall, incredibly stiff Marine. The girl looked to be in her early twenties and had bright red hair with a shock of blue dye at the front. "Is that a girlfriend I should know about?"

"We went out clubbing, once," Eric replied. "But girlfriend would be stretching it. She's a linguist, a really good one. Sort of a savant."

"I'm not sure what that means," Brooke admitted.

Eric thought of the linguist in the Cavern of the Dragons, stretching out her hand and directing the opening of the gates. Nobody had been able to figure out the puzzle, but it was as if the linguist was God-touched in some way. She certainly was strange enough.

"I'm not sure I can explain it, either," Eric admitted. "But she's special. Not retarded special, the other way. Gifted. Almost scary sometimes. We work with a lot of top-flight people but Miriam's . . ."

"I can see you like her," Brooke said, tightly.

"Not that way," Berg replied, grinning at her. "She's *way* too weird for me. But, yeah, I like her and admire her. Same deal with the guy she's dancing with. Sergeant Lyle. We call him Lurch cause he's so messed up. And tall."

"That's not very nice," Brooke said.

"Worse than you think," Eric said. "He got that way in a roll-over. Spent most of a year in therapy then nearly as much time convincing the Marines to let him back on active. *Then* he went back through Force Recon qual and operator training to get in the line units. Gotta admire that much determination. Good operator."

"And that means what?" Brooke asked. "For that matter, what are quarters? You said something about 'securing quarters.' I figure you don't mean the coins . . ."

"Quarters are where you live," Berg said, pulling Brooke towards the twosome. "Securing off-post quarters meant I got us an apartment."

"Why not just say you got an apartment?" Brooke asked curiously.

"It was the CAO," Berg replied. "That's how we talk. You'll get used to it."

"Two-Gun," the tall sergeant said. "And his lovely wife. Do I get a kiss?"

"Of course," Brooke said, lifting up on her tiptoes to kiss him on the cheek. He still had to bend over. The sergeant was tall and thin as a rail but with a wiry toughness that was apparent even in formal attire. "You're Mr. Lyle?"

"Sergeant Lyle," the sergeant said. "But you can call me Lurch."

"And this is Miss Moon," Berg continued, gesturing to Miriam.

"Miriam," the linguist said, shaking Brooke's hand then giving her a hug. "I'm so glad you two are together. You seem *so* right for each other. You're staying in Newport?"

"Norfolk," Berg corrected. "Housing in Newport is impossible. I was looking at a small house, but an apartment made more sense."

"I haven't even seen it, yet," Brooke admitted.

"Not how it's supposed to go, Two-Gun," Lyle said. "Wives are in charge of quarters."

"I'm letting her get her feet on the ground," Berg admitted.

"I wonder what sort of officers' wives club the new CO's going to run," Lyle said. "I heard it was pretty good under Mrs. Spectre."

"Just have to find out," Berg said. "But, again, I'm going to let Brooke get used to the whole idea first."

"What is an officers' wives' club?" Brooke asked. "I'm getting a bit lost here."

"The military is a specialized culture with a tremendous number of traditions," Miriam said, looking at her almost sorrowfully. "As with any subculture, it has its own language and customs. Some of them are unnecessary holdovers from days when it was often physically separated from civilization or at least its home civilization. Think of Army officers and their families stationed in cavalry outposts on the Great Plains or the Naval officers stationed in the Phillipines or even Hawaii before it became fully developed. Surrounded by strangers, many of them hostile and all of them from societies that were alien. The only social life they had was their own kind.

"Then there is the fact that military families face stresses unfamiliar to the culture that produces them. Police officers and firefighters face as many risks and during times of peace even more than the military. But if a firefighter or policeman is injured or killed in the line of duty, the families find it out almost immediately. And the officer's commander is there to bring the bad news.

"With the military, death or injury can occur so far away that it takes time for information to reach the families. And there is the unknowing. The waiting for news, good or bad, and so often convincing yourself that it's going to be bad."

"That I know about," Brooke said, finally really getting it. "I met Eric just before his last mission. And I was on pins and needles waiting for word."

"Quick work, buddy," Lyle said, doing the math.

"I asked her to marry me as soon as we got back," Berg said, grinning. "She made the mistake of saying yes. And almost the whole time, since, I've been in OCS."

"That sort of separation is normal in the military, unfortunately," Miriam continued. "Civilians don't have to put up with it, normally, and find it very strange. They don't understand the stresses even if they try to be nice about them. Often, they don't understand why the spouse puts *up* with them. So the military tries to help, often doing the opposite, with spouse support groups. They're generally organized by the commanding officer's wife, one of the duties that you'll have to take over if Eric ever reaches that lofty state. Sometimes there are severe generational clashes, but those are fading. There are always societal clashes, especially with newlyweds. Newly wed spouses often don't understand the point. That is, until they need the support of people like them. And, of course, as with anything bad leadership can make something like that truly horrible. In which case, they're generally voluntary."

"Yeah, but if she decides she's going to sit it out, a bad CO's wife will go complaining to her husband," Lyle pointed out. "Sometimes you can have a great CO and a horrible wife. Or the other way around. I knew one unit that wished its boss and his wife could change places. Nobody knew why she put up with the bastard."

"Eric, do you want to be a career officer?" Miriam asked. "Do you want to do twenty years and retire as a colonel? Or do you want stars?"

"I got all of that but stars," Brooke said.

"She's asking if I want to be a general," Berg said. "Sure, I mean I've thought about it. Who doesn't? But I'm not sure if I'm going to even re-up as an officer. I more or less have to do four years, but . . ."

"Brooke, would you prefer that he just do four years then get out?" Miriam asked, turning to the bride. "Or do you want him to be a general? Do you want him to wear stars?"

"I want him to do whatever will make him happiest," Brooke said.

"I feel the same way about Brooke," Berg interjected.

"Then, Brooke, you have to decide if you want to be Mrs. General Bergstresser," Miriam said, gesturing to the commandant's wife, who coincidentally was chatting with Brooke's mom. "If you do, behind every successful person is a strong spouse. Officers are no different, be they male or female. You have to decide if you're willing to play the political game and back your new husband, often at your own expense. There are tremendous sacrifices that military families make, long separations, bad housing, often a degree of hostility from the local community and lower pay than they can generally get in the civilian world. You'll spend years raising your children on your own, knowing your husband often as a stranger who drags in a bag of dirty laundry and leaves as soon as it's done. And if he continues in the vein he's chosen so far, never knowing when you'll get a call from his CO saying that he won't be coming home. A casket filled with parts will be lucky;

more likely it will just be weighed down with sandbags. And even if you have played the perfect wife, which will often be at the expense of whatever career you've chosen, you'll have lost the game. And you'll have little or no control of how that game's been played."

"This is a great conversation for a new bride to hear," Lurch complained.

"Mrs. Commandant probably had something she was planning on doing today," Miriam pointed out, shrugging. "Because her husband, for whatever reason, decided to attend this event, she had to give up her plans. It's the sort of thing he *had* to bring his wife to. And she *had* to go. Or he'd never have made commandant. And now he's leaving, without her."

"What?" Berg said, looking over at the door. The senior brass were quietly filing out, followed by their aides but not their wives. Weaver was with them, as well. But not Miller who was holding up the bar and apparently telling war stories. But he caught the exit, Berg could tell.

"That bodes poorly for us," Lurch said. "Because that looks like an emergency exit."

"And an emergency for the Gods eventually becomes our emergency," Berg said. "But I'm not even in-processed. So if you end up launching tomorrow, I won't be there."

"Be a shame to launch without our good-luck talisman," Lurch said, grinning. "But if we gotta . . . Oh, hell, I haven't had pre-mission, yet."

"Pre-mission on the cruise again?" Berg said, wincing. "I know that's going to be my lot. Just once I'd like to get pre-mission in in the normal timeframe."

"I, however, have had pre-mission," Miriam said, smiling.

"I wheedled it out of Dr. Chet as soon as we knew a mission was coming up."

"You're supposed to be in lock-up," Berg said, frowning.

"Different rules for technical specialists," Miriam said. "Brooke, you look as if you're still processing what I told you."

"I am," Brooke admitted. "And trying to catch up with the language."

"I can give you a dictionary," Miriam said, smiling. "I wrote it after the first mission. Nothing that violates operational security, but it might help."

"If you would, please," Brooke said, nodding.

"I'll e-mail it to you," Miriam replied. "Have you given any thought to it?"

"I sort of already did," Brooke said. "Eric and I were . . . Well, we were sort of on a date when he got a call and had to go."

"The term for which is 'recalled,'" Miriam said. "I was supposed to be presenting a paper that day; I remember it well."

"And then I didn't know what was going to happen," Brooke said, frowning. "I got one short message from him and sent him one."

"And did you talk to your friends, to your mother, about it?"

"Yeah," Brooke admitted. "And my friends . . ."

"Didn't get it," Miriam said. "And thus we're back to the spouse association. The point of such an organization, a well run one anyway, is that they *do* get it. There's a lot of claptrap associated with it, stupid parties that are sincerely lacking in men; dresses and hats and gloves, fortunately, have mostly gone the way of the dinosaur. But the point, under all the formality and the social overlay, is a group of people who are stuck in an unusual situation and have to adapt to it. A situation that the people outside that group, the friends they had back home for example, generally don't 'get.'"

"I get it," Brooke said, grinning. "What does your spouse, who I presume isn't military, think about it?"

"What spouse?" Miriam asked, holding up her left hand. Other than a ring in the shape of a spider on the middle finger it was unadorned.

"And, uh, you go on these . . . missions?" Brooke asked.

"I promise I won't steal your husband, Brooke," Miriam said softly. "He's a very nice guy and you make a great couple. But, frankly, he'd bore me to tears in a month, no more."

"Well thank you very much," Berg said.

"Two-Gun, you're a very nice young man, but you are very young and although you're very smart you're also very focused," Miriam said. "And not in areas I find interesting. From where I stand, that adds up to booooring."

"What about me?" Lurch asked when the group stopped laughing.

"Nice boy-toy, maybe," Miriam said. "Less than a month. Weekend at most. No, three hours. Max."

"You're very . . . frank," Brooke said.

"Only when it doesn't hurt people," Miriam replied. "Sergeant Lyle, were you hurt by that comment?"

"Not a bit," Lurch said. "You're pretty, but I've been around you when you're bored. No thank you. Crazier than a ferret on catnip."

"And the new ship doesn't have any pipes to paint!" Miriam wailed.

"You guys are nothing but in jokes," Brooke said. "Can you at least explain that one? And why people call him Two-Gun?"

"Gentlemen," the President said, shaking the admirals' and generals' hands. "Thank you for coming. Some introductions are in order. Bob?"

"Gentlemen, General Wang Zhenou, Army of the People's Republic of China," the national security advisor said, gesturing to an Asian gentleman in a polo shirt and jeans. "General Anatoly Karmasov, Russian Army," a short, heavyset man in country and western wear that looked a tad ludicrous, "and General Amjit Meennav," a tall, slender and dark skinned man in Sikh dress.

"Admiral Townsend, Chief of Astronautic Operations, and Admiral Blankemeier, Director of Astronautic Operations. General Holberg, Commandant of the Marine Corps. Captain Weaver, Executive Officer of the Alliance Space Ship *Vorpal Blade*. And, of course, Colonel Fordham-Witherspoon, of Her Majesty's British Government."

"And so we are gathered," the President said as a steward served coffee. "General Wang, would you care to lay out your initial statement?"

"The People's Government finds it unacceptable that the United States has concealed the ability to not only defy gravity but fly into space from the peoples of the world," the general said gruffly. "This is a direct insult to the People's government and all governments who believe in sovereignty and respect between nations."

"If you truly believed in sovereignty then you would not raise an issue with another country concealing such a thing," the Indian said in an Oxford accent to the Chinese general. "So your response seems somewhat hypocritical. What you really mean is you want it and you're trying to pressure the Americans to give it to you."

"I have a point of order," the Russian general said in a thick accent. "The Motherland's government has had knowledge, for some time, that our dear neighbors to the south were aware of the dastardly experiments on the part of the Americans. However, I am wondering why my esteemed colleague from the sub-continent is present."

"In other words, our subs weren't chasing the Americans so how could we know?" the Sikh asked. "At the insistence of their British 'colleagues,' the Americans brought us in on the secret some two months ago. And it's a bit broader than you're aware. So I would suggest you hold all your bluster and opening arguments for a later time, because, in the Adar vernacular, we are seriously *grapped*."

"Captain Weaver?" the President said. "I understand you prepared a briefing?"

"Actually, an overworked lieutenant commander in AstroOps prepared it, sir," Bill said, standing up. "I'm just giving it. Gentlemen, I give you the Alliance Space Ship *Vorpal Blade* Mod One," Weaver said, keying on the screen.

"One?" the Russian asked, sitting up.

"Oh, don't tell me you haven't noticed the changes," Bill said. "Your intel corps is better than that. The *Vorpal Blade One* was designed around the former USS

Nebraska. The engine, which I'm sure you're all itching to study, was an artifact the Adar found and we Americans got tinkered into a drive. Were we actually to release it for study, which we're not, trust me and my professional background when I say that you would find it as baffling and enigmatic as we have. It is so far ahead of our technology, it is not even funny. Magic is a better description. It is not only capable of normal space flight, but of warp flight."

He stared at the Chinese delegate as he said that and couldn't get anything from him. If the Chinese knew about the warp capability, the general wasn't letting on.

"Using it, we have accomplished two separate deep-space missions," Bill continued. "The first was a local area survey during which we encountered several astronomical issues, landed on a few planets, got ourselves beaten up thoroughly, encountered another friendly alien race and got ourselves beaten up even more thoroughly by a biological planetary defense system."

"Was this Dreen?" the Chinese delegate asked. The Chinese had not had any Dreen gates in their country. Since the war, however, there had been reports of occasional Dreen outbreaks. As with many countries, they had looked upon the Dreen as a potential biological weapon of enormous ability. And like every country that had tinkered with them, save the U.S. and Britain as far as Weaver knew, they'd lost control of the infestation.

Dreen spread-fungus was nasty. It actively tried to escape and would produce enzymes and acids until it found a combination that got it out of its holding vessel. Keeping the result from spreading was nearly impossible.

"No," Bill said, switching to the next slide. "The system was either designed by the Cheerick, this chinchilla-like species, or some older race. However, it was determined during the mission that the Cheerick could control it. It produces various ground and air combat systems as well as a space combat system termed dragonflies. They are capable of normal space operations and fire laser beams from their compound eyes."

"Oh, very good," the Russian said, starting to stand up. "This is some joke you play on us, yes?"

"General, this joke blew the hell out of our ship," Bill said tightly. "We were slag when we got back to Earth and that was *after* we did repairs on Cheerick. The dragonflies are no joke, especially with a couple of hundred coming at you."

"You were there?" the Chinese general said. "You were on this mission?"

"I was the astrogator, General," Bill replied. "We lost all but five of our forty-one Marines and about half of our Navy crew as well as numerous civilian scientists and *all* of our Special Forces scientific assistants. May I continue?"

"Please," the Asian said.

"The second mission was an emergency mission to determine why we'd lost contact with a colony," Bill said, bringing up another slide. It was of a standard harsh-world science station, bubble tents and rocky soil. "The planet was HD 36951 Gamma Five. It was an archaeological station that had been attacked by an unknown force. We determined that it had been destroyed by the Dreen and rescued one survivor. Then we found remnants of a battle in the Tycho 714-1046-1 system. Following the trail of one of the ships, we encountered another race, the Hexosehr.

"The Hexosehr had recently battled the Dreen and lost. The ship was the last major battle platform that defended a refugee fleet of handpicked survivors. Most of them were in cold-sleep and the Hexosehr had fled with over a million of them. Of course, that was out of a total population, on six worlds, of just over two billion."

"Barely your country and mine combined," the Indian said, smiling and looking at the Chinese delegate.

"If bodies was all that was going to help, the mujahideen would have won in Lebanon," the President pointed out. "Continue, Captain."

"We assisted their battleship in repairs," Weaver said. "And then went ahead to inform their refugee fleet that it had survived. The fleet had to refuel and was stopped in the HD 37355 system. The *Blade* assisted the Hexosehr in holding the system and, in fact, in stopping the Dreen task force. However, she was virtually scrap by the end of the battle. The Hexosehr roused their workforce and between the scrap metal from the *Blade* and their factory ships created a new ship from the ground up. Thus the A.S.S. *Vorpal Blade Two*. The rest of the briefing will be handled by Mr. Ascher."

"Information from the Hexosehr and a Dreen dreadnought we captured during the battle indicates that the Dreen are spreading rapidly," the national security advisor said. "They are spreading in every direction through what are called 'local bubbles.' In our direction, they are currently in the Orion local bubble, where most of the action the captain just described took place. There are two local bubbles between ours and that one. Hexosehr estimates, and our own, place the arrival of overwelming Dreen normal space forces at between twelve and twenty years. Best estimate is fifteen."

"*Bozhe moi*," the Russian muttered. "This is . . . not well news."

"That estimate assumes two things. That they do not find out the location of Earth and that even if they do they do not want to jump ahead."

"If I may add one note," Bill said diffidently.

The NSA nodded. "Go ahead, Captain."

"The Dreen, and the Hexosehr, use a warp technology that is similar to wormhole jumping," Bill said. "We're still studying it. But they jump, rather slowly compared to the *Blade*, from star to star. In normal space, the Hexosehr fleet will not reach our region for at least two years. The majority of the Dreen are farther out. If they found out where Earth was today, they would take at least two years to reach here, more like three, in any force. This is part of the full briefing documents we are turning over to your governments, as I understand it."

"The U.S. government, the British government and the Adar planetary government are all aware of this new information," the NSA said. "Our plan was to bring your governments in, through more or less normal diplomatic channels, next week. And, no, I'm not making that up. What we've been waiting on, frankly, is a documentary to be completed. Three, actually. One to assist the briefings of your governments and two for general consumption. At that point, the Hexosehr were going to be presented as well as the Cheerick ambassador to the Alliance. And it was intended to offer expansion of the Alliance to other

Earth governments. We're fully aware that we cannot stop the Dreen by ourselves. No combination of the U.S. and Britain can possibly do so. We know we were keeping you in the dark, but we didn't intend to do so for much longer."

"Frankly, this just jumped the gun by a week," the President continued. "The general audience documentary is complete. Would you care to see it? It's three hours long, intended to run for three nights. But the chairs are comfortable . . ."

"I would," the Chinese delegate said. "And you mentioned further information. Is this to be technical?"

"We're going to be depending on technology from the Hexosehr," the President said. "They are as far ahead of the Adar as the Adar are ahead of us. Perhaps further. It is Hexosehr technology that *might* permit humanity to survive. But it will require a world-wide effort, a coalition of the willing if you will. We have enough time to prepare. If we actually do so."

"That is the rub, isn't it?" the Indian said, smiling broadly. "The most effective economies on Earth, all pardons to my Chinese colleague, are the democracies. Can we sustain a fifteen-year buildup? If we did, we would win. Unquestionably. In fifteen years we could establish colonies, schools, training facilities, build a fleet beyond even the comprehension of the Dreen. We could put in *massive* defenses if we went to a full wartime footing for even ten years. We have six billion people on this planet and with what I've seen of the Hexosehr manufacturing ability, which is amazing, it would just be a matter of training space sailors and Marines. But can we?

Will we? Can we sustain such a push? At the cost to our economies? In the teeth of wailing as consumer goods become scarce?"

"*We* can," the Chinese delegate said. "If this doesn't turn out to be an elaborate tale."

"You'll be given all the data we recovered," the President promised.

"Let us see this documentary, then," the Russian said. "And could we have something stronger than coffee?"

"You're sure you're shiny?" Eric asked.

"I'm fine," Brooke replied, grinning. "Better than fine. Okay, a *bit* sore."

"I hadn't realized you were . . . weren't . . ." Eric said, trying to figure out how to put it delicately.

"Eric Bergstresser, I'm a *good* girl," Brooke said playfully. "And good girls wait."

"Oh, you're more than good," Eric said, brushing some hair out of Brooke's face. "You are amazing."

"So are you," Brooke replied, snuggling into his shoulder.

"Not all that amazing," Berg said. "I'm sorry this was all I could swing for a honeymoon."

The Holiday Inn, Seaside, in Virginia Beach was not exactly a five star hotel in some exotic location. But it also wasn't as expensive and if they'd taken the travel time to go to someplace like Cancun, it would have cut time out of the honeymoon.

"This is perfect," Brooke replied, nibbling his ear. "Wherever thou goest. I'm glad you didn't do something expensive."

"We might as well have just gone to the apartment,"

Eric argued. "Of course, the apartment doesn't have room service."

"Which we won't be using," Brooke said firmly. "We can go out long enough to find something less expensive."

"If you say so," Berg replied, puzzled.

"I suppose I should have talked about this sooner," Brooke said, sitting up. "But it's something Momma made me promise I'd do early. So here goes. Can you let me take over the family finances?"

"Whatever you want, honey," Berg said. "Right now, you could tell me to bark like a dog and I'd do it."

"I'm serious, Eric," Brooke said, pulling his chin up so he was looking her in the eye. "It's something Momma did when she and Daddy first got married and she made sure I'd promise to do the same. You're a lieutenant. Yes, that makes more than a petty officer, but not by all that much. And we're going to have babies coming along, probably sooner rather than later. We're going to have to be careful with money."

"Agreed," Berg said, shrugging. "Like I said, whatever you want. The only thing I spend money on, really, is my truck."

"Which may have to go," Brooke said, sighing. "If you're not too reversed on the payments, we'll need to trade it in on a family car."

"Ouch," Eric said. His truck was his one vanity. "If you say so."

"I'll make sure you have enough money to buy your rations in the officers' club," Brooke said. "And an allowance. But I'll warn you, I'm a penny-pincher. I hope you're going to be able to handle that."

"Yes, Brooke, I can," Eric said. "Now can we cuddle some more?"

"Please," Brooke said, sliding down into his arms. "Are we shiny?"

"I hate trying to figure money out," Berg said. "We're more than shiny. So we get a couple of family cars. I can handle that."

"One," Brooke said. "You're going to be gone a lot; you won't need one."

"Shiny," Eric said, blinking in surprise at the response. "One it is. You really are a penny-pincher, aren't you?"

"Enough to make George Washington scream for mercy," Brooke said, grinning. "When all the other girls would be buying stuff at the mall, I'd go along. But I never had the urge to get any of it. Way too expensive and you could find exactly the same stuff in thrift shops. Momma made most of my dresses and nobody could tell and I learned to sew early. It's just a matter of being really careful with money and you can look as if you're better off than other people while, in fact, not making nearly as much. You remember that conversation where Miriam was talking about your career?"

"Vividly," Eric said.

"Then that's the rest of the story," Brooke said. "I'm not willing to settle for second best. I want to be a wife first and I want you to *be* somebody. I'm more than willing to play the spouse game if you're willing to do what it takes to get stars. Are you?"

Eric thought about that for a few seconds.

"I don't mind doing the jobs," he temporized. "I mean,

that will mean lots of staff positions. But I can do those, I'm sure. I'll learn. But stars are a long way away."

"Every step of the way is going to matter," Brooke said. "Think hard if you really want to do it. I've seen the modern woman and I don't want that. I want to be a traditional wife. Oh, sure, I'll get a job. But I don't want to be double income, no kids, do you?"

"No," Eric said definitely.

"So I'm going to be following your lead, not the other way around," Brooke said. "And, sure, there might be some false steps along the way. Things might look bad from time to time. Maybe we'll have to change course and ask for directions. But I need to know where, in general, we're going. Is that to stars or not?"

"I've really got to think about that one," Eric said. "Right now, I'm just concentrating on surviving the missions."

"And *please* concentrate on that," Brooke said. "But I don't think it interferes, does it?"

"Not that I know of," Eric said, then paused. "Well, spec ops officers rarely make stars. But those are the guys who marry to it and never get out. Spec ops as a lieutenant or a captain? That's sort of like a good merit badge. I'm going to have to collect those, anyway."

"So concentrate on surviving the missions," Brooke said. "Please. But decide, sometime soon, if where you want to go is stars. Or if you're going to be a major success in the civilian world. It changes what I do, how I act. If you're going to go for a civilian career, I need to get a degree I can use to support you while you go back to school."

"Shiny," Eric said. "I repeat, you're amazing."

"You haven't learned the half of it," Brooke said. "Now, what was that you were explaining about positions?"

It had been a seemingly short three hours. The opening of the documentary—most of which was shot from surveillance cameras, external cameras on the ship and Wyvern systems—was definitely designed for the computer generation. Short clips of groups of people would zoom in on one, lay out a statistics and general information screen, then give deeper background about each of the characters. Then Commander Weaver was there, including his background in the Dreen War, which was open-source information. There were also several Marines and sailors as well as the commander of the ship, Captain Steven Blankemeier.

Internal surveillance cameras had caught several of the pre-mission briefings and a description of pre-mission physical, using some very nice computer generated imagery, was revolting enough that the Russian nearly lost his lunch.

Then there were the details of the missions. The more or less useless Dean's World, Runner's World with its deadly crabpus, nearly losing the ship and all the Marines. Some of the people the audience had been introduced to were suddenly gone—eaten, mangled, ripped to shreds. But the *Blade* went on.

The second hour covered the findings in Cheerick and again, people died, people who had been made to live and breathe during the earlier parts of the documentary. The Wyvern video from the fall of the science section was particularly vivid. The amazing biological defenses of the planet were detailed along with their utility to humanity, once they were fully understood. It ended with the return to Earth, startling the mission controllers with a giant crabpus mounted on the hypercavitation activator.

The third hour was the scramble to head to the lost colony. The documentary caught, vividly, the boredom of the long transit. But the viewers quickly got caught up in the battles around the unnamed stars. Captain Blankemeier, one of the central characters, was given a short bit where he referenced "battling on the arms of Orion." One of the internal cameras on the ship caught a blast of plasma ripping through the crew quarters, fortunately vacant. More caught lasers and mass drivers ripping the ship until she was virtually airless but still fought on. Wyvern video of Eric capturing the flagship was missing, so CGI and overlay techniques were used to simulate it. If anything, they looked better. The Mreee "sentient" controller of the task force brought a cry of surprise from the Russian, who bent forward to look closer.

The last hour closed with video of the shattered *Blade I* in space, then a discussion of the aid of the Hexosehr and finally a shot of the built-from-scratch *Blade II* setting down in Area 51, its alternate base.

"Admiral Blankemeier," the Chinese general said when the videos were finished. "It is amazing you are alive."

"It's amazing any of us survived," Blankemeier replied.

"Yes, but the one that I want to meet is, how is it? Two-Gun Berg," the Indian said, grinning. "What a warrior! Especially for an enlisted man. I am glad to see that you made him an officer."

And thus we uncover the weakness of the Indians, Weaver thought with a sigh. They just could not seem to get over the whole caste thing. And if you considered large portions of your population as sub-par, the intellectual value of that portion was lost. Who knew how many Einsteins and Booker T. Washingtons might exist among the Untouchable, who were *still* relegated to not much more than garbage collection.

"So what is next?" the Chinese delegate asked. "You say that we are going to get access to these Hexosehr? In two years? That is too much time. We need their technology immediately!"

"Actually, the Hexosehr are in the process of colonizing Runner's World," the President replied. "We established gates to get them there. Their ships won't arrive for a bit under two years. But we were able to move some of their fabricators through and, of course, their expertise. We are liaising with them now about how to portion out their personnel. They've made a study of our various societies and countries and are making many of their own decisions. They are an independent group, allied but with their own . . . how was it you put it? Ah, their own 'sovereignty.' What technology goes to what groups is up to them. But, yes, you're going to get access to it."

"And the *Blade*?" the Russian asked.

"No," the President replied. "We've considered the possibility of putting observers onboard or even a mixed crew. Subsequent to mutual defense treaties, we may consider it further. But it is an Alliance ship. The British have, thus far, declined to offer personnel but there is an Adar on board and shortly a Hexosehr. Until things change, politically, however, we're not going to put in Russian, Chinese or Indian crewpeople or observers. As to studying the drive, it's always been a toss-up between studying it and using it. For the time being, again, we're going to use it and study it as we can. Even the Hexosehr, after examining it intensively during the rebuild, admitted that they could not understand it. It violated several of their theories of faster-than-light travel, which were rather mature and now have to be rethought. So if we cannot figure it out, meaning the U.S., and the British cannot figure it out and the Adar cannot figure it out and the Hexosehr cannot figure it out, I strongly doubt that the Chinese or Russians, the ability of their scientists being noted, can do any better. Honestly, do you?"

"We *demand* observers," the Russian said. "The ship should be the property of all the world, not just one hegemonic government! It should be an international crew under a commander chosen by the United Nations!"

"Well, let's see," the President replied, grinning. "The Adar trusted *us*, being in contact with all of *you*, with the black box. We spent twenty *billion* dollars rebuilding a nuclear submarine and turning it into a spaceship. And we took all the casualties finding the Cheerick, the Hexosehr and the Dreen. So you'll understand me if I try not to scoff at your demand. And, frankly, we're going to completely ignore the UN in our preparations for the Dreen. I don't see what use a bunch of kleptocrats and tyrants are going to be to us."

"The Hexosehr will be sending a liaison and technical group to each of the countries joining the coalition," the national security advisor said diplomatically. "They will require appropriate quarters, which means suited to their physiology especially since they use a slightly different atmosphere. They will also require logistical support including food. Some Adar foods are mutually compatible. Most major Earth governments will get a Hexosehr ambassador. Those that join the coalition are the only ones that will be getting technical support. That is the *Hexosehr's* position, not ours."

"And this coalition?" the Russian said furiously. "I suppose that the Americans they will be the top dog, yes?"

"Each country will be expected to produce their own ships, fleets," the national security advisor replied. "Higher command structure will be a matter of negotiations. But American fleets will *never* be under the command of others, not even the British. We're more willing to consider higher command by Adar or Hexosehr. But only willing to consider it. The U.S. has a history of winning battles that cannot be matched by any country in this room."

"And losing wars," the Russian scoffed. "For that matter, who took Berlin?"

Just because Patton was ordered *to remain in place*, Weaver thought. But he managed to hold his tongue.

"It's not a matter for argument," the President said, clearly thinking much the same thing. "The American public is never going to accept a Chinese admiral over an American fleet. But that is for later. The completed documentaries and the reams and reams of video and sensor data they were derived from are assembled for each of you. As are the preliminary methods for getting in contact with the Hexosehr. We request that we be given one week before we release the information."

"I am not in a position to promise that," the Chinese general said. "This meeting was only to be on the subject of the spaceship you have, this *Vorpal Blade*. This new information will have to be considered by my government. We may request an extension of the information being released."

"We have indications that it's not going to be long before our news media gets to the bottom of what's going on," the President said. "Or at least some of it. So . . . consider fast."

"I have no clue when I'll be talking to you next," Eric said, brushing Brooke's cheek.

It was the time of day the military referred to as o-dark thirty, before even Before Morning Nautical Twilight, black as pitch, a time when normal people might stir but then roll over in bed and go back to sleep. Brooke had actually gotten up and driven him to headquarters. Eric had checked in the night before, officially coming off of leave in time but long after anyone could put him to work. But this was the start of his new career as an officer, his first working day. Between in-processing and duties, he had no clue when he'd be home, but if the new CO wanted him to participate in PT he wanted to be in in plenty of time.

"You'll be home when you are home," Brooke replied, then kissed him. "I promised not to bind you to the pasture. And I keep my promises."

It was a "thing" between them, a special code. During the last mission, Brooke had sent Eric a link to a flash animation done during the War On Terror. It was a series of pictures set to a song called "Homeward Bound," done in homage to a soldier who died in Afghanistan.

> *Bind me not to the pasture,*
> *chain me not to the plow.*
> *Set me free to find my calling*
> *and I'll return to you somehow.*

"Just try to call me in time for me to have supper waiting," Brooke said.

"I'll do that," Eric replied, trying not to grimace. He loved Brooke and she had some remarkable abilities for a girl fresh out of high school. But she'd apparently failed Home Ec.

"And I'll try to get it right this time," Brooke said, already learning to read subtle body-cues in her new husband.

"Your cooking is . . ."

"Awful," Brooke said, grinning. "I have to eat it, too, you know."

"I'm no better at it," Eric admitted. "But if I have to stay late, I'll probably eat in the mess hall. It's not that expensive."

"Shiny," Brooke said. "When I get home, though, I'm going to sit down and start reading cookbooks. Winging it is clearly not the answer. Now kiss me and have a good day."

Eric paused in front of the company headquarters building and shifted his jump bag on his shoulder. The company was housed in two "starbase" barracks, essentially multistory apartment buildings built in the 1980s, fronted by a two-story headquarters building. The headquarters was the only new construction, a rectangular windowless block with heavy security systems. Some of the stupider security measures, such as the timed doors, had finally been removed, but it was still a highly secure facility.

Eric knew the headquarters like the inside of his mouth, having spent more time there it seemed than in his enlisted quarters. The armory, the Wyvern room and all the briefing rooms as well as the company quarterdeck were all in that two-story structure. A Bravo Company soldier couldn't, officially, discuss even their training schedule in the barracks. Due to the black nature of their missions, every briefing, every discussion, just about every bit of training had to take place in the HQ building.

But it was a different building, now. Eric no longer had any place in the enlisted barracks save for an occasional inspection. This was his home for the rest of his career in the company. People who used to casually order PFC or Sergeant Bergstresser off on details were still in the unit, but the vast majority of them were now required to salute Second Lieutenant Bergstresser. It was going to take some—

"Morning, sir," First Sergeant Powell said, walking up behind him.

Eric turned and for just a moment froze at the salute.

"Morning, First Sergeant," Berg replied, managing to return it crisply.

"Forget something at home?" Powell asked, grinning wisely.

The tall, lanky senior NCO had been the Top-Dog of Bravo Company since Eric joined as a PFC. Over the past two missions, he'd sent Eric into some situations that appeared suicidal and in one case very nearly was. By the same token, they'd stood side-by-side against monsters that ate Wyvern armor like candy, trained side-by-side and traded good-natured insults to the extent a sergeant and a first sergeant could. If Eric could point to one person as a mentor in his professional development as a Marine, it was First Sergeant Powell. And now the first sergeant was saluting him.

"Just thinking that sort of thing is going to take some getting used to, First Sergeant," Eric replied. "The salute, that is."

"We salute the rank, not the person wearing it," Powell said. "But you wear it well. However, if you think you're doing PT this morning, think again. You're going to be doing paperwork all day long. And tomorrow and the next day ad infinitum. If you'd like one suggestion from an old soldier who's watched more than one LT grow or fail, it's: Find the time. But today you won't."

"Top, I'm planning on going on listening to your advice as long as you'll give it," Eric replied.

"Well, sir, then my advice is to take one more deep breath and report in," Powell said with a grin. "I mean, how hard could it be compared to, say, being crisped by plasma fire?"

"Yeah," Eric said, grinning back. "The *good* thing about being an officer is that the *next* time you tell me to do that I can tell you to *grapp* off."

"One thousand units of item 413 will be arriving later this afternoon, sir," Weaver reported to the captain.

"And you nearly didn't twitch when you said that," Prael replied, grinning. "How bad was it?"

Prael's office had an unlived-in look. He'd been the CO of the *Blade* for more than two months but the land-side office still only had a nameplate on the desk and a picture turned towards him. It showed a family group that Weaver presumed was Mrs. Prael and their two children. Unlike a lot of officers, he kept his domestic side completely separated from the military. And also unlike most officers, there was no "I-Love-Me" wall. Weaver had checked his service record and knew that he was a "plank owner" of the last Seawolf submarine constructed, but that plaque was also missing.

"The diet details are too gross to convey, sir," Weaver said. "But I'm glad to report that all of her dogs are in good health. Her mom's not doing so good, though. Care for the details?"

"No, but have the clerk write me a letter to the effect for my signature," the CO said. "It never hurts to keep on Clerk Click's good side. Maybe a box of chocolates."

"Seems like an awful lot to go through for a thousand rolls of space tape, though."

"Based on your last mission report, space tape is what keeps the *Blade* functioning," Prael pointed out. "And on the matter, sort of, of your last mission, you had an interesting phone call while you were gone."

"I cannot wait to hear what you define as interesting, sir," Bill replied.

"A call from Robin Zenikki," Prael said, in a much darker tone. "You recognize the name."

"*Washington Times*," Bill replied. "I haven't talked to

him in years, not since shortly after the Dreen War. And never on secure subjects, even to confirm or deny. It was always under orders to detail things that had already been authorized for disclosure. And all the conversations were prior to becoming an officer."

"Well, he apparently wants to talk to you," the CO said. "He said he'd call back but he also left a number. I'm hereby authorizing you and requiring you to contact him and see what he has to say. Don't let anything go in the opposite direction, understood?"

"Clear, sir," Bill replied. "I've done this before, sir."

"I suppose there's that," Prael admitted. "Call him. I want to know what he knows or suspects. But later this afternoon. We're headed to HQ."

"For?"

"Mission brief," the CO replied. "Finally."

"That was a quick in-process," Lieutenant Ross said.

Roger Ross was the executive officer of Bravo Company. XO is one of the more thankless positions in the military. The XO ensures that the unit is functioning, simple as that. It's the XO's job to make sure that the vehicles and other systems are working, that training schedules meet the myriad and often baroque requirements of higher, that the company has sufficient logistics to function, be that in garrison or in the field, that the unit is fed and resupplied in battle and that, in general, the unit works as a well-oiled machine. It's petty, detail work, often frustrating, generally without great reward and often with huge penalties for failure. But XO is also a necessary step at each level on the way to command duties. Without being in the position, it's impossible to truly understand the way that a unit functions, where the weak points are, what the probable problems are that will arise and how to fix them.

"Slow day, sir," Eric replied.

It was nearly the end of duty hours and Eric had been in-processing all day, a procedure that *could* have been done in a maximum of two hours. He'd gone to the medics and ensured that his shots were up-to-date, got a stamp. Went to payroll and ensured that his pay records were up-to-date, got a stamp. Legal and his will, got a stamp. Field equipment, got a stamp. At each of the stops, incredibly bored clerks, most of whom had little or nothing to do, spent about four times the necessary time to do each job.

"Call me Rog," the XO said. He was newer to the unit than Eric in some ways. The Marines on-board the *Blade* during the battle worked in damage control and most of them had died in those positions including the then-XO, Lieutenant Kolb. "Grab a chair. But now that you're back, I don't really have anything for you, yet. You still need to see the CO and get his in-process speech and he's on his way back from a meeting with General Zanuck.

"I *can* tell you about your duties," Lieutenant Ross continued, grinning evilly. "Now that you are here, and assuredly the most junior lieutenant seeing as the other two platoon leaders are first lieutenants, you get to take over the Dog Duties."

"Here it comes," Eric said, sitting down.

"Here are the unit VD reports," Rog said, sliding over a thick file folder. "Not much in the way of positives, but you're also required to do the mandatory training classes on prophylaxes and the paperwork showing that the classes have been successfully completed by all junior enlisted members of the company. Officers and senior NCOs are not required to attend but are encouraged."

"Yeah, like Top's going to take a VD course," Eric said, picking up the file.

"I would find it unlikely," Ross said, grinning. "Note that most of this stuff is database based. In addition to my other duties, I'll need to familiarize you with the company management system. I could wish you'd spent time as an operations sergeant or even a company clerk; that would have sped the transition to your new lofty status. As it is, I'll just hope that you learn quickly."

"I'm generally a quick study, sir," Eric replied.

"One can only hope," the XO said, sliding over another file. "Unit morale and welfare officer. You are in charge of the MWR inventory and will need to do a full inventory of same for turnover. You are also responsible for a monthly report on MWR issues with the company, including an itemization of MWR inventory usage and explanation of non-usage if it falls below a certain time matrix. Sports, especially, are highly encouraged by the Marine Corps so if the Marines of Bravo Company don't use their baseball bats and footballs, the commandant wants to know why!"

"Gung-ho, sir," Eric replied. "I'll try to make sure we play with the commandant's balls."

"Motorcycle defensive driving officer," the XO continued, sliding over another file. "There are nine motorcyclists in the company. You are to ensure that each is up-to-date at all times in their insurance and training on motorcycle defensive driving courses. Two of them haven't attended

MDDC, yet, so you're going to have to find them a slot in the next two weeks."

"Sir, we're leaving on a mission in less than two weeks," Berg pointed out.

"That's what makes your new job so *fun*," Ross replied, coldheartedly. "Not to mention mine. You will fill out the appropriate forms to point out that, due to exigencies of service, they were unable to fulfill their mandatory training and request an extension upon return and sign swearing and affirming on your soul as an officer that it's all true so help you God really. I will then review them, require you to fix any necessary corrections and the CO will then countersign them."

"At the rate this company loses people, most of them aren't going to," Eric said, chuckling. "Complete the course at a later date that is. I suppose there's another form we have to submit explaining that they're not in violation, they're dead?"

"Normally, if a young lieutenant said something like that I'd jump their ass," the XO replied. "In your case, given that you were around for most of those losses, I'll let it slide. But you might want to avoid saying that sort of thing around the troops."

"Wasn't planning on it, sir," Eric said. "Sorry."

"It is, however, true," Ross admitted, sighing. "I had no *grapping* clue the casualty rate of this unit when I volunteered. As XO no less. Where was I? Ah! Unit inventory officer . . ."

"HD 242896."

The briefing officer was a Navy commander, an old

one. The ribbons on his uniform indicated that he had never been anywhere or done anything that involved hearing shots fired in anger. On the other hand, he had several ribbons that indicated people thought he walked on water, up to and including *two* Legions of Merit. So either he was an A Number One kiss-butt or he was one of the boffins services kept around for their intellectual prowess rather than warrior spirit.

"Which means exactly nothing to me," Captain Prael said.

"Then *try* to keep up, Captain," the commander said dryly. "HD 242896 is an F9V, that means hot-green star, located between the constellations of Sagittarius and Orion, more or less in Taurus, in the night sky. It is important solely because during their retreat from the Dreen, the Hexosehr found an interesting installation around one of its gas giants."

"Define interesting," Bill said.

"This interesting," the commander replied, bringing up a slide.

Bill recognized the view as one that had been translated from Hexosehr sonar images. The Hexosehr used various sensors and then converted them to sonar terms, just as humans, for example, would convert the bounced radio signals of radar into blips on a screen.

Converting the result into visual images for humans was often a matter of art rather than science. And generally the art form was surrealist.

"What in the hell is that?" Captain Prael asked. It was a structure that looked a bit like an octopus mated with a walrus.

"That is the best image we've been able to create," the commander said. "But this facility was in orbit around a giant the Hexosehr were refueling at. Whether it was a fueling station for a dead race or a living habitat, a space station . . . Perhaps all of the above. The purpose of the facility was unclear. It was heavily damaged and in retrograde orbit. However, their brief survey of it did find this."

The commander reached into his briefcase and set a small black monolith on the table.

"Is that what I think it is?" Bill asked. "Because it looks a lot like the LBB that powers our ship. And if it is . . . make sure you've got a static protector or this entire city is going to be gutted."

"If it is, it is broken," the commander said. "The Hexosehr, knowing nothing about the technology, already applied electrical power to it. There was no result. Ditto various particle streams. However, the point is that the Adar found the LBB we now use on a star in the direction of Sagittarius. And now there is this facility. That indicates that the center of this predecessor race, the race that created the engine in the *Blade*, may be located near HD 242896. Given that they did not want the Dreen obtaining any technology from the race that built the facility, they attempted to destroy it. It was particularly adamant and resistant to even their chaos balls. They eventually increased its rate of descent and dropped it into the Jovian's atmosphere. They are unsure if that truly destroyed it or not. For all we know, it's simply sitting on the metal hydrogen center."

"Now that would be something to see," Bill commented.

"Indeed."

"How far away is this place?" Captain Prael asked.

"Four hundred and twenty-six light years," Lieutenant Fey interjected. He'd been tapping at his computer during the majority of the briefing. "I'd estimate twenty-three days transit. Fewer chill stops and better recyclers means we can make better time."

"Get out there," Admiral Townsend said. "Sailing orders are for nine days from now. Go to that star system first and check out the other planets. Then spread out. Standard orders. It's a scouting mission, not a battle, but if you run into trouble or something that you think needs fixing, use your own judgment. With the increased storage space on the *Blade II*, not to mention the Hexosehr recyclers, you should be able to extend your away time over a hundred days. If you find anything that's immediately useful, though, bring it back right away. By the same token, if you find anything that might be useful but you can't bring it back, destroy it. We don't want the Dreen using this race's technology against us. And speaking of the Dreen. Commander?"

"Note that the Hexosehr were fleeing through this region," the commander added. "The Dreen came from the general direction of the Triffid Nebula, which means towards Sagittarius as we see it. According to Hexosehr and our estimates, they probably have not started to colonize the region of HD 242896, but it is possible there are scouting forces in the area."

"So keep on your toes," Admiral Townsend said. "We want you back with your *Blade*, not on it."

※　※　※

"Commander. Could I have a word with you?" Bill said pulling the Navy intelligence officer aside as the brass filed out of the secure room.

"How can I help you, sir?" The Navy commander raised an eyebrow at Weaver. Despite his being the blatant parody of a TV character, Bill liked him. Especially the way the junior officer had told Captain Prael to *try* to keep up. Bill had almost laughed out loud, but had thought better of it.

"What do y'all plan to do with that LBB in your briefcase?"

"It's dead, Captain. The Hexosehr even think so. I guess it'll get stored somewhere back at Area 51."

"*Maybe* it's dead, Commander. Maybe. But the *Blade*'s LBB wiped out an entire star system without any sign of damage. I doubt whoever made it normally leave them just lying around ready to go. We got lucky with the first one. What if this one is just turned off?"

"Off?" The commander rubbed his open palm against the leather of his briefcase almost affectionately. "Hmm. Interesting point, sir. What would you suggest?"

"There's a little girl about to turn sixteen and I've been trying to think of what to get her for her birthday."

"Sir?" The Navy officer looked down at a note that Weaver was scribbling on a yellow Post-It. Bill could tell by the commander's expression that he recognized the name and phone number. Probably from other intelligence briefings.

"Tell her I said that this was all I could think of as a gift for the girl who in essence has the entire universe on *her* shoulders." Weaver smiled, handed the officer the note and walked off. "Happy sweet sixteen, Mimi," he said under his breath.

"Robin Zenikki."

Zenikki had been covering the Pentagon and the military for over three decades, knew everyone and had a Rolodex to die for. The only thing that surprised Weaver was that it had taken him this long to piece things together.

"Bill Weaver," Bill replied. "Long time. You never call, you never write, we never do lunch and then out of the blue . . ."

"Hey, Bill," Zenikki said, obviously grinning. "Like your new job?"

"Better than being a civilian consultant," Bill replied, leaning back in his chair and looking at the overhead. That he was a Naval officer was not classified information.

"I meant as the astrogator of a spaceship," Zenikki said.

"Being in the Navy is fun," Bill said. "Be aware that this conversation is being recorded. SOP in my new job."

"So we're going to play it that way?" the reporter replied with mock sadness. "I thought we were friends, Bill!"

"Like I said, you never call, you never write . . ."

"Well, you were kind of unavailable for comment when you went to that planet where all the Marines were killed," Zenikki said. "You know, the ones that were supposedly killed in a helicopter crash in the Mojave?"

"And I'm *still* unavailable to comment, Robin," Bill replied. "If that's all you've got, I suggest you take it to the UFO society. Or maybe *Weekly World News*."

"Are you denying that the U.S. has a spaceship that has

been in at least one battle?" the reporter asked seriously. "Because I've got one confirmation already."

"Your sources used to be better than that, Robin," Bill said. "Slipping in your old age?"

"So that's a confirmation?" Zenikki asked.

"Gimme a break," Bill said. "No, it's not a confirmation. Neither confirm nor deny. But if all you've got is some wild story about a spaceship and some dead Marines, I'd strongly urge you to refrain from making a joke of yourself."

"So you're denying that we have a spaceship capable of faster-than-light travel," the reporter asked doggedly.

"And your hearing is going, too," Bill said. "Neither confirm nor deny. Just suggesting you need to find the right market. Have you considered writing science fiction?"

"You've been a real buddy there, Bill," Zenikki said. "Let's do lunch. You buy."

"If I'm in town," Bill said then winced.

"So you're doing a lot of traveling?" the reporter pounced. "Off-planet?"

"Robin, do you know how many gates there are on Earth to other planets?" Bill said, deciding to lay a red-herring. It was dangerous, but potentially worth it if it threw Robin off for as much as a week. "Forty-seven. Do you know how many we have research colonies on? One less than we did six months ago. I'd suggest you look for some of your answers elsewhere."

"You're saying that you're mixed up with that research station that disappeared?" Robin asked hurriedly.

"Who is the military's number one expert on Looking Glass bosons, Robin?" Weaver said. "And that's all I'm going to say. Good night, Robin."

❈ ❈ ❈

"Filling Two-Gun in on his Dog Duties, XO?" Captain Zanella said as he walked through the office.

Captain James Zanella was tall, lean and fit with a sharply pointed jaw, high cheekbones, green eyes, black hair and an olive complexion. Any casting director would throw him out as being *far* too heroic looking to be a *real* Marine CO. The fact that he was also a capable one was the amazing thing.

His good looks were slightly marred from a mottling on his face, the only remaining indications that he'd been partially freeze-dried when his space suit was holed during the battle at HD 37355. Only quick thinking on the part of his RTO and a handy roll of space tape had saved his life. In that case, space tape really *had* been a life-saver.

Space tape, for the *Vorpal Blade* and the Marines that infested her, filled the venerable role of duct tape, hundred-mile-an-hour tape, rigger tape, what have you. The problem with using duct tape or its numerous brethren was that it simply did not work in space. The glue that worked so well in atmosphere just boiled away and in the incredible changes of temperature found in space the base material either froze and cracked or melted or sometimes both in quick succession.

Space tape, however, was the more wealthy and stylish child of the tape beloved of soldiers, sailors, Marines, airmen and anyone who has ever had to repair a '67 Chevy without the aid of baling wire. Space tape, Item 117-398-7494560413 in the Uniform Federal Logistics Database, or Item 413 for short, worked perfectly well in any conditions including under water. The just-short-of-miraculous glue of the tape would stick to *anything*, left no residue no matter how long it had been applied, worked in vacuum and had a temperature range from just above one degree Kelvin to just short of that of the surface of the sun.

And it was expensive. Oh My God was it ever expensive. Nearly one hundred thousand dollars per roll expensive. And the Marines and sailors of the *Vorpal Blade* still tended to use it very much like duct tape, up to and including keeping partial rolls tucked away in odd places "just in case."

When Captain Zanella had signed off on his first inventory in the unit and seen the prohibitive cost of the material, he nearly had a heart attack. For a few dozen rolls of space tape he could buy a Wyvern suit. He had blanched every time he saw the stuff and nearly screamed when he saw Marines using it to attach bits of equipment to their combat harness. He'd prohibited it from use under all but the most dire and fully official circumstances and ordered all rolls turned in on pain of pain.

Then his RTO had pulled out one of the many contraband rolls the Marines managed to retain and saved his life with it.

After that, he was a believer in space tape. If the Marines wanted to keep rolls, that was fine by him. As long as he had the budget, he'd buy all the space tape he could get his hands on. He still, however, prohibited using it to make hackysack balls.

"Just about done, sir," Lieutenant Ross said, looking up from the paperwork he was explaining.

"You're looking a bit fried, Two-Gun," Captain Zanella said.

"Just trying to figure out when I can see my new bride, sir," Eric replied, shaking his head. "There's . . . a lot of paperwork here."

"Every bit of which Lieutenant Ross has to review and I have to review and sign," the CO said. "Paperwork is what officers were created for, Lieutenant Bergstresser. It is our lot in life. Get used to it."

"I will, sir," Berg said. "Not complaining, just contemplating."

"Well, come on in and we'll get this over with," the CO continued, heading for the door of his office.

"Grab a seat, Eric," the captain said, sitting down behind his desk and contemplating his inbox. "See this?" he continued, gesturing at the overflowing pile. "That's just what I haven't caught up with, yet, today. Because I had to go over to Quantico. I'll be here until at least nine catching up. Lieutenant Ross will be here nearly as long. For the first few days, you're going to have much the same schedule and you'll probably take what you can home. Not all of that stuff is classified, fortunately. Honestly, though, even as much as I like and respect you, I could wish that the President hadn't stuck his nose in. If he hadn't, or if he'd just said 'Send him to OCS,' then we'd have done this the normal way. You'd have spent at least a year in one of the MEUs getting used to being an officer, *then* come back here."

"I think I'm going to be able to maintain a separation from my former teammates, sir," Eric replied.

"I don't," Zanella said. "And it's the least of my worries,

frankly. Force Recon officers are generally closer to their troops than officers in regular units. We spend too much time separated from large groups of other officers. If your platoon is in Thailand, it's hang out with the troops or be by yourself. And you never fly without a wingman in Thailand. That's not the problem. Problems. Comments?"

"Still waiting to find out what I'm going to do wrong, sir," Eric said.

"Good one, Two-Gun," Zanella replied, grinning. "Okay, if you'd been in an MEU, the stuff that just got dumped on you would have been spread more. Some of that in an MEU is MEU specific. The motorcycle thing would have an officer, a JO admittedly, in charge of it for the whole MEU. Ditto the MWR inventory, but a different officer. So JOs would spread the load and have time to adjust to it. Then, when an officer got to Force Recon and got handed the same shit all over again, just more of it, he'd have already developed the habits that would help him shift the load faster. You don't have that experience because you didn't spend time in the MEU."

"I guess I'll just have to learn fast," Eric said.

"And so many things," the CO said. "Among other things, that Direction of the President missed sending you to Officer Basic Course and Force Recon Officer Training. In both of those you would have learned more details of how to handle your troops in a combat environment *and* in garrison. OCS, necessarily, covers the broad spectrum. You were supposed to *really* be taught how to be an infantry officer, and then a Force Recon Officer, in those two courses. You've had neither. I've been reviewing the lesson plans of both and realizing just how much you missed. Including introduction to the CMS. You also haven't had any experience running troops. I know that you've had experience being a troop and think you know what it's all about. But from this side of the desk, things are different. Priorities, especially. So you're going to have to learn. Much of this I'm going to throw on Gunnery Sergeant Juda."

"He's back?" Eric interjected. The Gunny had been hit even worse than the CO during the battle. "Sorry, sir."

"He is, indeed, back," Captain Zanella said. "However, since his right leg is still missing a goodly chunk of muscle, he's somewhat grouchy. Hopefully he won't oh-so-subtly take it out on his new lieutenant. But part of any gunny's job is to teach the newbie lieutenant, that being you. In fact, given your position I'm sure that all the senior NCOs will tend to be helpful. Perhaps too helpful. Do you get my meaning?"

"Eventually, I have to learn to do this myself," Eric said. "Is that what you mean, sir?"

"More or less," Zanella said. "Just one of many traps, Lieutenant. There's one last trap I need to point out. I suspect it's the one you've probably already thought about. That trap is the trap of courage. You know where I'm going?"

"I don't take the door, anymore, sir," Eric said, if anything sadly. "I'm supposed to send others to take it."

"Not supposed to," the CO corrected. "Must. You *must* send others to take point. You don't lead from a bunker or from the ship, usually, but by the same token you have to place your Marines in the position of greatest risk. Their job is to kill stuff and blow things up. You lead from behind, to convey my orders and expand on them. I don't mind an officer who's willing to get his hands dirty, in fact I demand it. But the point on anything, be it loading the ship or fighting Dreen, are your Marines, *not* 'Two-Gun Berg the One-Man-Killing-Machine.' If you can get through an engagement without firing your weapon you're doing things correctly. And if I see you toting gear instead of figuring out what's supposed to be toted, next, I will damned well bust you back to sergeant. Are we absolutely, positively clear on this?"

"Clear, sir."

"I said the job of an officer is to do paperwork," the CO said, leaning back. "But that only covers part of the spectrum. The real job of an officer is to consider not 'what now' but 'what's next?' Your NCOs handle 'what now.' You tell them 'Take that room' and they take the room. You don't have to tell them how to take a room. They know that. Your job, while they're taking it, is to consider what's next. After that room, what needs to get done that's not an automatic trained reaction. Do you need to prepare defenses? Or is this a raid and you need to consider the problems of exfil? The job of the officer is to look ahead in time and be prepared for what time is going to throw at him. Leadership and all the rest comes quickly enough. If your troops realize that you know what you're doing *as an officer*. The first time that one of your NCOs says 'What now, sir?' and you have the answer they don't . . . that's when you start being an officer. Clear?"

"Clear, sir," Berg said. He'd had much the same speech in OCS, but he had to admit that Captain Zanella hit the high points better.

"On the ride out, I'm going to devote two hours a day to professional development," the CO said, sighing. "However, I seem to recall a Marine sergeant who had his head fairly firmly on his shoulders instead of up his ass. Try to keep it there."

"I'll try, sir," Eric promised.

"Now, you need to complete your training with Monsieur Ross then decide if you actually have time to go home tonight to do more than change clothes. See ya tomorrow morning."

"Most girls like you want to be waitresses," the restaurant manager said, looking Brooke up and down. "You could make way more money as a waitress."

"I know," Brooke admitted. "But I want to learn to cook. I'm hoping I can do some of that working in the kitchen."

"All I got is busser," the Italian said. "You're mostly going to be washing dishes, maybe chopping some vegetables. Even my choppers, they got professional training."

"It's why I'm applying here," Brooke said, smiling prettily.

"Damn, you'd make a good waitress," the manager said. "I don't know for busser. That's hard work and no pay, hardly. I don't think you'd last."

"I'm willing to work hard," Brooke said patiently. "But I really want to learn how to cook."

"*Maulk*," Antonio said, shaking his head. "I tell you what. I make you a waitress and *part time* chef. *If* you can get along with Fernando. I put you on Fernando's shift. Victor's gay but Fernando, he *like* ladies. He keep his hands to himself but you smile at him. he teach you some stuff. Rest of the time, you're a waitress. I need pretty waitresses. You don't last, you don't last."

"Thank you," Brooke said, smiling.

"It's these damned Hexosehr recyclers, sir. A CO_2 scrubber is easy. These, we don't understand how they work so when they break, and they do, we can't figure out how to fix them short of replacement."

Weaver was upside down, leaning over backwards, examining a piece of alien machinery and trying to act like the position was totally natural.

"It's an ionization separation system, Chief," Weaver said, pointing. "Filtration, ionization point, separation point, oxygen reconsolidation, compressor system. What's the issue?"

"The separator's not working," the chief said. Chief Petty Officer Dean Gestner, lead machinist of the *Blade II*, was stuffed into the narrow space between the ionizer and a bulkhead. Fortunately, he was a small guy. "We're getting a half a dozen toxins come through. Not just CO_2. Ketones, esters, you name it. Some of it gets thrown out in compression, but the separation's the problem."

"We got a spare separator around?" Weaver asked.

"Sure, sir," the chief said. "Four in spares baseside. But are we gonna have one when we're on the back side of Gamma Nowhere?"

"Point," Weaver said. "We're getting at least two Hexosehr tech reps on the next cruise. We were supposed to get them before now. Pull and replace this separator and hold onto it. We'll get them to examine it and tell us what's wrong and how to fix it. For that matter, have you asked Tchar? He's starting to get a handle on some of this stuff."

"No, sir," the chief said, grinding his teeth.

Unfortunately, the chief had the full measure of Napoleon complex that went with his size.

"Look, Tchar's around for a reason, Chief," the XO said. "He's an invaluable source of technical expertise. He won't be with us on this cruise, but he's going to be with us on others. If you can't handle working with an Adar I'll find a chief who can. Are we clear?"

"Clear, sir," the chief said.

"Pull it and replace it," Weaver repeated. "Then give it to Tchar to look at. Make sure we've got at least one replacement for each system. And ask Tchar, if he figures out how to fix it back to spec, how he did it and for him to write the repair manual. There's a bunch of this Hexosehr stuff we don't have repair manuals on, yet. Looks like we're going to have to write them."

"Got it, sir," the chief said as Weaver pulled himself out. The chief followed then stopped to brush some dust off his coveralls. "There's another . . . issue, sir."

"Yes?" Weaver said.

"This chick with blue hair came breezing into the shop yesterday and asked what we needed done," Gestner said. "I told her to get the hell out of my shop. When I did, I started getting grief from PO Morris and PO Gants. I've got that under control, but I just thought you should know. I don't think much of having women on a boat, sir, but if it's got to be it's got to be. But I won't have them in my shop."

Weaver looked at the chief blank-faced and wondered exactly how to handle this.

"Okay, Chief Gestner, here's the deal," Weaver said. "You just monumentally *grapped* up."

"*Excuse* me, sir?" the chief said hotly.

"Are you going to actually listen to why you *grapped* up?" Weaver asked. "From someone with far less time in the Navy and about five hundred times more time in *space* than you?"

"Of course, Captain," the chief said, his teeth grinding again. "I am *always* seeking the wisdom of my betters."

"Chief, that wasn't even on the edge of insolence," Weaver warned. "I'm serious. Are you actually going to listen? Or are we going to turn this into a dick beating contest? One that, I guarantee it, you are going to *lose*."

"I apologize, sir," the chief said, taking a deep breath. "I am listening."

"Miriam Moon is the ship's linguist, yes," Weaver said. "But on the last cruise . . . Look, she's ADHD. You know what that is, right?"

"So are both my kids, sir," the chief said, his brow furrowing.

"Incredibly smart little monsters that go ballistic if they get bored?" Weaver asked.

Gestner chuckled. "More or less describes them, sir."

"When Miriam gets bored, she starts wandering around the ship, being . . . annoying as hell," Captain Weaver said. "Since she's a civilian, there's only so much the CO can do about that. What we found out, more or less by accident, on the last cruise is that if you give her something to do, she does a spectacular job. Especially something mechanical. She completely rebuilt one system and painted every steam-pipe in the ship along with doing all sorts of minor jobs. Not to mention fixing the neutrino injector in the middle of a battle. The reason she breezed into *your* shop, Chief, is that it's more *Miriam's* shop than yours. She was a major part of the design team when the Hexosehr built this ship. And you got about twenty percent more relative space because of it. So you should be thanking her, not insulting her. And the reason Red and Sub Dude gave you grief was because they were trying to tell you the same thing. Knowing both of them, they were probably doing it badly, but that was what was going on. Now, you're going to apologize to Miss Moon, give her full access to your shop and utilize her. In fact, first thing to do is put her in charge of this thing and see if *she* can figure it out. But apologize first, sincerely. How you handle that with your people is up to you. If you're the type that can't lose face, you're going to have a hard time doing so. But you are *going* to apologize and you are *going* to utilize her or you're not a chief that can handle the *Blade*. Are we clear?"

"Clear, sir," the chief said. "You're serious."

"Yes, God damnit!" Weaver snapped, finally losing his temper. "I'm deadly serious! Hell, if she didn't already have a job and if I could figure out a way to do it I'd give *her* the machinist section! Among other things, she had the guys who worked in that section eating out of her hand last cruise! I'm *that* serious! Are we clear?!"

"Clear, sir," Gestner said, obviously nonplussed.

"I'm serious, Chief," Weaver said, calmer. "This is not a sub. It's a spaceship. It's a spaceship that gets into really weird *maulk*. I can't afford to have the guy who has to get stuff fixed in a funk because things aren't going according to routine or somebody's gotten up his nose. I need somebody who if he can't figure out a piece of strange alien equipment will figure out who *can*. If you can't get over whatever keeps you from listening to people's input, you're not for the *Blade*. Because nobody in this ship understands every part or can figure out every problem that crops up. And I need to know that in time to get a replacement. You're a good mechanic and your reports say you run a good shop. But the shop on this ship is unlike any other in the service. And if you can't get with the program, tell me now."

"I can do the job, sir," the chief said, frowning. "I really can."

"Be square with me, Chief," Bill said. "It's seriously different. Are you sure?"

"I'm sure, sir," Gestner replied.

"*Grapp* me on this and I'm not going threaten you with Diego Garcia or Iceland," Weaver said. "But I do suggest you ask Red or Sub Dude the story of Petty Officer Olson."

"Olson, sir?" Gestner asked.

"Ask them," Weaver said, dusting off his own coveralls. "Are we space ready with the exception of the separators?"

"Yes, sir," Gestner said. "I'll have a full report on down or questionable systems on the Eng's desk this afternoon. But the rest of it's minor stuff."

"Good to hear," the XO said. "Tell Commander Oldfield I'll need it on my desk by noon tomorrow. But do not dawdle on looking up Miss Moon, Chief."

"Yes, sir," Gestner said, frowning in thought.

❆ ❆ ❆

"This XO shit is for the birds, sir," Bill said as the CO entered his compartment. "What ever happened to the paperless office concept?"

"What's really funny about it is that most of the actual paper gets filed and forgotten," the CO said, sitting down across from him. "It's the stuff that we file electronically that gets looked at. Hell, mostly it gets automatically compared to norms and some computer sends up a red flag if it doesn't fit the model. Which is why—"

"We keep getting these stupid queries!" Weaver finished, holding up a form. "I wish somebody would tell the software we're no longer an SSBN with a crew of 157 and twenty-four missiles! We haven't filed our weekly paperwork on missile stability so this damned program keeps sending damned queries!"

"And we will until somebody comes up with a second model just like us," Captain Prael said. "When will the equipment status report be done?"

"By 1700," Bill said, holding up same. "I think we can squeeze in most of the minor repairs before we leave; I'm working on the budget and worktable now. But the only major issue is the separator and we're going to pull and replace that."

"What's this I hear about you having a run-in with Chief Gestner over Miss Moon?" the CO asked, holding out his hand for the preliminary report.

"I told the chief that Miss Moon was the most valuable resource the machinist's shop had on this ship," Weaver said. "And that if he couldn't figure that out, I'd find a chief who could."

"And did you discuss the threat to have him relieved with me, first, Captain?" the CO asked neutrally, flipping through the pages.

"No, Captain," Weaver replied. "I don't discuss every encounter I have on this ship with you. If you wish me to restrain myself in any negative encounter until I have solicited your advice, Captain, then I will do so."

"Get off your high horse, Weaver," the CO said, looking up. "I'm not Spectre Blankemeier and this is no longer his ship. In my ship we do things my way. And *my* way does not necessarily mean a civilian female running around fixing stuff. In case it's not clear to you, *Captain*, that's a major departure from normal activity in any military unit, much less a sub. And threatening a senior chief with being strapped to the outside of the hull for three days was not the conduct I expect of my officers. Am I clear?"

"Clear, sir," Weaver replied.

"I've been fully briefed on Miss Moon's activities," Prael continued. "Which does not mean I approve. Miss Moon is to restrict herself to authorized linguist duties if and when she is needed. I've sent in a memo for record recommending her replacement with a qualified *male* Navy candidate. We may be forced to carry her for this mission, but I see no reason why we even have her on-board. We're not carrying a science team, otherwise."

There was no question asked so Weaver kept his mouth shut.

"You're doing a decent job as an XO," Prael continued after a moment. "Decent, not extraordinary. Since you're a hard worker and unquestionably smart, I put that down to lack of experience. You were fast tracked to lieutenant commander then jumped twice to your present rank for, basically, being there. Yes, you did a good job as astrogator. That's to be expected. You've proven you're courageous. But that doesn't add up to being a Naval officer. If you were a real Naval officer you'd have handled things differently. So you can get over being a civilian wearing a uniform or . . . I believe the phrase was 'I'll find someone who will.' Are we clear?"

"Clear, sir," Weaver said, stone-faced.

"Comments?"

"XO to Skipper or Captain to Captain?" Weaver asked.

"Again, quoting, I think the phrase I'm looking for here is that was over the edge of insolent," Prael said dangerously.

"Captain to Captain it is," Weaver said. "This is your ship, sir, sure enough. And, yes, I was bumped up fast. That, sir, is because there are *no* other officers in the Navy with my training, experience or skills. And Miss Moon is on this ship because there are no other *people* with her experience or ability. Your job, in addition to your other duties, is to teach me to be your XO. And I'll do that to the best of my very high ability. I never do anything by halfs. But my job, Captain, is to teach *you* to be a *starship* commander."

"You're really going to push this, aren't you?" Prael asked.

"You already, mistakenly, referred to this ship as a sub, sir," Weaver continued. "It's not. It's a spaceship, designed as such from the keel out. It can go underwater but it's primarily designed for space. If you think of it as a sub, sir, you're going to get us all killed. Because there's a universe of difference between being at sea and being in space. One difference, is that if you're cruising the Pacific you don't suddenly run into a species that speaks by sonar and have to have someone to figure out how to talk to them. Have to have that or you're going to get blown away. Thus you have to have someone who can figure that out, no matter who that is. And thus we get to Miss Moon. Who completely redesigned faulty systems on the *Blade One* so that they were no longer faulty and figured out how to communicate with the Hexosehr and, and, and. The last 'and who' being that she was a primary member of the design team of *this* ship. Who is an asset you do *not* want to lose despite her being female and occasionally bat-shit crazy. I can't believe I'm having to explain this to you! You *read* the reports!"

"I'm going to have to ask for relief, aren't I?" Prael growled. "Because yes, I've read the reports. But it was Spectre's ship. It's mine now."

"If you asked for relief, right now, you'll get it, sir," Weaver said. "You'll find yourself off 'your' ship so fast it will make your head swim. We both know it. I'd get reamed for handling things badly but you'd be *gone*. Because there is no one else to do my job, sir. Which is to be XO, yes, but is primarily to keep you and this ship alive when we get where there's no air and the universe goes crazy. And you're going to do one or two cruises and then be gone, fast-tracked into a training position or, if we have them by then, a bigger ship. I'll still be here, probably still be XO, teaching your replacement. Because when we get out between the stars, sir, there are going to be *dozens* of times you'll turn to me and ask me what the *grapp* is going on. Just as, now, I have to turn to you, sir, to figure out Clerk Click and all the rest of this *maulk*. So are we going to make this work? Or not?"

"There has to be one boss on a ship, XO," Prael said fiercely.

"Agreed," Bill replied. "I'm not going to override one of your orders. Unless it's going to get us killed and you don't realize it. I hope that we don't hit that point. And I don't want to *grapp* with your confidence; a CO has to have it. But Spectre could maintain his confidence *and* ask questions, even in front of the crew. Can you?"

"We'll see," Prael said. "But the thing you need to figure out is that I've got nearly twenty years of experience as a Naval officer and this isn't the *Enterprise*. It's a U.S. Naval vessel."

"Correction, again, Captain," Bill said with a sigh. "It's an *Alliance Space* Vessel. Why couldn't they have chosen that for the actual name? And, sir, I have over twenty years of experience in the fields of engineering, quantum physics, optics, physics, astronomy and astrophysics. And, sir, as much as you may know about Naval bureaucracy and the play of wind and wave and how to calculate buoyancy, when we hit zero-G all that experience means exactly *dick*. And at that point, mine becomes critical. If you cannot handle that or if you cannot figure that out, then please request relief. Because if you're unwilling to learn, we're all doomed. As for me, I want to learn how to be a good XO. I'm more than willing to learn to be a good XO. I know that I'm still unqualified to be a CO and I'll be watching your moves to see how while learning my job."

"As I said, we'll see," Prael said, standing up. "Miss

Moon is still not to be given duties outside her specific area of expertise. At least for the time being."

"That's your right as CO," Weaver said, shrugging.

"And you think I'm making a mistake," the CO said.

"Several, actually," Bill replied. "You've undercut me with Chief Gestner which means that in the future he's going to think he can walk all over me. Any time he's unhappy with one of my orders he'll cry to the Eng who will, in turn, cry to you. He's also going to ignore my advice on interacting with Tchar, which will reduce his ability to get things repaired. And from his attitude, he's going to have a tough time interacting with the Hexosehr but that's just a guess. On the direct subject of Miss Moon, you're going to be subject to unintentional and intentional harassment during the cruise. And if you directly control her, such as confinement to quarters, you'll both lose the respect of the crew, especially those who are veterans of her previous cruises, and you'll almost undoubtedly get reprimanded upon our return for illegal restriction of a civilian technical specialist. Last, you're positioning yourself, mentally, to ignore my advice or, more probably, fail to access it. Given experiences from previous cruises, that is likely to be a bad thing. However, none of those are, at this point, critical issues that will kill us. So I'm raising no objection. You did, however, ask."

"You're going to be a pain in the ass, aren't you?" Captain Prael said.

"Apparently, sir," Bill replied, tiredly. "But as my momma used to say, don't ask me a question if you don't want the answer."

"Well here's one for your professional development,

Captain," the CO said. "We can have these sorts of differences in private, but you'd better damned well keep them to yourself around the crew."

"Aye, aye," Bill replied. He leaned back and shuddered after the door closed, rubbing his face. "*Maulk*. This is gonna be one *grapped* up cruise."

"This is *maulk*," PO Ian 'Red' Morris said, unbolting the separator from its mounts. "I know how to fix this piece of *maulk*. You've got to open it with a melder, though."

"And Gestner doesn't want to hear for melders," Michael "Sub Dude" Gants said, engaging the jack to lower the multiton separator. "Miriam'd have this thing fixed in five minutes," he continued, sucking in through his teeth.

"No *chither*," Red said, pulling his Number Two arm off and replacing it with Number Four. Two was good for small work but Four had more power. On each of the previous two cruises, the machinist had been hit by fire in, respectively, his right arm and right leg. He had a human prosthetic arm, a good one, and a Hexosehr prosthetic leg, a better one. He placed his prosthetic leg against the bulkhead, grabbed the hand-hold on the separator and pulled, rolling the massive piece of machinery out onto the deck. "He and the CO are going to be right sorry about that when we're outside."

"Sorry about what?" Chief Gestner said pointedly. Neither of the machinists had heard him arrive.

"Sorry you ignored the XO," Gants said, pumping the jack and lifting the separator up to the level of the carry-cradle.

"Keep your opinions to yourself, PO," Gestner said angrily. "I get lip from you like that again and I'll have you up on report."

"Chief, maybe you should just ground me now," Gants said, helping Red get the separator positioned. "Because, honestly, you're going to hear my opinions if you ask me a direct question. Gonna happen. You asked, I answered. If you consider that insolent, then you'd better ship me out now."

"Just get this thing replaced," Gestner snarled.

"Aye, aye, Chief," Red said. "What are we supposed to do with it?"

"Send it to dock for repair," the Chief said. "We don't have room to keep it on the ship."

"It's times like this I wish Macelhenie had survived the last cruise," Gants said as soon as the chief was out of earshot.

"It's times like this I contemplate the pleasure I would obtain by brushing old Numbah Fow across his face," Red said, holding up the massive prosthetic. "It'd be a right pleasure."

"Come on," Gants replied, shrugging. "Let's get this thing winched out of the ship and see about finding a spare."

"How the hell am I supposed to do that?" Lieutenant Ross said, looking at the directive.

"Excuse me, sir?" Eric replied.

In the last five days he'd seen Brooke exactly ten hours. At the moment he was using the computer station in officer's Admin to try to catch up on paperwork. The company was doing PT and when they got back there was a field evolution he had to lead. He'd rather be running, but the paperwork just wouldn't *end*!

"There's a new position called 'Vac Boss,'" Lieutenant Ross said. "He's supposed to be the go-to guy if there's an EVA. They're starting a training class in it, but the boss has to have vac experience. Right now, the guy with the most hours wins. So we, I, am supposed to compute the number of hours each member of the company has in vacuum and find out who is vac boss. It will probably turn out to be one of the sergeants who survived the last couple of missions. How the hell are we going to put them in charge of an EVA exercise? God, I need a cigar."

"Quickly," Berg said, shrugging. "The last mission we did all the *way* outside EVA stuff. The squids stayed by the ship. Hell, it's probably Corwin. Heh. That'd be funny. I wouldn't want Corwin in charge of a day-care center."

"That still doesn't tell me how to compute it," Ross growled. "How many hours do *you* have?"

"Whoa," Berg replied, not looking up. "Lots. Depends on how you calculate it. I'm not sure if the drop on Cheerick counts or not, but that was just a couple of minutes. Hours and fricking hours at Tycho 714. More at HD Thirty-Seven. Wrestling that comet . . . When the Karchava dreadnought got evacuated, couple of hours right there . . . Come to think of it, there's a vac indicator on the suits. That probably got dumped to the mission log; everything else was. Get Portana to pull the mission logs and look."

"I've got a better idea, Lieutenant," Ross said, grinning evilly.

"Oh, come on, sir!" Berg protested. "I'm swamped!"

"How hard could it be?"

"It not in the standard log," the Filipino armorer said, shaking his head.

On the previous cruise, Berg and the then-new unit armorer had gotten off to a rocky start, a little matter of, well, *everything* getting on each other's nerves. Since they bunked right by each other, Portana's habit of playing Filipino salsa music at top volume had led to Berg replying with Death Metal and country at same, which led to the rest of the compartment playing a medley of clashing tunes to the point that the CO and the first sergeant stepped in. Berg was big, good-looking, popular, easygoing and a West Virginia country boy. Portana was short, swarthy, caustic and Filipino. They'd managed to get past it during the course of the cruise and were now, to the extent a lieutenant and an enlisted man could be, friends. But it had been a long road to that point.

"It doesn't get logged?" Berg asked, shaking his head. "Okay, I guess we're going to have to . . ."

"It get logged," Portana said. "But it in deep structure. Got to get a program to parse it out. And mission log's encryp'ed so got to decryp' first. Not something you can just press a button and there it is. Gonna be work."

"I don't suppose . . ." Berg said, grinning.

"I got fifteen Wyverns to configure," Portana said. "You *know* how long t'at take. Not sure I'm going to be done by mission time. One being you new one. But, good news, you mission log survived. Well, right up to when you get all fried and stuff."

"*Chither,*" Berg said. "Dump the raw mission logs to my computer and I'll see what I can do . . ."

"Well, I guess it's good I'm working so late, lately," Eric said as he got in the truck. "How was work?"

"I'm trying to learn how to tell customers, 'Sorry, I'm married,'" Brooke said, sighing exasperatedly. "Actually, I just hold up the ring. But some guys can't take the hint."

"Try 'I'm happily married to a Force Recon lieutenant who'll bust your face if you don't keep your hands off me,'" Eric said, closing his eyes and leaning back in the seat.

"That won't exactly help with the tips," Brooke pointed out. "Not that this particular group of jerks left much of a tip, anyway. One of the other waitresses handles it just fine, but she's been doing this for a long time. I'm trying to figure out how she does it. But most of the time, it looks to me as if she really *is* willing to go home with them. Then if they get too crude she just . . . hammers them flat and they *like* it."

"It's a game," Eric said, shrugging. "Nobody *really* expects to go home with the waitress. Well, except The Envoy. You just have to come up with standard answers to the come-on. 'Sorry, but unless you can touch the back of your head with your tongue I'm not interested.'"

"Eric Bergstresser!"

"'Well, gosh, sir, I *would* go home with you. That is, if I didn't have a husband with the stamina of a lion and hung like an elephant . . .'"

"I could *never* say that!"

"Why? Waitresses said both of them to *me*," Eric pointed out.

"You . . . oh!" Brooke replied, shaking her head. She looked over at him and frowned. "Are you shiny, honey?"

"Beat," Eric said. "I got a new duty dumped on me today and it's kicking my ass."

"More VD reports?" Brooke asked, dimpling. "I never thought I'd say something like that in my *life.*"

Given that things like VD reports and MWR reports were anything but classified, Eric had willingly discussed those with her. He opened his mouth to reply then closed it with a clop.

"No," he said after a moment. "Something . . . else. One of the things I'm *not* supposed to talk about. Which is why I didn't bring it home."

"Shiny," Brooke said, restraining her curiosity with difficulty. "Did you hear there's going to be some sort of broadcast by the President tomorrow night? And that it's going to run over an hour?"

"No," Berg said. "What about?"

"Nobody knows," Brooke said. "The TV said it was on a matter of great importance that has been, up to this point, classified."

Eric's eyes flew open and he looked straight forward. Just then, his implant dinged.

"Tomorrow?" Weaver screamed, looking at his secure e-mail. He'd just gotten home and keyed on his computer to find the warning message."No, no, no, no!"

"Weaver," Prael said over his implant. "Back to the office, stat. We've got a secure link with the Secretary of Defense in thirty minutes."

"I'm on my way, sir," Bill replied, picking up his uniform blouse. "*Chither*! Why *now*?"

"Not by our choice," the Secretary of Defense said. "What the *Times* has been able to piece together about the *Blade* is coming out in the morning edition. What they don't know, though, is that we effectively lost the *Blade* and got a new one from the Hexosehr. They did, however, piece together the 'helicopter crash' with the first mission and speculate on casualties from the second. They don't know about the Dreen. Bill, you had some conversation with Robin. I pulled the transcript when I got the news. Anything you want to add?"

"I tried to throw him off-scent, slightly, sir," Weaver said. "Best I could do. I could tell he knew about the *Blade*, pretty solidly, and that we'd run into something that killed Marines. He didn't mention the scientific losses or the SF or the Cheerick or the last mission's results. But my contact report stated that he was going to do a piece on the *Blade*."

"They apparently got some video from our Russian friends," the Secretary of Defense said. "I'm sure the Russians will be running that one down. But this changes . . . Well, it changes everything. Commandant, I want Lieutenant Bergstresser available for Dog and Pony."

"Yes, sir," the commandant said. "I'll inform his CO."

"Ditto Spectre and you, Bill. Anyone else you'd suggest? Any of you?"

Weaver had a suggestion but given his rocky position with the CO he wasn't about to bring it up.

"That linguist," Admiral Townsend said. "Miss Moon.

Good looking, obviously articulate. And I've seen the way that she looked in the documentary. I especially loved the parts where she was repairing the ship on the last mission. Painted every steam pipe in the ship? That took determination, by God. It puts a human face on the whole thing. Cute lady who talks to strange aliens and still wields a wrench when she has to. What do you think, Captain Weaver?"

"Sounds good, sir," Bill said, trying not to sound strangled. "She's going to need a heads up, though. First, she'll need at least ten minutes to panic, then a day to do her hair. She might have to go home to see her usual stylist."

"We need to centralize this," the SecDef said. "Get all the people down here in DC. I know you're preparing for deployment, but this takes precedence. Get to work on this tonight." The video of the SecDef cut off leaving only the commandant and the CAO.

"I'll order up Bergstresser and, hell, one of the enlisted," the commandant said. "People always like junior enlisted for this sort of thing. I'm sort of shamed to say I don't know the Marine players all that well. Captain Weaver?"

"Lurch, sir?" Bill replied. As well hung for a sheep and all that. "That is, Sergeant Lyle? The guy who was injured in an accident and worked his way back to line. He's not all that articulate, but . . ."

"Good call," the commandant said, nodding. "Good human interest angle. The first sergeant's been on both missions, what's your read on him?"

"First Sergeant Powell is one of those rare NCOs that

really could take over as a commander, sir," Bill replied. "Smart as a whip intellectually—hell, he's got a degree from the Sorbonne—good common sense, experienced. But the company's preparing for deployment. Dragging him away may interfere."

"If the company commander can't do without his first sergeant for a few days, I need to find a new CO," the commandant said. "Sergeant Lyle, Lieutenant Bergstresser and First Sergeant Powell. Got it. Good line-up. I'm done. Out here."

"Since everyone *else* is asking," the CAO said, chuckling.

"Well, you've got myself and Miriam, sir," Bill replied. "Admittedly, Miriam's from the civilian science side. If you want enlisted personnel . . ." Bill paused and thought about that, running through the list and then chuckling.

"Something funny, Captain?" the CAO asked.

"Just imagining the COB being interviewed, sir," Bill replied. "'So you are the chief of boat? What's your name?' 'C-O-B.' 'How do you spell that?' 'C-O-B. Chief. Of. Boat.' Sir, in all honesty, no, I can't think of any others unless the CO wants to go. In that case, I'll stay back and get the boat ready to go. That's my job, after all."

"The Marines are sending enlisted people," the CAO said. "And Captain Prael hasn't been on the previous missions."

"Then I'd suggest Red, sir," Bill replied, then blinked rapidly, realizing he could not for the life of him recall Red's real name. "Petty Officer First Class Ian . . . Morris. Not particularly articulate, either, but with two prosthetics from two missions, he's not going to have to be."

"Get that done, Captain," the CAO said. "Make sure he's available and everybody gets down to DC tomorrow. Early."

"Aye, aye, sir," Weaver and Prael both replied, simultaneously. Weaver didn't look over to see his CO's reaction.

"Any questions, Captain Prael?" the CAO asked.

"No, sir," the CO replied.

"Then I'm out," the CAO said.

The screen blanked and there was an uncomfortable silence.

"You'd better get moving, XO," Prael said after a moment. "You've got a lot of work to do."

"Yes, sir," Bill said, standing up and walking to the door of the shield room.

"Weaver."

"Sir?" Bill replied without turning around.

"We'll talk when you get back."

"Yes, sir."

"Yes, sir," Eric said, nodding into the phone. "Yes, sir. Aye, aye, sir. Yes, sir. Understood, sir. Gung ho, sir. Yes, sir. Good night."

"You sure weren't saying much," Brooke said. She'd combed out her hair and changed into a nightgown but stayed up, yawning, as long as her husband did.

"I'm a lieutenant," Berg replied, finally getting a chance to strip out of his uniform. "We generally just take orders. The difference between a private first class and a second lieutenant is that a PFC's been promoted twice."

"What's happening?" Brooke asked. "Is it a mission?"

"Sort of," Eric replied. "But not the way you're thinking. I've got to go to DC tomorrow. Something came up."

"And you can't tell me what," Brooke said.

"Honestly, I probably could and get away with it at this point," Eric said. "But I'm still under orders not to discuss anything I do with anybody. Can you . . . ?"

"I'm fine with that," Brooke said, stretching in an arch that drew down the front of her already low-cut nightgown. "Among other things, I suspect it would be a long conversation. And I've got other things on my mind."

"What were we talking about?" Eric said, hurrying with his boots.

"Miss Moon," Weaver said as the slight linguist exited the Looking Glass. "I see you redyed your hair."

Union Station was the central hub for the increasingly defunct Washington Metro Line. The Chen Anomaly generated dozens of Looking Glass bosons per minute. They then proceeded on a path more or less parallel to the surface of the earth in apparently random zigzags and eventually came to rest. There they generally sat innocuously, still in rare cases opening up a gate to an unexplored world.

However, the millions of inert LGBs that the Anomaly had generated over the past years could be moved to another spot and then linked to any other boson of the same frequency. By moving two to two separate points that the movers wanted to link, a portal could be established between any two points on Earth.

Moving an LGB was no simple technical feat. The boson first had to be charged with static electricity using a massive Van der Waal static generator. The generator was similar to a plasma ball but much harder to construct, requiring a formed ball of metal with an absolutely blemish-free surface. Given that the minimum size to be of any use was over ten feet across, the first few had been enormously expensive. But as time went on, manufacturing processes and technologies improved to the point that creating one cost less than a million dollars.

Then the charged LGB had to be moved. To move it required massive electromagnets to maintain a holding field and the power to run them. But the value was there. Using more and more systems, gates were being opened at the rate of over forty per day in the U.S. alone. Even the first few hundred had killed the airlines as every hub airport got linked to every other. As time went by, those hubs were connected to more and more cities, more direct links were established and even links internal to cities became common.

Them that has, gets: Washington, DC, had become a poster city for LGB gates. A series of them had been set up around the city, each in pairs to prevent collisions, permitting rapid movement across the entire city by simply stepping through the right portals. There were over thirty on the Washington Mall, alone, and a coffee-table book that consisted of nothing but pictures of the reflected images lasted surprisingly long on the bestseller lists.

Furthermore, through Looking Glasses at the defunct Dulles Airport, the city was connected to other countries and even to Adar. More portals then moved the incoming to Union Station, which was the central hub for all domestic arrivals and departures.

Miriam Moon actually lived in Dalton, GA, and had taken over fourteen minutes to get to the portal in Washington, including waiting for the connecting portal in Atlanta. Bill, on the other hand, lived in Huntsville, AL, and had a direct link.

"It was getting washed out at the wedding," Miriam replied, surprisingly calmly. Bill had expected her to be nearly hysterical. He knew she'd be all right once she had to don her public persona, but he figured he'd have to hold her hand up to that point. "I'd been thinking about redoing it, was going to before we left. This just gave me a reason."

"Did you get any sleep last night?" Bill asked, gesturing to the escalator and taking the handle of her rolling bag.

"No," Miriam said, her voice shaking slightly. "But it gave me time to do my hair. And get over the panic. I could use something to eat, though. I was throwing up most of the night." The linguist *was* particularly pale.

"Well, everybody's waiting in the restaurant top-side," Bill said. "None of us has eaten, yet."

"I hope you weren't waiting for me," Miriam replied. "I nearly sent my regrets. Right up to the point I was getting ready to step through the gate."

"The CAO was rather pointed that he wanted you to be there," Bill pointed out.

"I'm not a Navy officer," Miriam replied tartly. "Greg Townsend can kiss my white butt if he thinks he can *order* me to do *anything*."

"I understand," Bill said, rolling his eyes behind her back.

"Don't you roll your eyes at *me*, Bill Weaver," Miriam said.

"Sorry."

"I think we should have gone public from the beginning," Miriam continued as they walked past a newspaper stand. Normally, there would have been a line for the *Washington Post*. Today, she was being heavily outsold by her more conservative brother. There was only one *Times* left on the rack and as they walked past, someone grabbed it and got in line. "Why do we always have to do things as a crashing emergency?"

"The Chinese and Russians asked for more time," Bill said. "I can imagine their reactions. We're going to have to wait until the third documentary until we know their full reactions."

"Hi, guys," Miriam said, slipping into the booth. "I need a waffle."

"You going to be shiny, ma'am?" Red asked. The group was in civilian clothes but everyone had a suit bag with them holding their uniforms. "The hair looks great, by the way."

"I'll be fine, Red, thanks," Miriam said. "How's married life treating you, Eric?"

"Good," Berg replied, shaking his head. "It's a bit of an adjustment, but . . . good. Really good."

"I need to give him a jar and a bag of jelly beans," Lurch said, grinning.

Eric looked around as the older members of the group, and Red, who was long married, all chuckled.

"I don't get it," Eric admitted.

"Get a jar," Red said. "A big one in your case, probably. And a bag or a dozen of jelly beans. Each time you fool around the first year of marriage, put a jelly bean in the jar. After the first year, each time you fool around pull out a jellybean and eat it. The legend says that no matter how many years you're married, you'll never empty the jar."

"And for some reason, you only put in the licorice ones," Weaver said. "Let's order, then I'll lay out the agenda. There's not much today, honestly. We're probably not even going to be put on display until after the third documentary comes out. But it's going to get rocky later in the week."

"Are you shiny, Brooke?"

Tom was one of the older waiters in the restaurant, a pro of the old school. Brooke had tried to learn his moves, but it was like a tyro painter trying to copy a grand master; it just wasn't the same. She knew she'd need decades of experience to come close. And, frankly, she'd rather be a cook.

"That documentary that's coming out tonight, the government one," Brooke said. "I think it has to do with my husband."

"Well, we've got customers to attend to," Tom said. "Try to stay in the groove."

"Groovy, Tom," Brooke said, looking at her orders and trying to recall what she knew she'd forgotten. "Salads to fourteen . . ."

"Drink refills on nine," Tom said, sliding past her.

"Thank you."

She checked her list, glanced at table nine and got

replacements for the drinks that were low. Two diet cokes and a coke, not too hard.

"How are you doing?" she asked the family.

"Irritated," the father said. "I need a scotch and soda."

"I'll get that right away," Brooke said, heading for the bar. It wouldn't break pattern too badly.

Unfortunately, the TV in the bar was tuned to a station that was broadcasting the "government documentary." Brooke wasn't addicted to the news but she'd caught a snip of two talking heads debating the idea of government-produced documentaries. Neither of them liked the idea. But the customers at the bar were clearly riveted and as she was putting in the bar order she heard a familiar name.

". . . Moon, ship's linguist. Miss Moon speaks twenty-seven languages fluently and put herself through college through modeling and painting portraits. A Renaissance woman par excellence, she is also a noted engineer and mechanic, often working on the ship systems of the *Vorpal Blade* . . ."

The next shot was a surveillance camera showing the girl Brooke had last seen in a daring Little Black Dress wearing a blue coverall, a big wrench in her hand, a smear of grease on her cheek and whacking away at some part in what was clearly a ship.

". . . Born in the small city of Waycross, Georgia, her father is a minister and her mother a school guidance counselor. With six degrees, including everything from forensic science to drafting, she is a critical member of the *Vorpal Blade* team.

"PFC Eric Bergstresser . . ."

"That's your husband, isn't it?" Tom asked, his eyes wide.

"Yes," Brooke squeaked, picking up the drink for table nine.

"Leave it," Tom said, looking over his shoulder. The restaurant was slowly emptying into the bar as more and more of the patrons came in to see what was going on. "Nobody cares."

". . . was born and raised in the small town of Crab Apple, West Virginia, where he lettered in track and field, football and basketball while also being the captain of the Central High School Physics club. He volunteered for the Marines and then for Force Recon and was the Distinguished Honor Graduate of his class in Force Reconnaissance Operators Training, one of the most demanding courses in the entire United States Military. A recent transfer to the unit, his presence was to be most fortuitous. Because while the missions of the *Vorpal Blade* required a team effort, if there was one outstanding member, one most valuable player if you will, it would be Two-Gun Berg."

"That's her husband," Tom said loudly, pointing at Brooke.

"Stop it, Tom!" Brooke snapped. "I need to go cover my tables . . ."

"They're all in here," Tom said, sighing. "I need to go get this sorted out. It looks as if the restaurant is moving into the bar for the time being."

"He's your husband?" one of the male patrons of the bar asked. In his sixties, he looked as if he'd been holding down the bar since the restaurant was opened. "So you knew about this?"

"Yes, he is and no, I didn't," Brooke said. "He never talks about his work. What *is* this?"

"We've got a ship that goes to other planets," a woman said over her shoulder. "Faster than light, that is. And not just where the gates go. The President introduced this thing and said that there was information in it that meant things were going to change, significantly."

"The stock exchanges are being closed the day after the last documentary," another patron said. "They just released the word today."

"These are the missions of the Alliance Space Ship *Vorpal Blade*," the announcer said stentoriously, to a view of the *Blade One* bursting out of the water. Then the TV cut to a commercial.

"Now *that* is an unfortunate acronym," the first patron said. "I see the hand of the Adar in there."

"I need to get back to work," Brooke said.

"Just cover the back tables in the bar," Tom said from over her shoulder. "I've got most of your people moved there. Bring the guy his drink."

"I'm sorry about this," Brooke said, trying hard not to cry. "My husband is one of the Marines on that ship. I never knew it until just now. It's sort of . . ."

"Don't sweat it," the father said, holding out his hand for the scotch. "I'm a retired Navy captain."

"Are you going to be okay, honey?" his wife asked. "Jim never told me things, too. But they didn't put most of them on prime-time."

"I'll be fine," Brooke said, sniffing. "I need to go check on your food."

She got her tables covered just in time for the commercial

to end and then got locked in again. By then the word had circulated that "the hero of the mission's" wife was one of the waitresses and her tables started cutting her some slack. Eventually, Tom pulled her off and just sat her at the bar as things heated up.

By the time the action ended she was crying and so were most of the patrons. Especially as the closing scrolled through the list of dead.

"Tomorrow night, the *Vorpal Blade* continues on her mission of discovery and uncovers both a great threat and a powerful ally. Until tomorrow, this is . . ."

"You've got yourself a good husband there," the Navy wife said, taking her arm.

"I knew that even before tonight, ma'am," Brooke said, wiping her eyes. "God, I must look terrible."

"Never better," the woman said. "It's tough living with a warrior, honey. But it's worth it. Hold on to what you've got. He'll be okay. Boys like that, well, they walk through raindrops."

"Thank you, ma'am," Brooke said.

"Lisa," the woman replied, holding out a card. "You call me. Have you met your CO's wife, yet?"

"No, ma'am," Brooke admitted. "We were supposed to have a get-together this weekend but it got cancelled."

"She needs to get on the ball," the woman said. "Especially after this. I'll make some calls. But if you need somebody to talk to, that's my number."

"Thank you, ma'am."

"It's Lisa," the woman said. "You call me. That's an order."

"Yes, ma'am," Brooke said, grinning through the sniffles. "Does a military spouse have to obey orders?"

"No," Lisa admitted. "But the smart ones learn to."

Eric looked at his phone and sighed, then flipped it open.

"Hi, honey."

"I don't know what to say," Brooke said calmly.

"I'm sorry I couldn't say anything," Berg said. "But they really blew it out of proportion."

"Five out of forty-one, honey," Brooke replied. "You said that much before, but I never really could understand that until tonight. All those . . ." Her voice started to break.

"Yeah," Eric said. "Honey, it's shiny, really it is. I'll be okay. I promise. Are you going back on yours?"

"Not even close," Brooke said. "But the other missions . . ."

"We can't talk about," Eric said. "That is an absolute. We got *seriously* briefed on that. There are international, heck *interstellar*, agreements on it. But the good news is that I survived. Or bad news. We've been talking to reporters all day on deep background. All of them wanted to know what the big news is. I got to where that was my mantra: The big news is that all of *us* survived. For the rest, you're going to have to wait."

"There wasn't really much about Miss Moon in this one," Brooke said, getting right to the important part.

"She ends up shining in the next two," Berg said. "I will say that. Honey, it's late. Get some sleep. I'll be home in a few days."

"You can just hop a Looking Glass . . ."

"I'm sitting in the Marine Annex Transient Officers'

Quarters by direct and personal order of the commandant," Eric said. "Who is fully aware that we've been married less than two weeks and even apologized. But I'm also not allowed to leave. Sorry, honey."

"It's shiny," Brooke said, sighing. "What's that thing about I knew this would come but I didn't expect it to be so soon?"

"Yuh warns 'em and warns 'em . . ." Eric said, laughing halfheartedly. "I love you, honey."

"Love you," Brooke said. "I guess I'll see you tomorrow night. Sort of."

"Night."

"So we may *not* have Hexosehr on the next mission," the CO continued. "Thoughts?"

"We need to figure out how to fix their systems without resorting to sending them to Runner's World for repair, sir," Bill replied, rolling his eyes. It was the middle of the night and whereas the CO was up, too, he was calling from the shield room in HQ. Bill had had to catch a cab to the Pentagon when he got the call and would have to catch another back to the BOQ.

Fortunately, the stream was audio only, but Prael caught the sarcasm.

"And I'd entertain thoughts on that," the CO said. "Captain."

"Sic Miriam on it when she gets back," Bill said. "The Hexosehr have *got* to have something on the order of repair manuals, they just need to be translated. She's a translator. *And* she has engineering background. Sounds like a perfect match and well within her standard duties."

"I notice that you didn't recommend her to the CAO," the CO said. "Any reason why?"

"Well, possibly because you were sitting right next to me and I was fully aware of your opinion of her, sir," Bill replied tightly. "Or did you think I was going to knife you in the back?"

"Point taken, XO," the CO said, just as tightly. "Look, Bill, let's bury the hatchet . . ."

In my head? Bill thought.

". . . You had some points I probably should have entertained more fully. We'll have a more detailed discussion of it when you get back. But . . . Uncle, XO, okay? You got me."

"It was never about 'getting' you, sir," Bill replied. "That's not my place, sir, and it's not my style. But, sir, every ship thinks that they're special. At least, every good one. But the *Blade* really *is* special. Not just because it's the only warp ship we have, sir. It's things like . . . Well, take Red Morris. He lost an arm on the first mission and a *leg* on the second and just keeps coming *back*. Every single Marine survivor of the first mission volunteered to keep going out. The four that are left are *still* there. The *Blade* has a nearly one hundred percent retention rate. You get people off the *Blade* with a crowbar or in a body bag. Heck, most of the time the losses end up being ash. And we just keep going out, again. My point being, and it's not just directed at you, sir, that that sort of culture is unusual even in the military. People just entering it—"

"It's a club," the CO said, musingly. "I hadn't really thought of that, I'll admit. The new people, even me . . ."

"Frankly, sir, you're all new meat," Bill finished. "The

ones that have been on these missions are the survivors, sir. I've been trying to stop it but I know that the old timers, all of a year, are looking at me when they should be looking at you. But when you start talking about the new Eng, Chief Gestner, people who not only haven't been there and done that, but have ways of doing things that, frankly, are built around something that no longer really exists to the *Blade* people—"

"Welcome to the new Space Navy," the CO said. "It's like the old wet Navy. But not."

"The tone was set when Spectre chose to keep going after Runner's World, sir," Bill said. "We were barely a day away from home, but we kept going, damage and casualties and all, sir. The crew that's done that know they can trust the people who have been there. And people like Gants and Red sure as hell don't know it about Chief Gestner. They'll respect the rank but they're going to have a hard time respecting the person. Especially when he's making decisions they have experience of being wrong choices. When we're thirty days out, it's just us. There aren't any tugs, there isn't any CVBG to call. It's just us. And you don't go 'well, I can't repair it so we'll just have to send it dockside.' Not when there are people who could figure it out, you just don't want to use them because of, well, prejudice."

"I'm getting the trend of this conversation, XO," the CO said.

"Sorry, sir," Bill replied.

"Like I said, we'll talk when you get back. Any idea when that's going to be?"

"Minimum of next Monday, sir," Bill said. "I'm set up

for *Meet the Press* on Sunday morning. So is Two-Gun. Frankly, with the buzz about these shows, the mission may be delayed or even scrubbed. That was a musing of the CAO, sir, but it's in the wind."

"Great," Prael grumped. "And on that happy note . . . I'm clear, here."

"Night, sir," Bill said, standing up and disconnecting the secure line. "*Maulk*. We'll see if I'm even the XO anymore after that little téte-a-téte."

The documentaries ran for three days, from eight to nine PM, Eastern Time. Each of the major cable news networks carried them as did Fox. The regular media chose to forego the honor. Which just meant that they got hammered in the ratings. Say what you will for the entire genre, the *Vorpal Blade* missions upped the ante of "reality programming."

Immediately following the third night came the first press conference. Miriam had been throwing up most of the day but was surprisingly calm as the moment approached.

"Hey, you going to be shiny?" Eric asked.

"Everybody keeps asking that," Miriam said. "I'm fine. Seriously. It's the waiting that's been getting to me."

"You and me both, sister," Red said as the CAO walked out onto the stage. "Here we go."

"You'll enter as the CAO introduces you," the lieutenant commander from Public Affairs repeated, unnecessarily. "March in in a military manner and take your positions in line."

"I don't march," Miriam said tartly. She was dressed

in a business suit that would have looked right in a courtroom. Over the past three nights, millions of viewers had seen her in everything from micro-minis to jeans to spacesuits to grease- and blood-covered coveralls but never a business suit. The heels, however, were consistent. Even her space suit had a three-inch heel.

"Except for you, ma'am," the lieutenant commander added hastily.

". . . the brave sailors and Marines of the *Vorpal Blade*. In order, I'd like you to finally meet, in person, Captain William Weaver, formerly astrogator and now executive officer of the *Blade II* . . ."

"I would rather die a thousand deaths," Weaver said, marching out of the group.

"Lee said that when he surrendered at Appomatox," Berg said, chuckling. "'I would rather face a thousand deaths, but now I must go.'"

"Petty Officer First Class Ian 'Red' Morris . . ."

"Make sure you emphasize the limp from the leg," the PAO officer said.

Red gave him a withering look and marched onto the stage, back straight and not the slightest trace of a limp. On the other hand, he'd made sure he was wearing his Number Two arm. The glittering stainless steel gave him that nice cyborg look. If he'd been wearing Number One, there wouldn't have been anything to see and somebody was bound to ask him to take it off to prove it was a prosthetic.

"Ship's Linguist, Miss Miriam Moon . . ."

"March indeed," Miriam said, swaying onto the stage. The business suit she was wearing was, arguably, as sensual as a potato sack. But she suddenly made it the number one wear for strippers everywhere.

"She just caused fourteen million hard-ons," Berg said, chuckling as the linguist sensuously slid into place, placed one hand on an outthrust hip and gave the camera a languid smile.

"Sergeant Joshua Lyle . . ."

Lurch wasn't called that just because he was tall. Try as he did, there was just too much damage for him to march or even stand perfectly straight. He lurched in a military manner across the stage, though, and took up a position of parade rest next to Miriam. The incredibly tall and awkward former parapalegic looked almost, but not quite, ludicrous next to the sensual and diminutive linguist. The reason it wasn't ludicrous was that the dichotomy was more in keeping with the term "diversity."

"First Sergeant Jeffrey Powell . . ."

"Time to show them how a *Marine* does it," Top said, popping to attention and stalking out. His steps were so perfect he could have been on the Marine Corps drill team and he stopped, turned and popped when he reached his place.

"And holder of the Navy Cross, Lieutenant Eric 'Two-Gun' Bergstresser . . ."

"I'm not even going to *try* to improve on that," Eric said, marching much more loosely to his position. It was still in a military manner but drew from his laid back nature rather than the perfect precision of the first sergeant.

"Ladies and gentlemen of the press, the representatives of the Alliance Star Ship *Vorpal Blade*."

Admiral Townsend started to open his mouth to ask for questions but paused at a slow clapping from the back of the room. In a moment it was joined by others and swelled to full applause. He tried not to react with shock but applause at a press conference was unheard of.

On the other hand, since a couple of changes of administration, and especially the Dreen War, the press had become less adversarial towards the military. During the Dreen War, casualties among the press were at about par with the units they were covering. That had a tendency to reduce tension on both sides, as the military grew to respect the reporters who went out to cover the news, no matter the danger to themselves, and the reporters saw that the soldiers were doing their damnedest to protect them. And the Vietnam generation of the press corps had mostly retired. Their replacements were liberal, yes, but the views were changing about the press and military, becoming less a matter of dragging down the military and more "Hey, they're our soldiers, too."

Still, *applause* at a *press conference*?

On the other hand, if humanity didn't get the next decade right, the world really *was* coming to an end. And the doumentaries *had* been pretty darned good television.

"Ladies and gentlemen of the press corps, being aware that these are not professional speakers, we will now entertain questions."

Eric was balancing two bags in one hand and fumbling to get his key in the lock when the door of the apartment banged open and Brooke swarmed up him to wrap her legs around his middle.

"I love you, I love you, I love you . . ." Brooke said, kissing him all over his face.

"I love you, too," Eric said, tossing the bags past her. "But right now I'm just wondering how fast I can get these clothes off."

"We need to get a jelly-bean jar," Eric said, running his finger down Brooke's neck.

"Oh, that old thing," Brooke said, shivering. "I forgot to ask what with one thing and another. How did Miriam hold up?"

"Throwing up a lot," Eric said. "But she made it every step of the way. And she rocked on *Oprah*."

"*You* rocked on the *Tonight Show*," Brooke said. "Even Leno was impressed."

"I am going to catch *so* much *maulk*," Eric said. "My new nickname's probably going to be Hollywood, and it won't be a term of endearment. I mean, until last week this was the deepest of deep black op. Now, all of a sudden, we're movie stars. And the whole thing was so successful, they're planning on repeating it after every damned mission! That means people are going to be thinking about the cameras instead of what they need to be thinking about. And the guys who got missed on the previous ops are going to be bitching about who got coverage and who didn't and—"

"Why don't you worry about that tomorrow?" Brooke asked. "I'll say this, I've got a new way to handle problem customers."

"Oh, no," Eric said, groaning.

"I had a guy say something very *coarse* to me last night

and I just looked at him and said 'My last name is Bergstresser. Two-Gun is my husband.' Got a hell of a tip, too."

"You're actually enjoying this, aren't you?" Eric asked.

"Honey, you're famous for being who you *are*," Brooke said. "You're the most dangerous fighter in the galaxy, the guy who captured a Dreen spaceship almost single-handed. Yeah, I'm enjoying being your wife."

"Well, in that case," Eric said, grabbing her. "I'm enjoying it, too!"

"Red," Captain Weaver said as they were about to go through the Looking Glass connection to the Newport News base. "A word."

"Yes, sir?" the machinist said.

"When you get back, you're going to catch a certain amount of flack," Weaver said. "But don't reply to it except in your usual and customary way. Being on TV does not make you immune to discipline. It especially won't make you immune to Captain's Mast. Just . . . be yourself."

"I've been thinking about that, sir," Red said. "I'm going to try. But I think things are going to be a little different, no matter what I do."

"Agreed," Bill said. "But pass this around: the first time I catch somebody trying to get their good side at the cameras, I'm going to make them regret the day they were born."

"Gotcha, sir," Red said, grinning.

"Let's roll."

"Hail, hail the conquering hero," Captain Zanella said as Eric, wearing PT gear, walked into Admin.

"That was a little bit more than I'd expected, sir," Eric said, hanging up the suit bag holding his uniform. "How bad's it going to be?"

"Oh, I understand that the gunnys are planning a celebratory fete," the CO said. "The lieutenants have their socks filled with rocks and the other platoons are trying to figure out just how to take you down a notch. That's when I can get them to quit posing for every security camera in the building. And you'll note the pile of paperwork on your desk. You really think you have time for PT?"

"Since that's all unsecure, now, sir, yes," Eric said. "I can take as much as I'd like home tonight. I honestly didn't ask for any of this, sir."

"I know you didn't, Two-Gun," the CO said. "And I'll try to keep the *maulk* storm to a minimum. Besides, the whole company came off smelling like a rose. *I* even got an honorable mention. For that matter, the first sergeant was right there in the middle of it. Which show was it where he went off on the similarities and differences between the coalition the Chinese are proposing and the Delian league?"

"One of the shows on CNN, I think," Eric said, chuckling. "That was when the whole 'degree in international relations from the Sorbonne' really started to stick in people's minds. Before that one, he was low on the ladder of invitations. After that one, everybody was clamoring to get him on."

"'In the modern world, a conscriptive and confiscatory condition between nations is unmanageable and unacceptable. The only choice is cooperation, willingness and enthusiasm. If humanity cannot raise such willingness, if we are so nihilist as to have forgotten honor, duty and sacrifice, then we are condemned by the universe to oblivion and deserve no less.' Damn, it sounded like he was running for office. And he'd get elected in a landslide. He really thundered that last bit."

"I actually saw a 'Powell for President' bumper sticker," Eric said, grinning.

"So did I, sir," First Sergeant Powell said grumpily, as he stumped into Admin. He was in regular duty uniform.

"No PT this morning, First Sergeant?" the CO asked, raising an eyebrow.

"I'm scheduled for a local morning TV show, sir," Powell growled. "I hope to be back by 0900 formation. And I told PIO that given our mission schedule this was the *last* one I'm doing."

"Gunny Juda can take it," the CO said. "But he's beginning to complain about your paperwork."

"I'm not *beginning* to complain, sir," Juda said as he walked in with Gunnery Sergeant Mitchell. "I've *been* complaining. Welcome back, Top, Lieutenant."

"The *Delian League*, First Sergeant?" Gunny Mitchell said, grinning. "I mean, you spent a good three minutes just explaining *that*!"

"I blame the fact that I had to on poor public schools," Powell replied. "And good day to you, too, Gunnery Sergeant. I ought to drop you for push-ups for simply mentioning the Mongolian cluster *grapp* that was last week. And I'd sincerely appreciate it if we could simply forget the whole thing happened."

"How can we?" Juda said, gesturing at the monitors

in the room. "Forget posing for the camera, Third's been trying to get in the best one-liners. Wilson noticed that the guys who were getting good coverage were the ones that had the sharpest retorts. It's getting *brutal* in the barracks, let me tell you."

"Right!" the first sergeant snapped. "Sir, permission to revise the training schedule!"

"What day?" the CO asked, grinning. "And why?"

"Today," Top said. "*And* tomorrow. Starting at the 0900 formation. Uniform changed to field gear and combat ruck load."

"Oh, hot diggity," Eric said. "You're talking a good, old-fashioned, Powell Pounding, aren't you, Top?"

"We'll need to scare up an ambulance," Powell said, with relish. "And a truck for the wounded. It's about time the company remembered who was boss."

"That would be me," the CO said. "But I'm in general agreement and can't think of anything that can't be moved around on the training schedule. Mandatory for the officers, by the way. Lieutenant Bergstresser, I hope you know where your combat gear is."

"Oh, *yes*, sir," Eric said, grinning. "Hey, Top, can I call cadence and set the pace?"

"We may switch off, Two-Gun," Powell replied. "If you remember how to march."

"Military decorum, First Sergeant," the CO said, still smiling.

"In that case: We may switch off, Sir Two-Gun."

Miriam sat at her computer console in the linguist's office of the *Blade II*, nearly motionless, staring blankly at the computer screen. The only lighting in the room came from the crack in the office door, and the dim blue-green from the monitor cast an eerily dancing silhouette of her slight figure against the bulkhead behind her. The only sound in the office was the tap tap tapping of the keyboard keys and a faint whistling of air rushing through the air conditioning vent. Her hands typed frantically, filling the open Word document in front of her with what might seem like techno-babble to the average reader, but on occasion the techno-babble had proven to be useful information to get them out of tight spots. So, Miriam had started writing it down, just in case.

". . . *as the scalar field consists of two stable neutral oscillations and two charged oscillations three of which can be described as massless and unphysical bosons while the fourth is the manifestation of the massive unstable particle with no spin or intrinsic angular momentum. A one-loop evolution diagram of the first order correction to this mass shows that it strongly couples to top quark fields and therefore typically evolves to top anti-top pairs. The addition of intrinsic properties to the massive boson creates a stable gauge entity from which metric structure can be manipulated . . .*"

Miriam hated to admit it to herself but being away from the *Blade* during the past few months had left her with a feeling that something had been missing. She realized upon her return that it was the voice from the ship. At first she had hated the voice as it had nearly driven her nuts. But it was becoming sort of an old friend to fill void periods of time where she usually got bored.

Sometime during the last mission Miriam had begun

hearing gibberish voices in her head. At first she had thought it was a faulty implant, but her reluctance to let the ship's sawbones crack open her skull forced her to keep quiet about it. After all, most of the crew already thought she was bat-shit crazy; hearing voices would only have put the purple icing on the fruitcake.

As time passed the voice finally went from gibberish to English techno-babble. Miriam soon realized that the techno-babble was indeed information that was somehow pertinent to the functioning of the *Blade's* alien drive system. Somehow, and for some reason, the little black box had chosen to dump user information into her mind. The information was about as useful, for the most part, as Chinese stereo instructions to someone who only speaks French and has never seen a stereo. Fortunately, in Miriam's case she spoke both languages and quite enjoyed music and every now and then she understood what the voice was telling her.

"*. . . it is inconsistent for the mechanism between symmetry breaking aspects to be unitary as . . ."*

"Hi, Miriam," Bill said, sticking his head in the linguist's office. "I was wondering, did you happen to get anywhere with . . . ?"

"Shhh!" Miriam said as she tapped one last set of keystrokes. The voice stopped.

"Miriam?" Weaver blinked his eyes to adjust to the darkened room. "Uh, you know, my grandma used to tell me not to sit too close to the TV with all the lights out or I'd go blind . . ." His voice trailed off as he realized Miriam wasn't paying attention. Or more like she was paying attention only in the way she did when she translated for someone.

"Sorry, Bill. I didn't want to lose my train of thought." She clicked the minimize box on the document she was typing.

"Uh huh." Bill nodded. "If now's a bad time . . ."

"And I was expecting to see you. We *have* manuals for all the Hexosehr systems," Miriam said. "They're not stupid enough to have given us the equipment and no repair manuals. It was mostly what I was doing on the way back, translating them all. I mean, they'd been autotranslated but that left a lot of ambiguity. What we *don't* have, I just discovered, is all the parts and tools we're supposed to have for them. They're all listed, they're in the required parts and tools inventory, we had them when we got back but now they're missing!"

"That's not good," Bill said, the air going out of his lungs in a rush. He walked around to look at her computer and contemplated the list. "Holy *Maulk*, that's a lot of stuff. And *none* of it's standard inventory. We're going to have to get it all straight from the Hexosehr."

"*You're* missing something," Miriam said, pulling up another list. Bill couldn't figure out what it was then noted that it was an inventory of "nonvital materials" removed from the ship for storage landside. "They *gave* us everything we needed when they built the ship. Enough to last for a cruise or two, at least. This ship was absolutely *turnkey* when we got it. But some idiot pulled it all off the ship as nonvital."

Bill looked at the annotations on the form and felt his blood pressure start to go through the roof.

"GE-E-E-E-E-ST-NER!"

"Where's Top taking the company?" Portana asked. "We're starting loading tomorrow!"

"I'm sure the first sergeant is cognizant of that, Sergeant," Berg said, grinning. "He's pissed people are mugging for the cameras so he's going to administer a Powell Pounding."

"Glad I got stuff to do," Portana replied. "You infantry types can have it. I don't have to go, right?"

"No, Portana, you get to stay back here," Berg said. "But I need you to do me a favor. A big one. I need you to run in town and pick something up for me. A sign. Then I need you to . . ."

2

"So where is it now and why doesn't this have your signature or mine on it?" Captain Prael asked.

"Equipment transfers of nonspecial inventory are handled below our level, sir," Bill replied.

"XO, if the most advanced Hexosehr technology isn't 'special inventory,' I don't know what is!"

"Yes, sir," Bill replied. "Agreed. Among other things, he shipped out fourteen hand melders. *Fourteen*. And a *fabricator*! A whole *grapping fabber*! I don't know what the street value of one would be but I'd put it as at *least* a million dollars. Possibly a billion. Punch in the design and it will turn out the most advanced microchips we make nearly as fast as a multibillion dollar plant! But it's not noted as being special inventory or even particularly expensive. It's not like they were trying to requisition a hundred rolls of space tape. It actually *opened up* our budget for material, probably the reason that Gestner and the Eng did it. This was a routine movement *out* into normal distribution channels. The problem being that none of the stuff is normal inventory. It doesn't even have Federal Stock numbers and nobody had any idea how to inventory it. I've tracked it as far as Newport Base. They didn't know what to do with it so they sent it to the main supply base at Norfolk. Norfolk, assuming it was surplus and out-of-date material, shipped it to the surplus and salvage yard. That's as far as I've gotten. I'm hoping that surplus and salvage can find it for us."

"Where did the tracking numbers come from, then?" Prael asked, frowning at the screen. "There's even associated costs. Low ones. Most of them are under a hundred dollars. *Including the fabber*? Jesus Chr—"

"Not sure, sir," Bill said, shrugging. "Not my department at the time."

"Damn," Prael said, shaking his head. "*Grapp* me. Okay, find this stuff. We're grounded until we get it back. And I now have to call SpacCom and explain to them that we're non-mission-capable until a couple of tons of unobtainium parts and tools get found!"

"With all due respect, sir," Bill said. "Sucks to be you."

Prael stiffened. "*Thanks*, XO. Send a message to the Eng and Gestner. Tell them I want them standing at my door in ten minutes. In the meantime, I need to go over to SpacCom and report on this little *grapp*-up in person. I'll probably be a couple of hours."

Since there were no hills of any significance in the entire Norfolk area, the first sergeant had promised to find some. The nearest, he'd opined, were in Richmond.

Most of the company had chuckled at what they took to be a joke. Richmond was eighty miles away.

The more experienced members of the company just groaned. You could do eighty miles in one day, if you counted a day as from when you woke up until you collapsed in exhaustion. The trick was alternating a slow dog-trot with a fast walk. With enough training, a person could do that trick until their body ran out of muscle to eat or they went stark staring mad from sleep-deprivation dementia. With First Sergeant Powell in the mood he was in, either was possible. Nobody had mentioned anything about busses once they *got* to Richmond. They'd have to come back, too.

It was somewhere around Williamsburg, just short of thirty miles into the march and all of six hours later, that Berg got to take over cadence. The problem being that the first sergeant, who had the most remarkable memory for lyrics and cadences Berg had ever experienced, had used up just about *everything*. Six hours of cadence calling that ranged from standard military cadences like "Yellow Ribbon" and the "Battle Hymn of the Republic" to rock and roll tunes with an appropriate beat. Hell, he'd even slipped in Britney Spears. If you worked with it, you could march to both "Oops, I Did It Again" *and* "Hit Me." "John Brown's Body" was buried back in Newport News. So were "Early Morning Rain" and "Yellow Bird," all twenty known verses including *all* the dirty ones.

But Top's musical tastes were *just* divergent enough from Eric's that Berg had a few Top hadn't thought of. Not eight hours worth, and they'd be going for a lot longer than that. But he could keep the company groaning out cadences for an hour or so just on Within Temptation, a few Manowar songs Top had missed, and Crüxshadows.

Hell, there was some ZZ Top that the first sergeant had missed.

But start with the good stuff.

"Languid waves of desperation fall before the rain," Eric sang, grinning at the groans from the experienced hands. "A vanguard to approaching war is born upon the sea. The icy breath of cyclones bent on raging our destruction, drills hard against the hearts of heroes, called here to defend. Double-time . . . march! Chorus, Marines!"

"What do you mean you don't know where it is?" Weaver said, trying not to whimper.

The warehouse was vast and filled with packing crates. If the Ark of the Covenant was buried anywhere, it was in this warehouse.

"How do you maintain inventory?"

"We don't, really," the warehouse manager said. "When stuff comes in it's dated and moved to a particular section. If it sits there for ninety days, it's put up to auction. Yours had been here less than ninety days, right?"

Bill looked at his forms and sighed in relief. Sixty days, maximum.

"It should have gotten here around the middle of July," he said. "You should have it."

"Mid July," the warehouse manager said, muttering to himself. "What did you say this stuff was?"

"Misplaced parts and tools," Bill said. "It's mostly in heavy plastic containers. They may look a little weird."

Hexosehr fabbers had no issue with curves so their output had a tendency to look a bit more organic than human manufacture.

"Oh, hell, I remember that stuff," the supervisor said, nodding. "We opened up a couple of the boxes but couldn't figure out what the hell it was. I figure somebody might buy it for scrap. Section Eighteen."

"Which is where?" Bill asked hurriedly.

"I'll take you over in my cart," the supervisor said, standing up and heading to the door. "But you're not going to be happy."

"Why?" Bill asked.

"This is Section Five," the man said, waving around the warehouse. "The whole warehouse, that is. Section eighteen's the same size. And all I know is that it's in there. Unless I can find the driver who put it away, you're going to have to get some people to come toss the place."

"Oh *Maulk*," Bill said.

"Oh double *maulk*," Bill repeated when they entered Section Eighteen. It was, if anything, more packed than the first warehouse. "I am so *grapped*. We are so *grapped*."

"What is this stuff, really?" the supervisor asked. "I'm sorry it took me a while to figure out who you are. You're the guy who was on TV, right?"

"Yeah," Bill said. "And if you can keep it to yourself, I'll tell you."

"Lips are sealed," the super said, taking a corner a tad fast.

"It's all the parts and tools the Hexosehr gave us along with the *Blade II*," Bill admitted. "The stuff you couldn't figure out? Well, if you did you'd think you were looking at magic. It was priced in the system as nearly junk value.

To say that was an underestimate is the understatement of the year."

"Cool," the super noted, slowing down and waving to a fork-lift driver. "Hey, Manuel! You remember some gray plastic crates and some other stuff that came in way back in July? Really odd looking stuff."

"*Si*," the driver said, pulling to a stop.

"You don't happen to remember where you put it, do you?"

"*Si*," the driver said. "Southwest corner. We get it wrong, *si*?"

"We get it wrong, *si*," the super said.

"I think so," Manuel replied. "You not see it, but when I lift it up, I see markings on the bottom. Not Earth markings. I think to myself, Manuel, this is something not right in here. So I set it aside."

"Oh, thank God," Weaver said, finally letting out a breath. "Where? Where?!"

"*Aqui*," Manuel said, spinning the forklift in place.

"YES!" Bill shouted as they turned the last corner. In just about the only empty corner of the warehouse, clearly kept separate, was a pile of gray shipping boxes and a very large wooden crate. "Oh puh-lease let that be the fabber!"

"Glad you're so excited," the super said, grinning.

"Can you imagine how embarassing it would have been if we went back to the Hexosehr and admitted that we'd *lost* all this stuff?" Bill said, jumping out as the cart came to a stop. "Yes!" he shouted again as he compared a stencilled on number to the list in his hand. "Yes! Yes! Oh, this is great! I need to see if that's the fabber."

"What in the heck is a fabber?" the super asked.

"A fabricator," Bill replied. He consulted the list and opened up a box, pulling out one of the hand-melders. Just as an oxy-acetylene torch could cut steel open or weld it with appropriate materials, the melder made a fine cutting device.

"We tried that thing," the super said. "It doesn't work."

"Didn't have the power module," Bill said, consulting the list again and pulling open another box. He slid the power module into place and then approached the wooden box. Keying the melder for a three centimeter cut, he drew it along all four sides of the box and then stepped back as the side fell away.

"Damn, that's some fricking saw," the super said, hands on hips.

"Yes!" Bill shouted, dropping the melder and sliding into the box to kiss the organic looking machine it had housed. "Oh, baby! Oh, baby!"

"Jesus, Captain," the super said, laughing. "I know you want to have its love-child but there are limits . . ."

"First Sergeant, we're going to have to find a quicker way back," Captain Zanella said as the company fell out in Mosby Park. "We've still got to load the ship and prepare for departure."

It was about three o'clock in the morning and they were, by God, in Richmond. They'd made eighty miles in under twenty-four hours, not a record but damned close. And not a one had fallen out. A couple had boots filled with blood, but they'd kept going.

"Yes, sir," Powell said. "I have that under control, sir."

"You've really dogged the hell out of 'em, haven't you?" the CO opined, looking around at the collapsed Force Recon Marines.

"Haven't started, yet, sir," Powell replied, pulling out a field ration. He pulled the tab to heat it, then dumped the contents in his mouth. "But we'll be back in good time."

"You're not going to even tell your CO?" the captain asked.

"Not short of a direct order, sir," Top replied. "But you're going to like it. Try not to act surprised. ON YOUR FEET, MARINES!"

"This is Mosby Hill," the first sergeant said, gesturing at the vista below. "It was part of the last defenses of Richmond during the Civil War, a *seven* degree slope at its steepest and one point five miles from top to bottom following Broad Street. I have *arranged* with the Richmond Police department to maintain one lane clear of traffic until six *AM*. From now until that time, we are going to learn to *love* this hill. Aren't we, Marines?"

"YES, FIRST SERGEANT!"

"We are going to love this hill as we have never loved a hill. And at six AM, when the police, alas, have to open the lane up, well, then it will be time to make our way home. But in the meantime, Right . . . Face! Quicktime . . . march . . . *Oh, I wish I was in the land of cotton, Old times there are not forgotten . . .*"

"Loving the Hill" is right up there with "Good Training" in the history of military sadism. What it meant was that the Marines of Bravo Company, United States Space Marines, would march down the hill quite peacefully then run, "double time," back up. One lane of Broad Street had been closed with police cars at either end to maintain it and barricades to ensure motorists didn't decide to use it anyway. The Richmond Police officers and the public workers who had set up the closure leaned on the hoods of their cars and trucks and watched as the Marines marched down, ran up, marched down, ran up, repeat to exhaustion or at least until six AM.

Shortly before that time, the first sergeant turned over the cadence calling to Gunnery Sergeant Juda, who was if anything more brutal than he, and had a quick conversation with the unit's most junior officer.

Which left Second Lieutenant Bergstresser as the cadence caller for the last climb.

"Quicktime . . . march," Berg shouted when the company was barely halfway up the hill. Already, behind them the city workers were taking down the barricades and preparing to open the road. The police cars had pulled well to the side and as the Marines passed them the officers waved and grinned, as if they knew a special joke.

"New cadence," Berg said. "Try to keep up.

> *"In the quiet misty morning when the moon has
>   gone to bed,*
> *When the sparrows stop their singing and the sky
>   is clear and red.*
> *When the summer's ceased its gleaming,*
> *When the corn is past its prime,*
> *When adventure's lost its meaning,*
> *I'll be homeward bound in time."*

Berg didn't have the greatest singing voice in the world, but it was good enough for the simple tune. And the words couldn't have been more heartfelt. As much as the Marines had been cutting up for the cameras, lately, much of it was simply pre-mission jitters. Casualties on each mission of the *Blade* had been so high as to be suicidal.

"Chorus!"

> *"Bind me not to the pasture,*
> *chain me not to the plow.*
> *Set me free to find my calling*
> *and I'll return to you somehow.*
>
> *If you find it's me you're missing,*
> *if you're hoping I'll return.*
> *To your thoughts I'll soon be list'ning,*
> *and in the road I'll stop and turn.*
> *Then the wind will set me racing*
> *as my journey nears its end.*
> *And the path I'll be retracing*
> *when I'm homeward bound again.*

"Chorus!"

A simple enough one to remember, and the Marines boomed it out as they approached the top of the hill and the long road home.

> *"BIND ME NOT TO THE PASTURE,*
> *CHAIN ME NOT TO THE PLOW.*
> *SET ME FREE TO FIND MY CALLING*
> *AND I'LL RETURN TO YOU SOMEHOW."*

But at the top of the hill, where they'd assembled before learning to love it, where they'd turned to begin the descent more times than they'd bothered counting, was something that hadn't been there ten minutes earlier. A Looking Glass, shining bright in the rising sun. And a grinning crew of techs who had just set it up.

Berg gave them a few moments to contemplate that, pausing as the Marines continued to keep time approaching the Looking Glass.

"By column of twos!" Lieutenant Bergstresser boomed, breaking the unit down until it was two abreast instead of four. The Marines, despite carrying a hundred and fifty pounds of gear apiece, having marched nearly a hundred miles grand total and with minimal sleep or food, did the maneuver flawlessly. Two by two they entered the Looking Glass to an unknown fate. For all they knew, it could have been pointed at another planet. But there wasn't a flicker from any of them as they approached the gate.

When Berg emerged, he had to chuckle. The other side emerged on the parade field in front of the company headquarters building in Newport News.

> "In the quiet misty morning when the moon has
>   gone to bed,
> When the sparrows stop their singing,
> I'll be homeward bound again . . ."

"By column of fours . . . Companeeeee . . . halt."

"I'm glad to see everyone made it," Captain Zanella said to the assembled Marines. "But it's what I expect of

Space Marines and you can recover on the ship. We have loading to do . . ."

There were some groans to that and he grinned, thinking that maybe he should revise the schedule he and the first sergeant had worked out. But, no, it was one of those times the CO got to be the good guy.

"I have convinced the first sergeant, however, that we do not have to start right away," he continued.

It was military leadership. Call it good cop/bad cop. The senior NCO in any unit was the bad cop. He was the one who assigned all the crappy details and meted out minor punishments. The officer, on the other hand, remained generally distant and only interacted when there were good things to be said and done. Except on the rare occasion where someone truly *grapped* up, in which case, like calling Dad in for punishment, you knew you were really *grapped*.

The first sergeant had punished the company for their grandstanding. Now the captain got to pat them on the head.

"You have the rest of the day off. Recall formation at 1700. We'll then commence loading. The majority of materials have been pre-loaded for us this time, the remainder will be doled out at 1700. Following the formation, platoon sergeants and leaders in my office. First Sergeant!"

"Okay, this has put a total crimp in my planning," First Lieutenant Javier Mendel said. Despite his Hispanic name, the lieutenant looked more like a poster child for the Waffen SS, tall and slender with blue eyes and short-cropped blond hair. However, in keeping with his name, he was a second generation immigrant from Peru. If the hundred mile ruck march had bothered the officer it wasn't apparent, he was still carrying his ruck on his back as he and Berg made their way into the heaquarters building. "I had *maulk* to do last night."

"You weren't married less than a month ago," Berg pointed out. "But when Top gets a bee in his bonnet, well . . ."

"Good training, though," Lieutenant Morris said. Morris was medium height with brown hair and eyes. He'd entered from one of the few Marine ROTC units and had never intended to be a Force Recon officer, it was just bad timing. Since he'd graduated in winter semester, his whole career had been out-of-schedule; newly minted officers were *supposed* to show up at the beginning of the summer. He'd completed his time as a platoon leader and was supposed to take over a company XO position in a different MEU. However, that unit was deployed when he became available. He had the choice of a make-work position until it came back or a course. The only course available was Force Recon. Once he joined the course, though, he'd just refused to quit and graduated as the Honor Graduate from Force Recon qual *and* FROT. Since he'd already had a platoon, he qualified as an FR platoon leader. And the FR platoon leader spot open had been in Bravo Company after its merciless first mission. At this point he had one mission under his belt in the *Blade* and was *still* refusing to quit. "Glad Top got it out of his system."

"OKAY, WHO IN THE HELL . . . ?"

"Had," Berg said, grinning. "*Had* it out of his system."

"TWO-GUN!"

"That would be Sir Two-Gun, First Sergeant," Eric said, as the three officers walked into the orderly room.

To approach the CO's office there were two choices. On one side, the side enlisted approached from, there was the gauntlet of the orderly room, held down by the company clerk and the operations sergeant. From there, if a person was worthy, they could enter Top's office. On the other side was the XO's office, the route normally taken by officers. In this case, since it was the shorter route and there was more room to dump their rucks in the orderly room, the officers had taken that route. Which was how they got to see the sign.

Someone had been busy while the company was gone. Before they left, the first sergeant's door had only a simple plaque: "First Sergeant Jeffrey Powell."

Now, over the door there was a large wooden sign which read:

> We pray for one last landing
> On the globe that gave us birth;
> Let us rest our eyes on the fleecy skies
> And the cool, green hills of Earth.
> —Robert Anson Heinlein

"You were addressing me, First Sergeant?" Two-Gun asked as he slipped his ruck to the floor. He had to admit he was grateful to finally have the thing off his back but he tried to keep the relief off his face.

"No, *sir*," the first sergeant said, grinding his teeth. "I would *never* address an officer in that manner. I believe I was addressing a smart-aleck sergeant I once knew."

"What's that from?" Mendel asked, setting his own ruck down. "Although, I agree with the sentiment."

"It's a long story, Lieutenant," Top said, then gave a reluctant smile. "It's a good sign, though, Lieutenant Bergstresser. I take it I *do* have you to thank."

"I was thinking about the sign the Legion has in its orderly room," Berg admitted. "'*You are in the Legion to die and we will send you where you can die.*' I kinda felt this was more appropriate. Lord knows it's true."

"That it is, sir," Top said softly. "That it is. But we've got work to do, sirs."

3

"Good to hear, Captain Weaver," Captain Prael said, grinning at the XO's tone. "Glad to hear you got it all back. You're going to need to arrange transportation . . . Okay, glad we're clear on that. And a working party to . . . I'll make sure the COB's aware of the importance. In case I wasn't clear, good job on all of this from tracking down the problem to rectifying it. . . . Yes, I'm fully cognizant of Miss Moon's part in this and appreciate that as well. She may not be the problem-child she at first seemed."

"So I've been thinking," Miriam said.

"*Oh*, those are scary words," Sub Dude replied.

"My belly's quaking for some strange reason," Red agreed.

The threesome were playing cards in the small space between the number fourteen and number sixteen chaos launcher. Technically a storage space for peripheral materials, it was strangely empty because the parts that *should* have filled it were sitting in a warehouse in Delaware.

"The CO's still not real happy with me helping you guys out," Miriam continued, ignoring the jibes. "And I got really bored on the last cruise. Worse, I had nobody to snuggle."

"You're not snuggling me or Red," Gants said, sucking his teeth. "Married. Damnit."

"So I *need* something to snuggle," Miriam continued, ignoring him again. "And the ship really *needs* a mascot."

"Oh, God," Red said. "This is getting worse and worse!"

"All I'm talking about is one little kitty," Miriam said. "It will take up hardly any room. Nobody will notice. Probably."

"And just what is this kitty going to eat?" Red asked. "We don't stock cat food."

"He eats raw meat just fine," Miriam said. "Don't worry, I got that covered. With my access, tweaking the supply orders was easy."

"Oh, God," Red said. "You hacked the supply system?"

"Duh."

"Okay, how are you going to get it on the ship, Smart Lady?" Sub Dude asked.

"All hands! All hands! Assemble by Hatch Three for working party!"

"I dunno," Miriam said. "Maybe in a Hexosehr cargo box I just happen to have and that looks just like the rest we're getting ready to load."

"*Damnit.*"

"PO, is it just me or are we loading a lot of provisions?" the mess specialist asked, heaving a leg of beef onto a large stack in the freezer.

"Stuffing every nook and cranny," the petty officer replied. "Going to be a long cruise."

"Yeah, but, this is one heck of a lot of meat," the mess specialist said. "I mean, more than normal, right?"

"Looks about right to me," the PO replied. "This is the *Blade* . . ."

"We don't turn back until we're out of food or Marines," the mess specialist said, sighing. "I guess we're going to be making a lot of chilimac."

"We got it all back," Bill chortled. "All of it. Every last item!"

"That's great, Bill," Miriam said, looking around at the piles of boxes. "Now all we have to do is figure out where it all goes, again."

"No problem," Bill said. "I just want to get it all back in the ship. Then we can figure out where it's going. I can see you're just as glad as I am, otherwise you wouldn't be here. Admit it."

"You're right," Miriam said, trying not to glance over at where Red and Sub Dude were joining the line of sailors loading the ship. "But I've got stuff I've got to do. See you later?"

"Absolutely," Bill replied. "And did I mention we got it all back?"

"I thought you said this was a *cat*," Sub Dude whispered as they broke away from the group and headed aft.

"It's sort of purring like one," Red pointed out. "Sort of."

"It's *way* too heavy to be a cat," Gants said, sucking his teeth furiously. "Unless you brought a menagerie."

"Just one little kitty," Miriam promised. "Is this far enough? I miss my Tiny."

"Over here," Red whispered, opening up one of the between-launcher supply closets.

The threesome entered the compartment, shut the hatch and then Gants hit the lock on the box.

"What kind of a cat—?" he started to say and then found himself flat on his back in the face of a joyous "MRAOWR!"

The beast on his chest was the size of a medium dog and weighed about the same. But that was where the resemblance ended. Snow white with black spots and blue eyes, the thing looked like an albino jaguar. And it had the power of one, having knocked him off his feet before he could get a sentence out or even scream. If it was a house cat, it looked like it must have been crossed with a leopard. It began licking his face like a dog, but with a vocalization that could best be replicated as "YUM! YUM! YUM!" It was *not* a reassuring sound.

"Can I push it off? Or is it going to rip my throat out?"

"Oh, Tiny's a big softie," Miriam said, pushing the cat aside.

"Is that some sort of bizarre genetic accident?" Red asked. He'd backed into the corner of the room since the cat was between him and the door. He was afraid to try to run in case it caused a chase reaction in the massive feline. "I saw this picture online one time . . ."

"It's a Savannah," Miriam said. "A cross between a Bengal and a Cervil. And his name is Titanus, after the lord of the Titans. I like to call him Tiny."

"Look," Gants said, scrambling to his feet and backing

to the door. "I don't know anything about any cat. We were not here. We disavow all knowledge of how a fricking monster catzilla got on the ship. My God, woman, where is he going to go to the *bathroom*? We don't happen to have the *Sahara* onboard!"

"Where does a sixty pound cross between a house cat and a mountain lion go?" Red mused. "Anywhere it wants. I'm thinking . . . Conn."

"He's potty trained," Miriam said with a moue. She knelt and grabbed the massive cat by the head, scratching it hard at the neckline. At which point, "Tiny" rolled onto the deck and onto his back to have his tummy rubbed. That required two hands for sure. "He goes in the potty. I wouldn't want to change *his* catbox."

"Like, in the can?" Red asked, straightening out of his crouch. "Really?"

"Oh, sure, that I've heard of," Gants said, sucking his teeth nervously. "But is he trained on a potty for a prototype, Hexosehr-built, *space*ship Miss Smartypants?"

"Well, *duh*."

"So it just eats raw meat?" Red said, holding out a slice of beef. It turned out that Miriam had doubled the meat ration of the ship. Normally, that would be impossible, but for some reason the ship had about double the regular freezer space. He had to wonder, given that Miriam had been involved in the design, just *how long* the girl had been planning on bringing her "little kitty."

"And organ meat," Miriam said.

"Okay, who in the *hell* ordered two tons of calf liver . . . ?"

"Oh, man, liver and onions, here we come . . ."

"You've pretty much got it licked, don't you?" Gants said, sighing.

"Thought of everything," Miriam said. "Trust me."

"Is this one of those times that as a good Marine wife I trust you that you were not carousing all night?" Brooke asked as Eric opened the door to the apartment. She was folding laundry in the living room with the TV set to Fox News.

"Yes," Eric said. "The first sergeant and the CO decided that everybody was getting too into their new roles as TV stars. So we had a ruck march."

"All night?" Brooke asked, alarmed.

"Yep," Berg said. "I caught breakfast at the mess hall and that was the first solid food I've had since yesterday sometime. The good news is that I've got the whole day off. I need to be back at 1700."

"That's . . . five o'clock, right?" Brooke asked. "Do you want me to get you something to eat? I would have fixed breakfast. I'm sorry I snapped."

"That was not a snap," Eric corrected. "A snap would have been 'where the hell were you last night?' And I'm fine. I need a shower. After that I'm sure we'll find some way to pass the time. Especially since lift-off is about this time tomorrow morning."

4

"Power for five knots," the CO said as the tugs released the lines on the ship.

Since its existence was supposed to be a huge secret, the *Blade II* had been docked in a standard subpen. Which meant a massive concrete box with overhead cover. Just flying out was out of the question. Arguably, she could have driven herself out, as she had done on previous occasions. But the tugs were standard and with the secrecy off, no longer an issue.

What *was* an issue was their sailing orders.

"Twenty degrees starboard," Prael said, gritting his teeth. The deep water where subs hid was to port. The main basin for Newport News was to starboard, the basin where the thousands, perhaps hundreds of thousands, of watchers had gathered to watch the world's first starship take off. "Let's kick it up a bit."

"Twenty degrees starboard," Weaver repeated. "Engage drive to one percent. Maintain water contact."

There was already a supplemental provision bill before

Congress for a new spaceport, a real one that didn't involve water. But it was still based at Newport News. The Navy had slid the entire plan across the table and, as far as anyone could tell, they were for once getting everything they asked for. Riding a tide of public opinion was a wonderful feeling.

"Why do I get the feeling that everybody wants us to burst out of the water?" the CO said. "Input, XO?"

"One option, sir," Bill replied. "Alternatively, rising ominously into the air, passing slowly over News and Norfolk then out to sea. Then kick it in to get out of the grav well faster. I really don't think we want to go supersonic at low altitude near a city. There are regs against it for that matter. And we can only go so far nose up without everyone falling sideways. We'll have the depth in the turning basin for a slight dip."

"I think we should go for the splashy exit," Prael replied. "People have gotten used to seeing it on TV, haven't they? Once we reach the turning basin, go to twenty meters, then we'll bounce out at about forty knots and accelerate to just under Mach One. Not as flashy as Spectre's runs, I'll admit, but we don't have *Akulas* to avoid."

Brooke watched as the ship carrying her husband first dipped into the harbor, then splashed out, heading upwards and outwards towards the stars. Her eyes were filled with tears, but she wasn't the only teary-eye done in the crowd by far.

"Calm down, Tiny," Miriam said, rubbing the cat's sides. "It's shiny. It's better than with Spectre."

It was a note of pure cat distress as the massive feline squatted on his haunches and howled at the overhead. But deeper and richer than any house cat. When it passed through a thick hatch and echoed through the ship . . .

"Captain Weaver?" Prael asked.

"Not . . . sure, sir," Bill replied, listening to the sound of bending metal that resounded through the hull. "But it *sounded* expensive."

"We need to know if we're spaceworthy, XO," the CO snapped. "Pilot, level off and drop the accel." As the ship leveled out the sound subsided. "Damage report."

"Pressure is holding at two percent over standard atmosphere," Bill replied. "No reports of structural damage. Sir, we've never heard that particular sound from the ship. Yes, it sounded bad. But it might have just been things settling. The inertial compensators don't kick in until we're out of the grav well and coming back we didn't maneuver very hard. My gut is saying bad things. Every sensor we have, every person we have on watch, is saying everything's shiny."

"I want the source of that transient tracked down," the CO said, nodding. "But if we're spaceworthy, then we're spaceworthy. Pilot, kick it back in."

As the acceleration climbed and the ship pointed upwards, the sound started up again.

"COB, track down the source of that sound," the CO said. "Find out what's broken in my ship."

"Aye, aye, sir," the chief of boat replied.

"Reaching exoatmospheric," Bill said as the feel of being pointed up fell off and the deck was once more "down." The artificial gravity created by the ancient artifact was just slightly under Earth's gravity. It was so slight a difference, most people didn't notice. It just made for a feeling of lightness. It kicked in automatically as the ship left Earth's gravity well.

"Pressure check," the CO said as the noise subsided. "I really want to know what that sound is."

"Pressure is nominal," Weaver replied as everyone's ears popped. The air was overpressured for the check then *slowly* reduced to a high oxygen content but low pressure. "We're not leaking, whatever it is."

"Very well," the CO said. "Astro?"

"One-Six-Eight mark neg Nine, sir," Lieutenant Fey said. "Course for Cheerick to pick up our dragonflies and their riders."

"It's times like this I really think I've stepped into wonderland," Prael said distastefully. "Pilot, course laid in?"

"Aye, aye, sir," the pilot replied. The recently promoted petty officer was a survivor of every battle the *Blade* had been in and *lived* to have his hands on the controls of the ship. "Second star to the right and straight on to morning."

"Just engage," Prael said with a sigh.

"How's it going, Two-Gun?" Captain Zanella asked.

The Marines were settling into place, but Eric was already done so he'd headed for the Admin office in the ship and settled down to catch up on paperwork again.

"Just fine, sir," Eric said, not looking up. "Bit strange to have a cabin, even if I am sharing it with Lieutenant Morris."

"Well, here's your course load and your homework

schedule," the CO said, handing over an SD chip. "I got a buddy who's an instructor at FROT to send me all his stuff and a syllabus. The OBC portion is open-source. The syllabus has us doing two hour blocks a day. And since they're both multi-week courses and we've got just this cruise to cover them, I'll be taking it pretty fast. And I won't be able to do all of it, so the XO is going to be doing some of the courses. Then there's the simulator portion. FROT now uses the actions on Runner's World and Cheerick as part of their exercises so you get to replay them as an officer. Comments?"

"What fun," Berg said, trying not to sigh. He'd slipped the chip into his computer and scanned the course load while the CO was talking. It looked like a couple of semesters in college to him. "I mean, aye, aye, sir."

"That's the spirit," the CO said, grinning. "If you want to blame somebody, blame the President."

"He gets blamed for enough, sir," Eric replied. "When do we start?"

"Fourteen hundred. You need to read the first portion by then so you're prepared."

That was barely three hours away. Berg looked at the mass of paperwork he had to catch up on and the courses he had to take and mentally kissed sleep goodbye.

"Aye, aye, sir."

Bill whistled to himself quietly as he went off watch. He knew he'd have to be back up in a couple of hours, given that he was going to be busy when they got to Cheerick working on arranging the dragonfly fighters they were picking up. Not to mention integrating the Cheerick riders. But being XO had some privileges. When he'd done previous cruises he'd been bunked with three other officers. This time, he had his own . . .

He paused and swore as he entered the corridor to his quarters. The damned *door* was missing. Of all the things the Space Navy was bringing over from the sub service, why did it have to be *this*?

It was a game the crew played. Sometime in the first week of the cruise, somebody stole the XO's door. Thereafter, the game for the XO became "find the door." Since the XO was *supposed* to know every nook and cranny in the boat, surely he could find one door?

Right then, Weaver swore he was going to win. The XO rarely did. Crews were ingenious at hiding the door. But he was, by God, going to Find the Door.

In the meantime, though, he had to go find a spare blanket.

"Get the ball," Red said, tossing the ball down the corridor, then turning back to the pump. "Jesus, when's Miriam's shift?"

"I dunno," Sub Dude said, pulling the pump out and looking in the pipe. "But I hope it's—"

"Mraow!" Tiny said, dropping the tennis ball.

"Damn, this thing's fast," Red said.

"What in the hell . . ." Chief Gestner said, his eyes wide. "What in the hell is that thing? It looks like a four legged Mreee!"

The felinoid Dreen slave race had tricked humanity, early in the war, into believing they were friends. Closing the Dreen gates, however, had required putting a planet buster bomb through a gate that led to their homeworld and as far as humans knew, wiping them out. Only on the last mission had it been discovered some still survived. Human attitudes towards the Mreee varied, with most pitying them. From Chief Gestner's expression, he apparently wasn't a Mreee fan. Or maybe he just didn't like cats.

"His name's Tiny," Sub Dude said, tossing the ball down the corridor. "He's the ship's mascot. We got infested with this weird rodent sort of thing on Cheerick the last time we were there. The only way to keep them down is Tiny here."

"Oh," the chief said, blinking. "So it's a cat?"

"Yeah, Chief," Red said. "It's a cat. It's a Savannah. You've heard of them, right?"

"Oh, sure," the chief said, clearly having not a clue. "Well, carry on."

"Will do, Chief," Gants said. As the chief turned the corner he let out his breath. "*Grapp* me. We're so *grapped*."

"Nah, I think he bought it," Red said.

"Bought what?" the COB asked, coming from the same direction the machinist chief had passed.

"Uh . . ."

"How's Tiny?" the Chief of Boat asked, taking the ball and tossing it down the corridor.

"Just fine, COB," Sub Dude said, his eyes wide.

"Don't worry about the yowling," the COB said, taking the ball and tossing it again. This time he bounced it off two bulkheads but the cat caught it in midair and spun on the floor hammering back. "He'll get used to maneuvers."

"Hope so, COB," Red said.

"If he's getting in the way of your repairs, send him over to Camp Watch. He hasn't got much to do."

"Will do, COB," Sub Dude said.

"See ya."

Bill paused as he entered the missile room since he nearly got hit in the head by a ball.

"Sorry, XO," the petty officer on missile watch said. "Watch out for—"

The ball bounced off the deck and hit the bulkhead just over the hatch, bouncing again towards the port bulkhead. A white streak went by Weaver's face and caught the ball midair, hit the bulkhead by the hatch with four feet, then launched off at least ten feet to land in the middle of the large compartment. Two bounds and it was at the end of the compartment, dropping the ball at the Camp Watch's feet and wriggling its butt in preparation for the next run.

". . . Tiny."

"What in the hell . . . ?" Bill said.

"He's for rounding up those rodents we picked up on Cheerick, XO," the Camp Watch said stonily.

Bill recognized the petty officer as a veteran of both missions of the *Blade*, one of about sixty crewmen who knew darned well they hadn't picked up any "rodents" on Cheerick. The ship, as much as possible, maintained quarantine on alien worlds for the express purpose of avoiding picking up a possibly pestiferous alien species that could be a problem on Earth. An alien version of kudzu, much less rats, would be unwelcome in the extreme.

For that matter, the *Blade II* had been made from scrap of the *Blade I*. There was no way in *hell* "space hamsters" had somehow gotten from one to the other.

So he had one of two choices, one of two types of XO to be. The first choice, since they were barely nine hours from Earth, was to report that they had an unauthorized pet onboard and turn the ship around. Hell, they could space the thing, he supposed, but he knew that would be a disaster on many levels.

The second choice was to go along with the cover story. Obviously, nobody who knew that there weren't any alien space rats on the ship had reported the presence of the massive cat. And at least he no longer had to worry that there was a serious structural issue with the *Blade II*. He now knew where the sound like bending metal had come from. And he suspected he knew who had smuggled the massive creature onboard.

"How's he doing?" Bill asked.

"Haven't seen any chee-hamsters in days, sir," the Camp said.

"Glad to see he's earning his way," Bill said. "Secure the missiles for landing on Cheerick."

"Aye, aye, sir," the Camp Watch said, tossing the ball then hitting the switches that ensured that no matter what a missile could not fire. "Missiles secured." He picked up the ball again and tossed it.

"Carry on," Bill said, exiting the compartment. "Chee-hamsters," he added with a giggle. "Chee-hamsters . . ."

"Colonel Che-chee," Captain Prael said. "Welcome aboard the *Vorpal Blade II*."

The *Blade* had been to Cheerick several times since returning from the mission where she met the Hexosehr. After the first few missions, the powers-that-be had determined that there were, in fact, no major hostile organisms to be picked up on Cheerick, including chee-hamsters, and had relaxed the once strict quarantine. Thus the greeting party had been able to meet Lady Che-chee on the underbelly ramp the *Blade II* sported.

"*Ig keek*, Che-Chee," Miriam squeaked. "*Ikki keek, Vorpal Blade Two*."

"Englik unkertank," the massive rodentoid squeaked. The Cheerick were bipedal, rotund chinchilla-like beings of about human height but significantly higher mass. "Skeakink uk . . . uh . . . hu-arker. *Keek eek krik skeek kree*."

"Colonel Che-chee has been studying English and understands it," Miriam translated. "She just has a hard time pronouncing most of our phonemes."

"Feel free to speak Cheerick, Colonel," the CO said. "I don't understand your language, yet, so I can hardly fault you for not being able to speak ours. If you and your pilots will accompany me to the wardroom we can continue this discussion in comfort."

"Uh, sir," Bill said. "Permission to speak."

"Go, XO."

"Sir, I would suggest that the Mothers accompany us to the wardroom," Bill said. "The chief of boat is on-hand to get your males settled in their quarters."

Miriam nodded at the series of squeaks and shrugged.

"She's the only Mother," Miriam said. "The others are all enlisted."

"Damn," Prael muttered. "I'd forgotten about that."

Cheerick females were larger and stronger than males and filled all senior roles. That is, once they were post-breeding stage. Breeders were sub-sentient and males were considered to be lacking seriousness and intelligence. Whether the latter was genetics or culture wasn't clear, yet, but all males were relegated to enlisted slots whereas Mothers, post-breeding females, were the officers and leadership of the society.

"In that case, Colonel," the CO said, "if you'll accompany us to the wardroom, the COB will get your men settled."

Colonel Che-chee squeaked at the nine males accompanying her and gestured to the COB. It was clear that they were getting a bit of a dressing down but if it suppressed them it wasn't apparent. They were all grinning and nose-wrinkling at boarding the human spaceship.

"Ko," Colonel Che-chee said after a moment, gesturing into the ship.

"We're going to want to run exercises on the run out to Taurus," Captain Prael said, once the group reached the wardroom. "And since we've never tried to keep dragonflies alive on the hull for this long, that's going to be an issue. We'll just have to hope they survive."

Previous missions of the *Blade*, besides bringing ambassadors back and forth, had included testing various ways to carry the Cheerick Dragonfly Fighters. The dragonflies had both a very fast normal space drive system and lasers for engagement. But their real trick was a force field, permeable to the lasers but apparently impermeable to anything else, that could absorb a good bit of punishment.

The organic fighter system would be a major force multiplier if they survived.

"The colonel is sure they will," Miriam translated. "Every test so far has been successful. Is there any news on how they work?"

The *Blade* had brought back a dragonfly after their first mission. It had died enroute, since they had no clue about how to feed it, but the parts were all still there.

However, human and Adar scientists had been stumped by the creature. It generated the lasers using a rather comprehensible chemical system. Part of its dietary requirements that the humans hadn't known was that it needed the base chemicals for the lasers, the dragonfly equivalent of vitamins. However, beyond that point, humans and Adar were scratching their heads. It had various parts that were probably its reactionless drive, antigravity generator and power source. But the power requirements for the dragonfly's proven range and acceleration were enormous and there was no fusion reactor in the thing's guts.

Live dragonflies had been delivered to the Hexosehr and they promised to look at them as soon as they got settled. But for the time being the answer was . . .

"No," the CO said to Lady Che-Chee, shrugging. "We still have no clue. Do you dislike providing support?"

Miriam winced at the blunt question, then chuckled at the reply.

"The short answer is: No," the linguist translated. "The longer answer is the Cheerick realize that if they didn't have the dragonflies, they would have virtually nothing to trade. As it is, with them, they can bring in scientists and specialists to advance their technology and culture. They're allies, but . . ."

"Alliances are based on mutual benefit." Prael nodded. "Good. Very well, the mission is to investigate an area we think a higher technology race once inhabited and try to find any technologies that may help in the war against the Dreen. The Dreen are known to be in the sector but it's believed in minimal force. We may not even encounter them. If we do, however, I intend to run rather than fight. This is a scouting and exploratory mission, not a raid. If we do have to fight, however, we're going to need to have your wing integrated. I'd suggest that we get down to particulars of how we're going to use you and your people . . ."

"Hey, Berg, I'm heading down to Kakki Town," Lieutenant Morris said, sticking his head in Admin. "You wanna come?"

Between loading the dragonflies and some diplomatic duties, the *Blade* was going to be on Cheerick for better than two days. Given that, and that the actual loading would be late in the action, the CO had authorized shore leave.

The Marines, especially, were looking forward to it. On-board the ship they had nothing to do but drill and while First Sergeant Powell was inventive, the drills became boring as hell quickly. This was the last friendly planet they could look forward to visiting for some time and just seeing sky from outside a Wyvern suit sounded good.

"I wish I could," Eric admitted. "But I am loaded to the max."

"Check with the Old Man," Morris said. "It's shore leave, man!"

"Sir, am I authorized for shore leave?" Eric asked after being given permission to enter.

"You're an officer now, Lieutenant Bergstresser," Zanella said, looking up from his monitor. "If you feel you have the time and you're not on a duty roster, that's up to you."

"Are you taking shore leave, sir?" Eric asked. He knew that that wasn't a straight "yes."

"I'm still up to my eyeballs in paperwork, Lieutenant," the CO replied, gesturing at the monitor. "The good part about a twenty day cruise is that I might be *almost* caught up when we get to our destination."

"In that case, sir, I will decline to take shore leave," Eric said, nodding.

"Thought you might."

5

"Ready to go?" Weaver asked.

Along with the rest of the *Blade*'s mission, Miriam and Weaver were scheduled to meet with the Alliance ambassador and the Cheerick Minister for Stellar Affairs. The Cheerick had been more than willing to be secret partners in the Alliance until the *Blade* went public. With the sudden change in status, the American government wanted to prepare the Cheerick for the onslaught of curiosity that was about to break out. And ensure that the partnership with the Alliance was solid.

Rather than have a direct portal from Cheerick to Earth, a third planet had a gate installed with another jump to Earth. The planet, which was still unnamed but referred to ubiquitously as Waypoint, also had a portal to Runner's World, which the Hexosehr were in the process of colonizing and reterraforming, and to Adar.

"Of course," Miriam said, hitting the hatch to the ramp and stepping out. "It's not like the queen will notice my hair isn't rolled."

"Queen Sicrac?" Weaver said, stepping onto a chee-board. "I wouldn't bet on it."

The boards, *chack-chack* to the Cheerick, or "sleds" earlier to the *Blade* crew, were just part of the strange dichotomy of Cheerick, a planet with a mostly medieval culture and technology mixed with tech so advanced humans sometimes felt like monkeys examining it. The boards simply appeared, scattered across the surface of the planet. A user, human or Cheerick, just stepped on the board and thought about where they wanted to go and how. The board responded perfectly, performing loops and banks that would make a swallow jealous, while generating some sort of "sticky" traction field that kept the user's feet firmly attached to the top of the board. They worked in deep space just as well as in atmosphere, had a high acceleration and inertial damping and, like the dragonflies, they had an unknown power-source. Although in the case of the boards it appeared to be unlimited; no board collected by the Cheerick had ever failed in recorded history.

The local monarchy maintained the boards as a royal monopoly and used them primarily for their cavalry arm. However, there were more than enough to trade some to their human allies and for transportation of distinguished visitors.

"Place hasn't changed much," Weaver commented as the two flew over the city with an escort of Cheerick air-cavalry.

"No, it's spread a bit," Miriam argued, pointing to the west where new construction, new homes, was clearly evident. "The big impact hasn't hit, yet, though. Start electrifying the city, bring in cars . . . It will be interesting to see how they adjust. This truly is a fifteenth-century culture. The shock of new technology is going to make things interesting."

"Gunpowder and the printing press are arguably the death of any aristocracy," Weaver said, sliding closer to the linguist's board. "I hope we can maintain friendly relations with whatever the successor government will be."

"That's the ambassador's problem," Miriam pointed out. "Ours is to make sure this government is going to stay on our side."

"*Ik ikki squee tik scrree!*" Queen Sicrac squealed.

"We were informed that your government was going to take some more months to release the information," the translator interpreted loudly.

The audience was taking place in front of the full court and Weaver hoped that the royal "we" form, which the queen had never previously used around him, was a result of the public display. If not, it did not bode well for their mission.

"Events forced my government's hand," Ambassador Cookson replied. "Our press had become aware of many details of the missions of the *Vorpal Blade*. Going public, as we put it, was a necessity rather than a choice."

"We have discussed with you the subject of your press," the queen said through the interpreter. "We comprehend the nature of the problem. However, it also forces our hand. We have not yet completed Our negotiations with the Tickreek. Are We to assume that there will soon be competing governments interfering in those negotiations?"

"Probably, Your Majesty," the Alliance ambassador replied.

"We will not have it," the queen said. "Until We are sure of their intentions, all embassies must remain under Our control. We will establish a trading community near Our capital and the new Looking Glass. All such emissaries will be relegated to that trading community until We are willing to open up full relations."

"So Mote It Be," the major domo boomed, thumping the floor with his pike.

"This audience is concluded," the queen said, standing up. "We are repairing to quarters."

"*Ick squeak*," a page said, touching Weaver's arm.

"He wants us to go with him," Miriam said, frowning.

"*Ik ikki squee!*" the rodentoid said as sotto voce as possible given the Cheerick squeal.

"Oh," Miriam said. "We're to go to a private audience."

"Ah, you're here," Ambassador Cookson said. Sarah Cookson was a long-service diplomat with experience in multiple countries and had previously held the position of Undersecretary for South American Affairs. Being both a senior female in the diplomatic service and with a flair for languages, she had been a natural choice for the position. Up until recently, the job of ambassador to Cheerick had also been both black and not a particularly important position. Weaver wasn't sure if she'd gotten the job as a booby-prize or because she was an optimal choice. But she had done an excellent job thus far and interacted well with the military, a rare feat among long-service diplomats.

"Where in the hell did she get the idea to establish a

controlled trade zone?" Weaver asked quietly. They were waiting to be presented in an antechamber off a smaller audience chamber. That chamber was, effectively, the queen's private office. Weaver had been there a couple of times on the first *Blade* mission and recognized the door.

"Hours and hours of discussions," Cookson replied, just as quietly. "At this point, I think Queen Sicrac has a better handle on human politics and international relations than most presidents and prime ministers. I'd hoped for something like this but it was her own idea. She got it from the Japanese."

"That's what it sounded like," Miriam said, biting her lip. "But that sort of thing isn't going to hold as well these days. Other governments are going to be livid about it."

"As long as the Alliance continues to support it, what are they going to do?" Weaver said. "We're the only ones with ships, we control the portals . . . I can think of some complicated ways around it, but they'd be technically hard if not impossible."

"So have I," Sarah said. "But as you pointed out, smuggling an LGB would be difficult. One can't pass through a Looking Glass. As to it holding, the queen is well aware that it's a stop-gap measure. She's mostly struggling to control the changes in society that are going to come with the new technology. New tech coming into a society like this is so destabilizing it can be horrible. By establishing an economic zone she can control the rate of change to an extent. Even if it holds for one generation it will help."

"*Ik squee, ik*," the major domo said at a knock on the door.

"She'll see us, now," Cookson said. "Here goes."

❊   ❊   ❊

"Kottander Beeeel," the queen said, holding out both hands. "*Ik squee, squeek tik.*"

"The Queen welcomes her Sister in Battle," the translator said.

"Thank you for seeing us, Queen Sicrac," Bill said, taking both hands and placing them together with his.

"What do you think of the trade zone?" the queen asked through the translator.

"Probably the best choice you could make, Your Majesty," Bill replied. "I don't know how long it will hold, but it will help your people adjust to the changes."

"It's more than that," the queen said. "Much more. We are in the process of making alliances with most of our long-time enemies. With your technology we are both a preferred partner to our former enemies and militarily unstoppable. They can see the truth clearly and may not like it but they are agreeing to binding treaties. If your many countries flood onto this world, making their own side-alliances, it will make my job much harder. That was the deciding factor. I'm aware that it will not hold forever. But if I can create a unified planetary government, or even something close, then my Daughters will be in a much stronger bargaining position when your other countries finally come calling."

"There is that," Bill said, nodding. The nice thing about smart monarchies was that they tended to think long-term.

"I am also aware that political change is inevitable," the queen said, holding up a book. Bill recognized it as a popular book on the development of western civilization.

"I cannot speak your language, but I can read it well enough. Ambassador Cookson has been most helpful in obtaining books about your world and its politics. I have read so much my eyes are bleeding but I think I have a handle on what to expect of your competitors. Many of them, frankly, could be a better short-term partner. Those who support dictatorship over democracy, for example, or simply are enamored of 'realpolitik.' I expect your government's more liberal elements to begin pressing for political change in my country very soon. Perhaps in the next change of your administration. Perhaps even earlier. The trade zone, again, will permit me to control that. Having looked at the facts, a representative republic is an excellent system in the long-run. In the short run, while such monumental change is taking place, with a society that is based on duty obligations and has limited under-standing of personal choice, it is a potential disaster. We are far more likely to fall into the trap of a personality cult than a true republic. Which is why I'm going to hold it off for as long as possible. The citizenry must first become educated, technology must take hold, we need a stable middle-class. *Then* we can discuss becoming more democratic by steps. Do you agree?"

"Actually, I do," Bill admitted, blinking. "But our media is probably going to disagree. Which means they will foment a political crisis out of it, for the ratings if nothing else."

"Which is why they are going to be carefully controlled," Queen Sicrac said. When she'd said it there was a squeal Bill had come to recognize as humor. "But subtly. Your media is lazy; they tend to stay near the best restaurants.

Given the traveling conditions on this world, I do not see many of them straying much beyond the capital even if I permit it. And your liberals are enamored of the 'noble savage' concept. We will show them the kindly agrarian society of Cheerick, the happy harvesters in the fields. The clean skies, the happy workers, the wonderful environment. We will provide them with . . . stringers, I believe the term is. They will gather the 'real' news and it will be news that we carefully feed them, just as insurgents and dictators did on your world. We are, of course, establishing manufacturing centers. But We are requiring them to be well away from the Looking Glass. And We have started a program to move the unemployed of the capital to Chakree, which is our primary factory center, to become the workers in the factories. I intend that by the time your press comes to this planet, they are going to find nothing but fuzzy little rodents that look cute and are having a lovely time under their benevolent queen."

"Ouch," Bill muttered. "How long do you think that will hold?"

"About five years," Queen Sicrac replied, adding a nose wrinkle that was the equivalent of a shrug. "But that's long enough for some of the technology to take hold and it gets us past the initial crisis. And, as I said, your press is most remarkably lazy. There is only one gate on this planet and for the time being I intend for that to be the only gate. Give them a good story, and I intend to give them many good stories, and they will remain near the Looking Glass and their supply of . . . scotch and vodka, yes? In the meantime, the stringers I provide will bring them the videos of battles to overthrow vicious dictators, crying

Cheerick children liberated from the lands of my enemies, kindly Cheerick liberators. Oh, I will throw in the occasional negative story about my own country, but with luck I'll come off smelling like a rose."

"And the Alliance?" Bill asked.

"I have also studied the reports you brought in about the Dreen," the queen said. "And studies of the effect of the war on your planet. As I said, much much much reading. I will support the Alliance as sturdily as possible, because although we are not in the direct path of the Dreen to your world, we are high on the list after you fall. One of the requirements that I'm building into the alliances is supplying fighters for the dragonflies. Since we control the methods of production for them, and for the Demons—although I try to downplay that to my new friends—it is simply a matter of getting trained fighters to control them. We receive enormous payment for each dragonfly and rider. I don't intend to cut off my source of funding for the many programs I have going."

"You've got a lot on your plate, Your Majesty," Bill admitted.

"I had able advisors when you first arrived," the queen said. "I admit that they are getting stretched. I'm always looking for good material. Care for a job?"

"No, but thank you," Bill said.

"Pay's good," the queen pressed. "Living conditions are excellent. I regret I cannot offer you concubines, however. Interspecies and all that. The offer is extended to Miss Moon as well, of course."

"I enjoy what I'm doing at the moment, Your Majesty," Miriam said, dimpling. "I, too, must respectfully pass."

"Captain Weaver? You're sure? I can see about arranging concubines."

"Again, I too must respectfully pass," Bill said.

"Oh, well, offer is open," the queen said. "You can send the message to your President and thus to the Alliance that as long as I can hold this lash-up together, the queen of Cheerick is your ally and all that. So anything that they can do on their end to try to give me some breathing space would be heartily appreciated. Because if I have to deal with labor organizers and the Communist Party, not to mention transnational progressives, the Earth media and the French, then I'm going to be hard put to supply space fighters."

"I'll ensure that they get that message loud and clear, Your Majesty," Ambassador Cookson said. "In fact, I will include those words, precisely, in my report."

"Very good," the queen said. "You have things to do, I have things to do, and things to read, so I'm afraid this audience must end. Good luck on your next voyage. What is the mission?"

"Looking for an extinct race that had advanced technology," Bill said. "Some of it is still around; the drive in our ship for example. We're hoping we can pick up some more bits in a particular region of space."

"Hopefully Lady Che-chee will be of use," the queen said, waving at the door. "Now I really have to get back to paperwork."

"Thank you for your time, Your Majesty," Ambassador Cookson said, backing to the door.

"Just go ahead and walk out," the queen said. "All this backing and scraping gets tiresome."

❊   ❊   ❊

"How do we know if this is edible?" Machinist Mate Second Class Kulpa asked, looking at the fruit.

"It is," Gants replied, sucking his teeth. "When the *Blade* was refitting here we practically lived on that stuff. It's not bad, but you can have it."

The two machinists had been given a three-hour shore leave and had barely made it past the market that had sprung up by the ship. When the Cheerick heard that the humans were being permitted to visit, they had swarmed out in huge numbers for a glance at the aliens and to make money off of them.

"We don't have any of the local money," Kulpa pointed out.

"They mostly barter," Gants said, shrugging and holding up a necklace. "You think Vonn would like this?"

"It's pretty," Kulpa admitted. "What the hell do I offer?"

"Got any idea how much nickel content there is in a nickel?" Gants said. "Like, none. But it's still worth more than that fruit to that vendor. Copper's like hard currency to them. Show them something with actual silver or gold in it and they'll freak out; they won't be able to change it. These people are *poor*, man."

Kulpa fished in his pockets and came up with a handful of change. He handed over a few pennies and after considering them carefully the Cheerick handed over the fruit. It looked a bit like an orange but when Kulpa pulled off the rind he found the interior to be more similar to a pear. The taste wasn't like anything he could describe, vaguely pineapply.

"Weird," he said as Gants completed his negotiations. He'd traded a butane lighter for the necklace of some sort of purple shells with the luminousness of pearl.

"True tale," Gants said, picking up one of the fruit and tossing the vendor a dime. "Back in the days when Africa was just starting to get explored, the traders would park their ship and set out some stuff on the shore. Steel hatchets, knives, stuff like that. The natives would come down, put some of their stuff out and move the piles around. A whole elephant tusk of pure ivory by ten knives or so. The traders would go out the next day and move stuff around again. Three knives by the tusk, say. That would go on until the piles didn't move, then everybody would collect their stuff and leave."

"Slow way to get stuff," Kulpa said. "I'd rather just swipe my ATM card."

"Sure," Gants said. "But then the traders would take back the tusk of ivory to London or Antwerp or wherever and get several *thousand* knives for it. Or the money equivalent, anyway. They made money hand over fist. That was worth waiting around in the tropical heat for."

"Why didn't the natives just steal the stuff?" Kulpa asked as they stopped by a troop of Cheerick acrobats. Admittedly, the rotund rodentoids weren't a patch on the Cirque du Soleil, but they seemed really happy over the few quarters in their bucket.

"Oh, the guys on the ship would point a cannon at the clearing," Gants said. "Just to keep everything honest. And if they went on shore and tried to steal all the native stuff, well, a spear from the jungle is a permanent souvenir. Trade's about contracts, in that case maintained by spears and cannons. Hasn't really changed, much. Just gotten faster and more complicated."

"So, what do you think it's going to be like having these guys on the ship?" Kulpa asked as the Cheerick pyramid collapsed in a pile of squeals.

"Probably hardly see them," Sub Dude replied. "Time's about up. Time to get back to work."

Red looked up from the motor he was working on at a series of high-pitched squeals from down the corridor.

One of the Cheerick dragonfly pilots had turned the corner and come face to face with Tiny. The cat was in a play-pounce position and the Cheerick, even though he outweighed the cat by at least a factor of nine, clearly wasn't sure he wasn't the intended prey.

"Throw him a ball," Red said, tossing same down the hall.

At the skittering sound behind him, the cat turned on his tail and launched through the air, overshooting the ball and spinning again. With another pounce he had the ball and ran it back to Red.

"Go ahead," Red said, holding out the ball to the Cheerick.

The rodentoid came down the corridor and took the ball, sending it bounding down the corridor to bounce off a coaming. Tiny loved that since he had to turn in mid-run, leap off a bulkhead and catch the thing in the air. He ran it back to the giant rodentoid and dropped the ball, wiggling his butt in anticipation.

"Feel free," Red said, turning back to his pump. "I'm kinda busy right now."

6

"Ship status, XO?" Captail Prael asked.

"All personnel returned from shore leave," Bill said. "All critical systems functioning. We're clear for take-off, sir."

"Straightboard shut?" Prael asked.

"All hatches closed and locked," the COB replied.

"Pilot, make course for HD . . . 242896," the CO said after a moment's pause. "XO has the conn. XO, please call Miss Moon to my office."

"Thank you for your assistance on Cheerick," Prael said as Miriam entered his office. "Sit, please."

"Just doing my job, sir," Miriam said, sitting down.

"And now we don't have one for you until we potentially encounter another alien race," the CO said. "And that's what I wanted to talk to you about. I'm aware that on your previous cruise you spent a goodly amount of your time working on maintenance. But the ship is working perfectly well. It's practically brand new, after all."

"I was there when it was built," Miriam said.

"And then there's the matter of the crew," the CO said. "While the older crew is perfectly used to dealing with you, the others are from the sub service. For some very good psychological reasons, women have never been allowed in subs."

"That is arguable," Miriam said. "But I'll take it as a given for this discussion, since I can see where it's going."

"There is a large and fully functional science wing in the ship," the CO said. "And we're not carrying a science team. It is also directly connected to the wardroom and the officer's areas. I do not mind you interacting with the officers, however after much thought on yours and Captain Weaver's arguments to the contrary, I'm going to require that you stay out of the crew and Marine areas. If necessary, we will return to Earth to drop you off."

"That *won't* be necessary," Miriam said, standing up. "But I'm going to make a pronouncement, Captain. The day is going to come, and probably soon, when you are going to regret this conversation."

"I'll live with that," Prael said, gesturing at the door. "Thank you for your time."

"Hey, Port-man," Eric said, walking into the Wyvern Room.

In the *Blade I* the Wyverns had been housed between the remaining missile tubes of the converted sub. In the *Blade II*, a special room had been constructed. Still three stories high, it was easier to get the massive armor in and out of the room than it had been in Sherwood Forest, for which everyone was grateful. Lifts raised the armor up and down and in the central floor there were multiple airlocks for deployment. There also was a broad corridor to the underbelly ramp on the ship for ground deployments.

"Hang on!" Portana said, tossing a ball through the hatch. "Quick! Shut the hatch!" he added as a white streak went through Eric's legs.

Eric did as he was ordered, despite being an officer, and then looked at the armorer quizzically.

"What was that?" Berg asked.

"Tiny," Portana replied, growling. "Damn t'ing."

"Why is there a giant cat on the ship?" Eric asked. "And when we're alone it's okay to forget the 'sir,' Port-man, but . . ."

"Sorry, sir," Portana said. "Somebody brought it on to catch those chee-hamsters you picked up the first trip. It mostly take up time playing fetch. An' I don' see no chee-hamster, ever."

"They're nocturnal," Eric said after a brief pause. "It's like cockroaches; they only come out when there's no light. So you'd only see them right after you turn on a light in a compartment. Glad to see we finally got something to keep them down. Now, I'm up for simulator training."

"Got it licked, sir," Portana said. "Runner's World. Been there . . ."

"Did that from the front, Port-man," Eric said, accepting the mission-chip. "Now I got to learn how to manage the battlefield."

"Come!" Bill shouted at the knock on the hatch.

"XO, we have an issue," the Eng said.

"And that is?" Bill asked, not looking up from the

consumption report. They were going to have to stop by a gas giant and pick up some water and pressurized O_2 within the next five days . . .

"Number Two air recycler just dropped offline," the Eng said, swallowing. "Number One is down to eighty percent. If it drops below sixty percent efficiency, it will drop off, too."

They were in deep space more than four days from the nearest known habitable planet, the air of which was only barely breathable. And even with one recycler at eighty percent, they'd be breathing soup in no more than a day.

"I sure hope you've figured out how to fix this thing by now, Chief," Bill said, flexing his jaw. "Or we're all going to be breathing off spare O_2 by tomorrow morning."

"If you can tell me what a covalent shear screen is, sir, I can probably fix it," the chief snapped, holding up the printed out manual for the Hexosehr system. "But since I've got no clue how it works, I'm having a hard time even figuring out what's wrong."

"This, I think," Red said, holding up what looked like a wire-mesh screen. Portions of it were a brilliant metal that reflected the overhead with shades of violet. But others were black and apparently covered with a tarry substance.

Three machinists had the failed recycler torn down and scattered across the deck, trying to figure out how to fix it while Red and Sub Dude were inside the guts up to their waists.

"I got more of that stuff," Sub Dude said in a muffled tone from deep inside the device. "Do we have spare covalent shearing screens in parts?"

"Covalent . . ." the chief muttered, flipping through the book. "How do you spell that?"

"Polar corpuscle looks fried, too," Ian said, holding up a metal piece that looked vaguely like a kidney. "What's going to fry that?"

"Look, we don't have time to figure this out," Weaver said, grabbing his remaining hair. "Just pull the thing and put in the spare."

"What spare?" the Eng asked.

"When we were having problems with it on Earth, I told the chief to pull that one and keep it around," Bill said. "It was still working, it was just marginal. So where is it, Chief?"

"I had Red and Gants pull it," the Chief said. "Red, where'd you store the spare recycler?"

"You told us to send it to depot maintenance, Chief," Red said, back up to his waist in the recycler. "It's in Norfolk."

"I told you to store it and work on it in your spare time," Chief Gestner said.

The clinking from inside the machine stopped and then both machinists slid out as if teleported.

"You told us, Chief, to send it to depot maintenance," Gants said, gritting his teeth. "Send it to depot. That is what you told us to do, Chief. We sent it to depot. It's in Norfolk. You didn't say anything about working on it in our spare time. *You* said send it to *depot*."

"I don't like your tone, Machinist," Chief Gestner snapped. "You will jack it up!"

"I don't like yours, Chief," Bill snarled. "I gave you a direct order which you, in turn, failed to ensure was carried out! So trying to shift the blame to a couple of petty officers is . . . Petty beyond belief!"

"Whoa," the Eng said, holding up his hands. "What we definitely don't have time for is to get into a he said/he said! The point is, we do not, in fact, have a spare onboard. Is that correct, Chief Gestner?"

"Yes, sir," the chief said, glaring at the XO. Unable to take out his fury on the officer he rounded on the machinists. "You two, back to work."

Gants gave him one more fulminating look then slid back into the depths of the alien machinery.

"Then we need to get this one working," Weaver said. "And we then need to pull the other one down and get *it* working. And if you cannot figure out how to spell 'covalent,' Chief Petty Officer, you had better damned well learn. I'll sell you a clue: It starts with a C, just like coc . . . Chief!"

"Eng," Weaver said as they left the compartment. "I want it reflected on the chief's evaluation report that he was given an order to maintain a critical component and whether there was a damned miscommunication or not, it was his responsibility to ensure that order was carried out."

"I don't think this is the time to be bringing that up, sir," the Eng said. "When we're past the crisis we can determine the mistakes that were made. I'll remind you, sir, that as the person responsible for all aspects of this ship, it reflects poorly upon your own actions that you did not ensure that that order was fulfilled. I, for example, who am responsible for all the *engineering* aspects of the ship, was unaware of it, sir. Because you dealt with the situation directly, rather than working through the department heads. That is what we're here for, sir, to ensure that all orders are carried out."

"Duly noted, Eng," Weaver said, grimacing. "But that order was given and it was not carried out. And I want that to be reflected in his evaluation report."

"Also duly noted, XO," the Eng said. "But on the subject of us running out of air, sir? I would entertain suggestions from my superior in this matter, sir. Because while I can spell covalent, I, too, have no *grapping* clue what a covalent shearing screen does."

"*Grapp, grapp, grapp . . .*" Gants muttered.

"He's gone," Red said from outside the device. "The behanchod."

"I was actually talking about this *grapping* Hexosehr piece of *maulk*," Gants said, grunting then yelping. "*Grapp!* Work, you Hexosehr piece of *maulk!*" he shouted, banging on something in the depths of the machine.

"It's not going to work with its guts spread all over," Red said, looking at the system inventory. "Damnit, we don't *have* any shearing screens! They're listed as a capital item! They're not supposed to break down, apparently."

"Well, they sure as shit have," Gants said, sliding out another piece of machinery. "And will you look at that?"

"What is it?" Red asked, picking up what looked like a painting canvas. Like the shearing screen, it was covered in a black tarry substance and holes had apparently been eaten in it in spots. Unless it was supposed to look like chemical moths had been at it.

"I have no *grapping* clue," Gants said. "But I'm pretty sure it's important."

"We are so *grapped*," Red said, slumping back against the recycler. "We have no *grapping* clue what any of this *maulk* is or how to fix it. How could we go into space not knowing how any of this *maulk* worked? Were we *grapping nuts*?"

"It's Hexosehr stuff," Gants said, sliding back out and sitting up. "It's magic. It's supposed to work like magic. Magic doesn't break."

"Well, if we're not all going to die of asphyxiation, we'd better figure out how to fix magic," Red said.

"And who is the most magical person on this ship?"

"It breaks the covalent bonds in ketones and esters," Miriam said, not looking up from rubbing Tiny on the stomach. The linguist looked terrible. Her skin was gray, hair was frumpy, her tone listless and her eyes bloodshot. She was also wearing glasses, which Gants had only seen a couple of times in all the time he'd known her. "That breaks them down to CO_2, nitrogen, oxygen and water. When the covalent shearing screen broke down, you started to get organic acids which ripped up the carbon cracker, that thing that looks like a painting canvas. That breaks CO_2 and carbon monoxide down into carbon and oxygen then transports the carbon to a holding compartment. You did check the carbon holding compartment, right?"

"That's a regular maintenance item," Gants said. "But I never knew where it came from."

"So the CO_2 and organics detectors recognized the system was broken," Miriam continued, "and shut it down automatically. Otherwise we'd be breathing that black stuff."

"Ma'am, we're hours away from breathing pure carbon dioxide and days away from air," Gants said gently. "We really need to figure out how to fix this thing."

"I'm no use," Miriam said. "I'm no use to anybody. Just ask the captain."

"Ma'am, we really need your help," Gants said, swearing mentally at the new CO and his stupid order. "Ma'am, if we can't figure this out, we're all going to die."

"Everybody dies sometime," Miriam said.

Oh, maulk, Sub Dude thought.

"Ma'am," he said, carefully, looking at the cat stretched across her lap, "Tiny's got to breathe, too."

Miriam glared at him for a moment, then frowned, her brow furrowing.

"There's not supposed to be build-up on the covalent shearers," Miriam said. "The only way that you'd get that is if molecules with polar bonds were getting through. The covalent shearers can't break polar bonds. Check the polar corpuscle. It's probably detuned. Check the point and dwell settings. As to repairing the covalent shearer and the carbon cracker, you can't repair them perfectly. But you can take them and cut them up and run them through the fabber on a recycler setting. The parts will come out clean. Use a melder to join them and you'll get about ninety percent efficiency. See if that works."

"Damn, Gants, you are a genius," Bill said, looking at the humming recycler.

"The efficiency's high enough I recommend tearing down the other one and repairing it, sir," the Eng said.

"Concur," Bill replied. "Good job, Eng, Machinist. Damned good. How'd you figure out the polar corpuscle was screwed up?"

"Oh, it was pretty obvious, sir," Gants said, sucking his teeth. "I mean, that's the *only* way you could get build-up on the covalent shearer, right sir?"

"Point and dwell settings?" Bill asked, shaking his head. "Why didn't I think of that?"

"Not your job to figure everything out, sir," Gants replied.

"Point," Bill said. "Now I have to wonder what's going to screw up next. . . ."

"Well, that was different," the CO said, setting down his fork.

Captain Prael felt it important that the ship's officers have at least one meal together each week. It was an opportunity to talk shop and cover the minor stuff that might not be getting the attention that it deserved.

Normally, the meals were fairly good. Admittedly, shipboard fare was never exquisite; after a few weeks all the fresh food was gone and it pretty much came down to three-bean salad and chili-mac. But the sub service was well known for the quality of their meals. With nothing to see but steel walls, twelve on and twelve off, day in and day out, keeping up morale could only be done with good food. So if it wasn't four star, it tended to be the best that was possible.

But there was a vast range of difference between a four-star meal and . . .

The current meal was listed as "Spinach Fandango." Bill had never previously heard of spinach fandango and if this was spinach fandango he never wanted to hear of it again. He picked up some of the greenish-gray glop on a spoon and held it upside down. Despite repeated attempts, he could not, in fact, get it to fall off. No matter how hard he shook it. "Stick-to-your-ribs" was an understatement. This stuff could be used for spackling.

"I've been hearing some rumblings from my department about the quality of the chow," the Eng said. "Since it hadn't been all that bad up here, I just put it down to the usual grumbling. If this is what they've been getting consistently . . ."

"Sir?" the gunnery officer asked, diffidently. Like children, lieutenants junior grade were meant to be seen and not heard and he knew it. "Shouldn't we still have some fresh vegetables? We were on Cheerick three days ago and I thought we got a shipment of fresh stuff."

"Yes, we should," the CO said. "And I'm beginning to wonder if this isn't some sort of prank. But I know how to find out. XO?"

"Sir?" Bill said, diffidently tasting the stuff. It didn't taste nearly as bad as it looked, but that was just because it looked so very, very, *very* bad. It only tasted *very* bad. Filling, though. One taste was all it took to kill his appetite.

"In addition to your other duties, you will take random meals in the enlisted mess," the CO said. "Morale of the unit depends, among other things, on the best possible food, all things being equal. I wouldn't describe this as the best possible food, would you?"

"No, sir," Bill replied. "And aye, aye, sir. I'll get to the bottom of this."

"That wasn't what you was supposed to have," Chief Petty Officer Duppstadt said. "You was supposed to have the spinach salad and goulash. I'll find out where that went, instead, sir."

The ship's galley was not, admittedly, the most amenable compartment on the *Blade*. A steamy hell of boiling pots, sizzling pans and ovens running full blast, it recalled the Harry Truman expression. And Bill admitted that he was ready to get out of the kitchen the moment he stepped in.

"That's not, in fact, the point," Bill said, patiently. "Was the spinach fandango the meal for the enlisted mess?"

"Yes, sir," Duppstadt said. "It's a favorite."

"It's a disaster, Chief," the XO said angrily. "The stuff should be used for vacuum sealer! It's a noxious *glue*."

"It's one of my specialties, sir," the CPO replied, his face tight. "I've been making my spinach fandango whenever I got fresh spinach for over twenty years, sir!"

"Wait, you used fresh spinach for that . . . that . . . glop?" Bill snarled. "You used precious *fresh food* for that indescribable, unholy *mess*?"

"I ain't never had no complaints," the chief replied, mulishly. "*Captain*," he added, sarcastically.

"Was that an insult to my rank, Chief Petty Officer?" Bill said quietly. "Because if you think you can be insolent because I'm not a 'real' Naval officer then you'd better think twice, chief or no chief."

"No insolence intended, Captain," the chief said.

"Then you'll refer to me as 'Sir' or 'XO,'" Bill said. "'Captain' in a surly tone of voice will not do, Chief. Now do you seriously think that that mess you just slopped up is a palatable meal?"

"This isn't DC, sir," the chief said. "There ain't no four-star chefs on no sub. And I ain't had no complaints in over twenty years."

"Then consider this your first," Bill said. "And you are about to receive orders, which you will abide by, chief or no chief. From here on out, the officers will receive the *same* food as the enlisted tables. No difference, Chief. I will be eating with the enlisted ranks by the order of the CO, who is your *second* complaint in 'over twenty years,' by the way. And you had better start cracking the books, Chief, because if this is your best dish, you're going to find yourself sorry and sore by the end of this cruise. You are *not* going to poison this crew as long as *I'm* the XO. I've got enough troubles on this ship without having everyone down with a case of the 'I'm dying from Chief Duppstadt's so-called food!'"

"Jesus Christ," Weaver swore under his breath as he left the mess compartment. "What *else* can go wrong?"

His eyes crossed momentarily and he shook his head.

"Tell me I didn't just say that," he muttered as a mess specialist walked by.

"You okay, sir?" the mess specialist asked, looking at him askance.

"Just fine, just fine," Bill replied. "Carry on."

※   ※   ※

"XO's talking to himself," the mess specialist said, shaking his head and spooning up something called "goulash" that Duppstadt said was a "speciality."

"Never a good sign," the PO next to him said.

"Heard the cooks talking," the missileman said, sliding his tray onto the table. "XO's talking to himself."

"Damn," the ship's medic said, shaking his head. "We're only three weeks in. Never a good sign."

"Better get your syringe ready," the missile tech said, grinning.

"Carry it with me always."

7

All machinists on a nuclear boat were "nukes." That is, they had been through the Navy's brutal Nuclear Power School after learning their other craft.

Thus PO Gants had been through a course that was the near order of a bachelor's in nuclear engineering. Even if most of the time he felt like a glorified plumber.

However, that meant that most of his time was *not* taken up with glorified plumbing: It was taken up with watching the many readouts related to the power system of the *Blade II*. Eight hours out of every day everyone on the ship stood "watch" with an additional four hours of "duty." (Glorified plumbing.) What "watch" meant depended upon the speciality. But in Gants' case it meant watching a large number of readouts from, on this watch, Fusion Engine Two, which were *not* supposed to be fluctuating.

With a nuclear power system, such as had been on the original *Nebraska*, Gants would have known not only what any fluctuation meant directly but the thousands of additional issues it would cause.

However, the *Blade II* had fusion engines. He'd read the manual on fusion engines, understanding a surprising amount, but he could not really be called, in his opinion, fully certified. Then again, there were no humans that he considered "fully certified" on Hexosehr fusion engines.

So when one of the waterfall displays, vertical colored readouts that ran from green at the top through yellow then red, started flickering, he wasn't positive if it was the first signs of cataclysm or just something "hinky."

The whole fusion conversion system was a bit of a mystery, frankly.

In nuke boats radioactive fission released heat which boiled water which turned turbines which made electricity. Which was why one name for nuke boats was "tea kettles."

The way that fission works is a "slow" neutron is captured by uranium 235 turning it into uranium 236. This destabilizes the uranium atom which then breaks apart, fissions, into, usually, barium and krypton gas and energy. Lots of energy. The fission releases 200 *times* the amount of energy in the neutron and, notably, gamma rays and more neutrons. The new neutrons continue to break up more uranium, thus the "chain reaction" part. The excess energy is mostly in the form of heat.

The heat is transferred to water (or in some cases sodium or helium) which in turn is run via pipes through other water. That water, turned to steam, drives massive turbines. The turbines directly drive the propellers and also produce electrical power.

In a fusion boat, helium three (He3) atoms were fused together. Like a fission reaction, that produced heat. It also produced plasma, atoms that had been stripped of their electrons. He3 was used because, unlike deuterium and hydrogen, it produced no secondary radiation.

Instead of boiling water, a secondary Hexosehr system grabbed the stripped electrons for electricity as well as used the generated heat to produce more through the "heat converter" unit. About 90% of the generated energy was captured and turned to electricity. Which was good since too much heat in a spaceship was a bad thing. Using the Hexosehr systems gave them four times as long between chills as the *Blade I*.

The whole thing was encased in a magnetic containment bottle. The containment bottle was, in fact, bottle shaped, having an opening on one side. That led to the plasma conduits and the heat transfer system, which had their own magnetic containment. The helium 3 that fueled the thing was inserted through rapidly opening and closing "holes" in the magnetic containment bottle.

Input: the He3. Output: the total power released in the fusion bottle. Throughput was how much electricity was scavenged. There was an "input" side of throughput from output that was measured as well.

What he was seeing, every five seconds more or less, was a slight drop in throughput. Just a flicker. Fusion Two was set at 80% output, a good level for fast cruising. Every now and then throughput dropped about two percent.

What was bugging him was that if the throughput was flickering, the output should have been. And there should have been other systems showing a fault.

But only throughput was flickering. Actually, input power of the throughput systems. Which meant about two percent of the output was disappearing. Somewhere. To be specific, somewhere *in* the bottle. Given that the power contained in the bottle was nearly as much as had destroyed Nagasaki, two percent of it disappearing was . . . problematic.

He reached up and touched a control, bringing up the numeric readout of output for the last few hours. Sure enough, he could see where the output started flickering. About ten minutes ago. It wasn't visible with the waterfalls or the numeric readouts.

He sat back and contemplated that for a bit.

"Got a problem, Gants?"

The lieutenant of the watch was a nuke. He had a degree in nuclear power and had been through the same school, albeit for officers, as Gants. He had more theoretical knowledge than the machinist and Gants acknowledged that. But, like Gants, his training was in *fission* not *fusion*. They were *not* the same.

Gants, therefore, didn't answer directly. He called up the same screens while he thought and pointed to the changes.

"How can you have a two percent drop in throughput but less than one in output?" the lieutenant mused.

Gants had started off thinking the same thing. But he was bugged by something.

He pulled up a detail of the containment bottle. The readouts were designed for fairly large-order changes and he was looking for very slight ones.

Dialing down he finally found what he was looking

for, thought about it for a moment and reached out like a cobra to hit the SCRAM button, shutting down the fusion reactor.

"What?" the LT shouted. "What are you doing?"

"We were about to lose containment, sir," Gants said, calmly, as alarms started to scream throughout the ship.

When Weaver reached the engineering compartment, the Eng, the lieutenant of watch and Chief Gestner were bent over the panel for Fusion Two while Gants was standing off to one side, his arms folded.

"What happened?" Bill asked.

"Gants SCRAMed the plant, sir," Chief Gestner replied as the CO trotted into the crowded compartment.

"Why?" Prael asked.

"He says we were about to lose containment," the Eng said, looking at the readouts. "I don't see it. We were getting output fluctuations and one of the bottle cells was two percent out of alignment, but I don't see that causing a containment failure."

"What do you have to say, Petty Officer?" the CO asked just as Weaver said: "Which one?"

"XO," the CO said. "I have this."

"Yes, sir," Bill replied.

"PO?" the CO asked, looking at Gants.

"There was a drop in throughput intake with a lower drop in output, sir," Gants said, shrugging. "And the number three containment series was down two percent. Only the number three . . ."

"And that caused you to SCRAM the reactor?" the Eng asked angrily.

"Damned straight," Weaver said, turning pale. "Oh, *hell*, yeah."

"Okay, sir," Commander Oldfield said, grabbing his head. "What am I missing?"

"Gants?" Bill asked.

"Pinch bottle reaction, sir," the PO replied, his face stony.

"Pinch bottle . . ." the CO said, then turned pale as Weaver. "Damn it!"

"Pinch bottle . . ." Gestner muttered, flipping through the manual. "M . . . N . . ."

"Try looking for 'discontinuous lobular reaction series,' Chief," Bill said furiously. "Look under 'Critical Emergency Conditions.' The bottle was out of alignment, causing the primary reaction mass to form in a non-smooth fashion. The whole thing is a hydrogen bomb *trying* to go off. It's a barely controlled *sun*, Chief Petty Officer! The magnetic containment prevents the power from destroying the ship. It only works if the power is maintained uniformly across the interior of the bottle. When you get a pinch bottle reaction, you've got most of your power forming in a small area that places undue stress on the local containment cluster. And when that portion finally fails, as it will, the whole thing goes 'boom' in a very unfun fashion. But a two percent drop in the third series doesn't explain that."

"I know, sir," Gants said, clearly tuning everyone else in the room out. "The only thing I can figure is that the primary optical drivers are out of alignment, but they show as aligned."

"Well, my recommendation is that the system remains down until we figure out the fault," Bill said.

"Concur," the CO said. "Eng, I want my fusion plant working. Which means fusion explosions going on *inside* the containment bottle not *outside*. Soon. We're going into a partial chill while you work on it. If you can't get it up, this mission is a *scrub*."

"Okay, sir, I'm buggered if I can figure this out," Chief Gestner said quietly.

The portions of the fusion bottle that could be taken apart had been taken apart. The compartment that held the actual fusion reactors was a "clean" room since the slightest contamination would just make the problem worse. In fact, the first check they'd made was for contaminants in the injection series and the fuel. Both had come up clean.

"Unfortunately, Chief, so am I," Commander Oldfield said with a sigh. "And with it down, we're going to take nearly *twice* as long to get back to Earth as we did coming out."

"Injectors are cleaned," Red Morris said, walking over. "Lasers are aligned. Software is nominal. Mags meet specs and are aligned. Fuel is to spec. What next, sir?"

"Put it back together and see if it comes up properly," the Eng said confidently. "If not, we'll go to secondary methodology."

"Which is *what*, exactly, sir?" Gestner asked as the machinists got to work putting the fusion reactor back together.

"Damned if I know," the Eng admitted.

"And we have ignition," Gants said, his clean suit still on.

"Power to ten percent," the Eng said, looking over his shoulder.

"Power to ten percent, aye," Gants said, bringing up the power on the system. "We're going to need somewhere to put it soon, sir."

"Somewhere to put it, aye," the Eng replied. "Route power to main engine. Chief, tell maneuvering they're going to have to start running for us to see if this is back in spec."

"Got it, sir," Gestner said.

"Forty percent, sir," Gants said.

"Shut it—!"

Before the words were out of the officer's mouth Gants had hit the cut-off switch.

"Bigger surge than before, sir," Gants said, pointing to the replay. "That one was *close*."

"Concur," the Eng said, then sighed. "I need to think on this one. . . ."

"Gants, tell me you put this thing together right," Gestner said.

Gants was attempting to carefully insert the injector bore into the fusion engine's wall. The injector wasn't actually secured, it simply slipped in. Various jokes were made about it, especially since it very definitely could *not* be lubricated.

But the point was that it had to fit precisely. Which the petty officer could not do with his hands shaking in anger. So he set it down very carefully; the slightest scratch on its surface would make it *impossible* to insert.

"Chief, with all due respect, you carefully and completely supervised the disassembly of the fusion engine," Gants said, breathing deeply and trying not to lose it. "You then paid just as close attention to the checks, the adjustments, the tests and the reassembly. Not to mention the *second* disassembly. If I did anything wrong, please feel free to tell me *right now* as I'm doing *the* most fiddly *part* of the *second* reassembly, Chief Petty Officer!"

"We're all frustrated, Gants," the chief said, for once placatingly.

"You know why I'm *really* frustrated, Chief?" the petty officer asked, picking up the injector.

"I don't suppose it has something to do with a certain linguist," the chief said, sighing.

"If there is one person on this ship who could maybe figure this out, Chief . . ."

"Fine," Gestner said, throwing his hands up. "I see nutting! I hear NUTTINK!"

"Oh, no, Chief," Gants said, finally getting the damned thing aligned and slipping it in. "Not this time."

"Gants . . ." the chief warned.

"What? Are you suggesting that *I* disobey a direct order of the captain, Chief Petty Officer?"

"You're going to push this, aren't you?" Gestner said.

"I'm not pushing, Chief," Gants said, getting the injector seated. "The manual is very clear on that. Just ease it in, don't push."

"*Grapper*," Gestner muttered.

"That would be Petty Officer Grapper, Chief Petty Officer," Gants said with a grin as the chief stomped out.

❃ ❃ ❃

"I don't know," Miriam said.

The chief had brought with him all the records of the repairs, which in true Nuke Navy fashion meant every single step had been documented and recorded. What had taken nearly a day to accomplish and what the chief had to admit to himself would have taken a professional nuke officer an hour to review had taken the linguist twenty minutes.

"That's not good to hear," Gestner replied.

"I would have thought you'd be happy to hear I'm stumped," Miriam said, flipping back through the pages.

"Not when the ship is on the line, miss," the chief said. "You're sure you don't know . . ."

"Oh, I know what was happening," Miriam said. "The injector had gotten misaligned. It probably was misaligned from when we left and slowly shifted out of position more as it was used. There's a record of a strip-down and repair, normal maintenance, done two weeks before we left. I'd guess it wasn't properly aligned then. That caused a bubble reaction. What I don't get is why it's still malfunctioning. Realigning the injector should have fixed it. Could you do me a favor?" Miriam asked, looking up and grinning winningly.

"Of course, miss," the chief said. "What do you need?"

"Bring the injector to the science section," Miriam said. "Oh, and the third sector battery of electromagnets. I think I might know what is going on."

"Miss, this is the last magnet," the seaman said, setting the fifty pound device down carefully on a table.

Miriam had opened up the clean room in the science section and was bent over the electron microscope.

"Thanks," she said absently. "Can you get Chief Gestner and PO Gants for me, please?"

"Yes, ma'am," the seaman said, darting back through the blower.

"Odd . . ." Miriam muttered.

"Hey, Miriam," Gants said as he stepped into the clean room. He and the chief had both donned new coveralls, masks and hoods before being swept for any remaining particles.

"Catch," Miriam said, tossing him the injector.

"Holy shit, ma'am," Gants said, catching the priceless item carefully. "Without that . . ."

"Since it's useless, even if you dropped it we wouldn't have a problem," Miriam said, grinning like a cat. "Okay, you had one problem. That caused another problem and that caused a third. Ready?"

"Go," the chief replied.

"The injector was almost certainly misaligned before we left," Miriam said. "You need to be clear that tolerance is in the micrometer range. More like nanometer range. I'll come up with a better aligner for it so we don't have the problem again. I think the Hexosehr use a microsonic system that's better than what we use for alignment. But I'll come up with something."

"Okay," Gestner said. "But what are the other problems?"

"When the injector shot the He3 into the fusion bottle, that put undue stress on the third magnet battery.

Among other things, it meant that some particles were getting through the magnetic bottle. Those, in turn, degraded the material of the magnets and their support. What happened then was that as the magnets had to work harder, they started . . . pulsing. They weren't designed to put out the extra power continuously so they were putting it out in fluctuations."

"That loss of power I was seeing?" Gants asked.

"That was *very* late in the process," Miriam replied. "It was actually a sign that things were about to go critical. No, this would have been indetectable to our instruments. But that caused a blowback condition, particulate mostly, which was hitting the injector. Which in turn . . ."

"Degraded the material of the injector," the chief finished.

"Yes," Miriam said. "It's only noticeable under electron microscopy and even then I had to use a crystal flux spectrometer. But the edge of the injector is heavily degraded. So. You're going to need to replace all the third sector magnets, all their supports including feedback systems, physical supports and power supports. *And* the injector. *That* should fix the problem."

"I'm not sure we have all that in stock," the chief said.

"*That*, Chief Gestner, is why you should be glad the XO found the fabricator *you* nearly left on Earth. It has every part small enough to reproduce in its database. Go see if you can figure out the shiny buttons."

"Humming along nicely," Captain Prael said, looking at the fusion reactor. "Good job, Eng."

"Thank you, sir," the engineering officer said blankly.

"Chief Gestner and PO Gants were critical in determining the nature of the fault and methods of correction."

"What was the problem?" the CO asked.

"Misalignment of the injector system led to a chain failure, sir," the Eng said. "We're doing up an SOP change and . . . personnel are working on a new alignment system that will prevent a recurrence."

"I'll make sure you get a letter on this," the CO continued. "And do some up for the critical crew."

"Yes, sir," the Eng said, wondering if he dared slip Miss Moon into the pile. Probably not.

"Now if things will just hold together for a *little* while longer . . ." the CO muttered as he left the compartment.

8

"Okay, that's weird."

"Define weird," Petty Officer First Class Guy Fedele asked, looking over the chaos gunner's shoulder.

Part of the redesign of the *Blade II* had been to create a full-scale Combat Information Center instead of a small Tactical office. The CIC featured a mix of Hexosehr, Adar and human technology and included both information positions and fighting positions.

In this case, the control center for the port-side chaos ball guns. The Hexosehr system fired balls of what had only been translated as "pure chaos." They disrupted molecular bonds through a process that was only slightly exothermic but very definite, cutting through layers of the most refractory armor as if it were air. They didn't blow ships up, but they put great whacking holes in them. Unfortunately, the one that the Hexosehr had hastily refitted the *Blade I* with was only good for putting relatively small holes in ships and would only penetrate a few dozen meters. When the *Blade* had used a single one against Dreen dreadnoughts, it had taken dozens of hits, each requiring the *Blade* to penetrate the enemy's brutal fire, to get a kill, which was one of the reasons that the original *Blade* had been scrapped.

However, the *Blade II* had been fitted with twenty of the Hexosehr prototypes per side, creating a broadside that could punch holes most of the way through a fair-sized asteroid.

"I was running the watch check on the port side battery," the gunner said. "I got a fault in Number Seven gun. So I ran it again. No fault. But I was careful . . ."

"Which is good," Fedele said. "So you ran it again."

"And I got a fault in Number Nineteen," the gunner said. "Fault Eight-Twelve: Failure to properly communicate. The gun got the order, communicated that it got it, but its test response wasn't received."

"Same fault on Seven?" the PO asked.

"Yep," the gunner replied. "That was when I muttered."

"Run it again," Fedele said.

"It takes—"

"Seven minutes to do the full response test," Fedele said. "I know. But run the level-two diagnostic. I want to see exactly what it's reading."

"Shiny," the gunner said, bringing up the options box and pressing the appropriate icons. "Gonna be a while."

"I'm not going anywhere."

"Okay, now I'm *creeked*," the gunner said. "PO!"

"I'm looking at nothing," the petty officer said, looking over his shoulder again.

"No *chither*," the gunner swore. "But here's the log. Two Eight-Twelves, two different guns, right in a row."

"And nothing on the full diagnostic?" the PO asked unnecessarily. "That's weird."

"That's what *I* said!"

"Okay, you're not doing anything but looking at blank screens and playing solitaire," the PO said. "Run a level one every twenty minutes. I want to see what's going on. I'm getting that suboptimal feeling . . ."

"Lieutenant Bergstresser, these results are not what I call optimal," Captain Zanella said, examining the data from Eric's Wyvern simulation. "You managed to lose your entire platoon four times."

"Yes, sir," Eric said stoically. He'd been hitting the scenario, on and off, for a week. "Sir, I've rethought that scenario several times. I'm not sure it's not a lose-lose proposition. Absent the heavy weapons that I brought into the mission, the crabpus are very difficult to defeat."

"They don't do that sort of shit in real training," the CO said. "If you're thinking this is that *Star Trek* thing, the Kobe Mashu or whatever . . ."

"Kobayashi Maru, sir," Eric said.

"It's not that," the CO continued. "The only thing you teach people by a lose-lose proposition is to lose. That's been proven over and over and we don't do it. It's stupid. I've figured out three ways to win it at both the platoon and company level. Admittedly, you guys got caught flat-footed by it, but there are ways to win without Two-Gun Berg and his smoking cannon-pistols. You're getting too focused on individual actions. You need to keep an eye on the whole picture and maneuver your squads more fluidly. I'm going to rotate you back to easier scenarios so you can get a better feel for handling multiple axes."

Captain Zanella didn't put it bluntly, but what he was saying was that Eric wasn't ready for prime-time. It was not a comforting thought.

"Berg!" Miriam said, walking into his quarters.

"Jesus," Berg said, pulling up his sheet. He'd been lying in his bed doing the unending reading the CO had assigned and was wearing only underwear. "Knock for God's sake."

"I'm bored," Miriam said. "I've been going crazy. Then I thought to myself, '*Eric's* an officer, I can talk to *him*!'"

"Miriam, I love you like a sister," Eric said. "But the CO's on my ass right now and I've got a bagillion tons of homework and paperwork to do. I just don't have the time. I'm really sorry."

"I can help," Miriam said, picking up a book. "Ick. Military stuff."

"I didn't think you were prejudiced against the military," Berg said, surprised.

"I'm not," Miriam replied, setting the book down. "I just get bored by it really quick. Tell me a story?"

"Once upon a time there was a lieutenant who got busted because he got several crappy evaluation reports," Berg said. "Because he didn't do the homework the CO required."

"That one's boring," Miriam said.

"It's also going to be my life story if . . ."

"I can take the hint," Miriam said. "There has to be

somebody on this ship I can talk to! *Something* I can play with!"

"I thought that was why you brought a cat," Berg said as she stood up.

"Oh, that rat," Miriam said, frowning. "He's always off playing fetch with the crew. He hardly stops by anymore, the traitor."

Tiny tossed the creature through the air, bouncing it off the port bulkhead and then pouncing on it again as it squeaked in distress. He'd discovered they tasted terrible and gave him a tummy-ache, but they were more fun to play with than a ball, which he never would have believed.

This one, though, had quit playing. So he carried it to the head, expertly operating the lever handle, then dropped it in the commode. Hitting the lever to flush, he watched the weird purple arthropoid spin round and round, then down the drain.

He flushed the toilet a few more times, just to see the water swirl, then got bored.

They seemed to always be where it was dark, so he set off down the corridor, searching for more. One of these days he was going to figure out how to open the hatches with the round wheels, but they were harder. There were probably lots of the little creatures in there.

"Morning, sir," Sub Dude said, sitting down by the XO. All the rest of the mess was keeping as far away from the officer as possible.

"Morning, Gants," Bill said, taking a sip of coffee. Navy coffee was almost legendary in its wholesome goodness.

Chief Duppstadt had even managed to *grapp* that up. "This is . . ."

"Awful," Gants said, taking a sip. The coffee managed to be both weak *and* bitter: a tough combination. "Yep, that's a Dumpstadt special, all right. I swear he gets up for each shift just to ruin the coffee."

Green eggs. Scrambled eggs oxidize upon contact with the atmosphere, causing the green coloration. But it takes a certain amount of time. Which meant that the eggs had been prepared at least an hour beforehand and kept warm instead of "just in time" in which case they would have been yellow. Well, white and yellow and runny, but not green and brown and runny.

The bacon appeared to have been given a brief glance at a griddle and then dumped into a pile of grease. There was toast, if you could call the stale, rocklike hardtack toast.

"Am I gonna have to get in there and run the damned kitchen myself?" Bill asked.

"Probably, sir," Gants said, eating the green eggs and horrid bacon with if not relish then at least determination. "Chief Dumpstadt apparently knows what sailors want, and this is it. You ever had his spinach fandango?"

"Please," Bill said, his stomach turning more at the thought. "I think I'll just have cereal."

"Isn't any, sir," Gants said. "Seems someone has been pilfering it. The chief's cut it off until we catch up on stock levels. This is breakfast, take it or leave it."

"I'll see about that," Bill said, standing up with his nearly untouched platter of food. "It seems that the chief and I are going to have to have another talk."

※ ※ ※

Bill decided that the only choice was to change the venue, which was why the next conversation was in his office.

"Chief, I think we have a failure to communicate," Bill said, having failed to offer the chief petty officer a seat.

"What's wrong now, sir?" the chief asked angrily.

"Well, let's see," Bill said, ticking off items on his fingers. "Green eggs that were runny and cold, bacon that was so underdone you could hear the squeal from the pig and toast that could be used as a throwing weapon. Oh, and did I mention the coffee? How do you get it unpalatably bitter *and* so thin you can see your spoon to the bottom of the cup? That, I'll admit, was *genius*."

"The guys like their bacon rare," the chief said plaintively.

"I think we have a different definition of rare, Chief," Bill said. "Rare means it has at least hit a griddle, not been *waved* over it to get the *frost* off! And I doubt that you took a poll before letting that *inane* comment slip from your lips. By the commanding officer's order I am now taking *every* meal in the enlisted mess, Chief, until you can actually learn what has apparently escaped you in 'over twenty years' which is to cook a *palatable meal*! And you're going to do that, if I have to sit in the kitchen and help you flip the damned burgers! Are we *clear* on this, Chief? Do you *understand* me? Am I getting through to the two brain cells you might *actually* have? Because if I'm not, I will find the lowliest cook and put him in charge of the kitchen and I am morally *certain* than he could not do a WORSE JOB! I'll be back for lunch, which I see is fried chicken. Try to read a cookbook between now and then or by GOD we will be having this conversation again and it WILL be reflected in your evaluation!"

"Conn, preparing to EVA through Hatch Seven."

"Go EVA through Hatch Seven," the COB replied, hitting the remote control. "Depressurizing." .

"Seals good. Prepared to EVA."

"Opening outer doors."

"Tallyho to the beasts!" Colonel Che-chee said, the Hexosehr translator in her suit transforming her words into high-pitched English.

Even the newer *Blade* had to stop from time to time to "chill." Space was a poor radiator of heat, being vacuum, and the *Blade II* built up heat slowly despite the astonishing efficiency of the various Hexosehr systems. A human nuclear power plant got less than ten percent of the actual power the plant produced, the rest turning mostly into waste heat. Thus the need for massive cooling towers and a nearby source of water. The Hexosehr He3 fusion plants translated 98% of their total output into useable power, which was considered theoretically impossible prior to meeting them.

However, even two percent of the energy of a fusion plant was a lot of heat. The *Blade* had exterior vanes that radiated some of it and a glaseous heat-sink that collected more. But from time to time the ship still had to stop and "chill." The "chill" was not as extreme as the original *Blade*; the engine stayed up, providing artificial gravity in some way. But the output of the plant was dropped to only two percent of full power and in an hour or so the ship cooled off in the cryogenic conditions of deep space.

Given the conditions, though, chill was a great time to

try out the dragonflies. The beasts, attached to support lines, had continued to live for over two weeks, much to the surprise of everyone involved. The nutrient feed was very close to identical to what their production cavern fed them, but everyone had expected them to die from the supernal cold of deep space or the long duration on the hull. However, they were hanging in there.

Designing a spacesuit for Cheerick had been another technical hurdle surmounted by the increasing number of scientists and engineers backing the *Blade*'s missions. Cheerick rarely wore clothing, since it was unpleasant with their fur. The space suits were, therefore, more like space armor, being hard-shells with carefully sprung flex-points. It was also hoped that if the shields failed, the armor might afford the dragonfly riders some survivability. They looked, in fact, very much like the JIM suits that deep ocean divers wore, an egglike shape with legs and arms sprouting out from it. They'd immediately been christened Humpty-Dumpty suits.

Lady Che-Chee used the jets on her Humpty suit to scoot over to her dragonfly, then assumed her mounting position. Like the boards, the dragonflies generated a sticky traction field to keep the rider in place. Unlike the boards they, fortunately, had an inertial stabilization field. Otherwise, their acceleration of a thousand and a half Earth gravities would have torn their riders in half.

"Dragonfly one rider in position," Lady Che-Chee said. "Release clamps and feeding tube."

The feeding tube broke loose first with a small jet of lost nutrient. Then the clamps that held the dragonfly's feet to the hull released.

"Tallyho," Colonel Che-chee said. "All riders in place and form on me."

The *Blade* was parked in deep orbit around an M class dwarf star, well inside its dangerous heliopause but outside planetary orbits in the region called the Oort Cloud.

The dim red star was less than half the diameter of Sol and at about five thousand astronomical units from where the *Blade* was parked so the local "sun" was merely the brightest spot in the sky.

Oort Cloud material was extremely dispersed but with the right instruments it was possible to find a comet or two even when they were separated by the distance between the Earth and Mars on its closest pass. The target for today was just such a comet, one about the size of that believed to have caused the extinction of the dinosaurs. Wiping it out was possibly going to save some nascent race in this solar system. Assuming that *any* species arose on a planet around an M class star. The things were as common as ants at a picnic but they had narrow life-belts, short periods of potential life-development and darned few rocky planets. From a human perspective, M class stars were the teats-on-a-boar-hog of stars. Unless you needed a comet to blow away where *nobody* was going to watch.

"Telemetry?" Captain Prael asked.

"Suit transponders nominal," the fighter combat controller replied. "Triangulation is good. Thirty percent above optimal."

"That's good," Prael said, punching in a code. "Dragonflight, maneuver test first. Entering maneuver Delta-Three. Engage."

Delta-Three was a simple combat approach maneuver

with three changes in vector. Designed for approach to a firing enemy, the maneuver was more a test of the Cheerick ability to follow orders.

On the heads-up display inside the Cheerick riders' helmets a karat appeared with a marker for acceleration. The idea was for the Cheerick riders to follow the karat as it moved across their visor and accelerate or decelerate as the indicator ordered.

Two separate screens in the CIC noted positions of the riders, one on vertical and one on horizontal. If you had the head for it and could keep an eye on both screens at more or less the same time, you could tell where something was in three dimensions at all times.

Prael was used to thinking in three dimensions; it was the essence of submarine combat. What he was not used to was thinking *fast* in three dimensions. Submarine combat was very rarely fast, it was a matter of slow stalk and *rare* fast run, the latter always planned well in advance and well understood.

But it wasn't really necessary to keep up when the Cheerick attempted the maneuver. On either board they were all over the map.

"Cease exercise," the CO said, trying not to sigh. The Cheerick had only recently encountered any technology more advanced than the steel sword and mould-board plow. Expecting them to jump straight to understanding icons was idiocy. "Colonel, do you want to return and work this over or just talk to your people out there?"

"We will continue," Colonel Che-chee responded tartly. "I would suggest Delta-One to start and a maximum of ten gravities of acceleration. I will explain to my people what is about to occur and then walk them through it. Slowly."

"Very well," the CO said. "Tell me when you're ready." He looked over at the TACO, Alexander White, and shrugged. "I guess even a hinky fighter system is better than nothing."

Weaver sighed. "Define hinky."

The job of an XO, as noted, was to ensure that the ship functioned so that the CO just had to order it around. His was the tedious task of making sure that the personnel files were updated, that there was enough food, that the systems were working. Guns were pretty important to a warship.

"Hinky," the Eng said. "The port side chaos ball generator system has been having random malfunctions when we run tests on it. We're not sure why."

"I assume you've been running down the malfunctions," Weaver said. "Where's the fault?"

"We've been trying, sir," the Eng said uncomfortably. "But the problem is that the system is partially Hexosehr and part human."

"I know that, Eng," Weaver said dryly. "I was part of the design team. Is it in the interface? That tested out perfectly well when we installed it. For that matter, it was working when we were on Earth."

"It's one of those intermittent things, sir," the Eng said. "We get a fault in the feedback system, then when we try to run it down it's gone. The TACO put the gun teams on it when it first cropped up. They eliminated it being in the software and they pulled down three of the ball generators and couldn't find any fault readings in them. So I put two electronics mates and a network mate to work on it. They couldn't find any physical faults in the system. Then the whole port side crashed the day after they got done. And then it came back up on the first restart and worked like a charm all day. Now we've got faults again."

"I'm pretty sure it's not the software," Bill said. "By the time we got to designing that, the Hexosehr had been over our software protocols pretty thoroughly and they wrote most of it. All I can suggest is keep looking. I know who I'd suggest to look at it . . ."

"Miss Moon, right?" the Eng said, somewhat sarcastically.

"O ye of little faith," Bill said sourly. "She's been driving me crazy. *She's* going crazy being cooped up in an empty science section. And, yes, that is who I'd put on it if it weren't for the CO's orders. You might get some fresh ideas in there, bring in some people you normally wouldn't. About all I can suggest."

"Fresh faces," the Eng said, shrugging. "I'll think on it, sir."

"I want to know right away if *anything* goes wrong with the guns," Weaver said, turning back to his computer. "You know the way out."

9

"*What* are you doing?" Weaver asked, rubbing his stomach and yawning.

It was two hours before his shift started and he'd been up late trying to catch up on paperwork. But he'd decided there was only one choice in the ongoing battle with Chief Dump—Duppstadt, which was to check on every meal before it was cooked.

Two hours was about right for the cooks to be just starting their preparations, but when he arrived four cooks were dumping scrambled eggs into containers, sliced bread was piled on the counters drying out and that horrible greasy bacon was already, supposedly, "cooked" and was piled in masses, the majority of it swimming in grease.

Bill had barely been able to conjure how Duppstadt could possibly have achieved his feats of culinary legerdemain. Now he had a clear vision. So clear he stood dumbfounded, just blinking at the startled cooks.

"Are you shiny, sir?" the lead petty officer asked.

"What in the hell do you think you're doing?" Bill asked, broken out of his stasis. "Breakfast doesn't serve for two hours."

"Chief Duppstadt's orders, sir," the LPO said, stone-faced. "Get everything prepared in advance then clean the kitchen for inspection. Thirty minutes before chow's up we have an inspection of the kitchen, so we have to have everything prepared in advance. Sir."

Bill looked at the food and couldn't figure out what to do. His first instinct was to tell them to dump the stuff and start over, but that would be a huge waste, one whole meal down the garbage chute. Given that the limiting factor on the *Blade's* endurance was quite simply *food*, he couldn't do that.

"And where is the chief?" Bill asked.

"He gets here for inspection, sir," the LPO said. "We'll be ready for you to inspect in an hour and a half or so. Sorry it's such a mess, but we were . . ."

"Cooking," Bill said. "The idea, though, LPO . . . Oh, never mind. When the Chief arrives for 'inspection,' tell him that it's cancelled and he is to report to my office. I will expect him in one hour and forty minutes from now, not one hour and forty-two."

"Two *hours*?" Bill shouted. "You're having the cooks prepare the food *two hours* in advance so you can run some damned *inspection*?"

"I keep a clean kitchen, sir," Chief Duppstadt said, standing at attention and looking at the bulkhead behind the officer. "Always have, always will. Won't have no filth in my kitchen, sir!"

"No, you just *serve* it!" Bill snarled. "Chief Duppstadt, listen to me very carefully. Here is the revised schedule for your kitchen. You will begin your meal preparations at the latest possible moment to have food on the table for the shift's designated meal times. You may then, when the service has been completed, clean your kitchen and inspect; then you will begin preparations for the next meal, repeating this process. If I ever go down there and find two hundred pounds of eggs prepared two hours in advance and cooling, I will upon our return to Earth ensure that you are sent to the coldest, nastiest, most forsaken outpost the United States Navy has to offer, be it on Earth or off. As something other than a cook. And you had better figure out how to actually apply both eggs and bacon to a griddle for long enough that they *cook* or so help me God I'll have you strapped to the exterior guns for the duration of the voyage! If I'm feeling merciful, and I rarely am after eating your *slop*, I will afford you the luxury of a *spacesuit*!"

It had to be done.

Bill was just at his wits end. Systems breaking that nobody knew how to fix. Crew on the edge of mutiny over the food. More paperwork than could be done by a legion of clerks and the CO riding his ass Every. Single. Moment.

He just couldn't take it anymore. He HAD to blow off some stress somehow. He was starting to figure out why submariners were such practical jokers. He'd considered that solution and rejected it. There was a better way.

He picked up the guitar, tuned it carefully, then kicked on the speakers. There was a dull thump that rattled the few nicknacks on a shelf. The curtain that had replaced his door fluttered in the sudden pressure change then settled slowly, quivering as if in anticipation. Or, perhaps, fear.

When under stress, Weaver liked to blow it off in one of several ways. His preferred method was going on long mountain bike runs. But that was sort of out on the *Blade*. Second to that was his karate fetish. He'd considered checking to see if any of the Marines had serious hand-to-hand skills but never quite had the time.

The last was to play guitar. Play it very loud. And headphones just weren't the same.

"WHAT THE HELL IS THAT?" the torpedoman screamed.

He'd been just about to insert a microchip into one of the ardune torps. The chip had failed a diagnostic and since it controlled the ardune release, that was considered "ungood."

Ardune was the Adar name for what humans called "quarkium," a material made up entirely of unique quarks. What type of quark, up, down, strange, charmed, didn't really matter. The thing about quarks was, they were the building blocks of matter. But they had to pair up to form "normal" particles like protons and neutrons.

A mass of "unique" quarks acted much like the neutrons in a fission reaction, breaking up not just atoms but their building blocks and, along the way, releasing lots of energy. Essentially all the energy in the matter. And since they still couldn't bind, they kept going and going and going.

Antimatter worked on the basis of Einstein's famous $E=mc^2$. But antimatter only hit regular matter and converted all the energy once. Quarkium did that and kept going.

It was brutally dangerous stuff. Also lovely for causing explosions. Which was why the torpedoes and missiles in the *Blade* used the stuff. But an uncontrolled release would be . . . ungood.

Fortunately, he hadn't quite gotten it seated when the room began to vibrate. He was afraid the harmonics might just shake the whole damned room apart.

"'MISSISSIPPI QUEEN'!" the torpedo room chief shouted back. "BY *MOUNTAIN*! ONE HIT WONDER FROM THE '70S! GUITAR'S NOT BAD BUT I DON'T KNOW WHO IN THE *HELL* IS SINGING! HE SOUNDS LIKE A VULTURE THAT'S JUST FOUND A WHOLE ELEPHANT CARCASS!"

"XO, in my professional opinion, I find that your singing is an undue stress to the crew and a potential safety hazard," the CO said balefully. He'd been a victim of part of the concert all the way back in Conn, which was a third of the length down the ship from the XO's quarters. "In the future you will refrain from playing your music outloud just as the rest of the crew must. That, by the way, is an *order*, XO."

"Yes, sir," Bill said.

"Dismissed."

10

"Come on in," Berg said at a knock on the hatch to his quarters.

"*Ik squeak,*" the Cheerick in the opening said, waving to him.

"You want me to come?" Berg said, looking up from his studies. "Shiny. I guess."

The Cheerick seemed to get lost part of the way to wherever he was leading the lieutenant then found the compartment he was looking for. After a knock he waved Berg into the quarters.

"Perk," Lady Che-chee said. "Come."

"Lady Che-Chee?" Berg asked, confused.

Lady Che-chee's stateroom was larger than the one that he shared but she was, after all, a colonel. Not to mention a personal friend of the Cheerick monarch.

What surprised Berg was the books. The room was absolutely packed with them. They filled all the few bookshelves and more were piled on the deck.

Thinking about it, he really shouldn't have been surprised. Lady Che-chee's manor had been similarly filled with books and even ancient tablets from early Cheerick history. The lady was a renowned soldier among the Cheerick but at heart she really seemed to be a scholar.

However, the weird part was that most of them seemed to be in English. He spotted multiple military manuals, biographies and histories of Earth civilizations in the collection as well as some stuff that looked like military fiction.

"Kit," the colonel said, pointing to a human sized station chair. She picked up a device and squeaked into it for a moment, then held it out and hit a button.

"Welcome to my quarters, Lieutenant Bergstresser. I am gratified that you have been made an officer, even if you are a male. Your prowess in battle is great. It is to be hoped that your sex will not interfere with your thinking. But you humans are different so perhaps you can be wise as well as brave."

"Thank you, ma'am," Berg said, confused by the device as well as the summons. "May I ask what that is?"

"Hexosehr translator," the colonel said, speaking directly through the device. "I just got it delivered before we took off. We weren't sure if the Hexosehr could make it in time. It works for translating Cheerick to English and a couple of other human languages and to Hexosehr and Adar. So, I wanted to ask, how do you like being an officer?"

"I'm starting to regret it, frankly," Berg said. "I'm spending most of my time pushing paper and the rest trying to catch up on professional studies."

"It's always like that as a junior officer," the colonel said. "But think of it as an investment for your future. The goal is always command, that's what makes all the necessary bull*maulk* necessary. What are you studying?"

"Small unit employment," Berg said.

"Which manual?" the colonel said. "I've been studying your Earth methods and tactics. I find many of them novel and others things that I've been proposing for, oh, years! I had most of your military manuals sent to me even as I started to learn to read English. I probably have it here, somewhere."

"Marine Small Unit Tactics," Berg said. "FMFM 6-4 Marine Rifle Company/Platoon Operations."

"Got it," the colonel said, pulling out a book. "Yes, this one I have read. I believe I understand it rather well and can probably help you. I have more experience in small unit operations than I like to think about."

"Thank you," Berg said.

"I need a favor, however," the colonel admitted. "My riders are simple people, all males, alas. And they are having a hard time understanding space combat."

"Well, ma'am," Berg said, uncomfortably, "I'm not sure I understand it all that well."

"No, but you have more of a grasp of human technology," the Cheerick replied. "We need to have a way to practice that does not just happen outside the hull."

"Use your simulator," Berg said, frowning.

"What is a 'simulator'?"

"Holy *chither*," Berg muttered. "You guys don't have simulators? A simulator is just that, if that thing's translating right. It's a thing that simulates what you do in your job.

We Marines have simulators for both Wyvern combat—
we actually just climb in our Wyverns for that—and for
unarmored combat. We do part of it just on a computer,"
Berg added, gesturing at the monitor on the colonel's
desk. "For more of it there's a small simulator on the ship
where we can simulate entry training, for example."

"We have no such thing," the colonel said, frowning.
"There were none put on this ship that I know of."

"I'm pretty sure there weren't," Berg admitted. "Which
was one hell of an oversight, pardon my language." He
thought about it for a second and then grinnned. "But I
can think of somebody who could help . . ."

"Oh, sure," Miriam said when the problem was put to
her. "You guys just follow the icons on your HUD. I can
work up an interface for your helmets. Actually, you're
going to have to use the suit; there's no separate helmet.
But it should work just fine."

"That . . . sounds as if it would work," Lady Che-chee
said, sighing. "I say that as if I understood what you were
saying. I lie. This . . . this . . . 'technology' is so hard for us
to *understand*! Just the fact that pictures appear is too
much like magic! Technology is a sword or even one of the
new steam power engines. These I can understand, barely.
But computers? Electronics? Heads-up-diplays? These
are magic!"

"You get used to it," Berg promised. "It hit humans
pretty fast and hard but we got used to it, too. And then
the Adar came along . . ."

"Just one problem," Miriam interjected pensively. "The
control of the dragonfly is entirely mental. I can't think of

any way to get that to work. I could talk to Doctor Chet and see if he's gotten anywhere on it, but . . ."

"I'd already thought of that," Berg said. "Ever use a flight simulator program?"

"No," Miriam admitted.

"Well, when you push the stick, you're thinking where you want the plane to go," Berg said. "Sometimes, when you don't understand what you're doing, you're just really, really *wishing*. Especially just before a crash. But the *thought* is there. I don't see why it would affect the interaction with the dragonflies. Of course, the guys are going to end up trying to use a stick when they're flying the dragonflies. But that shouldn't be a problem. Heck, maybe mount one for them so they have something to hold onto . . ."

"Are we sure this is going to work?" Colonel Che-chee asked. "Even a Mother must consider face, as you humans would put it."

The Cheerick pilot ready-room was set up much like any ready-room in history, a series of auditorium-style chairs with a dais at the front, a podium and a massive plasma-screen monitor. The major difference was that the chairs were oversized for a human. They were even oversized for a Cheerick; they had been designed to take pilots wearing their suits.

"It should work fine," Miriam said. The colonel was in the front row and the diminutive linguist was up on the dais, punching in the scenario. "Just remember to use the joysticks I installed in your suits. Otherwise the computer doesn't know where you're trying to go. I've set this up for a very simple movement. We'll take it nice and slow . . ."

※   ※   ※

". . . Okay, now that I've disconnected the arm controls on the suits for training, this should work perfectly. And I'm sure we can get Crak-chee's arm reconnected in no-time. I'm not so sure about the damage to the chair . . ."

Colonel Che-chee was panting inside her suit and the thing was filling with shed. The furry Cheerick shed massively, especially when stressed and she was *very* stressed. Flying a dragonfly was a matter of thinking where you were going. They had been working hard enough that control of the "joysticks" had become second nature, but she still wished she could simply think the maneuvers. There was also the fact that the Cheerick were not naturally a hunting species. They had derived from omnivores, true, but omnivores that got most of their meat from carrion and very small game. They did not have the natural chase reaction that even humans posessed. And whereas in humans, following an icon with the eyes was so automatic as to be hard-wired, indeed hard to ignore, the Cheerick had to concentrate on it.

But not only was she following the damned dancing karat, she could spare enough time to check her . . . "monitors" and her riders were staying in perfect sync. They were flying as if they were crack cavalry on boards, which was where she'd drawn them from. Finally, it was coming together.

"Cease exercise," the human linguist said in perfect Cheerick. "Colonel, that was very nearly flawless."

"Very nearly flawless and flawless are two entirely different things," Colonel Che-chee said to squeaks of dismay over the open frequency. "Attend me, *males*! You dishonor your family names by your male whining. We will do this until we are perfect or I will return you to your families branded as failures! Miss Moon, please set the exercise up again. We continue . . ."

The Dreen fighter was banking back and forth for all it was worth but Colonel Cheerick almost had it locked. Finally, it crossed her firing path and she willed the laser to flash out and destroy it, unthinkingly pressing the firing button at the same time.

The seedlike fighter belched air and water and lost power then erupted in flame.

"Team One come to one-one-four mark neg nineteen," a robotic voice chimed. "Bandits at one-one-three mark neg seventeen."

"Ka-che, you will stay on my tail this time," the colonel snarled. "If I look back and you are not in position again, you will . . . You will clean the head for a week." Normally, she'd have had him shovel out the stables. Coming up with an alternative was tough. There was nothing like shoveling the stables to center a cavalryman's attention.

"Yes, Colonel," the wingman replied.

The colonel had automatically followed the icon while delivering her threat and even anticipated it, the vector coming unthinking to her after having spent so many hours in these "simulators" her quarters had almost become a distant memory. But she was coming to enjoy the game, especially now that the linguist had thrown in enemies to fight. The Cheerick were not natural predators, but the instinct of battle came easily to them.

Males battled over females, females battled for territory. Battle was battle.

"Dreen fighter at two-two-seven mark nine," Ka-che said. "Closing on my tail."

"Flight nine," Colonel Che-chee said. "Bandit seven."

"On it," the other flight called, closing the Dreen fighter which had locked onto her wingman. "Target destroyed."

"Well done, Nine," Colonel Che-chee said. "Target locked . . . firing . . ."

"Okay," Captain Prael said, leaning back in his chair and interlacing his fingers behind his head. "Let's try this again. But unless we just sit in place for a week and train these guys, I don't see where those dragonflies are going to be any use except strapped to the hull to give us a shield."

"We can always hope, sir," the TACO said.

"Colonel Che-chee," the CO said, pressing the comm button. "Let's take this slow. Entering maneuver Delta-One. Engage."

"Holy *maulk*," White said as the ten dragonflies followed the projected path as if they were drawing it. At the completion of the maneuver, though, they broke up, seemingly randomly. Then, as the tracks of the dragonflies scrolled across the screen it was apparent they were performing a complex maneuver, first forming a diamond then a square then a circle and finally a snowflake pattern.

"Is that a bit better, Captain?" Colonel Che-chee said.

"Much," Captain Prael said. "I'd say you'd been practicing, but I know you haven't been EVA since our last stop."

"There are things called simulators, you know, Captain," the colonel replied, sweetly.

Prael blinked in surprise for a moment, first locking onto the fact that there were, as far as he knew, no simulators for dragonfly combat on the ship and then on the fact that the Cheerick knew what a simulator *was*.

"We can't simulate the mental process," the CO said, frowning. "The interface . . ."

"If you use a joystick, you are *thinking* where you want to go, Captain," Colonel Che-chee interjected. "It wasn't even that hard to create. The suits work perfectly well as simulators with some minor modifications."

"And who did the . . . ?"

"Miss Moon was kind enough to do it for us, Captain," Colonel Che-chee said. "As well as set up the . . . network and simulations. She is a most *remarkable* human. But, of course, she is *female*."

"I'll keep that in mind, Colonel," the CO said, his face tight. "Now, since you've clearly been practicing, let's work up to some harder maneuvers . . ."

The dragonflies shifted through complex patterns, overlapping their shields against simulated Dreen fire. As each shield became weakened, a recharged dragonfly would interpose, moving the weakened one back in a pattern the Roman Legions would recognize. From time to time they would open up like a flower as the side of the ship burst out in simulated chaos fire, then close to cover the vulnerable side of the ship. All the while they stayed inside the small space that separated the hull and the edge of the warp field, even maintaining position when the ship exited warp to fire.

"And . . . complete simulation," Captain Prael said.

"Whew, even *I'm* sweating after that one. Good job, Dragonflight. Simulation says barely three percent of the Dreen fire got through. You just saved a bunch of lives on the ship."

"But we're barely shedding, Captain," Colonel Che-chee said. "Is that all you've got?"

"Unfortunately, we're done chilling, Colonel," the CO said, trying not to grin. He had to constantly remind himself that the Cheerick Mother had first gone to war before he was born. "Time to come back to the barn."

"Well, I suppose we can always go back to the simulators," Colonel Che-chee replied. "Back to the barn it is."

"Colonel," Prael said, nodding. "I intend to keep drilling with your people but you've done one hell of a job. I'm truly impressed."

"We would not have been able to do as well if it had not been for the simulators," the colonel said, sipping a fruit drink. "Captain, I do not want to interfere in the running of your ship, but . . ."

"But," the CO said, grinning in a rictus. "You're going to."

"No, I'm going to simply tell you a story," the Colonel said. "Once upon a time there was a young officer who was very sure of herself and her place in the world. She had been an officer for some time and knew the ways of battle. That was true. But she still did not understand the ways of males. That would be the ways of troops to you. She considered them sub-chee, things to be used as pawns in battle and for the use of Breeders. Servants and such. Not real people."

"I don't think I'm that much of a misogynist," the CO said, nodding, "but please continue."

"Then she received à batman from an older officer who was retiring," Lady Che-chee said, reminiscently. "He was an old male for a fighter, much scarred. She considered him much like any batman, a person to be bidden and which had to be constantly ridden on even the simplest task. Oh, he could brush fur well enough and was useful for carrying armor, but not really chee. Do you understand me?"

"I'm with you," the CO said, taking a sip of coffee. "So what happened?"

"Then the officer was put in charge of one segment of a large battle, separated from her superiors. And the enemy was simply better. More motivated, more *elan* as the French put it. The officer's troops, caring little which overlord dominated them, were breaking. And the young officer was confused and unsure, not being used to losing. She froze in the midst of battle, with lower ranked Mothers asking her what she should do. And she did not know. And then the batman said something very simple and seemingly pointless. And he touched her. Kicked her, actually, in the back of the leg and said: 'If you can't punch them in the snout, step on their foot.'"

"And you realized that men had brains," the CO said. "Miss Moon has brains aplenty. What she doesn't have is a lick of common sense. And she drives me nuts. Then there's the fact that it's proven that males have reduced logic in the presence of sexual cues. Miss Moon, quite consistently, wears clothing that is one huge sexual cue. It throws off the psychology of the ship and interferes with the working of the crew. Sorry, but I won't have it. What happened to the batman? Retired with great seniority and a farm, I hope."

"Oh, I had to kill him for the offense of striking me," the colonel said. "But I did so sadly. He really *was* quite good at brushing fur. But he also made me realize that, yes, males were not sub-chee. They saw what was going on around them and responded on the basis of it. From then on I paid much more attention to my males and I was rewarded for it with performance. I'm not talking about Miss Moon at all, you see, Captain. At least, not directly. The problem is not Miss Moon, exactly. But you might want to have a quiet talk about her with one of your junior males. You would find something surprising."

He was just about the most junior seaman on the ship, a sensor tech straight out of A school. He never would have been considered for the mission if it wasn't for the fact that the *Blade*'s sensor systems were so new, nobody senior had any experience on them. Half the crew was like that, guys straight out of A school who were the only people with a clue how their systems worked and not much of one.

"Sit down," Prael said. "You're not in any trouble and you're not going to get in any trouble for anything that's said in this compartment. I'll add that I'd like you to keep quiet about what we talk about, but I figure that will last three days and then you'll let something slip. And you won't get in trouble for that, either."

"Yes, sir, Captain, sir," the seaman said, sitting down at attention.

"I'd say calm down but I know you're not going to,"

Prael said, grinning. "Here's the deal. I've been hearing some rumors about the crew and Miss Moon. I need to know the substance of the rumors. Again, no matter what you tell me, nothing will leave this compartment. No Captain's Mast, no articles. That is guaranteed. Do you believe me?"

"You're the CO, sir," the seaman said, really sweating now.

"So, what's going on with Miss Moon?" the CO asked then waited.

"Sir, I think I'm going to stand on my Article Thirty-Two rights," the seaman said after clearly dredging the phrase out of buried memory.

"Look, seaman, nobody is going to get in trouble," the CO said. "Unless I don't get any answers. And I think you can give me those answers. So if I don't get any answers, then there's trouble. Simple as that. No trouble for answers, lots of trouble for no answers. Especially once I get to the bottom of what's going on. So *talk*."

"Sir," the seaman squeaked. "It's nothing . . . bad. Honest to *God*, sir!"

"So what is 'it'?" Prael asked.

"Sir, I'm straight out of A school," the seaman said, desperately. "I was distinguished graduate. I've got two years of college. I was getting a physics degree but my scholarship ran out. I figured, do a few years in the Navy, get the money to go back. When I took the tests they said I could pick anything and there was particle sensor tech! The description was like a dream! The transfer credits are going to wipe out my junior year! So I went for that and I did really good. I *did*, sir!"

"I've seen your evaluations," Prael said sympathetically.

"But it's not like I've got my masters, sir!" the seaman said. "And the damned petty officers don't know *chither*, pardon my Adar, sir. They barely understand what the particles are, much less the physics of the interactions. So then the damned sensor starts giving me these really funky readings when we're in deep space and I report them and they tell me to run a diagnostic and I've got faults that I don't understand and they don't understand . . ." He trailed off desperately, not wanting to admit that he'd violated a fully lawful order. Doing so, especially since the ship was in what was referred to as "combat condition" didn't just mean Captain's Mast, it could mean a full court-martial.

"So you took the problem to Miss Moon," the CO said, nodding.

"And she pulled up the design of the system, told me what the problem was, a bad power module of all things, and I could fix it, sir!" the seaman said. "I'm sorry, sir. I know I violated orders by associating with her, sir, but I got the sensor system working again. And it's not like I'm the first one to do it!" He clapped his mouth shut on that, a horrified expression on his face.

"So just how many visitors has Miss Moon had?" the CO asked dryly.

"Sir, at this point I'd really like to stand on my rights," the seaman said. "If anybody finds out I told you . . . Sir, they can get brutal out there, you *know* that!"

Horrible practical jokes were endemic to the sub service. As one submariner put it, "If we don't like somebody, we *will* drive them completely insane. And get away with it."

On the previous cruise a particularly disliked crewman had been found strapped to the hull. He'd been there for at least three days, effectively in sensory deprivation, and had to be kept sedated for the rest of the voyage.

Much like a prison, "squealers" were particular targets. The seaman was in for a psychological pounding applied by masters of the trade if the word got out he'd informed on anyone else.

"I'll let you stand on that one," the CO said, nodding. "If you let slip what this conversation was about, I *officially* know nothing. I don't like it, but I know nothing. Out."

The seaman seemed to break the speed of light out of the office.

"Damn," the CO said. He knew what was going to happen, eventually; the question was how to do it so that it didn't make him look like an ass. Normally, he didn't care about that sort of thing. But with a crew, they had to think their CO always knew what he was doing. In an emergency, in combat, they could *not* be questioning his judgment. And he was beginning to realize he'd made a monumental error in that area. Come to think on it, that was almost precisely the term that the XO had used. Damnit. "Conn, CO."

"Conn," the watch officer replied.

"Get me the COB."

"So half the crew's been visiting Miss Moon to get their technical problems resolved," the CO said.

"Half would be an exaggeration, sir," the COB said. "The missile techs understand their systems just fine. And laundry and mess aren't having any issues. Well, Mess is, but the XO's on that and I doubt Miss Moon can cook."

"*I'd* say that's half the crew," the CO said sarcastically.

"Well, *all* the rest haven't been to see her, sir," the COB pointed out. "Just the ones that have hit a brick wall with something."

"They couldn't ask the XO?" the CO said. "He's a whiz-kid."

"With all due respect to both you and the XO, sir," the COB said, "the XO's usually really busy and is generally one grouchy son-of-a-bitch on this cruise. The crew steers clear of him if they can. And, frankly, I think Miss Moon has a better technical understanding of a bunch of the systems, sir. She's also a lot easier to talk to and pleasant on the eyes. I mean, seriously, sir, if you had the choice of asking Commander Weaver a question or Miss Moon, which would *you* choose?"

"And you don't have an issue with that, COB?" the CO asked angrily. "Direct disobedience of orders? Private time with a female on a submarine?"

"As to the first, sir," the COB answered, his face hard, "*officially*, I don't know *maulk* and will say so in front of *any* court you care to send me up before, *sir*. And unofficially, which I was thinking we were talking, the stuff's getting *fixed*, sir. We'd have turned around two weeks ago when Fusion Two was acting funky if it weren't for Miss Moon. And you and the XO barely *heard* about that one, sir. You responded to the SCRAM then went back to your regular work and got a report it was fixed. All done. Not *how* it got fixed, which was people who shall remain nameless trooping in and out of the science quarters the whole time and an hour run on the fabricator to fix a busted injector and some magnets that nobody *but* Miss Moon could figure out. And didn't the Eng hear nothing nor wonder about the engineering guys running in and out of the compartment every five minutes! For that matter, it all started because we wanted to be able to breathe, sir. You'll recall when the recyclers went down, sir? And nobody knew how to fix them?"

"Except Miss Moon?" the CO asked.

"She at least could figure it out, sir," the COB said "As to the second, sir, I've been keeping an eye on it really close. The whole crew considers her something between a mascot and a good-luck charm. More than half the crew worships the ground she occasionally trods. If anybody thought about raising a *hand* to her, the rest of the crew would space him and you'd have one guy permanently AWOL."

"Christ, COB," the CO said, shaking his head. "This has got to get under control. The problem is I gave that order and maybe it was stupid but the Navy's got to have orders."

"Beyond my paygrade, sir," the COB said, letting his CO dangle.

"Thanks so very much," the CO said. "I am now off my Captain high horse. I would entertain suggestions how to get out of this predicament. Because, yeah, we need Miss Moon on-board. I give. Uncle."

"Let it slide for now," the COB said. "Ignore it. I'll keep it to a dull roar. I've had to handle Miss Moon before and she's got more horse sense about people than you know, sir, pardon me. She sees what's going on and she's not going to make waves. First chance you get, let her off the hook and she'll let you off. If she backs you with the crew and I back you with the crew, well, sir, then you're golden."

"And *are* you backing me with the crew?" the CO asked.

"That hurt, sir," the COB said angrily. "You're the CO, sir. When I heard about the guys going to Miss Moon, I checked into it and realized there weren't no choice. When some *maulk*-for-brains complains about having to sneak around I dress him down right proper, sir. The chiefs are on it, sir, *all* of them. But, yes, you're going to need to climb down sometime, sir. This ship isn't going to make it to Rigel much less Taurus if we don't have Miss Moon's assistance. She's the only person that understands half the systems. We should have shipped with a full load of Hexosehr tech-reps filling the science quarters or at least a dozen human and Adar eggheads. Hell, even Tchar's gone! What we've got is Miss Moon and an XO that's new to his job and scrambling to figure it out. Do *you* know how to fix a busted particle sensor, sir? *I* don't. Or a covalent shearer? The nearest guy who's sure to be able to is about a hundred and twenty light-years off. So, yes, you're gonna have to climb down. It's just . . ."

". . . Us," the CO completed. "And Us includes Miss Moon."

"Yes, sir," the COB said.

"Message received, COB," the CO said, nodding at the door. "Not that we had this discussion. But you can be sure I'll take the first opportunity to climb down. But it's still against my better judgment. Women shouldn't be on subs."

"Sir," the COB said, sighing, his hand on the latch of

the hatch. "This ain't a *submarine*, sir. Sometimes I sore wish it was. Things were a *grapp* of a lot simpler."

"Serious improvement, Eric," Captain Zanella said, nodding at the results. "Serious improvement. The use of Bravo team was . . . Oh, hell, it was damned brilliant."

"Thank you, sir," Eric said stoically. He'd checked on similar runs by the other officers in the company and found that, despite the CO's pronouncement, they lost the engagement on Runner's World on average 80% of the time, losses ranging from losing a full platoon to the entire company and attachments. And that average included the CO. Eric had gotten to the point where the engagement was becoming childishly simple. Of course, he wasn't about to tell the CO that he'd gotten advice on fighting crabpus from a Cheerick.

"Are you sure the blades on the armor work that effectively?" the CO asked. "Closing seems . . ."

"Well, sir," the lieutenant said, "if you can't punch them on the snout, step on their toes. It works, sir. I've punched them myself."

"How's the homework?" the CO asked.

"I'm four days ahead," Berg answered. "I considered taking a break, but if I continue at the current pace I can be caught up at least one week before we reach the mission area, which will give me time to get back in shape. Right now I'm sorely out of reg for PT."

"Don't exhaust yourself, Lieutenant," the CO said. "Gung-ho will only carry you so far."

"Wasn't planning on it, sir," the lieutenant said. "I'm not even close to tired."

11

"Does this cat ever get tired?"

Lieutenant Commander Clayton Oldfield was a long-service "nuke," having primarily worked fast attack boats. However, with the changes made in the *Blade*, and especially in the *Blade II*, he was as good a choice as any for the job of engineering officer. Frankly, nobody really understood the *Blade*'s new systems except the Hexosehr and while he was glad they finally had repair manuals, the sections on the ball guns were impenetrable to him despite a Ph.D. in nuclear physics.

The commander was also not a cat person. He currently had no pets but if anyone asked he'd probably admit to preferring dogs. So the intensity with which he'd taken to the Savannah was as much a surprise to himself as anyone else.

"Not that anyone has noticed, sir," Sub Dude said.

"Where do you get one of these guys?" he asked, tossing the ball down the corridor.

"From a breeder," Red said. "All you need is about four thousand dollars and a good home."

"That much?" Commander Oldfield squeaked, provoking a cocked head from the cat. Tiny stopped and licked a spot hurriedly then paused, ready to pounce on the evil tennis ball.

"CO's coming!" Sub Dude whispered from down the corridor. He was tracing the fault on another part of the system and could see the approach from his chosen spot.

"*Maulk*," the commander muttered, looking around. He flipped the ball into a supply compartment and Tiny bounded after it, tackling it as it bounced off one of the bulkheads.

The Eng quickly shut the compartment and leaned on it, flipping open the Hexosehr manual and perusing it with an intent expression.

"Good afternoon, Eng," Captain Prael said, striding down the compartment.

"Afternoon, sir," Oldfield replied. "Great weather we're having."

"If you mean vacuum, yes," the CO said, furrowing his brow. "Have you got the problem figured out, yet?"

"I think it's a quantum instability in the wiring interface," the Eng said, frowning. "The pre-generator has to be kept online at all times and the dimensional flux field is destabilizing the strong force bindings in the wiring. We may have to back the molycirc interface away from the generation point. I'm also wondering about structural stability from the effect."

"Could that be what was causing that strange bending noise on take-off?" the CO asked.

"Possibly, sir," the Eng said, just as Tiny started a pre-yowl in the compartment. The hatch, however, was thick steel and Tiny never really sounded like a cat, anyway. "And then again, perhaps not. We're still getting it from time to time."

"Air in the sewage lines, sir," Red piped up. "I'm telling you, it's either air in the sewage or maybe in the water lines. I heard it on the *Georgia* one time."

"It's a bit of a debate, sir," the Eng admitted. "But so far there is no indication of structural damage."

"I'm hearing it, now, aren't I?" the CO asked.

"Yes, sir," the Eng admitted. "And that's one indication that it wasn't structural."

"Well, track it down," the CO said. "It's annoying."

"Will do, sir."

"Whew," Red muttered as soon as the CO was out of the gun compartment. "That was close."

"*Air* in the sewage lines?" the Eng asked. "Air in the *sewage* lines?"

"Hey, sir, I could tell you were frozen," the machinist said. "And I think I found the problem." He held up a wire and pulled. The insulation stretched and then tore, revealing that the copper was just dust. "You were right."

"What do you mean I was right?" the Eng said.

"That *maulk* about quantum flux, sir," Red said. "This stuff is being degraded by something. Want to bet it's a side effect of the generators?"

"But I was making that up!" the engineering officer said. "*Maulk, maulk, maulk, maulk, maulk*. That means we have to completely *redesign* the damned interface! And get it installed in transit! On both sides of the ship! How in the hell are we going to do that?"

"You're joking, right?" Red said. "Not about what we've got to do, sir, but about how we're going to do it. You're joking."

"No, I'm not," the Eng replied. "We're shorthanded as it is and the only person on this ship who could do a complete redesign is me. And I simply do not have the time."

"Okay, he's not joking," Sub Dude said, sucking his teeth. "Sir, who designed this thing in the first place?"

"The Hexosehr," the Eng snapped. "But we didn't get the tech reps we were supposed to have!"

"Let me rephrase," Gants said, shaking his head. "Who was in every single meeting handling the translation of our needs and interjecting her, and that's a hint, comments on modifications. Who did most of the conversion of Hexosehr three-d sonar imagery into CAD? Who, sir? Who, for that matter, made all of the blueprints. Take a guess."

"Damnit," the Eng muttered. "Okay, I need to talk to Miss Moon. And the CO."

"So now you want my help?" Miriam asked. "I've been going stir-crazy in my cabin since we left Earth and now you want my help? Is that what you're saying?"

Captain Prael clenched his teeth and carefully did not point out that he knew for a fact she was getting at least *daily* visitors.

"Yes," he said. "I, we, would like your help."

"Shiny," Miriam replied. "I'll get right on it."

"That's it?" the CO asked. "No request for grovelling? No snide remarks?"

"I don't do snide," Miriam replied. "And just asking is probably killing you. Don't worry about it. I'm used to men thinking that just because I'm pretty I have to be stupid. So I do the redesign and you have to, at least to yourself, eat crow. Being good is the best revenge anyone can have. Make that extraordinary."

"Then thank you," Prael said, trying hard not to growl. "When can we get the design?"

"Sir, I'd estimate at least a week," the Eng said unhappily. "And redoing the installation will take much longer. I'm not even sure it's feasible, given that we only have a limited quantity of molycirc."

"I'll have it tomorrow," Miriam replied. "And it will take into account how much molycirc we have."

"You're joking," the Eng said.

"I will see you tomorrow, Engineer," Miriam said. "I have to get to work."

With that she stood up and stomped out of the wardroom, four inch heels clacking furiously.

"No way," the Eng said. "No way in hell. Sorry, sir, but there's entirely too much detail to change. Doing that many CAD drawings is something that you'd usually give an entire team. And that is if you knew how you were going to change it. I'm still trying to figure that part out, and I've been doing this for twenty years."

"Then we'll see who eats crow," Prael said, nodding. "I admit I'm torn. Everyone talks about how that little weirdo walks on water; seeing her taken down a peg would not make me unhappy. On the other hand . . ."

"We have to get the reinstallation done on both systems," the Eng said, nodding unhappily. "And that, right there, is going to take more manhours than I can spare. The faster we get the plans . . ."

"Well, even if she's done in a week, that will probably give us enough time," the CO said. "Bring this to the attention of the XO, tell him that we got started on fixing it on his sleep shift and keep me apprised."

"You're joking," Weaver said, yawning.

"No, we're going to have to completely redesign and rebuild it, XO," the Eng said unhappily. "The CO and I discussed it while you were off watch. About six hours ago."

Like a lot of the professional officers on the *Blade*, Oldfield didn't think much of his new XO. Yes, he knew that Weaver had done some terrific things—fight giant octopus thingies, space battles, first venturer into the treacherous shoals of outer space, save the world for that matter—but a person who had worked his way up the ladder had a hard time taking seriously a guy who had been fast-tracked to the Eng's current rank and then bumped twice since. *Nobody* was that good. Besides, the guy was just a grouch.

"The design's going to take at least a week, whatever Miss Moon says," the Eng continued. "And as for the reinstallation . . ."

"Man, y'all are damn funny sometimes," Weaver drawled. "By y'all I mean y'all wet navy characters. This here's the *Blade*, Eng. Hellfire and damnation. We don't diddle around with taking a week for something like this. Ain't got the time, there's always some alien space beast or enemy fleet trying to wipe us out. Can't just go back to dry dock and let the contractors handle it. It's figure out the problem, fast, or die. And you say you told the CO at least a week for *Miriam* to do the plans? That *maulk* is just *grapping* funny."

"Yes," the Eng said, his face tight. "Do you find that questionable, Captain?"

"*Maulk*," Weaver said, laughing. "Hell, yeah, I find that questionable. You do know she's written about half the peripheral coding in AutoCAD, right? And that the company sends all their Alpha test systems to her, since she's the fastest user they've ever tracked, right? That they had to rewrite one whole generation just because she proved she could crash it simply by going faster than the program could handle? And that she's got enough classes to count for Ph.D.s in mechanical and electrical engineering *and* was the lead designer on this ship? A ship we designed, every last bolt and fastener, in *less* than a week? Most of it drawings that *she* did?"

"Oh," the Eng said, his eyes wide.

"I'm kinda surprised she's not already—"

"Hi, Bill," Miriam said, walking into the XO's office. "You want to look over this redesign? I think I managed to fix it. It was my fault to begin with, I think. I figured out a way to run the circuits and cut off thirty percent of the circuit length. But I'll admit I was hurrying the last time. I've been thinking about it since . . ."

"Be glad to, Miriam," the XO said. "I think the Eng was just going to have supper. The menu would be a form of rook."

"You're joking," the CO said, looking at the blueprints laid out on his desk. "The Eng said . . ."

"The Eng was unaware of some of Miss Moon's less

notable features," Weaver said dryly. "I think he was paying too much attention to her butt and too little to her brain."

"This is . . ." Prael was a nuclear submarine officer and had, in fact, come up through the engineering department. Like the Eng, he had a Ph.D. in nuclear engineering. He knew CAD drawings, used the program and knew how long it took to create something like this. Yes, she had started from extant drawings, but it was often more work to "fix" something in CAD drawings than to start anew. He flipped up the pages one by one and estimated how long it would have taken him to do something like this. More like a month, frankly. A day per drawing most likely, given the detail level. "Unreal," he finally said. "I would have said impossible. And she did this in *six hours*?"

"Sir, I'm going to say something that will come across as insulting and is not intended to be," Weaver replied carefully. "May I continue?"

"Go ahead, XO," the CO said, leaning back in his chair. "What's one more insulting thing? This seems to be the week."

"The original crew of the *Blade*, of whom Miriam was a member, was chosen from the absolute *top* of their respective fields," Weaver pointed out. "Miss Moon is one of the top linguists in the world, with a host of secondary skills, some of which are obviously as sharp or even sharper. Dr. Robertson, our biologist, was world-renowned and, again, multiskilled. Dr. Dean, God rest his liberal soul, was a brilliant planetologist and geologist even if he *couldn't* figure out not to run under a herd of rampaging giant crabpus. The CO, who admittedly was a fly-boy, had a string of walk-on-water reports, never had an airman request transfer when he was a carrier commander, was a former Blue Angel and an instructor at Top-Gun. Even the individual members of the crew were chosen from the best of their rank in the sub service and the Marines were all hand-picked for the job."

"And you're saying that the current crop is not?" the CO replied dryly.

"You were, obviously, sir," Bill said tactfully. "The CO of any nuclear sub is carefully chosen and the CO of the *Blade* more so. You're someone who's been pre-tapped as a future large-ship commander or an admiral. But . . . There's a difference between a large-ship commander, even a very good one, and someone who is at *genius* level in their field. It's like being pregnant; you can't be a little bit genius. The replacements are not being chosen from that genius caliber. It's another disconnect between the old hands and the new. Miriam, clearly, is at that level."

"By the same token, you're saying you are," the CO pointed out.

"I think I'll just stand on my record, sir," Bill said, smiling thinly.

"So why aren't you commanding?" the CO asked, smiling just as thinly back.

"Because I haven't had a slot as XO," Bill said. "And, hellfire, it's way more demanding than I realized; I can see why you need to do the job before you command. But the real reason is that I can do a better job where I'm at at what the Navy wants me to do."

"Which is teach me the realities of the Space Navy?"

the CO asked. "That we have to put up with the occasional flake because sometimes we really need her?"

"Or him," Bill said. "When we've established forward bases, when a ship isn't invaluable, when there's the choice to put into dock and fix something major that's screwed up, then it will be more . . . mundane. More like the regular Navy. In the meantime . . ."

"It's just us," the CO said, nodding. "We're a hundred fifty light-years from Earth and more from any ship that can tow us home. What? A year and a half for a Hexosehr ship to get here even if we could ask?"

"Deep space, sir," Bill pointed out. "The Hexosehr can't come out here short of a specially built ship. And then it would be more like . . ." He paused and did some numbers in his head. "Thirty years."

"Thanks for pointing that out," the CO said sourly, then paused. "Really?"

"Sir, if we have a major failure we cannot correct we are as dead as a sub at the bottom of the Pacific," Weaver said. "Deader. They could get to a sub in the Marianas Trench faster than they could get to us. Absent Hexosehr, the only people who have any chance of figuring out something really bad are myself and Miss Moon. We're both here, I guess, to teach the crew how to keep this lash-up running. But I'm up to my eyeballs in work and . . ."

"I've actually had this lecture, XO," the CO said tightly. "From at least one unexpected source. Okay, please kindly ask Miss Moon to oversee the reinstallation. And from this point forward, she has the run of the ship. Except Conn. I will not have her on the Conn."

"I'll pass that on, sir," Weaver said, nodding.

"I'll climb down that far and no farther," the CO stated, emphatically, *knowing* in his heart he was dooming himself to failure. Again. Sooner or later he'd have to have Miriam on the Conn. Damnit.

"Well, there's one part that doesn't work," the Eng said, as he brought the plans back to Miriam's office. "There's more molycirc in use than we have."

"Had to do it that way," Miriam said, not looking up from her computer. "When Red and Sub Dude pulled all the wiring the damage was well back from the generators. I think I know why, but it's complicated."

"I was once considered a geek," the Eng admitted. "Try me."

"Okay, what do you know about coordinate covalent bonds? They're sometimes called *dative bonds*," Miriam asked.

"That's when you have one atom supplying both shared electrons to the other atom it's covalently bonded to, if I remember correctly."

"Well . . . close enough. But without Ligand Field Theory I'd be afraid to delve any deeper into that aspect of it. What do you know about chaos?"

"I work in the Navy," the Eng said with a grin. "And on a more serious note, I did some control theory in my dissertation that had some systems of coupled differential equations that would go chaotic from time to time."

"Well, that's more of the nonlinear dynamics view of chaos where under conditions such that all potential Fourier series frequencies are present you get a system that jumps around like nuts and is wildly tending toward disorder that sort of agrees with the understanding of the classical second law of thermodynamics. What we have here is something different termed fundamental cosmic chaos."

"Uh huh." The Eng, of course, *had* taken it as though Miriam were being condescending.

"Chaos at a cosmos level is more a fundamental of the universe that strongly contrasts with the second law of thermodynamics. In fact, wild complex systems of systems that are seemingly completely random and chaotic often generate order from within the randomness. Think, oh, fractal screensavers but really more related to Schwartzchild boundaries."

"What does this have to do with the molyc—?"

"It has *everything* to do with it," Miriam said as she pushed one of the purple strands of alien metal. "The chaos generator actually *does* generate chaos. What it does, well at least what we *think* it does, is to create a sphere of uncertainty on the fundamental cosmic level. In that sphere there is nothing but the pure randomness of the vacuum energy fluctuations of creation and annihilation on the subnuclear scale. Within the sphere everything is broken down to its fundamental components and then set asunder following the rules of uncertainty and randomness. What the Hexosehr must not have realized is that the little black box creates a very thin shell around the ship of *its own* randomness at the event horizon of the warp bubble. Bill could explain that better, he's the expert in General Relativity and warp theory, but I believe he would agree that it is a Planck-length-thick shell where absolute fundamental cosmic chaos and uncertainty exists.

It works by generating nanosecond conditions of total chaos, a moment where we could be truly anywhere in the universe or possibly the multiverse, then resetting reality so that we've made a very small movement within the time-space continuum probably because that movement is relatively chaos energy minimal, that is it approaches the highest probability of reality that we don't move at all. There is a region of vacuum energy fluctuations coming into and going out of reality. Maybe the Hexosehr realized the bubble wall was there, but they didn't realize that it was going to interact with the quantum fluctuation fields the chaos generators created. The result was that from these two colliding regions of chaos driven by different sources there was a mutual order that was created. That order was a Ligand Field phenomenon. Oh, I said I wasn't going to discuss Ligand Field Theory, didn't I?"

"Uh," the Eng said, staring blankly at Miriam.

"But skipping trying to explain Ligand Field theory, the effect was the creation of ligands or coordinate covalent bonds under conditions that were stochastically unlikely absent the chaotic interactions of the fields and now seem to be stochastically certain. In other words: The coordinate covalent bonds that were created throughout the molycirc shouldn't be possible in this universe. The molybdenum and rhenium transition metals simply *don't work that way*. The chaos field phenomenon caused them to form quadruple coordinate covalent bonds which became powdery brittle in the weak chaos fields that were escaping the chaos ball generator's shielding. There was also some di-tungsten hexa hydro pyrimido pyrimidine ligands that formed but not as many. The spectral analysis of the degraded molycirc showed a bunch of odd materials. I'm making a really detailed record because there are some covalent bonds that might theoretically be useful. Some of the materials have structures and properties more similar to rare elements than molecules.

"Bottomline: The molycirc couldn't take the stress of the chaos generator field after the fractal odd order phenomenon occurred within the material's matrix. Oh, there was also some issue with lanthanide contraction, but it was less catastrophic than the other phenomenon. I think the lanthanide contraction was supposed to be stabilized by the molycirc and the chaos messed that up. Secondary effect rather than primary."

"Oh."

"At least that's what I think happened. Might wanna run it by Bill when you get the chance."

"Okay," the Eng said, his eyes wide. "But I think you're going to have to run it by him. You lost me at Planck-length shell and fundamental cosmic chaos. I can't even pronounce the di-tungsten hexa . . . hydra, uh whatever you said."

"Being a linguist makes saying chemical compounds easier for me. I can show you the equations and the spectral analysis if you'd like to see them," Miriam said distantly. She was only half listening to the Eng at this point.

"No, that's shiny," the Eng said. "Actually, on second thought—"

"I just fired them over to your e-mail," Miriam said. "Anyway, we can produce the molycirc we need in the fabber. It's slow, it's about the slowest thing the fabber makes, which is why I left it as the last part we're going to have to replace. But we can do it. We just need a source of osmium. We also need some molybdenum but there's so much chromoly steel on the ship that won't be a problem."

"A source of osmium?" the Eng said. "I don't happen to have one on me . . ."

"Then find one," Miriam said. "I'm sort of busy here."

"Yes, ma'am," the Eng replied, snapping to attention. "I'll get right on it."

"Osmium?" Captain Prael asked.

"A heavy metal," Weaver said distantly. "Atomic number 76 on the periodic table, atomic weight 190.23, in the platinum group, extraordinarily dense due to the lanthanide contraction."

"Which, apparently, we have to stabilize," the Eng noted.

"I know what osmium is," Prael snapped. "More or less," he added, less assuredly. "I *used* to know all this . . ."

"So do I," the Eng said. "And all the rest. I mean, I knew it was a lanthanide but I had to go look it up again to refresh my memory."

"Lanthanide?" Prael said. "That's what uranium is. It's not radioactive, is it?"

"No, sir," Bill replied. "Lanthanides just have higher density than their position on the periodic table would suggest due to contraction of their electron shells. Most of the heavy metal radioactives are lanthanides, but all lanthanides are not radioactive."

"I did find out it is a bugger to extract from all the other metals it's usually associated with," Commander Oldfield said.

"That's not an issue," Bill said, looking up. "The fabber will handle the extraction."

"How?" the Eng asked curiously.

"If I knew that I'd be making gigabucks back on Earth," Bill said. "Or a Hexosehr. But all we need is some osmium ore."

"And where are we going to get some in deep space?" the CO asked. "That's the issue. I'd really like to have all my guns working before we get to an area where there might be Dreen."

"Asteroids," Weaver said. "Comets. Osmium is one of the deposition metals that geologists look for to determine major impacts along with iridium. I think we need to go asteroid mining. What's the nearest solar system?"

"How much of this stuff do we need?" Chief Gestner asked.

"A lot," Miriam replied. "Almost five kilograms."

"That's a lot?" Gestner asked.

"Uh . . ." Miriam temporized.

"That's about sixty thousand dollars worth," Sub Dude said, chuckling. "Think gold mining, Chief. Stuff's actually more expensive than gold."

"Holy *maulk*," the chief said, his eyes wide.

"The problem is, we're going to have to run through a *bunch* of ore to get that," Miriam said. "The fabber will discard the waste, but it's going to get messy. We'll probably do it in two phases, one that just extracts the heavy metals then another that takes that and makes the molycircs. And this fabber's maw is small. So the stuff's going to have to be broken down into . . ."

"Skull-sized pieces," Red said. "More or less. You can get your head in the fabber if you sort of turn sideways . . ."

"Yeah, shiny, I get the idea," the chief said. "That's really going to *grapp* up my shop."

"Not if we move the fabber out," Sub Dude pointed out. "Miriam, didn't we use this model in vacuum when we were working on the ship?"

"It's vacuum rated," Miriam said. "Everything on the ship that's Hexosehr is."

"So we do it on the hull," Sub Dude said, shrugging.

"So the plan is we do the fabbing on the hull?" the chief asked. "In vacuum?"

"Makes the most sense," Red said. "That way we just leave our mess behind."

"Shiny," the chief said. "And we need head-sized nodules, which means breaking up an asteroid to get them. So, who gets *that* job?"

12

"Lieutenant Bergstresser, congratulations," Lieutenant Ross said as Berg walked into Admin. "You'll be pleased to know that I took the numbers you finally got me for vac time and crunched them."

"Sorry it took so long, sir," Eric said, stretching. "I was kind of busy with all the stuff the CO dumped on my lap."

"Understood," Ross said. "But don't you want to know why congratulations are in order?"

"I assume because you finally got the paperwork filled out, sir," Eric said, sitting down and turning on his computer.

"That as well," Ross said. "But the reason that congratulations are in order to you, Lieutenant, is that you have a new title."

"Oh?" Berg asked, wincing.

"It's called Vac Boss," Ross said, chuckling. "An analysis of all the numbers on the entire ship, including veteran crew, indicates that you, Lieutenant Bergstresser, have the most time in death pressure. By about an hour, which is pretty good. Or terrible, depending on how you view space."

"Whenever possible from inside a ship, sir," Eric replied. "Why do I think this is going somewhere bad . . . ?"

"Breaking something up in space is a nontrivial exercise, sir," Eric said, looking over at Weaver.

The *Blade* had entered three star systems in the area, poking carefully to ensure the Dreen hadn't gotten there, yet, and looking for a suitable asteroid field. Many systems didn't have them because of Jovian interactions and the fact that some of the stars were particularly poor in metal formation. They found a good one in the third system and after more hunting found a large asteroid that according to penetrating radar had a high density, a good sign that osmium might be present.

"We had a fun time with a comet last mission," Weaver admitted. "And he's right. You can't just blow it up; the bits continue with the velocity imparted to them by the explosive. Which is high."

"There has to be an answer," Prael said, looking at his XO and the most junior officer on the ship. Berg looked about twelve to the captain and he wasn't sure he trusted him outside the ship, much less in charge of the entire exercise. "We need nodules that are approximately head sized. No more than eight inches on a side."

"Eight inches," Berg said, looking at the bulkhead thoughtfully. "Commander Weaver, isn't that about the cutting distance of one of the melders?"

"About that," Bill said. "But we're going to need a lot of ore, Two-Gun . . ."

"We need to break it down and then break it down again," Berg said. "We'll need all the boards. *And* the dragonflies."

"The idea, Colonel, is to cut it up," Berg said, standing on his board and looking at the asteroid. It was shaped vaguely like a peanut, a common look for asteroids he'd noticed, and about a hundred yards long. "We need the smallest chunks you can get without starting any particular chunk on a hard trajectory. Your lasers are going to impart movement energy to this thing. We want it moving as little as possible. And be careful, there are boards flying around."

Practically the entire company had been rolled out on their golden surfboards and the officers and NCOs were circling the asteroid, considering the mission they'd been given. It wasn't a standard Marine mission, but as Captain Zanella pointed out it was pretty much on a par for Space Marines.

"We shall see how this works," Colonel Che-chee said, aiming her dragonfly at the rock. "Firing . . ."

"They're just not powerful enough," the lieutenant reported. "Even with three of them firing at the same point, they're barely scratching the surface. Based on their rate of cut, my calculations say that it will take more than a month to break it down to the point the melders can start cutting. Then there's the smelting process."

"Too much time," Prael said. "We're supposed to have been to the target by then and started our survey. We need a faster solution."

"Well, sir," Berg said. "I'm thinking that we might have to blow it up and then try to catch the pieces."

"That would be ugly," Weaver said, shaking his head. "Those pieces are not going to be going slow. And we'll have to drill the thing, anyway. Maybe we just find a bunch of smaller rocks. That would be time consuming, but . . ."

"We need the lasers to be more powerful," Miriam said, shrugging. "We just make them more powerful."

"You mean they need to be brighter not more powerful," Weaver said.

"Pedant," Miriam replied, sticking out her tongue. "But you're right, brighter."

"That just might work."

"And that means what?" the CO asked.

"Well, we don't really have the capability to increase the power, which is in watts, of the laser beams themselves," Weaver explained. "But, we do have the capability of focusing the beams and making them brighter on target meaning more watts per square meter. We need a BMG mirror . . ."

"XO?" the CO said. "BMG?"

"Uh . . ." Bill said.

"Big Mother*Grapper*, sir," Berg responded, trying not to grin.

"Oh," the CO said, obviously trying not to grin as well. "Go on."

"The . . . mirror will have to be perfectly reflective so it doesn't absorb enough of the beams to heat up and destroy itself and has to have a tight focus, very tight. We'll shine all the lasers on the mirror and then focus all the beams down to a centimeter sized spot on the asteroid. That should be enough irradiance on target to cut it."

"So . . . it's like frying ants with a magnifying glass?" the CO asked.

"More or less, sir," the Ph.D. in optics said, trying not to wince.

"Why didn't you just say so?" The CO was beginning to have visions of the Death Star firing multiple beams out that combined into one, which consequently destroyed Alderaan. "We'd need a bunch of silicon for the glass I assume?"

"No, sir. We don't need any glass at all. In fact, I'd recommend against glass and that we make the mirror out of Zerodur or AlBeMet."

"Albe . . ."

"Aluminum-beryllium metal, sir. We've got plenty of stuff lying around the ship that is made of aluminum and/or beryllium. Toss some of that in the fabber and regen us a blank of AlBeMet that we can hog a mirror out of. Zerodur is a composite, hmm, better stick to AlBeMet." Weaver ran his fingers through his thinning hair in thought. "We could build a very thin mirror out of AlBeMet without noticing the loss of material at all and the material is much better suited for the purposes here than glass or Zerodur. We're going to need to fab a mirror that is ten meters or so in diameter though," Weaver said turning to Miriam. "Can the fabber make that?"

"Well, it can make pieces and then we honeycomb them together and meld them outside," Miriam said. "We'll just have to make hardware to mount them together and point it."

"And cool it," Weaver added. "That much irradiance and the mirror will get hot hot hot. Wait, melding might cause wavefront errors on the mirror that we don't understand. Better to just leave it as a honeycomb."

"I'm beginning to hear the words 'space tape and baling wire' in my head, XO," the CO said.

"This used to be my day job, sir," Bill replied. "There ain't gonna be no space tape on *my* mirror, that you can depend on."

"How will we point it?" the CO added. "Can we attach something that big to the ship?"

"Uh, sir, that would be harder to do, I think. Besides, the ship vibrates like hell and we don't want any excess vibrations on the mirror if we can help it. Even AlBeMet has a natural frequency. Think of a fat lady singing and a crystal wine glass." Weaver thought for a moment and chewed at his lower lip. "We should just take the EVA thrusters off of a couple of suits or a probe and make this thing a free-flyer. We can hand launch it off the *Blade* and remote control for pointing. This way we ain't pointing the dragonfly lasers back at ourselves. That would be safer. Okay, you're right, there may be space-tape involved."

"And then the beams will be able to cut the rock?" Colonel Che-chee asked.

"We'll just have to see," Bill replied. "I need to go off somewhere by myself for a while and do some math. Wish I had a beer to go along with it."

It took more than a day for Weaver to simulate the mirror design on the ship's computers. It took another day just to fab and assemble the honeycomb pieces of

AlBeMet into a ten-meter diameter primary mirror. The biggest issue was keeping it clean since the slightest bits of dust or fingerprint oil or any impurities on the surface would be a place for heat to gather and then a point where the mirror could be damaged and possibly even destroy itself. The surface also had to be manufactured with a precision of millionths of a meter tolerance. Fortunately, the fabber was good for even stricter design requirements. Bill and Miriam had overseen the entire project. While Bill completed the optical design and engineering of the mirror, Miriam developed a control system out of retrofitted thrusters from the EVA suits. And, since Miriam had difficulty lifting hardware much larger than a bowling ball, she had enlisted the help of her two favorite engineering and machinist lackeys, Red and Sub Dude.

Since moving it from the science section outside would have required moving the pieces through the ship, and thus coating them with gunk, Red and Sub Dude cleared out a section of Engineering near the elevator and then planned for it to be evacuated per Captain Weaver's orders. The evacuation of the room would boil off most finger oils and impurities as well as suck out dust particulates. In other words, they sucked it empty to clean it.

"Captain Weaver, we've got the mirror component area cleared and wiped down and I guess we're ready to evacuate it sir," Sub Dude Gants alerted Bill, who was arms deep in the fabber pulling out the latest mirror holder and cooling junction.

"Good, that makes what now, Eng? Thirty-eight?" Weaver asked Oldfield standing on the other side of the alien machine at the fabber control console.

"Uh, Thirty-nine. Still twelve pieces to go. And then we can start on the mirror pieces," the Eng replied.

"Okay then, it is as good a time for a break now as any other." He turned to the machinist's mate as he stretched his neck. The mirror holders were damned heavy and lifting them for the last four hours as they rolled out of the fabber was giving him a serious pain in the neck. "Sub Dude, you and Red lock all these down and let me know when you are done. Then we'll go to zero gravity and suck out the clean room."

"Yes sir."

"ALL HANDS ALL HANDS PREPARE FOR ZERO GRAVITY!"

"Well, evacuating the room sucked most of the dust out of it and boiled off most of the oils and other contaminants. We used dry and clean air from bottles to fill the room to a slight overpressure so when we open the doors it will blow any contaminants out not in." Miriam adjusted the cleanroom suit booties over her spike heels and taped them down as she explained to Captain Prael what they had been up to for the past half of a day. Miriam jerked slightly from a static shock as she touched the metal doorfacing of the airseal, grounding herself.

"I see," the CO grunted.

"But the room isn't large enough to assemble the mirror and then get it out of the elevator. After all, when it is all said and done the mirror will be over ten meters in diameter and will weigh almost a ton." Miriam unzipped the makeshift airseal and stepped through, motioning the

CO to follow. She then resealed the plastic seam and turned to the door.

"I got it." The CO was already ahead of her and once he saw the seal close he turned the bulkhead door to the left, opening it. A rush of cool air washed over them as they stepped through the hatch.

"So," Miriam continued. "We'll have to make certain the components are clean here and that we know how to put them together. And then comes the fun part. Somebody who can handle things delicately will have to go outside and assemble the mirror in space."

"And who might that be?" the CO asked.

"That'll be me, sir." Weaver looked up from a checklist of components and systems where he was testing the physical mating of three honeycomb pieces. Red and Gants were straining against the weight of the large assembly pieces as Weaver attempted to mate them together while wearing spacesuit gloves. "There's nobody else on board who's really qualified for it."

"Man, I wish we could modify the gravity to about half in here," Red complained.

"Good idea," Bill wondered if there was a way to get the little black box to do that as he fiddled with an over-sized screwdriver. Letting his focus drift for just a second was enough for him to nearly drop it onto one of the reflective segments. "*Maulk!*"

"Maybe we should take a short break, sir?" Machinist's Mate Gants smiled. Even though the room temperature was specifically kept at sixty-five degrees Fahrenheit he was starting to sweat under his cleansuit.

"Good idea. Set'er down." Weaver backed away from

the components slowly and began sliding his EVA gloves off.

"Problems, Bill?" Miriam smiled even though she was wearing a doctor's mask over her face and nobody could tell.

"I've done EVAs in suits and Wyverns but nothing that required this level of intricacy," Bill said, shaking his head. "This is why astronauts like the ones who built the International Space Station trained in neutral buoyancy tanks for months before a mission like this. Spacesuit gloves are just damned hard to work in, even the Adar-designed ones."

"Are you saying this is undoable, Captain?" the CO asked unhappily.

"I don't know why we don't just fab some better designed gloves for you Bill?" Miriam said nonchalantly. "We could base them on the Hexosehr suits."

"Why in hell didn't I think of that already?" Bill said, tapping his head with the back of his hand. "Duh. I'll do that now for a break. Miriam, you want to get started with the ACS?"

"Why I'm here," she said with a smile. "The software is finished and just needs testing. Red, do you mind helping me get those attitude control system thruster boxes up onto the workbench?"

Red waved his number two arm assuredly at her. "Right away."

"The gloves work even better out here than they did inside," Bill said as he gently tightened the last mirror component into place.

"How much longer until we are ready to test the ACS?" Captain Prael radioed back.

"As soon as Gants and I disconnect the umbilical from the *Blade* we'll hand launch it. ETA, say fifteen more minutes, sir," Weaver replied. "Miriam, when we get a break I think we should seriously consider redesigning and fabbing some new EVA suits from the Hexosehr design."

"Roger that, Bill." She didn't have the heart to tell him that she had already done it.

"Okay sir, the umbilical is away from my end." Gants held the long cable in his left hand, keeping one hand on the large optic floating above his head; his magnetic boots gave him a solid footing against the *Blade*'s outer hull. "Red, you can reel it in now."

"Roger that," Red responded over the com link.

"Easy now, Sub Dude. Let's walk her around the hull and up to the top of the sail just as we planned," Weaver said, sweat beading on his forehead. "No worries."

"Why don't we just fly her, sir?"

"That's what the COB asked yesterday when I came up with this procedure." Weaver took the first steps very slowly, pulling one boot free from the magnetic grip it had on the ship's hull and then allowing it to *kachunk* back down.

"So, what did you tell the COB, sir?"

"'Cause if the ACS software isn't just right, or the thrusters misfire, or any number of things happen, we don't want to take the chance of bumping the mirror into the ship. We get it to the top of the sail, push it away from the ship and let it drift away slowly. If we are at the top of the sail it is less likely to hit anything else. That is sort of standard operating procedure for deep space probes: launch 'em and check them out right after they clear away from the launch vehicle. If we find that there is some software problem we have the whole long trip to the deep space destination to fix it. It's better than waiting till you get there to figure out that you've got a problem."

"Makes sense, sir."

Bill focused on making his steps slow and continuous and if he ever felt the slightest tug backwards from Gants walking slower he would pause in place until the pressure went away. Bill liked that level of mental and physical unity and focus. Lately it had all been paperwork and murky personnel problems. This sort of zen state had been hard to find and he'd missed it.

The trek across the hull of the ship and to the top of the sail while carrying an extremely fragile, highly reflective laser relay mirror seemed to take an eternity, but they finally made it.

"Ready for the maiden voyage of the Frumious Bandersnatch," Bill laughed.

"The Death Star has cleared the planet. I repeat the Death Star has cleared the planet," Gants added as the giant optic floated into space away from the *Vorpal Blade II*.

"So you are saying that Miss Moon isn't perfect?" the CO asked as Captain Weaver entered the conn.

"I never said she was, sir. Not her fault, though. The ACS algorithms were based on a *model* of the mirror system.

A rough model. We didn't take a lot of time going from CAD to dynamics modeling. So when we turned the thrusters on, the thing got itself in an off-nominal flight condition and that is why it went into the wild spin." Weaver sat down at the control station and exhaled slowly. "I half expected something like this."

"And you are certain it is all under control now?"

"Fairly so, sir. The spin actually gave the genetic algorithm Miriam generated what it needed to learn how to control the thrusters and steer the mirror. We should test the thing a time or two before we put anybody or dragonflies out there in front of it with lasers going though."

"Indeed."

"The Death Star has cleared the planet," Berg muttered to himself as the dragonflies took up a ring formation larger in diameter than the rock behind them and pointed in the direction toward the large mirror floating in space fifty meters in front of them.

"What was that, Lieutenant?" the colonel asked.

"Nothing, ma'am," Berg said. "Whenever you are ready."

Berg had been up for two days just doing the planning and rehearsal on this operation. Even the first test had moved the asteroid, slightly, so it was going to have to be stabilized. The only way to do that was with Marines "holding" it with rock spikes, which would put the Marines in the area of laser fire.

Berg had been a big reader of SF back before he joined the Marines. And he couldn't help but think about how blithely the old time SF guys talked about "asteroid mining" as if it was going to be the easiest damned thing in the universe. *Grappers*.

Safety drills, emergency drills, operational techniques: the operations order on this mining op looked like a battalion night attack and was just about as complicated. And the entire thing had come down on the vac boss. It was a good thing he'd caught up on his homework.

The ship had been moved back because the mirror and dragonfly combination had only been tested with one dragonfly and it was unknown if the mirror could withstand all of them firing together. Weaver and Miriam both agreed that the math looked good, but sometimes experiments didn't follow the math. For all they knew, the entire assembly was going to go sky high as soon as the dragonflies opened fire. A possibility that had been built into the operations order.

Colonel Che-chee opened fire first, then the other dragonflies in turn, one at a time, with a twenty second pause between each to make certain that the mirror was going to withstand the heat.

"EVA, cooling system is compensating for the heat well," Weaver looked at some readouts on his console back on the *Blade*. "Clear to add the next beam, Two-Gun," he transmitted to the lieutenant.

"Conn EVA, add next beam, aye," Berg said, looking at his controls. The thruster system on the Death Star, as it had come to be known to all, had been designed to allow remote adjustment of beam from the *Blade*. Since the cut was the most dangerous part of the mission, Berg had taken the responsibility on himself. He knew that at some level he'd chosen to "do the door," but he also knew that other than Commander Weaver he was the one most qualified. He started drawing the beam across the narrowest point of the rock, the beam slicing deep into the refractory metal of the nickel-iron asteroid.

"EVA, Conn. Cease fire. Target is shifting."

"Cease fire, aye, Conn," Berg said. "Colonel, cease fire. Team Four, realign this rock back to initial position."

Prior planning prevents piss poor performance, Berg thought. *So far, so good.*

". . . Sir, we are just having to realign after about every minute or so of firing. This will take too long if we have to do that," Berg said.

"Wait one, Two-Gun. We're working a fix."

If Captain Weaver was on the problem he'd figure it out, Berg thought. After ten minutes of sitting patiently though, he was beginning to wonder.

"EVA, Conn. Two-Gun, the problem should be fixed as long as you keep a Wyvern at three circumferential points about the target. One at twelve, four and eight o'clock and I'm taking remote control of their thrusters, got it?"

"Wyvern at twelve, four, and eight, aye, sir." Berg ordered the reorientation of the Wyverns. "Remote control, aye. Colonel, let's try this again if you please."

This time the beam tracked flawlessly where Berg pointed it and he did not have to worry about the motion of the rock in space. Somehow the BMG was tracking with the body as it moved from being blasted by the focused laser beams.

❈   ❈   ❈

It took nearly two days of hard work to cut up the asteroid into "head-sized chunks." Two days while most of the company cycled in and out of the ship, the machinists manning the fabber had regular breaks and Berg ended up having none at all. Space was an unforgiving bitch and it was up to the vac boss to make sure that everyone remembered that. Berg was constantly moving from the cutting areas, where Marines unfamiliar with the power of the melders nearly ended up breaching their suits, to the airlocks where tired and logy Marines were less-than-careful with their seal protocols. He had to constantly figure trajectories and power for the various Marines moving the rocks, keep rocks from hitting other Marines and, most especially, ensure that nobody got in the way of the cutting laser, which would slice through a Wyvern like a sushi chef through fresh tuna.

But in two days, instead of two weeks or two months, Sub Dude straightened up with a chunk of silvery metal in his suit-gloved hand.

"That's it," the machinist said, turning it back and forth. "That's five kilos of purest osmium."

"Right," Berg said, sighing in relief and looking around. The dragonflies were still at it, cutting carefully into a car-sized chunk stabilized by three very nervous Marines. More Marines were cutting the smaller pieces smaller and smaller. But they had what they'd come for.

"All teams," Berg said. "Suspend EVA operations. Marine teams, move back to the ship by the numbers. Team Two, recover the mirror and start breaking it down per procedure. Madame Colonel, your people are your own."

"I think we can make it back to the ship, Lieutenant," the colonel replied. Even with the Hexosehr translator the humor was evident. "We've done it enough at this point."

"Safety first, Colonel," Berg said, surfing over to where four Marines from his own platoon were carefully recovering the large mirror. "Good job, Shingleton," he added as the team leader corrected a hold by one of his people.

It was the most time Berg had spent with his platoon since the voyage started and the necessity of his position had forced him to treat them just like the rest of the company. But the individual members and teams had performed flawlessly, doubtless a result of having the exacting Gunny Juda in charge.

"Thank you, sir," the corporal replied.

Having no clue what an officer said next, Berg surfed off to check on the teams reentering the ship. Guys did the stupidest things in the airlock, it was amazing.

"So that's the Old Man," Dupras said. "'Good job, now get back to work.'"

"What do you want?" Shingleton growled. "A medal? You break this thing and I'll make sure you get a medal: right up your rectum."

"Two-Gun Berg," Lyle said, jumping team frequencies. "Don't cross him or you'll end up in a world of hurt."

"I've never seen him down on the troop level," another Marine chimed in. "Not even in the gym. What's he do all the time?"

"Practices killing people and breaking things,"

Sergeant Corwin said. "So like Sergeant Lurch said, don't cross him. Hell, even Top thinks he walks on water."

"I heard that march to Richmond was his idea," one of the Marines said. His tone was, if anything, respectful. You didn't join Force Recon if you didn't to an extent love pain and there were few things more painful than an eighty mile forced march.

"Wouldn't be surprised," Lyle said. "He's a glutton for punishment."

"Oh, *grapp*," Berg said, collapsing in his bunk. "If I never have to smell the inside of my Wyvern again, it will be too soon."

"Dude, you just oversaw more hours of space-walk than NASA has done in its entire *history*," Lieutenant Morris said. "With *zero* incidents of any note. Hell, NASA has had more seal accidents in less time than you just had under worse conditions! As a second lieutenant, if that right there doesn't get you a walk-on-water evaluation, the CO's just got it in for you."

"He's got it in for me, all right," Eric said. "You're not going to believe this, but . . ."

"What did I tell you, sir?" First Sergeant Powell said.

"You were right, Top," Zanella said. "That kid really *can* walk on water. Jesus. I was just comparing notes. In fewer man-hours, NASA had four times the level of life-threatening incidents. And they never tried to mine an asteroid with jury-rigged alien technology."

"And, of course the penalty for a job well done . . ." First Sergeant Powell said, grinning.

"I told him to have the entire mission report on my desk by the beginning of next watch," the Marine captain said, grinning. "Now, if he can do that, I'll give him an OER that makes him look like Jesus Christ come back to life, rapture and all . . ."

"So," Captain Prael asked, first thing next shift. "When are the guns going to be back up?"

The ship had left the unnamed F type star as soon as the fabber was secured below and was back on the way to the target area. But with the destination less than a week away, and starting to enter potential Dreen territory, the CO wanted to make sure his guns were going to work.

"Oh, they're already up, sir," Weaver said, yawning. "The fabber finished spitting out the last of the critical molycirc an hour ago. We're continuing the run to make sure we have spares in the event of another emergency. And of course we'll need it if we take combat damage; that's not the only place that requires molycirc."

"Wait," the CO said, blinking. "What about the rest of the guns?"

"They were fixed before we even started mining, sir," Bill said. "And you haven't lived until you've seen Miriam in a coverall and four-inch heels, bent over a hatch running molycirc . . ."

"Miss Moon . . ."

"Participated in the reconstruction, sir?" Bill asked. "I think that would be a yes. I had Chief Gestner log her hours and I ended up forcing her to work no more than eighteen hours at a time. I'd say that she probably did about twenty-five percent of the work herself, sir. Chief

Gestner and the Eng agree on that estimate, by the way."

"What, do I have to make an all hands announcement?" Prael asked, throwing his arms up. "Okay, I get it. She's amazing."

"And cute," Bill said, grinning. "Don't forget cute."

"Fine, I want to have her love child," the CO said, shaking his head. "I'll add that to the announcement."

"ALL HANDS, ALL HANDS . . ."

"What the *grapp*?" Chief Gestner said, his eyes wide.

"Hey, Chief," Sub Dude said, clapping him on the shoulder. "Welcome to the Space Navy. Things are different here."

13

"I simply have to get some sleep," Miriam said. "And Tiny won't leave me alone."

"You've been so busy, lately," Red said, sympathetically. "He misses his mommy."

"I know, but he won't go to sleep," Miriam said, her eyes red. "I need to finally get these contacts out. I need to sleep."

"We'll take care of him," Red said.

"No, he'll just come scratching at my door," Miriam said, desperately. "Here," she added, handing the machinist a package with Japanese kanji characters on it. "Give him some of this and he won't leave *you*."

"What is it?" Red asked, looking at it dubiously.

"Japanese catnip," Miriam said, yawning. "He likes it."

"Shiny," Red said, patting her on the shoulder. "Get some sleep."

Miriam finally lay down and closed her eyes, glad to have the dreaded contacts out as well. Unfortunately, she was blind as a bat without either glasses or contacts and she hated doing mechanical work with her glasses on. She needed to get some safety glasses in her prescription, but they looked so dorky and she'd spent too many years being considered an ugly geek . . .

". . . *uncertainty levels within the vacuum fluctuation will interact at causal nodes whereas metric control becomes distorted via . . .*"

"Shhh! Not now, I'm tired." Miriam told the voice. It obediently subsided as her head hit her pillow.

It occurred to her just as sleep enveloped her that she probably should have pointed out to Red that he shouldn't give Tiny *too much* of the Katty-Man, which was to catnip what super-concentrated hash was to marijuana. Even with his size, even *one* of the little silver packages could make him . . .

But by then it was too late.

"Wow, he really likes this stuff," Red said, chuckling.

"He looks really stoned." Sub Dude laughed as the cat flopped over on his side. "How much did you give him?"

"I figured he was big," Red said, shrugging, "so I gave him all four packages."

"He should be out like a—" Gants started to say just as the cat leapt to its feet and let out a howl like a fire-engine. "*Holy grapp!*"

"Catch him!" Red shouted as the cat screamed his way out of the compartment.

"Good luck," Gants replied. "I was not here. I have never *heard* of a giant, stoned, hyperactive catzilla . . ."

※ ※ ※

Space, the final and all that . . .

Four of the main screens in Conn could be set to external view and Captain Prael had to admit that the view was spectacular. But there were still times he pined for the view of the inside of a sub, nothing to see but steel walls and . . .

AND A HOWLING STREAK OF WHITE AT SHOULDER HEIGHT!

"Holy *maulk*!" he shouted, damned near peeing himself in surprise. For just a moment he caught a flash of feline shape at the far end of the Conn and then the thing was out the hatch headed for CIC. "COB, what did I just see?"

"That would be a Savannah, sir."

"Not a white streak that sounds remarkably like the ship breaking up?"

"No, sir!"

"And just what is a Savannah, COB?"

"A cross between a Bengal housecat and a Cervil wildcat, sir. Males are generally docile and have doglike personalities if neutered young. In this case, it would be a Savannah named Titanus. My guess is that somebody gave him too much catnip. I will investigate the phenomenon."

"Are you telling me that someone brought a genetic freak of a housecat onto *my* ship?"

"No, *sir*!" the Chief of Boat replied. "I would be telling you that someone brought a *massively-hyper, sixty-pound* genetic freak of a housecat, nicknamed Tiny, onto your ship, sir. He's for hunting down the chee-hamsters, sir."

"Oh," the CO said then paused. "Chee-hamsters?"

"They're pests, sir. Picked them up the first time we

were on Cheerick when the ship got torn up and we had to set down for repairs. Leave droppings all over, get into the food . . ."

"I've got the picture, COB. Well . . . keep him off the Conn."

"Will do, sir."

"COB, I have another question."

"Sir?"

"What else do I need to know about?" the CO asked carefully. "People covertly visiting Miss Moon to have her read tea leaves and butcher chickens so that this Hexosehr technology will work. And now a monster cat that hunts some rodent I've never heard of. Anything else?"

"Nothing any CO needs to know, sir," the COB replied.

"That was not a No, COB."

"Yes, sir."

Sigh . . .

14

Weaver hit Save and closed the form, then opened the next. But it was the usage estimate on food consumption . . . and he'd already done that one. Copy sent to the CO.

Weekly compilation of maintenance and repairs . . . No, that's done. Sent.

Payroll . . . checked and sent to the CO.

He3 usage estimate . . .

He looked through his to-do list, knowing that there had to be *something* to do. He'd been running around the ship checking on repairs, fixing personnel problems, shouting at cooks and generally killing himself for the last three weeks. There was no way that he was . . .

"Christ," Weaver muttered, running through the list. There wasn't anything to do. He couldn't ask the Eng for the spare parts inventory for at least another two days, there wasn't a single department issue to "mediate" or otherwise deal with . . . "I don't have *anything* to do."

So what did an XO do when he was actually caught up on paperwork? Weaver thought back and decided that what his previous XOs had done was go out and find out what was wrong that *wasn't* getting reported.

Which meant inspecting the entire ship until he found someone's ass to chew.

He might actually find the door to his quarters.

"This is why you've been restricting the cereal ration?" Bill asked, holding up the box of generic breakfast cereal. A hole had been nibbled in the side and the cereal dribbled on the floor of the galley. "I thought you said that it was pilfering?"

"I run a clean galley," Chief Duppstadt said mulishly.

Over two weeks, by daily abuse, Weaver had gotten Duppstadt to raise the quality of food to the level of "edible" if not "pleasant." The reality of Naval regulations was that even the CO could not relieve a chief for simple incompetence unless it was mission threatening. And after looking at Duppstadt's record, Bill figured out why Duppstadt was in the galley; it was the one part of a ship that was not life-threatening. How he had made chief in the first place was the real question. How anyone had let him cook in the sub service, which was normally renowned for the quality of its food, was totally mind-boggling.

But now he had him dead to rights. Bill had asked him in a previous shouting session why he couldn't at least provide cereal to the sailors, spacers, whatever, and the chief had told him, point-blank, that someone was pilfering. Bill had even assigned the Master-At-Arms to investigate.

What he had found, though, going through one of the supply lockers and not-at-all looking for his door, was that rats had been at the food. Rats. In *his* ship. This was what he got for spending so much time doing paperwork. Rats. In *his* ship.

"Chief, rats in the supplies are not a reflection on your galley," Bill said, for once kindly. "If anything, they're a reflection on me. But we need to get them tracked down. Have you set traps?"

"Yes, sir," the chief admitted. "But they don't go for them."

Bill almost made the comment that if the chief was putting his food down as bait he could understand that but refrained.

"How are you baiting them?" Bill asked, biting his lip.

"Leftovers, sir," the chief said. "But they don't seem to be going for them."

Must . . . keep . . . straight . . . face . . .

"Try something different, Chief," Bill said. "I hear oatmeal and peanut butter works. Maybe some cereal. Cheese is, of course, traditional. Perhaps they're not . . ." *Connoisseurs? No that would be ARE connoisseurs . . .* "meat eaters. And what's the point of having a cat if he's not catching the rats?"

"Won't have that filthy beast in my galley, sir," the Chief said, stoutly. "Won't have it. Filthy things, cats. Lick their own butts."

"Well, we need to get rid of them," Bill said. "We only have so much food."

He considered the problem, then shrugged.

"They can't be hiding in the walls. They have to be in the compartments. I'll get some hands down here to turn out the foodstocks and try to find them. And . . . where the food is stored away from the kitchen I'll have Tiny participate. Maybe he can catch some of them."

"Okay, this is *maulk*," Sub Dude said, picking up the case of cans. "We're rat-catchers, now?"

"Orders is orders," Red said, picking up two cases with his Number Four lifting arm. "And I don't want to be eating rat droppings."

"Well, I don't think there are any . . ." Gants said, then jumped back as a purple blur went past his feet. "What in the *grapp* was that?"

Tiny, though, had pounced at once, slipped a paw into a narrow crack between two boxes and fished out the creature. He flipped it out into the corridor and then chased after it.

"That wasn't no rat," Red said, following the cat. "Tiny, bring!"

The cat caught the little beast and ran over, dropping it at the machinist's feet. But as soon as the thing hit the ground it took off, fast, faster than any rat the two had ever seen. Red never even got a good look. Tiny pounced again and brought it back over, holding the squirming thing out in his jaws.

"What the *grapp* is that?" Gants asked, his voice hushed.

It didn't actually look like a rat, more like a purple crab or spider.

"I'm not touching that thing," Gants added, backing up.

"I got it," Red said, grabbing it with his number four arm and squeezing slightly. The shell of the thing cracked and it went limp. "I think we need to report this, though."

※ ※ ※

"What in the hell is *that*?" Weaver asked, holding up the plastic bag containing the body of the spider-thing.

"Chee-hamster, isn't it, sir?" the Eng asked.

"Chee-hamsters are more yellowish," Bill said. "And furry. This looks sort of like a crabpus. But not really. I'm not sure *what* it is."

"Well, it's what's been getting into the chow, sir," the Eng said. "Once they got to moving boxes, Tiny caught two more."

"Sir, if I may," Red interjected. "Tiny obviously recognized them; he chased them like he knew what he was doing. I think he's been chasing them for some time."

"What this *is*, is a quarantine violation," Bill said, sighing. "That means we're all in quarantine when we get back unless we can determine that it's from a nonthreatening biosphere. And since we don't know *where* it came from . . . Hell, just when we need a biologist . . ."

"Miss Moon?"

"Forensics isn't biology," Miriam said, looking at the thing in the bag. "Cute, though."

"They're getting in the food," Bill said. "And we need to know where they came from; Colonel Che-chee didn't recognize it. If they're from an unknown biosphere, we're all in quarantine for thirty days when we get back."

"That wouldn't make me happy," Miriam said. "Well, I've got the whole bio lab just sitting there. I guess I'll use it. If Tiny catches any more that live, save them for me."

"Successfully adjusted to system HD 242896."

The *Blade* had stopped in deep space, done a complete weapons and sensors check and chilled. This was potential Dreen territory; if the enemy was present the CO wanted the option to either fight or run as seemed most prudent.

"Sensor sweep," the CO said, holding down his position in CIC. Lieutenant Fey had the Conn with Captain Weaver at the secondary Conn in Damage Control near Engineering.

"No unusual particle emissions," the TACO said after a moment. "All nominal for an FV9 star."

"Conn, make course for the referenced Jovian," the CO said.

"We'll have to find it first, sir," Lieutenant Fey replied over the comm. "We weren't actually given its trajectory by the Hexosehr. Doing a planetary sweep at the moment. Permission to take the ship into the edge of the warp denial zone. We can sweep better from in near the star."

"Move her in, Conn," the CO said, his face blank. Item One on his report: The Navy needed a better class for COs of spaceships. "TACO, any sign of Dreen?"

"No sign of any other ships in the system, sir," the TACO replied. "No neutrino or quark emissions over nominal for the star."

"Stand down to Condition Two," the CO said. "Captain Weaver to the CIC."

"The best way to find the planets is still reflectance, sir," Bill said, looking at the information starting to come up on CIC's monitors. "The telescopes spot them automatically. We can get some from gravitic anomalies and standard astronomical distances. But mostly we have to just look, so looking with the sun behind us works better. The first time around we had a heck of a time but we learned from it and the algorithms are better, now. But we won't be seeing anything on the other side of the sun, obviously."

"CIC, Conn. We have the indicated Jovian spotted as well as two more Jovians, one super-Jovian and two rocky planets."

"Head for the indicated Jovian," the CO replied. "We'll do a sweep of the other side of the sun after checking it out."

"I'm not spotting any other installations in orbit," Lieutenant Fey said. "And the Hexosehr buried the other one."

"Wonder if it's still down there," Bill said, gesturing with his chin in the direction of the Jovian. "Be funny if it's sitting down on the metallic hydrogen bottom."

"Metallic hydrogen?" Prael said. "Oh, yeah. The egghead said something about that. How do you get metal out of hydrogen?"

"Lots of pressure, sir," Bill replied. "You've had chemistry, sir. Three states of matter."

"Solid, liquid, gas," Prael said. "Four with ions."

"Yes, sir," Bill said. "Ice is solid water, fog is gas and, well, water is liquid. Any material known has, potentially, all three states. But for you to get solid hydrogen requires sufficient pressure, say the pressure of the gravitational force of a gas-giant, pressing the hydrogen atoms together until they're a solid. Nominally, due to their configuration and position on the periodic table, a metal. Metallic hydrogen."

"Got it," Prael said then paused. "Let me guess. If the pressure gets higher, say more mass . . ."

"Then you pass the pressure threshold of the material, bits of hydrogen start to fuse and you have a star," Bill finished. "Super-massive Jovians, there's one in this system, are very close to stars. The pressure is so high that it generates some internal kinetic energy so they're not actually as cold as they should be for their position in the system. There's a theory that you could find some bodies that are right on the edge of both, sort of fusing but not really willing to be a star. Those are one class of white dwarf."

"And so much of the planetology lecture of the day," the CO said. "Plan."

"We'll approach to low ball-and-string orbit on each of the rocky planets and major moons," Bill said. "From there we can do a ground-penetrating radar sweep as well as a computerized visual sweep. Both will be looking for straight lines. They don't tend to form in nature but civilizations always seem to have them. If we find one, we'll consider the imagery and try to determine if it's an artifact or just an anomaly. If we think it's an artifact, we land and deploy the Marines."

"And who is the 'we' who are checking on the hits?" the CO asked.

"The intel section has an imagery specialist, sir," the XO reminded him. "He'll check them."

"Oh My God."

Julio Plumber hadn't been quite sure what an "imagery analyst" was when he signed up, but he By God learned in

A School. It was a guy who was going to go blind, early, from looking at satellite shots. When, rarely, satellite shots were shown to the media they were always carefully labeled and the clearest shots possible. The media didn't get the shots that were just a blur of movement or a shadow that might be a rocket launcher and might just be, well, a shadow.

And they sure as hell didn't get one hit every ten seconds of various rock formations.

"Chief, I'm getting swamped here," Plumber squeaked. "I could look at this stuff for the rest of my natural life and not catch up."

"What you got?" the chief asked, looking over his shoulder at the oversized monitor.

"*Chither*," Plumber said exasperatedly. "I don't care what anybody says, you get straight lines in nature. I got ridges, lots of ridges, I got recently cracked boulders. I got landslides. I got a couple of things I don't know what they are but they're not ruins I'll tell you that. And I got more than I can look at in a million years."

"I'll bump it up," the chief said with a sigh. That meant to the XO. "Makin' bricks without straw."

"That's the Navy way, Chief."

Miriam was not a biologist, but she could hum the tune and do a few of the dance steps.

Fortunately, the *Blade*'s biology department was as automated and modern as anything on Earth. There were many benefits to information technology and automation, but they all came down to the word "productivity." Since it was anticipated that the *Blade* was going to be doing major science missions—an anticipation that had mostly been unrealized—and given that the maximum number of science crew was restricted, making the science section as productive as possible had been the goal.

Thus, rather than slow and tedious "wet" chemical analysis, a full chemical work-up could be obtained by sliding a small sample into a chamber. Molecular Resonance Imaging, gaseous chromatographic structuring and even atomic level X-ray analysis was automatic. Pop in the sample, wait twenty minutes and you had a full description of every molecule in the sample, complete with three-dimensional topology. The device was state-of-the-art, very capable and, because it was in the *Blade*, very small. It was, thus, very very expensive. "No expense spared."

Knowing what you were looking at, though, was something else.

But before any of that, Miriam could start on the one part she really knew: Dissection.

"It's not a spider," Miriam muttered.

"Would you like to record this analysis session?"

One part of the bio section Miriam did *not* care for was the new Vocal Interactive Network. Vinnie was a pain in the ass unless you turned him all the way off. He wasn't an AI, just a bloody "smart" program, but the programmers had tried to make him as much like an artificial intelligence as possible. Which just meant he was a revolving busybody.

"Vinnie, leave me alone," Miriam said, pinning down the carapace of the alien bug.

"Procedure 419 dash 587 dash 326 Delta indicates a preference for recording of all analysis sessions."

"I know that," Miriam said. "I don't want to talk to you right now, Vinnie. Go away."

"Recommend initiate procedure 419 dash 587 dash 326 Delta."

"Shut up, Vinnie," Miriam said, positioning the laser scalpel.

"Procedure 419 dash 587 dash 326 Delta is highly recommended but can be overridden by following procedure 876 dash 239 dash 12540 Alpha. Do you wish to initiate procedure 876 dash 239 dash 12540 Alpha?"

"Oh, God!" Miriam snapped. "Okay, okay! Vinnie, initiate procedure 419 dash 587 dash 326 Delta recording of analysis session!" The alternative was a five minute procedure required to turn the damned thing *off*.

"Initiating procedure 419 dash 587 dash 326 Delta," the program responded happily. "Full audio and video. Please maintain running commentary for thoroughness. Beginning Procedure. Step One: Ensure quarantine of biological specimen."

"Quarantine ensured," Miriam said.

"Analysis indicates that specimen is not in quarantine zone. Ensure quarantine of biological specimen."

"Skip," Miriam said. "Quarantine breached."

"Quarantine breach logged and noted," the program replied as blast doors slammed down. "Quarantine field activated in science section. Quarantine breach report sent to Ops. Step Two: Ensure safety of session personnel. List materials used in session."

"Laser scalpel," Miriam said with a sigh. "Pins. Probes."

"List by stock number," Vinnie said, primly. "Item one:

Laser scalpel. Two possible systems. Item One: Bogdan Slicer Laser Scalpel, Federal Stock Number . . ."

Miriam got up from her stool, placed the arachnoid in the refrigerator, then walked to one of the computer stations. Sitting down, she cracked her fingers and started typing.

Three minutes were required to hack into the administrator permissions on the mainframe. Another ten seconds were required to find the core of Vinnie's program. The voice in the background, which was still requesting information, shut off abruptly. It took about an hour to reverse engineer the program, find the appropriate sections, rewrite them, then recompile and debug. There weren't any bugs.

"Vinnie, this is Miriam Moon, Ship's Linguist," Miriam said, standing up and going back over to the refrigerator.

"Yes, Mistress," the program replied in a deep Transylvanian accent.

"I'd like you to record this dissection session and record any results from the analysis of this organism," Miriam said.

"Yes, O Great One."

"Oh, and drop the quarantine restrictions," Miriam said. "These things are all over the ship."

"It shall be done."

"Begin recording," Miriam said, laying out the creature. "Analysis of aterrestrial organism tentatively designated *astroarachno titanus* common name Tiny's Space Spider. Creature is approximately ten centimeters from mandibles to tip of carapace. Exoskeleton color is purple shading to red in places. There are two eyes and a complex but truncated set of antennae. Creature has ten tri-segmented legs and two scorpionlike claws, each claw approximately three centimeters in length. Claws overlap, indicating cutting ability. Body is multisegmented and doesn't conform to arachnid body type. The carapace is flexible." She drove pins through the edge of the carapace and slid a laser scalpel down the center, just opening up the abdomen.

"Space Spider has book lungs with closure points on exterior. Removing sample of internal fluids for analysis."

She sucked up a bit of the fluid with a pipette and carried it to the analysis chamber.

"Begin analysis of internal fluids," she said, shooting the sample into a chamber.

"By Your Command!"

15

"I would have sworn this algorithm was good," Bill said, looking at the results. "Hang on."

He brought up an underlying subprogram and ran a validation on some of the matches.

"See, this ridge shows as a valid match," Bill said, shrugging. The ridge was now outlined with a purple shape that shaded to light blue. "Seventy percent positive. I can bump the stat up but then who knows what we'll miss? At ninety percent the system misses the Great Wall of China."

"Which mostly ain't straight, sir," the chief pointed out.

"Which is why it doesn't just look for straight lines, Chief," Bill replied tightly. "We're going to have to do an eyeball sort. That's all there is for it."

"Sir, I've only got two eyeballs," the imagery specialist pointed out. "I'm just glancing at most of this stuff, but . . ."

"We'll have to get more eyeballs on it."

"Captain Weaver to Biology Lab," the 1-MC bellowed. "XO to Biology Lab."

"Get the Marines on it," Bill said. "They're just sitting there."

"So what you're going to be looking at," Eric said to the assembled platoon, "is stuff from the scopes. Most of it's going to be ridgelines, rivers, stuff like that. But if you see anything that looks strange, kick it to me. If I agree, I'll kick it up to the specialists. Try to use your brains, but let me make the final determination. Queries?"

"Sir?" Lance Corporal Wagner said, raising his hand. "Are we going to land on this planet?"

"Not unless we find something worth checking out," Eric replied. "So hit the bunks; we're going to be at this for a while."

"That was quick," Bill said, walking into the lab.

Miriam had the space spider laid out on a dissection table and was peering at a screen filled with chemical and biological notations.

"I thought you'd like to know what we were dealing with as soon as possible," Miriam said. "But you might have to figure it out."

"Why?"

"Because I don't know if I'm figuring any of this out right," Miriam admitted. "Some of it's certain. This is a Class Four biology."

"That's Dreen," Bill said, blanching.

"I said it was Class Four," Miriam replied. "I didn't say Dreen. It's not Dreen. I don't know where it's from. It's more like Nitch. The only thing that I can find that's close to the *design* is Nitch but they're Class Three. Alien unknown organism."

"Great, we're in quarantine for sure," Bill said, sighing.

"Maybe, maybe not," Miriam said, pointing to one of the biological readings. "There are no, and I repeat no, microorganisms in this thing that have any important effect on Class One biologies. So there's no chance of us catching an alien space plague from it. The real biologists on Earth will have to double-check me on that, but this thing is the cleanest organism I've ever seen."

"Not following," Bill admitted.

"Okay," Miriam said, sighing. "You have any clue how many viruses you're carrying around right now?"

"None as far as I know," Bill said. "I'm not sick."

"Thousands," Miriam replied. "And I'm not talking about individual bodies. I'm talking about *species* of viruses. Most of them have, apparently, no effect. Some of them might even be doing good things; scientists still aren't sure about a lot of them. Then there's your gut, which is packed with E. coli. Most . . . poop is actually E. coli bodies. Human beings are so chock full of little germs and bacteria and viruses and stuff that it's surprising we have room for the muscle and stuff."

"Didn't know that," Bill admitted. "But this thing?"

"It has four viroids," Miriam said. "Best I can do on naming them. They're not anything like our viruses. Class Four doesn't even use DNA for one thing; it uses third juncture structures, closer to proteins, for genetic replication. The best description is that these are little packets that reproduce, but they can only reproduce on

Class Four biologies and if I'm reading this right they're some sort of enzyme producer that only attacks certain chemical structures. I don't know what the chemical structures are, but they're not human or other terrestrial proteins."

"It was eating my cereal," Bill said.

"Getting to that," Miriam replied. "It has some more stuff in its gut. Not just its equivalent of E. coli but some bacteria-*like* organisms. Closer in organization to Archaea but, again, using Class Four structures. Six of them. *One* of them can break down terrestrial sugars. You know how you can eat Adar food and not get fat?"

"Been on the Adar diet for a long time," Bill said.

"Well, these can break down our sugars and convert them into its version of ATP," Miriam said. "Badly. They can barely sustain themselves and it seems to release secondary materials that appear toxic."

"So if they eat too much they die?" Bill asked.

"I'm not sure they die," Miriam said. "I think they just don't enjoy the experience much. I tested the toxins on some of the neurons that were still functional. The response, if I'm reading this right, looked like a pain response."

"That's . . ."

"Weird, I know," Miriam said. "But it looks as if this thing would have little or no interest in, for example, entering terrestrial biologies and ripping them apart. If I'm reading all this right, it would find it actively unpleasant to try."

"That's good to hear," Bill said.

"Yup," Miriam said. "I even tried it on Adar food and

got the same responses. I don't have any Class Four biological material to test it on, so I don't know what it would do to a Class Four biology. But all the biologies that we're . . . friendly with don't seem at risk."

"All good news," Bill said, letting out a sigh. "I was really sweating quarantine."

"And you might, still," Miriam said, looking at the enigma on the dissection table.

"But you said . . ."

"I haven't gotten to the really good part," Miriam said, waving the XO over to the table. She picked up a probe and spread the carapace, using the probe to point to a bit of purple stuff.

"What am I looking at?" Bill asked.

"Reproductive organs," Miriam replied. "Here, here, here, here, here . . ."

"Uhmmm . . ."

"No," Miriam said. "That's not normal either. And all of them had some formed embryos in them. I'm not sure if they were dead or just . . . hibernating. Some of them seemed to be active for a short time. But this thing looks as if it's supposed to breed faster than . . . Well, a hamster would go 'Whoa!' And they're parthenogenic. Which means . . ."

"They don't need other spiders to breed," Bill said, breathing deep. "*One* of these things could . . ."

"Wipe out a world," Miriam finished.

"I need a bottomline here, people," Prael said, trying not to look at the linguist. He recognized, now, that he needed her. It didn't mean he had to like it.

"I don't think we can give one, sir," Bill replied. "Miss Moon is not a biologist."

"I've discussed the findings with Dr. Chet," Miriam said. "He's confirmed everything I found and does not consider them a threat. But it will be up to the science team on Earth to concur."

"We've caught four more," Bill said. "Miriam."

"They've been given various Earth and Adar foods," Miriam said. "Some of those are compatible with the Hexosehr. The only thing they'll eat of Earth foods is cereal. They avoid the sugary ones, going for the blandest stuff we stock. And even then they don't like it."

"Put a big pile in the cage and they'll go over from time to time, nibble on it, then lie down," Bill said.

"And I was able to confirm that it's painful for them to eat," Miriam said. "They only do it to survive, poor things. I wish I had some Class Four biologicals to feed them."

"I'd prefer that we keep their numbers *down*, Miss Moon," the CO said. "They are still a huge potential biological hazard. Anything else?"

"They hibernate in vacuum," Miriam said. "When exposed all their external openings close tight and they curl up. Their carapace is remarkably resistant to exfiltration. I don't know how long they can maintain it, but I've put them in hard vacuum for fifteen hours and revived them. At this point, it's how I'm storing them."

"So we can't even kill them by evacuating the ship," the CO said grumpily. "Where did they *come* from? Cheerick?"

"No, sir," Bill said. "No way they came from Cheerick."

"I think it was my fault," Miriam admitted.

"How?" the CO asked.

"The asteroid mining," Miriam said. "I think these things can last a long time in vacuum. Maybe for years or even centuries. There was probably one sitting on the asteroid. Who would have noticed?"

"Uh," Bill said, shaking his head. "I think there's a more probable explanation, if that's the case."

"Go," the CO said.

"Last mission we got some material from a comet. We really didn't use any quarantine procedures since what could you get from a comet?"

"Oh, yeah," Miriam said happily. "I wouldn't be surprised if they could get some nutrition even from comet ice. There's a hint of complex organics in it! Wow! Glad it's not *my* fault."

"So am I, Miss Moon," Prael said, gritting his teeth. "But to get back on point. This does not appear to be a threat to the ship?"

"No, sir," Bill said. "Not to us. But they're a threat to *somebody*."

"How's that, XO?" the CO asked.

"Gotta make a *Star Trek* reference, sir," Bill said, grinning faintly.

"I'll survive," the CO replied.

"If they got the right food, they're worse than tribbles. Tribbles didn't have claws that catch."

"Nada, CO," Bill said. They'd been at the process for a week, checking out all of the rocky planets and the bigger moons, even if they were outside the standard life-zone. "The only thing that seems to be in this system was that installation the Hexosehr trashed."

"So we keep looking," the CO said. "Suggestions? Astro?"

"HD 243170 is a G0 type star, very similar to Sol in other words, about four light-years away. That would be my next suggestion."

"XO?" the CO asked.

"Concur," Bill said. "Main sequence stars have longer life-zone periods than any other type of star. Theoretically, they're the most likely to have developed life. My only query is about that point. We're looking for a star-spanning species; they could be anywhere."

"In which case HD 243170 is also the closest star," Lieutenant Fey pointed out.

"Which was why I concurred," Bill said, shrugging. "We're just going to have to start from here and expand out. It's going to be slooooow . . ."

"Oh God," Berg moaned. "I can't believe I'm longing for some nice exciting paperwork."

The guys in the platoons had been told to send *anything* that might be an anomaly on to their chain-of-command. Then they'd been told to send stuff that only really looked like an anomaly. Which meant that Berg was only getting a file every minute or so. He was currently looking at a suspicious hill, if by "suspicious" you meant looking remarkably like Little Round-Top, tree-cover included.

The nice thing about this shot, admittedly, was that the *Blade* had finally found an apparently uninhabited planet that looked remarkably like Earth must have prior to the advent of civilization. The closest possible magnification even showed trees that looked like . . . well, trees. Broad-leafed, coniferous . . . If there was ever an Earth Two, it was the planet they were currently surveying.

"I know what you mean, man," Lieutenant Morris said. "I wish just one of . . ."

"One of what?" Eric asked, pulling up the next shot. This one, he had to admit, was interesting. It looked sort of like . . .

"Eric," Morris said in a strangled voice.

"I think I've got . . ."

"I don't *think*," Lieutenant Morris said. "I *know*."

"Calling that thing a ruin is a bit of an understatement," Captain Prael said, whistling faintly. "That's a . . . A . . ."

"That would be a city, sir," Weaver said, looking at the zoomed back shot of the area. "A big one. And it's not the first one we've spotted, just the largest to date."

It was hard to tell that the collection of odd-shaped mounds was a city unless you looked at the penetrating radar. When those shots had been pieced together, it was apparent that buried under about forty feet of silt and loess was a massive urban region approximately thirty miles across. The larger mounds were piles of rubble from immense buildings over a kilometer across at the base. Foundations for lesser buildings could be seen stretching out from those megastructures.

The ocean was now well away from the structures but the city might have once rested at a seaside. One side certainly had that terminal look. That meant that the planet had, probably, been warmer given that in twenty million years a sun tended to cool, slightly. The planet currently had extensive icecaps which might have been liquid in that earlier time.

"Do you think it's their home planet?" the CO asked.

"Sir, I wouldn't begin to venture a clue," Bill replied. "We don't know what these guys looked like, how they lived, what they ate or what happened to them. But the point is, we're looking at a ruined *planet*. One that has more territory than we can effectively survey just in this one shot. And one, by the way, that's perfect for humans as far as I can tell. Gravity's slightly lower, oxygen's a tad higher. It's actually paradisical."

"You just said a big word, XO."

"Sorry, sir."

"Gravity's lower?" the CO said. "The *Blade*'s gravity is . . ."

"Even lower than that, sir," Bill replied. "If we assume that they would design a drive that gave the same gravity as their home planet, sir, it actually mitigates against this being it."

"I wonder what their home planet looks like, then," the CO said.

"If we ever find it, it will be interesting."

"The majority of the ruins are under forty feet of soil," Captain Zanella said. "Which means we are not going to be digging; that's way too much to move. What we are going to do is look for any surface remnants we might find. Platoons will cover their designated search boxes and we'll keep it up until we find something or Captain Prael calls off the search."

❈   ❈   ❈

"Remember that scene in *Star Wars* where they're chasing each other on those bike things?" Dupras said, weaving his board around a massive broad-leafed tree.

The area where the city had once been was covered in trees. They looked somewhat like hemlocks but rose nearly ninety feet off the loam-covered forest-floor. Over the external sensors could be heard the sound of birdlike creatures fighting for territory, calling for mates. A deep, rumbling croak like from a frog the size of a mastadon occasionally echoed through the woods. Nobody had spotted the source, but there were various bets on what it was going to look like.

"Yeah," Staff Sergeant Carr said as they came to a large stream and started to parallel it. "And I remember them crashing a lot. So be careful."

"I'm being careful, Staff Sergeant," Dupras said, sliding around another tree. "I'm being so careful I'm the model of carefulness. But I gotta say, I wish this was as far as we were going. This place is great. Gotta get rid of some of the trees, though."

"Yeah, I don't get all the trees," Lance Corporal Rucker interjected. "Where are the fields? It's just, like, trees for miles and miles and miles. I was looking at the shots and I didn't see one open area in this whole part of the continent."

"The whole eastern seaboard used to be covered in trees," Sergeant Bae, the Bravo Team leader, answered. "It's been clear cut at least five times since you Westerners arrived. Ecologically destructive bastards."

"And the Chinese aren't?" Carr replied, grinning.

"Oh, hell, so was China until we clear cut it," the

sergeant replied. "But that was thousands of years ago, not hundreds, so it's all shiny."

"Staff Sergeant?" Dupras said, suddenly. "I'm sorry to interrupt your wrangling like an old married couple, but I think you need to see this."

"It's some sort of support member for one of the buildings," Eric said, looking at the shots from the portable ground penetrator. The meter-square box didn't have the power of the radar on the *Blade* so it only revealed structures down twenty feet or so. The member faded into the depths well below that.

The part that extended above ground, jutting out of the stream like a transluscent rock, looked like a log made of glass. It was apparently untouched by the elements, about a foot across and the portion that could be sounded for was at least forty feet long. It was a jutting enigma, a relic of a race gone for so long that their most massive works were buried under the dirt and silt of millennia, with only this glassine remnant whispering: *We were here.*

"My name is Ozymandias," Gunny Judas said.

"Sorry, Gunny?" Eric replied. "What was that?"

"I barely recall, sir," the Gunny said. "Something I learned in school. A poem about a ruin in Egypt. The only part I can remember is the part that goes something like: My name is Ozymandias. Look upon me ye mighty and despair. But the statue it's about was ruined and faded by time."

"Habitable planet and all those ruins right in the line of Dreen advance," Captain Prael pointed out sourly. "But we found nada of any use so we're done here. We'll leave it to generations of archaeologists if the Dreen don't trash it. Next?"

"HD 242647," Lieutenant Fey said. "G2 class star, just short of nine light-years away."

"XO?"

Bill looked at the star map pensively, then shrugged.

"Technically, Astro is right," Bill said, frowning.

"But . . . ?" the CO asked.

"But I'm wondering if we should bet on the ponies, sir," Bill said. "The *Blade*'s engine was found on the rocky planet of an F type star and so are two other facilities that are believed to be from the same race. Another, though, is on the sole rocky planet of a B, a blue star. Okay, so this *city* is around a G class. But all the stuff we've found that's *useful* has been around other classes."

"And . . . ?"

"HD 34547 is a blue seventeen light-years from here," Bill said. "If I'm wrong, I'm wrong and we blew a survey. But my point is that it's *not* a G class star."

"Whoa," the sensor tech said as the ship exited the heliopause. "TACO!"

"We're getting major readings, sir," the TACO said, pointing at the display.

"Hmmm . . ." Captain Prael said. "Dreen?"

"They don't match the Dreen readings we have, sir," the TACO said, shaking his head. "And they're way off the scale. If that's a Dreen ship, sir, it's the size of a *moon*."

"Got this triangulated, yet?" the CO asked cautiously.

"Right in by the star, sir," the sensor tech answered. "Less than one AU. Inside the warp-denial bubble."

Sufficient gravity caused the ship's warp drive to refuse to work. For Sol the warp-denial point was between the orbits of Mercury and Venus. For this more massive star, it was at nearly one astronomical unit, the distance from Earth to Sol. However, the surface temperature of a planet at that distance would be closer to Mercury's. Whatever was generating the energy was relatively close to the blue-white star.

"Actually, sir," the tactical officer continued, looking at the readings, "it appears to be in a non-Keplerian orbit. Not even that, it looks like it's just *sitting* over the star, directly out of the plane of elliptic."

"Well, we're here to find stuff from that race," the CO said. "Makes sense that it would be something that was big and put out a lot of particles. So we check it out. We have a visual, yet?"

"There's a flicker there," the TACO said, zooming in the scope. "There's something there, but *what* is the question. We'll just need to get closer."

"Conn, CIC . . ."

"Whoa," Bill said, looking at the swelling image on the screen. "That looks like . . ."

"The world's biggest Christmas tree," Prael finished.

The ten-kilometer object was tapered like a fir, either made of glass or some similarly translucent material and colored in wild shades of red, purple and green. Different "branches" were different colors and either were pulsing or picking up refractions from the blue star. The base of the "trunk," and there did appear to be an extension, was pointed towards the star with the tapered "top" pointed into deep space. And it was, in fact, just *sitting* at the absolute north pole of the star.

"Distance to object?" the CO asked.

"Three AU," the TACO said.

"Sir, recommend . . ." Weaver started to say.

"Conn, CIC," the CO said. "Hold it right here. Way ahead of you, Captain Weaver. We don't know what that thing is or what it does and I'm not getting any closer until we do."

"It's pretty, I'll give it that," Prael said.

The *Blade* had moved around the system getting images of the giant "tree." There was, indeed, a section of "trunk" on the inner side. Temperatures in that region should be nearly four hundred degrees Celsius on the surface. However . . .

"And weird," Bill said. "I don't believe these readings. Nowhere on the surface, including on the side pointed to the star, does the surface temperature get above a hundred degrees Celsius."

"Conn, Astro."

"Go," the CO said.

"We've got another anomaly and you're not going to believe this one . . ."

16

"Oh, now that's just too rich," Bill said, shaking his head at the planetology monitor.

The ship had not lifted with a full science complement, but it had brought some specialty personnel. Astroman Darryl Figueredo was an astronomy-mate, once one of the most obscure members of the Navy's wide-flung bureaucracy. Since man had gone to sea the stars had guided him and even with the advent of GPS the Navy had continued the tradition of teaching stellar navigation. Stars changed position ever so slightly on a constant basis which was why the Naval Observatory put out constantly updated tables detailing how to use *their* current position to find a *ship's* current position. Somebody had to do the viewing, the calculating and fill out the paperwork. Since that was what enlisted men were for, the Navy had an insignificant number of enlisted people with just that specialty.

With the abrupt shift to a space Navy, the specialty had become far more important. However, there were still only a handful of astronomy-mates in the Navy. The school was being ramped up, but in the meantime . . .

Darryl pushed his glasses back up his nose and shrugged.

"Sir, I just find the stuff," the astronomy-mate said. With gray-green eyes and chocolate brown skin, Darryl was a second-generation Dominican and still retained a trace of his family's islands accent. But since he had also been the captain of his school's astronomy club, getting this job was a dream-come-true. Admittedly, if he had his druthers he'd have been doing it from a nice safe observatory on Earth, but you went where the Navy sent you. "It's up to somebody else to figure it out."

So far the astronomy-mate had found only four planets in the system, a rather paltry number even for a blue-white star. But that was only the most minor part of the strangeness.

All four planets were super-massive Jovian gas-giants, planets that were right on the edge of being stars themselves.

All four were in exactly the same Keplerian orbit, circling the blue-white at a distance of two Astronomical Units, just a little greater distance than Mars is from Sol.

And they were, as far as the instruments could determine, perfectly spaced.

"I'm starting to wonder what this race *couldn't* do," Bill said, swearing faintly under his breath. There was no *way* that the orbits could be natural.

"And if you think *that's* weird, sir," Darryl added, "take a look at the spectral readings from the planetary atmospheres."

The majority of a Jovian's troposhpere was hydrogen and helium and that was the case with these planets: Atmo was 86% hydrogen and 13% helium. And after studying literally hundreds of them since the *Blade* went out, it was well understood what the mix would be depending upon the type of star that was in the system and the distance the gas planet was from that star. For Sol-like stars, Jovians between about three to fifteen AUs were mostly like Jupiter or Saturn and consisted mainly of hydrogen and helium gases in the outer layers. Deeper into their interiors were liquid metal hydrogen and very few other materials. Gas giants that had orbits out past fifteen AUs typically had hydrogen and helium in their tropospheres but also had other compounds like methane and ethane there as well. Deeper in those large gas planets were water and ammonia ices and even rocky materials.

In the case of these planets, however, the numbers were just . . . off. High levels of krypton, neon, and argon were present in planet one. High levels of sodium and neodymium in planet two.

"Metals in one planet, nitrogen in that planet, noble gases xenon, krypton, and . . . argon?" Bill said, swearing again. "It's 4% *argon*?"

"The planetary chemistry has been tailored, sir," the astronomy-mate said, pushing his glasses up his nose again. "I did the math while you were on your way down. That's more argon in that planet's atmosphere than the mass of the Earth. Be interesting to find out where they got it. Given that I've found no rocky planets or moons in the system, sir, they might just have converted it from those, assuming they could change huge masses of one element into another. Based on normal blue-white solar systems, the mass transfer is about right."

"I *so* didn't want to hear that."

"This entire system has been tailored," Bill said, shaking his head. "And that thing has to be why."

"The question is . . . what is it?" Prael asked.

"A weapon," Bill said. "Nobody expends *that* much energy on anything else. Their version of a supercarrier is my guess."

"Something that can destroy this part of the galaxy?" Lieutenant Fey interjected. "There's enough power there."

"This is reality, Lieutenant," Captain Weaver replied, "not an Xbox game. Think about propagation time. Even if it could destroy 'this part of the galaxy' it would be a while before the destruction got anywhere, don't you think?"

"There may be a data point for that," the TACO said. "A weapon that is. We've detected what look like meteoric impacts away from the surface. I think it has some sort of shield."

"I'm surprised they left any asteroids in the system," Bill muttered. "They sure seem to have cleaned up otherwise."

"So much for getting close, then," the CO said, ignoring the muttering.

"Not . . . necessarily, sir," Bill replied, breaking out of his reverie. "There are various types of theoretical shields that will stop a meteor but not a vehicle that's going slow enough. Not saying that's the case, but it's possible."

"How do we test it?" the CO asked.

"Well, the dragonflies are just sitting there."

"It's important to approach from the shade, Colonel," Bill said. "It's going to get really really hot if you don't."

"So you have repeatedly told me, Captain Weaver," Colonel Che-chee said. "I will make that approach."

The ship was in orbit around the star at three AU from the tree while Colonel Che-chee and her wingman accelerated towards it.

"Approach slowly," Bill reminded her.

"I will endeavor to avoid being smashed, XO," the colonel said.

"Flight One, follow the ball," the fighter control officer said, punching in deceleration orders. "More, more, stationary relative. Ready to advance, Colonel?"

"Quite," Che-chee said.

"That's about where we think the shield is, sir," the FCO said to the hovering officers. "If it's really a shield it's a big one, extending nearly a kilometer from the tree."

"Given its size, that's not all that far," the CO said dryly.

"But it's far enough we can fit the ship inside it," Bill said.

"Point."

"Flight One, two hundred meters to shield," the control specialist said. "One fifty. One hundred. Fifty . . ."

"That is an odd sensation," Colonel Che-chee said. "All my fur just lifted."

"Flight one is inside the theoretical shield zone," the control specialist said.

"Keep them inside it," the CO replied. "Colonel, are

you willing to go try to look over the edge at the sun? Be aware that if this shield doesn't work the way it seems to, you're going to get fried. You will *not* survive."

"Then I will let the male take the risk," the colonel replied. "That is what males are for. Vector?"

"Dragonfly five approaching edge of Limb One," the control specialist said. "Maintain heading and course. Reduce speed. Prepare to decelerate and reverse. Five, four, three . . ."

"No effect," Colonel Che-chee reported. "I'm moving forward."

"Careful, Colonel," the CO said.

"Ka-kre reports no ill effect," the Cheerick said. "But he does ask why the sun is so dark . . ."

"Why put something like that that close to the sun and then put a shield on it to reduce solar input?" Lieutenant Fey asked.

The shield acted as a polarizer on the side pointed to the sun, essentially a giant sunglass lens, reducing solar input to marginal levels.

"Prevents long-term degradation, I suppose," Bill said. "But the point is, the thing didn't react to the Flies. In fact, there's no indication that it even knows we're here. You'd expect some sort of automated defense system."

"Degraded?" the CO asked. "If it's from the same race it's over twenty million years old."

"Massive power output," Bill pointed out. "The shield's still working and there's apparently a reactionless drive to hold it where it is, sir. If this thing has had any degradation effect from sitting around for a bunch of million years, you'd think one of those systems would have gone."

"And we still have no clue what it is," the CO said sourly.

"The Tum-Tum Tree, sir," Bill said, chuckling. "God knows we're all in uffish thought."

"What?" Captain Prael snapped.

> *"He took his vorpal sword in hand:*
> *Long time the manxome foe he sought—*
> *So rested he by the Tumtum tree,*
> *And stood awhile in thought.*
>
> *And, as in uffish thought he stood,*
> *The Jabberwock, with eyes of flame,*
> *Came whiffling through the tulgey wood,*
> *And burbled as it came!"*

"I never thought of you as a quoter of poetry, XO," the CO said, frowning.

"'Jabberwocky,' by Lewis Carroll, sir," Bill said. "When the Adar named this thing the *Vorpal Blade* I looked it up and memorized it. If there was ever a Tum-Tum Tree, that's it. The way things are going, I'm looking for the gimble in the wabe."

"Well, let's hope the Jabberwock doesn't come burbling for us, here," the CO said. "Next step?"

"Send in the Marines?"

"So what kind of particles are we looking at?" Lieutenant Bergstresser asked.

Captain Prael looked nonplussed at the question and turned to Weaver.

"Lots of neutrinos, quarks, pentaquarks and fermions," Bill said. "No neenions."

"Didn't think so, sir," Berg said, grinning, then turning serious. "But that sounds a lot like the output of the engine, sir."

"Similar," the TACO admitted. "Not exactly the same, though. It's possible, however, that a part of the power source is a black box system."

"Colonel Che-chee didn't detect any entries on her flyby," Bill continued. "But that's what you're looking for. Hopefully, this thing has an intact control center, maybe even some clue as to what it does. Take your platoon down to the surface and look for an entrance. Just for giggles, I'd suggest that you start on the trunk extension. More particles seem to be coming from that area. But we don't have a lot of resolution at this distance. Stay in contact and continually feed us data."

"Roger, sir," Berg said.

"This is a recon, Lieutenant," the CO said, looking over at Captain Zanella, Berg's commanding officer. "Don't do anything rash."

"Wasn't planning on it, sir," Berg said.

"You know why you're doing this, right?" Captain Zanella asked. "You're our most experienced space hand and the best Marine we've got with particle readings. But you're not a physicist and you're not Superman. Just get in there, get the readings, try to find a hatch and get out."

"Yes, sir," Berg said.

"Good luck, son," Captain Prael said, standing up and holding out his hand.

"Thank you, sir," Berg said.

"Second Platoon, Bravo Company will approach the anomaly from the out-system direction in line, Team Bravo, Headquarters, Charlie and Alpha in sequence. Upon reaching the tip of the anomaly, teams will spread in echelon to cover one hemisphere of the anomaly, Bravo left, Charlie left, Headquarters forward, Alpha right, and will proceed upwards towards the spread end. Teams will maintain head-down position and use laser rangefinders to maintain one hundred meters separation from the anomaly. Open personnel separation as proceeding to maintain maximum spread across the hemisphere. Upon reaching maximum spread, platoon will reconfigure and move to trunk portion, performing a close sweep of the underside and trunk region. In the event that no opening is found, platoon will then move to the opposite hemisphere and do the same actions in reverse, regrouping at the tip and then proceeding back to the ship.

"Conditions: This is space, people. Conditions inside of the shield are reported to be nominal spatial conditions. Outside the field and in direct line to the star, suit temperatures will briefly rise to over four thousand degrees and turn the wearer and suit into an expanding ball of atoms. Do not get outside the shield.

"Communication: All sensor systems including but not limited to particle sensors and visual sensors will crossfeed to platoon radio transmission operator. RTO will ensure constant communication with the ship and will retrans all sensory data to the ship on specified frequencies. Teams will monitor platoon net at all times. Teams will not enter other teams' nets unless specifically ordered to do so. Teams will not communicate on platoon or command nets unless specifically ordered to do so.

"Safety: Pairs will check all seals prior to entering EVA chamber. Pairs will check for seal closure and leak upon draw-down of atmosphere. If all checks are good, personnel will then and only then exit chamber on boards, maintaining separation. Individuals will maintain minimum ten meters separation while in movement on boards. Weapons will be safed with no round in the chamber. In the event of failure of seal during EVA, individual will be placed in secure-bag and team will return with individual to the ship, opening bag *only* upon *full* resumption of normal pressure.

"Commander's Intent: It is the intent of the commander to gather information from the anomaly and find an opening to same while staying alive doing so. This is a reconnaissance mission, only. Platoon will take no pro-active actions in the event of finding out-of-standard readings or an opening. In the unlikely event of threat we will back off and call for support. Are there any questions?"

"Sir?" Corporal Shingleton said, raising his hand.

"Go."

"Are the particles dangerous?" Shingleton asked.

"No," Berg said, looking over at Gunnery Sergeant Juda with a raised eyebrow. "To repeat, all that has been observed is penta-quarks, fermions, quarks and neutrinos. Anybody know what that output resembles?"

"The ship's engine, sir?" Lance Corporal Kaijanaho asked.

"Correct," Berg answered. "You've got the same things going through you right now, Corporal. I want a report from you on the output level of the ship's engine in the Marine quarters under normal use by Monday."

"Yes, sir," Shingleton said, wincing.

"A coherent one," Berg continued. "Any other questions? No, then let's get it on. Gunnery Sergeant Juda, a moment of your time?"

". . . Don't know diddly about particles, sir," the gunnery sergeant admitted. "So I'm having a hard time getting them more advanced than they already are."

"My fault," Berg said. "I should have been checking into it. When we get back, shoot me their most recent scores in standard particle identification. I may have to give some classes."

"Yes, sir," Juda said. "They're good Marines, sir, but . . ."

"There are good Marines, Gunnery Sergeant," Berg said quietly, "and then there are good *Space* Marines. The two are not necessarily synonymous. We need to get it on. We'll discuss this later."

"Platoon, hold position."

Up close the Tum-Tum Tree looked less like a tree and more like a bunch of pagoda roofs stacked on top of each other. Each layer had multiple points of equal size with more points on each layer as the layers got larger. There were five at the very end, by the sharply tapered point, then eight, fifteen . . . If there was some sort of mathematical sequence there, Berg wasn't getting it.

It was also spectacular. Each of the "branches" that led to

the points fluoresced in a cascade of colors, shifting through most of the visual spectrum. There was no definite light source; it played from somewhere in the translucent depths of the thing. There seemed, however, to be a more intense line of the color in the depths, as if something was pulsing the colors into the branches like blood through veins.

Berg swung around, getting particle readings, and then frowned. The particles waxed and waned with the colors, pentaquarks being the most prominent line at this range. He had no *grapping* clue what that meant.

He also knew what he wanted to do but knew, as well, that he couldn't do it.

"Gunnery Sergeant," Berg said. "I need someone to go down and make physical contact with the surface. They're to touch it, lightly, and get particle readings from up-close. They are not to touch it if they determine there may be a threat."

"Aye, aye, sir," Juda said.

Lance Corporal Antti-Juhani Kaijanaho was a second generation Finnish immigrant born and raised in Orange County, California. With dark hair and eyes, a wide-flat face and very slight epicanthic folds from some Lapp ancestor, he had eventually just started spouting gibberish that sounded vaguely Asian when people asked him if he was Chinese, Japanese, Korean or Cambodian. His favorite had been one guy who had been absolutely sure he was Mongol and wouldn't take Finn for an answer.

When he had joined his first Force Reconnaissance unit his team NCOIC had looked at his face and name and said: "Kaijanaho. Japanese, right?"

"Finn, Staff Sergeant," he had responded, proud of his heritage. At the confused expression he had followed up with his standard expansion: "You know, where reindeer come from?"

Most members of a Force Recon team had their "team name," the nickname assigned by the team through some mystical process that involved a concensus of a short name or phrase that defined that person's personality and position. He had come to regret his standard explanation a few months later when the magic moment came for him to be assigned his team name.

Kaijanaho lifted "up" to the surface of the thing carefully, using his laser range finder to determine how close he was and his approach speed. Up close, it was nearly impossible to tell how far away the thing was; there was no real depth perception possible. As he closed he grew more entranced by the wall of color above him, shifting in multiple hues. As he got to nearly arm-length it was apparent that what looked like one shade was, in fact, millions of hues mixed together, flowing just under a translucent surface like billions of multicolored blood corpuscles.

He reached up one Wyvern claw and, lightly, almost reverently touched the surface. It was hard but where he touched the light seemed to draw around, following his finger . . .

"Blitzen?" Sergeant Champion barked. "Readings?"

"Uh . . ." Kaijanaho replied, entranced by the swirling colors.

"Lance Corporal Kaijanaho!" the sergeant barked again. "Atten-hut!

"Sorry, Sergeant," the lance corporal said, closing his eyes and lowering the claw of the suit. "Up close this stuff is hypnotic. My apologies."

"Accepted," Champion said. "Gimme some readings, Prancer."

"Just lots of pentaquarks, Sergeant," Kaijanaho said. "Actually, at this range I'm getting some slight alpha particle readings. Those are hazardous but the rad level is very low. About like a tritium watch face. No gamma or beta."

"Shiny . . ." Champion said after a moment. "Pull back to your position, Rudolph."

"It's pretty hypnotic from up here, too," Berg admitted.

"Agreed, sir," Gunny Juda replied. "Orders?"

"Continue the sweep," Berg said. "Onwards and upwards. But since I've spent, like, no time with the teams, can you explain why Lance Corporal Kaijanaho has three team names? And why they all seem to refer to Santa's reindeer?"

17

Eventually the Marines reached the point of full spread. At that point, the diameter of the "tree" was nearly six kilometers and the small unit of Marines could cover hardly any of the surface. However, it didn't seem to matter. One spot was as good as any. Everywhere it was just color and points.

"All units, hold position," Berg ordered as they approached the edge of the tree. "Gunny, the Flies tried this out so call me an old maid, but I'm not taking the whole platoon into the direct light of this sun until I'm sure it's clear. Send a point."

"Aye, aye, sir."

"All clear, sir," Sergeant Champion said. "The sun's sort of . . . Well, it's not *too* bright. And no hazardous rads. Levels are nominal as hell."

Stars put out more than heat. The solar wind was composed of mostly protons, some alpha particles, and even a few electrons as masses of particles swept out from the fusion of hydrogen into helium and helium into still more massive particles. Radiation in space was always a hazard and this close to a blue star they should have been sleeted with the equivalent of several hundred *thousand* chest X-rays.

Instead, the retrans from the sergeant's particle detectors said that the only generator in the area was the massive Tum-Tum Tree. The shield was absorbing or reflecting *all* the hazardous radiation from the nearby star. That had been one of Berg's main concerns. The Cheerick suits had particle detectors, but to say the least even Colonel Che-chee was no expert at reading them. The lieutenant had been more worried about radiation than the possible heat.

Berg advanced the platoon up the slope and into the light of the sun, then tuned his sensors on the surface of Gunny Juda's suit to get a reading. The surface temperature of the suit in the shade had been minus one hundred and fifty-seven degrees Celsius. As it entered the light from the super-hot star, which should have kicked it up to over a thousand degrees Celsius in an instant, it climbed to eighty-three degrees and stuck there. Hot, but the suit's chillers could handle it easily.

When he came in sight of the sun he could see why the responses had been so varied. The sun *looked* extremely hot and bright. But there was an edge to it, like the watery sunshine of an ever-so-slightly overcast winter day that mentally translated as nonthreatening. And the actual power-input levels, inside the shield, were about the same as the suits experienced from Sol in Earth orbit.

The view from the top of the spread was spectacular,

the sweeping rear side dropping to the "trunk." Berg got a sudden moment of vertigo and realized this must be what a spider felt like on a real Christmas tree. A very, very, very small spider. More like a mite.

"Slow and easy down the back side," Berg ordered. "Maintain one hundred meters from the tree and proceed to the joining of the trunk."

"Sir," Lance Corporal Fuller said, "we're losing contact with the *Blade*."

Fuller was the designated platoon RTO. With the complement of Marines on the *Blade* being so small and the commo being so integrated, the position was a secondary one for the Charlie Team cannoneer. All it really meant was that he was carrying a long-range laser transmitter tuned to communicate with the *Blade*. But while the system was line-of-sight . . .

"Put in a retrans box," Gunny Juda growled before Berg could open his mouth.

"We need to hold up while he does that," the LT pointed out. "Platoon, hold position."

The retrans box was the size of a Vietnam era radio but had interplanetary range. Fuller pulled it off his armor and then looked at the edge of the tree.

"Gunny, there's no place to affix it," the RTO pointed out.

"Time to find out how miraculous space tape really is," the gunny replied. "You *do* have a roll with you, don't you, Lance Corporal?"

"Uh . . ."

"Here," Berg said with a sigh, reaching into the cargo hatch on the back of his suit. "Use mine."

Space tape once again proved its miraculous nature by sticking to the surface of whatever the tree was made of. Fuller extended the transmission wand and the receptor mirror and backed his board away from the edge.

"All done, sir."

"Let's move," Berg said. "Platoon, continue approach to the trunk."

As they got closer, particle emissions climbed sharply. But there still was nothing of a hazardous nature. The closest to it was a sharp spike in neutrinos, but neutrinos were so small, fast and slippery that until the Adar came along the only way to detect them was with massive quantities of a special solvent in undergound tanks. The rest was stuff that had even less effect. But it proved that something very strange was going on in the interior of the massive artifact.

"Anybody see anything like an opening?" Berg asked as they approached the face of the trunk. The trunk itself was just under nine football fields in diameter, bigger around than the largest stadium on Earth. The Marines were dwarfed by the massive construction of the tree.

"Negative here, sir," Staff Sergeant Carr commented.

"Negative, sir," Sergeant Champion replied.

"Nada, sir," Sergeant Eduardo Bae finished.

"Okay, let's head down the trunk to the end," Berg said. "Maintain separation, et cetera."

The major particle output seemed to come from the joining of the main tree to the trunk and fell off, sharply, as they headed to the very "bottom" of the tree. Reaching the end, Berg didn't even pause the platoon, just sent them in a swoop to the very underside.

In that configuration, the shadows of the boards could be seen sweeping across the luminescent underside of the construction and it was the shadows, as much as anything, that pin-pointed a change in the surface of the thing.

"Sir . . ." Gunny Juda said. "Did you see . . ."

For just a moment as one of the shadows swept over the surface a line was revealed.

"Platoon, halt," Berg said. "Let's back up and see if we can get that again."

By maneuvering the boards around it was eventually possible to get the same effect, showing a thin line and a slight change in surface texture on one portion of the underside.

"Gunny, send a point team."

"Even if there's a door there," Corporal Sam Dupras complained, "I don't see no controls."

The Alpha team lance corporal rifleman was from Pladgette Parrish, Louisiana, and it showed in a thick Cajun accent.

"We just have to find the door," Staff Sergeant Carr replied as the threesome closed on the line. "So can it."

"I don't know if that's a door or just some sort of—" Lance Corporal Robert Rucker started to say just as an the material of the surface dilated away, revealing opening that was wide and deep enough to take all three boards. In fact, it looked as if it was tailored to take the threesome. Alas, with the flickering walls, the smooth, curved sides and the shadows of the boards, it looked not unlike a toothless mouth. "Urk."

"Lieutenant Bergstresser," Staff Sergeant Carr said. "We appear to have found a door."

"Openings occur, apparently automatically, whenever someone approaches one of those lines, sir," Berg said over the laser link to the ship. "We've traced the outline of the full area. It's more than seven hundred meters *wide*, sir. Most of the bottom appears to open. It's possible this thing is some sort of space dock."

"Fascinating," Lady Che-chee said, leading her dragonfly forward, then backing away as a tailored opening appeared. "And you haven't entered?"

"We don't have orders to, ma'am," Eric replied. "In fact, we have orders *not* to."

"Dragonflight, Second Platoon, this is CIC," the ship's CO said. "Dragonflight, maintain station. Marines, send one, repeat one member of your unit into one of the openings. Have him enter then attempt to exit and report."

"Just opens right back up, sir . . ." Lance Corporal Kaijahano said. "I don't know what happens if I go forward, though. Want me to find out?"

Kaijahano took a deep breath, then mentally sent his grav-board forward towards the inner wall of the compartment. As he did, his O_2 sensor began blinking, indicating rising exterior oxygen levels and he felt himself pulled sideways from artificial gravity. Since he could see no vents in the smooth walls of the alien airlock, he hadn't a clue where the O_2 was coming from. But by the time his board just about touched the wall, the O_2 pressure was actually *higher* than safe for humans. By the same token, the gravity was only about 80% Earth normal. Lighter even than the artificial gravity of the *Blade*. He twisted his board to align and continued forward, slower than a walk.

Just before the board touched, the inner wall dilated to reveal a glowing tunnel that curved to the right. That would be to the closer wall of the tree from his current position. He wasn't sure what that meant, but this was as far as he was supposed to go. He backed up and the door closed. Backing up more and the oxygen level dropped precipitously to death pressure, the outer door opened and he was back in space.

"Sir, all I gotta say is that whoever designed this thing knew what they were doing . . ."

"How are your consumables, Lieutenant?" Captain Zanella asked.

"We're all at better then seventy percent, sir," Berg replied. "If we're not surveying the surface, we've got plenty. And I've been considering Dancer's report from the airlock. That level of O_2 pressure is dangerous for humans, but our suit systems can back it down easily enough. If that's what the whole structure is like on the inside, sir, we can stay in there indefinitely from an air perspective. Well, as long as our scrubbers and power hold out, but that's weeks, sir. Heck, we can actually *resupply* on Class O."

"The problem, Lieutenant, is that you're out of communication with the ship while anyone is in there," the Marine CO replied. "We're considering it on this end. Hold your position until you have further orders . . ."

". . . send them in and have them look around," Bill said. "Two-Gun's smart and cautious. He's the best guy I could think of to lead this."

"The problem is that I'm feeling more and more like a monkey in a reactor compartment," Captain Prael replied. "We're pushing buttons and we have no clue what they do."

"Sir, we were sent out to find technology," Weaver argued. "This is technology beyond anything we expected. We need to find out what it is, what it does and if possible how to control it. Better yet, how to move it. As it is, it's right in the region we can expect the Dreen to occupy in the next five years. The one thing I can guarantee is that Space Command does *not* want this thing, *whatever* it is, falling into Dreen hands."

"Do you have any idea what it is or what it does?" the CO asked.

"No, sir, but we've barely scratched the surface!"

"I have to agree to that," Prael said, frowning. "Captain Zanella, you've been mostly quiet during this debate."

"I hate the idea of possibly losing a platoon, sir," the Marine said. "But that's what we're here for, to check things out. There's no reason for us to be on the ship if we're not going to do our jobs. If you want my vote, sir, I vote for going in. Carefully. Send one team in, have them recon forward. If there is no negative effect, then send in the rest of the platoon. Give them a specified time frame to investigate. If they don't report back? Then we have a problem."

"Shiny, Captain," Prael said. "That sounds like a plan."

"This is as far as we got in the time we had, sir," Staff Sergeant Carr said.

The tube had turned to the right in a long, smooth curve. Based on inertial guidance, they had to be near the edge of the trunk. However, Berg could see a second curve, back to the left, up ahead.

"Good job, Staff Sergeant," the lieutenant said. "Gunny, rotate the point."

"Whoa!" Corporal Shingleton gasped from his position fifty meters in the lead. There was another sharp turn there and whatever the corporal had seen had stopped him in what had been a smooth approach.

"Report, Corporal," Sergeant Bae snapped. "'Whoa' is not a useful comment."

"It's . . . Sergeant, you gotta see this!"

"Now . . . that's something."

The corridor ended in a massive cavern which must have taken up most of the width of the trunk. There was still a walkway, though, a shimmering ribbon of nearly transluscent material that arched upwards towards the ceiling and followed the right-hand side of the immense enclosure.

Far below Berg could see more walkways and semi-transparent extensions out into the opening, like wings extending from the walls. There were dozens of them, some small, some very large. It took him about ten seconds to realize he was looking at . . .

"That is one *hell* of a space dock," Gunny Juda said, awe in his voice. "You could park a dozen *Blades* in this thing at once, sir."

"Yeah, Gunny," Berg said, trying for a stable and serious tone. "But this is probably less than five percent of the total area of the tree. Most of the trunk, yeah, but not most of the *tree*. This thing's not purely a space dock."

Oh, grapp *this*, he thought. He knew that he was supposed to let other people take the risks but he just had to try this for himself.

Stepping gingerly off his board he tested the firmness of the tunnel floor first. Solid as a rock.

"Sir, what are you doing?" Gunny Juda asked over the command circuit.

"Having fun, Gunny," Berg replied, walking forward to the opening. He balanced on one foot, not the easiest thing to do in a Wyvern, and carefully tapped the semi-transparent bridge. Seemed solid. "Get ready to catch me."

"Sir, I can do that," Staff Sergeant Carr said.

"Got it, Staff Sergeant," Berg replied, stepping fully onto the bridge.

The view was more than terrifying. It was better than eight hundred meters straight down to the curved "bottom" of the tree. But he wasn't about to let that stop him.

"I'm wondering if these people really *used* this thing," Berg said, walking forwards. "I mean, this is one long damned . . ."

"Sir, slow down!" Gunny Juda snapped.

Berg stopped and turned around and was surprised to find that in just a few short strides he had separated from the platoon by nearly a hundred meters. He hadn't noticed any effect of acceleration as you'd get from a moving sidewalk and the walls were so far away there was no perspective for speed.

"Now that's interesting," Berg said, starting to walk back. Going in that direction, it was apparent that just a few steps accelerated him to much faster than running, but he slowed automatically as he approached the opening. He paused there and looked at the edge of the narrow platform. He squatted down and extended his claw outward towards the edge. It hit a barrier and he nodded. "Thought so."

"What's that, sir?" Gunny Juda said.

"No handrails, Gunny," Berg said. "That meant either a race that was suicidal or something we couldn't see. There's a force field there. You *can't* fall off this thing."

A few experiments determined that, in fact, the entire tunnel had the same system, which seemed to be a side-shoot of a reactionless drive system. The surface of the tunnel and the bridge moved under the foot just as a slidewalk would, but had some type of stabilization field that mitigated all the normal effects. The slowing as he'd approached the tunnel entry, moreover, was an effect of the crowding at the entrance. With no one blocking the entry, a user continued through at a rate of nearly thirty miles per hour, while walking at a normal pace. Users moving at different speeds, one a slow walk, one a fast walk, moved at relatively different speeds on the speedwalk. And the one time that two Wyverns collided at a relative speed of nearly fifteen miles per hour, there was no indication of contact, no clang of metal hammering on metal, no bruising, no flailed chests; the field eliminated the effects of inertial energy entirely.

"Sir, we're getting on for time," Gunny Juda said. "Damnit, Donner, get your ass back here!"

"Incoming, Gunny!" the lance corporal said from near the top of the bridge. He got the Wyvern up to a max-speed run and the gathered Marines at the opening flinched as he came in like a rocket. But just before he got to the gaggle he screeched to a slow walk as if he'd hit a brick wall. "YES!" he shouted, holding both claws overhead in victory. "One hundred and twenty miles per hour in a WYVERN suit! That *has* to be some kind of record!"

"God damnit . . ."

"Try Cupid, Gunny," Kaijanho said with a sigh. "You haven't used that one in a while . . ."

"God damnit, Comet!"

"That one's actually appropriate. Can I keep it?"

"I'm not taking the ship in there," Captain Prael said, shaking his head. "Not going to happen."

The dragonflies had been admitted through a large airlock directly into the cavern. They had landed on the platforms, checked them out with interest and then returned. They had also determined that whereas the whole cavern was not pressurized, the platforms were, invisible force fields holding the air in but somehow letting the dragonflies and their riders through. The size of the field was large enough, on one of the medium-sized platforms, to cover the whole *Blade*.

"Well, sir, what we've found so far is the parking garage," Weaver said. "And I'd say that's exactly what this is, sir. It's the parking garage for whatever the Tree really is. It might be a repair dock, but so far we've seen no signs of that. Just stuff for moving people. I'm starting to rethink my suggestion that this is a weapon. There is no sign of control of entry."

"So what is it?" the CO asked.

"Short of doing a thorough survey, sir, I'm not sure we can find out," Weaver told him.

"Suggestions?" Prael asked, looking around at the group. "Anyone?"

Berg wasn't really happy being at a contentious meeting with the CO of the *Blade*. He was, by far and away, the most junior officer on the ship and as such he kept his mouth shut.

"Is it still your intent to go get Hexosehr advisers, sir?" Captain Zanella asked.

"Yes," Prael replied. "This is too big and too advanced for little old us to figure out."

"That will take at least two weeks, sir," Captain Zanella pointed out. "A period during which there should be little or no threat to the ship and nothing to investigate."

"You're suggesting I leave the Marines," the CO said.

"Sir, while you are gone we can be surveying the structure," the Marine said. "By the time you get back we could have found a control room or something similar for the Hexosehr to investigate. If we just go with you, we'll have to do it when we come back and we'll have lost two weeks."

"Not to mention two more weeks with the Marines cooped up on the ship," Bill said, keeping in mind some of the more unpleasant incidents on the last two voyages. He frowned in thought for a moment and then continued. "Frankly, CO, we probably should leave a larger group. Call it a prize crew if you will. While there are no indications that we can comprehend anything about this technology, a few technical people would be in order. We're going to need to set up a full base station for the Marines, anyway. The Marines are going to require some logistical support."

"This all assumes I'm going to leave the Marines," the CO pointed out but nodded. "Which actually is a good idea, Captain Zanella. And the logistical support is on point. While the Marines could probably survive for two weeks without it, they are going to need a base station, which means leaving some mechanics and electricians at the least. XO, come up with a plan and have it on my desk by end of shift."

"Yes, sir," Bill said with a sigh.

"Damn," the CO muttered. "If we have to offload, I'm going to have to take the ship into the docking bay."

"Approaching force field in ten seconds," the pilot said.

"Reduce approach speed to one meter per second," the CO said. "Let's take this nice and slow."

"One meter per second, aye," the pilot said, reducing their forward velocity. "Fourteen seconds . . . Ship entering field . . ."

"XO?" the damage control talker said. "Forward torpedo room is reporting odd effects . . . really odd effects . . ."

"Conn, Damage Control," Bill said automatically. "Reporting odd effects from forward."

"Define odd effects," the CO responded just as the damage control center entered the field.

"That is a good question, Captain Prael," Weaver responded, taking the meerschaum pipe out of his mouth for a moment and stroking his Van Dyke beard. "Precisely defining it, however, is much more difficult." Weaver looked at his pipe and, despite being a violent non-smoker, stuck it in his mouth and puffed. "I suspect . . . (puff, puff) that what we are experiencing . . . (puff) is an induced (puff, puff) hallucination . . ."

The damage control section was still the same, a mass of readouts on conditions throughout the ship, five seamen and petty officers to handle communications and orders and four steel bulkheads. But at the same time, it was . . . different. Bill knew the reporting system like the back of his hand and looking at it now he still understood it. But all the controls and readouts had changed, becoming much more garishly colored, with formerly muted reporting screens now being covered in blinking green lights and yellow arrows. The whole room had changed, becoming darker and more sharp edged at the same time, as if it were seen through some sort of odd lens. The petty officers were wearing ornate uniforms, including brim caps, that he recognized as wrong and yet correct at the same time. The seamen manning the consoles had shrunk in size to be almost childlike and simian at the same time.

What really bothered him, though, was that much as he could recognize there was a major, even catastrophic, change going on on the ship, the most he could muster was a quiet sense of academic interest.

He also found a tweed, patch-elbow jacket and a

turtleneck sweater, clothing he wouldn't normally wear in a million years, to be oddly comfortable.

"Mr. Weaver to the Wardroom!" the CO barked over the 1MC. "On the double triple-time! We have a level nine emergency! Set Condition One throughout the ship! All hands! All hands! Man Your Battle Stations! Report Undue Effects! Report! Report!"

18

"Holy *grapp!*" Sub Dude squealed. He looked at the wrench in his hand and couldn't figure out why the hand holding it looked like a black leather glove. "What the *grapp's* happening?"

"That is unclear," a bass, robotic voice said from over his shoulder.

Gants turned around and squealed in fear, dropping the wrench and climbing up the bulkhead to look at his friend from the overhead.

"Red? Is that you?"

"I do not know," the cyborg replied, his head rotating upwards with a whir of motors. While still the same height, Red now was about half covered in glittering metal and had a metal skull for a head. All he was wearing was a pair of electric purple pants and metal and leather boots. "Is the orangutan speaking to me my good friend and brother-in-law Michael Gants?"

"The what?" Gants asked, looking at his hand again. Then he noticed that his forearm was covered in orange fur and it was strangely . . . long. "YAAAAH!"

"As I always suspected," the cyborg said, looking downward again, "deep down inside you *are* a monkey."

There was a roar from down the corridor and deep in Gants' primate bones he knew what it was.

"I should go determine Tiny's condition," Red said, straightening up with a whir and a click and marching down the corridor.

"Be careful!" Gants squealed. "I didn't like the sounds of that! If this is happening all over the ship . . ."

"Lieutenant Bergstresser, what happened to your hair?" Morris asked.

Berg looked in the compartment's small mirror and blanched. His formerly buzz-cut haircut was now long, black hair that stuck out on either side like uneven wings. The hilt of what looked very much like a claymore jutted over one shoulder. Looking downward he also determined that he was now unquestionably armed, in violation of regulations, the weapons being dual glittering pistols with mother-of-pearl hand-grips. He had never seen them before in his life but somehow *knew* that they were "laser" pistols that shot a green beam that would disintegrate any sufficiently small enemy. Given that lasers didn't do that, his mind was having a hard time with the image.

"I have no idea!" Eric replied, spinning in place and gesturing with one hand held upwards, his fingers in a weird pointing position. "But My Great Enemy And His Army of Darkness Approaches! Call out! The Space Marines!"

"What Is! Going On!" the CO shouted, waving his arms

in the air dramatically. He was wearing a purple and orange jumpsuit that was skin tight and revealed that he'd apparently gained about thirty percent in body mass, was now about seven feet tall and looked like the Terminator, complete with one eye that had been replaced by a red-glowing laser emitter. "This is! Unacceptable! Completely unacceptable! This cannot be accepted!"

The wardroom now had orange walls and a screen on the back bulkhead that showed a mass of trajectories that appeared to have nothing to do with *anything*.

"As I was (puff, puff) saying," Weaver replied, calmly, leaning one patch-covered elbow on the edge of the table. "The first theory (puff, puff) that must be entertained (puff, pause, ponder, puff) is that we are experiencing a mass hallucination . . ."

"All I want to know!" the CO barked, his laser emitter shining in Weaver's eyes, "Is How! We Are Going! To Stop this!"

"I would recommend," (puff, puff . . . pause . . . ruminate . . . puff . . .) "that we extract the ship from the field (puff, puff) and investigate the results . . . (puff.)"

"Well, do it fast!" Miriam snapped from the hatch. "I can't find anything to wear but these stupid school-girl outfits!"

The linguist was astride what looked like a white saber-toothed tiger. She was wearing a complete school-girl outfit from the saddle-loafer flats to the plain blue tie. If anything, compared to most of her wardrobe it was muted. The worst part, though, were her . . .

"What has occurred to your eyes, Miss Moon?" Bill asked, puffing politely.

"I don't know!" Miriam shrilled, rolling eyes that took up most of her face around the room. "The weird part is, I can't get contacts in them but I still can see normally! I should be blind as a bat. Tee-hee!" she added, clapping her hands over her mouth. "Oh, God, did I just *giggle*?"

"And now the effect is explained . . ." Weaver said, leaning one elbow on his station chair and taking a puff off his pipe while rotating his whole body to look at the over-head. "We have entered . . . *the anime zone*!"

"Okay, now that we're back to normal," Captain Prael said. "Can anyone explain what just happened?"

"Hang on a second, sir," Bill said, making a face and sticking his tongue out. "I need some coffee or something to get the taste of this damned pipe smoke out of my mouth!" He spat without actually ejecting matter and winced. "God, that's nasty!"

"Captain Weaver," the CO replied, sighing. "If you could focus for just a moment?"

"I think it was some sort of effect from the interaction of the drive and the protection field," Miriam said, stroking Tiny's belly. If the cat was affected by the recent experience, it was not apparent. Of course, his anime image was probably what he thought he was anyway. "It has to be the drive, given that neither the Marines nor the dragonflies had a similar experience when they approached the station. Hallucination? Change in reality? Who knows?"

"How?" the CO asked. "That doesn't seem physically possible!"

"Well . . ." Bill said, still working his mouth. "Remember

that discussion of chaos as related to the effect of the ball generators on molycirc and other materials, sir?"

"Vaguely," the CO said.

"The drive generates a thin field of absolute chaotic unreality at the edge of the drive field," Bill said. "Essentially it's an event horizon generated by the micro black hole the drive generates then somehow expanded to enclose the ship. Stephen Hawking postulated that at the event horizon of a black hole, anything was possible. Even the impossible. It is likely that the generation system of the Tree is interacting with the warp field in chaotic terms and creating unreality from reality."

"That tells me *so* much," Prael growled.

"And it's just a WAG," Bill added. "God, that's a nasty habit. If it's not a hallucination, and again an experiment to determine reality doesn't come to mind, then it had to be perfect quantum chaos somehow adjusted to a functional reality. Interesting effect, I'll add. If we could induce it to occur by command, we might get some enhanced effects from the weapons, given the sort of things you find in anime. Or not . . ." he added, looking at the CO's expression.

"But why . . . the specific changes?" the CO asked, frowning. "I hope that it's not some sort of wish-fulfillment thing. And why *anime*?"

"Well, this is just another WAG," Bill said. "More like a GWAG. But the reality of what we do is closest in . . . Miriam?"

"The nature of the *Blade* missions is closest to the archetype of anime in people's minds," Miriam said. "I think that's where you're going."

"That would be it," Bill said, nodding. "If the field picks up on general thoughts, underlying beliefs if you will, then the closest to the reality of what we do that most people are familiar with is the archetypes you find in anime. I feel like babbling about Jungian archetypes, but when you hear that phrase you know someone's completely lost it. Skinner will eventually be mentioned and then you know someone's really off their meds."

"So why were we . . . What we were?" the CO asked. "I hope that deep down inside I don't really think I look like I looked. I'm fairly certain Miss Moon doesn't."

"God knows I hate pipes," Bill said, spitting again. "Yuck. How can anyone smoke that foul stuff?"

"Anime has a set number of standard tropes," Miriam responded. "Captains of ships are always big, fierce looking men, often bullying. Scientists wear tweed or oddly patterned jumpsuits. Enlisted sailors are generally either monkeys or dwarfs. All women have huge eyes and only three or four acceptable 'looks.' I could have wished for the laser-cut-leather free-wheeling mercenary type but I got Suzie Schoolgirl instead. I wonder what the Wyverns looked like under the effect. Oh, and when you find the guy with the winged haircut and the sword, you know who the main character is."

"Well, it wasn't anyone in Conn . . ."

"I'm glad you've got your haircut back under control, Lieutenant Bergstresser," Captain Zanella said. "But what was all that about the approach of your 'Great Enemy!'?"

"Sir, I have no idea, sir," Berg replied, staring at a point six inches over his CO's head and locked at attention. "I am unable to fully recall the events that occurred while we were under the effect of the shield, sir. All I can recall is that it had something to do with someone betraying and murdering my father, sir. And something about once being his best friend and for some strange reason finding 'the umbrella of light.' Given that my father is still alive, sir . . ."

"Well, it was terribly dramatic," Zanella said dryly. "There I was, preparing to fight a great battle to the death against an overwelming enemy force and then . . . Zap, we were out. Stand easy, Lieutenant. I don't think any of us can be held responsible for what went on in the field. Otherwise the first sergeant will never live it down."

"I was just a spider, sir," Powell growled. "A big purple spider."

"Yes, First Sergeant," the CO said, still dryly. "But it was that strange silver web you were sitting in that somehow seemed to be connected to all of us and how you lightly tugged on the strings, sending us hither and yon against our will, that still bothers me . . ."

". . . it still bothers me, but the bottomline is that we're going to have to go back," Captain Prael said. "We've got to drop off the away team. Since the effect stopped as soon as we'd cleared the field, hopefully the away team will not be . . ."

"Stuck in the condition the whole time we're there?" Bill finished. "Yes, sir, agreed. I have to state that if the effect continues, I'm going to have to temporarily turn over command to Captain Zanella, sir. My . . . alter-self is not functional as a commander. He's pure advisor. I don't think I could even engage in combat much less direct it. I'd be all 'this is fascinating, I must figure out the equations . . .'"

"Well, we're still going to have to go back in," the CO said. "I'm going to order a stand-down for long enough for you to try to adjust the unloading plan based on the effects. Try to figure out how it will reduce the efficiency of unloading."

"I actually saw no true reduction in efficiency, sir," Bill pointed out. "Everything continued to work more or less as it normally would. If anything, there were some enhancements. But I'll try to plug the effect into the plan. I'd better get to work."

"One thing to keep in mind is that I may not have coveralls," Miriam pointed out.

"At least you kept more-or-less the same body shape," Bill replied. "Did you hear about Sub Dude?"

"Three meters . . ." the pilot squeaked. Under the effect of the anime field, the petty officer had shrunk to the size of a large child and had a vaguely monkeylike appearance and long, pointed ears. He also tended to hoot when excited. "Whoot! Whoot! Two meters . . . one . . . Touchdown. Wheeeee!"

"Landing jacks deployed and locked," the COB said. He was wearing an outlandish Naval uniform that would have looked well in a Gilbert and Sullivan play, had an eye-patch and was adjusting one of the landing jack controls with a hook. "Leveled on platform, shiver me bones!"

"Reduce counter gravity to fifty percent!" the CO

barked against his will, watching the monitors. The
landing platform was about six inches thick, nearly a
hundred meters across and appeared to have no structural
supports. Under the artificial gravity of the docking bay,
there was no way it should have been able to support the
weight of the *Blade*. "Mr. Weaver, effects?"

"The platform . . . (puff, puff) appears to be holding.
(Puff) Remarkable stuff."

"Begin! Away Team! Deployment!"

"Nice thing about this shape, wawk wawk wawk
waaaah," Gants said, dragging a huge pile of bundled
rations behind him as he knuckle-walked down the
ramp—despite the changes in form, his space suit still
fit—"We're strong! Strong! STRONG!" He paused and
began beating his chest with flapping arms, hooting
"WHOO! WHOO! WHOO! WHOOT!"

"I concur," Red responded in a monotone. He had three
similar bundles, one in either hand and one held by a
head-strap. He'd put on his space suit and it had immediately disappeared. A short experiment, though, determined
that he was able to survive the mildly toxic atmosphere of
the space station. What was going to happen when the
effect changed was uncertain. "But we mechano-humans
are stronger."

"Cyborgs," Gants muttered, continuing in his knuckle-
drag. "Can't live with 'em, can't trade 'em in for parts."

"Wyverns," the cyborg responded. "Clear the Way for
our Betters."

The Wyverns had increased in height, being now over
fourteen feet tall instead of nine. They also had more

angularity to them, looking something like glittering silver medieval Japanese warriors. Where the black sensor pod had once rested was now a demon face with red-glowing eyes. Besides their standard weapons, which were now "blasters" instead of heavy machine guns, all of them were wearing dual swords on leather belts.

The last two Wyverns, though, were different. The second to the last was a gigantic mechanical spider. Thin trails of webbing could be seen connecting its feet to all the other Wyverns and when it stopped and jerked on one, a Wyvern broke away from the pack to take up a stationary guard position.

The last Wyvern was shorter than even a standard one, small enough it was a wonder anyone could fit in it, had no face but did have a round "helmet" with multiple horns coming out of it and for some reason a long beard jutting out from under it. On its back was a leather rucksack that was nearly the size of the whole Wyvern. It was armed with two large axes and a massive hammer with a head half the size of the entire suit.

"Arrh!" the Wyvern growled. "When I find out who's done this to me, I'm going to pound them into a red gooey pulp, by Moradin's Beard!"

"Portana?" Red asked, suddenly dwindling to Tonka-Toy size, his voice coming out in a squeak. "Is that you?"

"Aye, by Gigli's Silver Pick!" Portana growled. "What's it to yah, Tin-Man?"

"I was simply inquiring," Red replied, back to normal size.

"Even my space suit is a school-girl outfit," Miriam said, giggling again. "Oh, God."

The space suit was skin-tight but had a modest skirt, a button-down shirt and tie and the boots were saddle-loafers. Through the clear visor it was apparent that her eyes were back to filling most of her head.

"It'll be fine when the ship leaves," Gants said, knuckle-walking over to her and patting her on the fanny. "Whoot! I touched her butt! I touched her butt!"

"Hands off!" Miriam snapped, backhanding the orang.

The strike should have barely been a love-tap. Instead, the machinist was knocked head-over-heels and rolled at least ten feet. At the end of the roll, he sat up and shook his head comically.

"Whoa! She's got a slap like being kicked by a Wyvern!"

"Get back to work," Chief Gestner snarled. The chief had transformed into a lumpy troglodytic humanoid with three eyes and a mouth full of sharp triangular teeth. He also was carrying a whip but had so far refrained from using it. He snapped the bullwhip through the air, though, making a nasty swish-crack! "Back to work, monkey!"

"I'm an ape," Gants protested, scurrying to his pile of rations and knuckle-dragging them off the ship. "Not a monkey."

"If I want to hear any lip from you, monkey, I'll squeeze your head until it pops," the chief snapped. "Move it! Move it! Schnell!"

"Oh, thank God," Weaver muttered, looking around at the assembled away team. It was apparent when the ship cleared the field; everyone was back to normal instantaneously. "Condition of the people whose suits modified?"

A temporary shelter had been erected and the four sailors, including Red, who had suits that were either nonexistent or sufficiently modified as to be dangerous had been sealed inside.

"All back to normal, sir," Captain Zanella said via the external speaker on his suit.

"Okay," Weaver boomed, turning up the gain on his suit. "In that case, I'm leaning in the direction of induced hallucination. I've got a question for everyone. When we were in the effect, did anyone change to a guy with winged hair, a chin you could use as a metal punch and probably wearing a sword?"

Virtually every Wyvern sensor-pod tracked around until they were looking at Lieutenant Bergstresser.

"What?" Berg asked. "So I was in a race against time to find the Great Umbrella of Light with which to defeat my Great Enemy who had killed my father, married my mother against her will and was bent on universal domination? Sue me. You guys all were *with* me *then*!"

"That's what I was afraid of," Bill muttered. "Damn, I *hate* being a secondary character . . ."

19

Away Station Anime, so named by universal acclaim, had been set up on the edge of the landing platform between two of the entrances to the interior of the station. It was as good a place as any, given that the entrances had no more protection against potential depressurization than the space dock. As far as anyone had detemined, there were no interior air-tight hatches. Of course, with the way that the thing was constructed they might be everywhere.

The station was fourteen sealed bubble tents, each with its own airlock and internal "safe pods," essentially air-tight bags that could be used in an emergency. The bags partially inflated so that they were personal tents inside the bubble tents and were standard sleeping quarters.

The Wyverns, however, could not enter the tents, so the Marines were forced to don respirators for the short walk to their Wyverns. O_2 toxicity was variable and based on genetics and body chemistry. Some people could handle O_2 at very high partial pressures, the equivalent of sixty feet underwater or three times Earth's atmosphere. Most people, however, reacted negatively at just double pressure or the equivalent of thirty feet. The station's atmosphere was at the equivalent of forty feet, so in an emergency some of the station personnel might find it survivable.

So far, nobody had tested it out.

"Captain Zanella, we're established," Bill said. "What is your plan on surveying?"

"I'm going to start slow, sir," the Marine replied. "I'm going to put the platoons on shift. One platoon exploring, one platoon on standby in case of emergency and one platoon down. The exploring platoon will break up into teams and be given quadrants of the station to explore. We have no real feel for how the interior is set up, so I'm going to have them start with short penetrations and then return to report. If we find that going is easy, we'll expand."

"Works for me," Bill said. "Tell them to keep an eye out for anything odd . . . well, odder than normal for here, and if they find anything report back. I'll be down the platform a ways."

Bill opened up the camp-chair, then laid his guitar case across his knees. Given the immensity of the cavernous space dock, he was far enough away to mute the effects of his playing while still being close enough that he was available in an emergency.

With the CO gone there was *nobody* who could tell him to stop playing! Ah, the heady air of independent command . . .

Opening up the case he removed the guitar and the four speakers, then set everything down and laid the speakers out for maximum spread.

Last he sat down in the camp-chair, again, slung the guitar strap around his neck and turned on the instrument. There was a faint "thump" as the speakers came on-line.

He twanged the E string and then slid his finger down the string, listening to the effect. Damn, for all its immensity, the place had AWESOME acoustics. Even this muted, he could hear a perfect echo of the sound.

He ran through a short riff, noodling along and tuning, getting the feedback just right. He tested the mike system . . . "Mee, mee, mee, mee, meeeeee . . ." then removed a set of receiver plugs, put them in his ears, set the volume to "Ridiculous" and let 'er rip . . .

"Holy *grapp!*" Red shouted. "All that's coming out of those little speakers? I've been in heavy metal concerts that weren't this loud!"

"We gotta do something!" Gants shouted back.

"You're darned right we do!" Miriam said, holding her own ears. "If I have to listen to this 70s *chither* much longer I'm going to jump off the edge of the platform!"

"I wouldn't mind it so much if he just wouldn't *sing!*" Red screamed.

"ANNA GADDA DA VIDA," Weaver screamed, his eyes closed and grooving to the music. "ANNA GADDA DA VIDA. ANNA GADDA DA*VIDA*! ANNA GADDA DAVIDA—"

He started at a tap on his shoulder and clamped one hand over the guitar strings, pulling out an earplug.

"Yeah?" he asked.

"Sir," Gants said diffidently. "I'm not sure you're aware of how loud that is at the base, sir. With all due respect . . ."

It was one of those command moments, a moment when an officer has to decide what sort of leader they are. Do they take into account the needs of their people? And if so, to what extent? Do they choose to be loved or hated and feared? An officer on independent command has God-like powers of life and death. Are they to be Patton or Bradley? Spruance or Nimitz? Nelson or . . .

"Message received," Bill replied, putting the earplug back in. "Call me if there's an emergency. *There's a lady who's sure, all that* glitters *is gold . . .*"

20

"Oh, thank God we're away from that," Lance Corporal Ken Smith said. The moment the Marine team stepped into the corridor, the sound of the continuing concert cut out.

"I don't mind being in rock concerts," Sergeant Tye Day admitted. "But the XO's just about good enough for a warm-up band, not the main show."

"Playing's not so bad," Lance Corporal Ruoff added, looking at the deck of the cylindrical corridor. "I just wish he wouldn't sing. So how do these things work? Floor looks solid to me."

"They said you just walk," Day replied, taking a tentative step. "That didn't take me far," he added, beginning to walk.

"Uh, Sergeant?" Ruoff said. "Wait for us."

Day rotated his sensor pod and saw that he'd already advanced thirty meters.

"Cool. Okay, we're supposed to go in for fifteen minutes or until we see something odd," the sergeant said, looking at the luminescent walls and flexible flooring.

"Whatever 'odd' means around here. Keep your eyes open for threats. Let's go."

"Sir," Captain Zanella said over Weaver's implant. "The first entry team is overdue."

"Damn," Weaver said, setting the guitar on the deck and standing up. "How long?"

"Only five minutes, sir," Zanella replied. "But it was to be a fifteen minute penetration."

"I'll be right there."

"If they're not back in another fifteen minutes we'll have to find out why," Bill said. "We'll take the rest of the platoon and set in a retrans system. Drop Wyverns along the way to maintain commo. One team in the lead."

"Permission to lead that, sir," the first sergeant said.

"Granted, Top," Zanella replied. "I'm wondering what got them?"

"They could have poked the wrong button for all we know," Bill said.

"Captain Zanella," Gunnery Sergeant Vankleuren said over the company frequency. "I'm picking up scattered transmissions from the team."

"Retrans," the CO snapped.

". . . it's to the left!"

"Right!"

"Damnit, Sergeant, I've seen this same intersection four times now!"

"Well, if you have a better idea of where we should be going, Lance Corporal, just be clear about it!"

"I am! Go left!"

"Day," the CO snapped. "What happened?"

"Sir . . . This place is a maze . . ."

"According to our inertial systems, we were barely three hundred meters from the docking bay, sir . . ."

"Inertial systems aren't going to work on the slidewalks," Weaver said dryly. "They damp inertia. You could have been ten klicks away for all you knew."

"I tried to maintain a comprehensible route, sir," the sergeant continued, miserably. "But there were forks, by my estimate, every twenty meters or so. I stayed on the right-hand fork for a while but then the guidance system said we were going back to the docking bay so I took a couple of lefts and then . . ."

"You got lost," Captain Zanella said sternly. "So much for spatial awareness, Sergeant."

"Sir, there's no landmarks in there," Day protested. "And with the way that the slidewalk works, there's no *feel* for where you are."

"This is going to be a problem," Bill said. "I can see the sergeant's point."

"Ball of twine," Miriam said.

"Probably the only solution," the XO acknowledged. "But do we have that long of a ball of twine?"

"You mean, lay down a string behind you?" Captain Zanella asked. "There are the safety lines for the Wyverns. They're monomolecule lines but they're only about eighty meters long. We're not going to get far with just those."

"Hook a few together," Bill said, shrugging. "See if there's a way to mark the turns. Space tape sticks to this stuff. Work it out. I'll be down the platform . . ."

❄　❄　❄

"And tape . . ." Lance Corporal Strait said, slapping a square of space tape on the left-hand wall as they turned left at a fork. "Any idea where we're going, Sergeant?"

"If I knew that, Strait, I'd be a genius," Lyle replied. "But so far nobody's found anything but corridor. There has to be something at the end of . . ."

"Whoa," Corporal Hamilton said as the corridor debouched into an open area. The circular chamber was about twenty meters across and filled from deck to overhead with glowing crystals. Like the walls, the crystals fluoresced in a waving pattern of pastel colors. There was another opening to the side, presumably going to a similar corridor to the one they'd just left.

"Okay," Lyle said. "We found something."

"But what?" Weaver asked, touching one of the crystals, lightly. "Miriam?"

"Your guess is as good as mine," the linguist replied, walking through the crystals. "Power system? Living quarters? A computer? There does not seem to be any defined pattern to their layout; they almost look randomly spaced . . . No . . . There's a pattern but I think it's . . . I've seen it before . . . I think I can see the equation . . ."

"I'll leave you to it," Bill said. "Captain Zanella, keep a team present while Miss Moon investigates this . . . anomaly. I'll be back at the platform . . ."

"*Amazing grace, how sweet the sound,*" Miriam sang, cross-legged on the floor and surrounded by equation filled papers. She was sure there was a reason for the layout of the crystals, but every energy system she'd considered didn't fit. And when she was severely puzzled, she either had to play music in the background or sing. Since she didn't have her MP3 chip with her, singing was the only choice. *"That saved a wretch like me . . ."*

"Ma'am!" Staff Sergeant Danny Robbins said over the comm. "Ma'am!"

"What?" Miriam asked, breaking out of her reverie.

"Damn," the staff sergeant said. "It stopped. That crystal you were leaning against just started to light up. Light up more, that is. It was sort of pulsing. I'd suggest you move away from it."

"Send me your recording," Miriam said, standing up and backing away from the pillar.

When she saw the video of the pillar of crystal pulsing she cocked her head to the side.

"How long had it been doing that?" Miriam asked.

"Not sure, ma'am," the sergeant admitted. "We were watching the entrances. I just turned around to check on you and it was pulsing like that."

Miriam watched the pulses for a moment and they were oddly familiar. Repetitive and . . .

"Oh My God," Miriam said. She turned on her external speakers and sounded a clear, high note. Among so many other skills, the linguist had perfect pitch and was an operatically trained singer. All seven of the pillars lit up, each turning a separate bright shade. As she held the note, going stronger and lighter, the pillars followed sync with their lights and the note seemed to be refracted by some sort of an echo effect, becoming a chord.

"That was pretty," Robbins said.

"And I'm beginning to wonder if that's not *all* it is," Miriam replied, making a moue.

"Do it again," Weaver said, watching the lights play on the pillars fade.

"*We wrestle not against flesh and blood but war against the powers of darkness . . .*" Miriam sang. The pillars flashed ripples of color through their depths, catching every tone and subtone of the hymn and turning it into glorious light. "*But we are mighty through God by the Blood of His Son that has rendered the Enemy Powerless.*"

"Cool," Weaver whispered. "Let me try: *If I leeeeave here tomorrrrrrow, Would you still remember meeeee . . .?* Huh . . . ?"

The pillars flashed to the words but the colors were muted, dull and even muddy in places, colors interacting unpleasantly.

"Why'd it do that?" Bill asked, confused.

"Uh, sir?" Staff Sergeant Robbins said, wincing. "No disrespect is intended, sir. But while you're pretty good with a guitar . . . You really should leave the singing to Miss Moon. Sir."

"Sir, with all due respect, if you're in here we'll be out of commo," Captain Zanella said, twitching slightly as Weaver tuned up the guitar. Everyone was starting to twitch when the guitar came out.

"I won't be long, Captain," Weaver said, hitting the E string, then running up the notes. On the A string, one of the pillars looked a little odd, and listening to the note again Weaver realized it was just slightly flat. "I'm conducting an experiment."

"Sir," Staff Sergeant Robbins said from the corridor outside the music room. Fortunately, he didn't have to shout since something was muting the "music" being performed within. "I'm aware that we really should have the CO of the away team immediately available at all times. But if he's in there, he's not out on the platform."

"Point," Zanella replied. "Right. Set up a series of retrans boxes so we can get ahold of him at any time. And let's hope he *stays* in there."

"We've found nine of these music rooms so far," Captain Zanella reported. "A couple slightly larger with a larger number of crystal pillars, but essentially the same. Tests indicate that all of them respond to musical notes. Response seems to be highest to well replicated opera and classical. The worst response is to rap."

"Well, they respond to music," Bill said. "They really like 'In-A-Gadda-Da-Vida.'"

"At least something does," the Marine muttered under his breath.

"Excuse me, Captain?" Bill said.

"Nothing, sir. However, there are no more advanced findings. Just these music rooms. And they appear to have no external effect. Colonel Che-chee has a Combat Space Patrol up and they've seen no external response nor have sensors indicated higher levels of particle emissions."

"How far have you spread out?" Bill asked, muttering under his breath. "*Anna Gadda Davida . . .*"

"That's hard to determine, sir," the Marine said, wincing. "But I estimate a kilometer. I also estimate, based on the best readings we can get from the inertial nav systems, that the music rooms are close to the tips of the Tree. And they seem to be found most easily by taking lefts at the forks. The one team that experimented with taking only right-hand turns at the forks found none and ended back at the dock."

"I'm starting to think that the gravity in the tubes is always down for the tube but may not be in the same direction as the space dock," Miriam said. "You'd never know if your spatial orientation was changing in the tubes. That being the case, some of those right-hand tubes may be going 'up' to access more of the music rooms on the far side of the Tree. So far, this place seems to be some sort of a music training facility."

"I hope that remark wasn't pointed in my direction," Weaver said, still upset that that crystals didn't like his singing.

"Not at all," Miriam replied. "You play a very good '70s rock and roll guitar. Admittedly, that's the same as saying Chief Duppstadt makes a fine spinach fandango but *as* spinach fandango it's not all that bad . . ."

"Oh, thank you *very* much," Bill snapped. "I suppose I should be playing some European electronic *chither*?"

"To each her own," Miriam said, grinning.

"This isn't getting us anywhere," Bill replied. "Captain, have your teams spread out further, concentrating on rights. Find more of the alternate exits to the docking bay, since we can see a bunch of them. Possibly use the boards to move to higher levels. Try to get forward. There has to be a control room or an engine room *somewhere*."

"Aye, aye, sir," the Marine said.

"I'm off-watch," Bill continued. "I'm going to go put my head down. Wake me if there are any new reports or emergencies."

"If I see one more of those crystal caves . . ." Corporal Shingleton muttered.

In a week of constant searching, the Marines had developed a feel for the layout of the corridors. Constant rights eventually brought you back to the docking bay. Throw in a few lefts and you ended up on different levels. More lefts and you eventually found a music room. If you got to the far side of the bay the pattern reversed. The interior of the Tree was like M.C. Escher come to life and if you could think in surrealism it was simple.

With the pattern more-or-less understood, the need for laying out wires and space-tape markers reduced. Permanent space-tape markers were installed at various points so when, not if, the Marines got lost they had directions to return to the base.

This, though, was the most advanced recon to date. With the pattern understood, the team was attempting to penetrate to the far end of the Tree. However, they'd found that it was increasingly hard since there were more and more of the music rooms, or "crystal caves" as the Marines called them. Missing them was getting harder and harder.

"You got your wish," Lance Corporal Lynn Eakins said. "Got a cave."

"Take a right," Sergeant Bae replied, striding along behind the point. Eakins was in the lead by thirty meters with Shingleton bringing up the rear.

"Is it getting brighter?" Eakins asked as they came to another fork. "Left or right, Sergeant?"

"Left," Bae said, musingly. "Probably another cave but—"

"DREEN!"

"It appears to be a small force of Dreen ground-fighters, sir," Captain Zanella said. "Eakins took a thorn in his armor but he's only lightly wounded. The other two escaped without injury."

"But we've got Dreen on the station," Bill said, wincing. "We need to move the camp to a more secure spot. Move it to the rear-most cave. Leave one platoon to provide security for that move. You're in charge of that. I'll go forward with Lieutenant Ross in command of the Marines."

"Sir, with all due respect . . ."

"We *cannot* lose both of us," Bill replied. "And if the Dreen have found the control center, I want to be there, Captain. So follow your orders."

"Yes, sir."

"It was just forward of here, sir," Sergeant Bae said, pointing to a red-marked square of space tape on the luminescent wall. "There were two turns, we went left at each of them."

"Lieutenant Morris, leave one team here to maintain control of this intersection," Lieutenant Ross said. "Lieutenant Bergstresser, your platoon has the lead."

"Aye, aye, sir," Berg said. "Gunny, point team."

"Champs, you're up," Gunny Juda said. "And I'll be right up your ass."

"Teams will enter the open area described by Sergeant Bae," Berg said over the platoon freq. "Charlie center, Alpha left, Bravo right. Order of targeting will be cannoneers to thorn throwers, riflemen to dogs. Do not engage any unrecognized type unless they present a notable threat. Teams will advance with maximum speed to the open area, eliminating resistance in the corridor by constant fire and movement. Use the boot, don't piss on them."

"Gung-ho, sir," First Sergeant Powell said. "You heard the man, Champs. Let's go kill us some Dreen."

Sergeant Champion wasn't watching his speed indicator; he was too focused on the targets in the corridor. The Dreen had apparently laid out dog-demons as security and there was one every thirty meters or so. More as they approached the open area. He'd gotten three so far but there were two together, using the corridor to charge him at lightning speed . . .

"Get the left," Powell shouted as a wall of fire came by Champion's suit.

Champion bit down on his trigger, sending a stream of .50 caliber rounds down the corridor, but he could not track in on the charging demon . . .

"*Chither!*" he shouted as the demon latched onto the leg of his suit and flipped him onto his face. Their contact may have had no inertia to it, but the low-slung, powerful alien was more than capable of lifting a Wyvern suit off its feet.

"Got it," Kaijahano said, firing a single cannon round into the dog-demon's exposed back.

"We got company," First Sergeant Powell said, dropping to a knee and firing down the corridor. "Sir, the entry is blocked. Too many to bull through."

"Platoon," Berg said calmly, "take positions and open fire."

"How many of these things *are* there?" Ducksworth asked rhetorically. The corridor was getting piled up with bodies of Dreen, mostly dog-demons.

"A lot," Champion replied. With his mangled suit-leg, he could only fire from the prone but it didn't really matter. His team was belly down, side by side with him, while Bravo took a knee and Alpha was standing. The wall of fire had the Dreen stopped in the corridor and there were no more forks, but that didn't mean there wasn't a way around. If there were enough of them, and under an intelligent controller, they could use the corridors to bypass the blocking position and hit them in the rear.

Of course, then they'd run into Third Platoon, who were patiently waiting for an opportunity to get it stuck in.

"Or not," Champion said as the wave receded. "Sir, we're out of targets."

"Either they're out of bodies or the controller has taken a different choice," Berg said. "Hold your position . . ."

". . . stopped," Berg said over the command freq.

"We still need to get into that room," Weaver replied.

"How's your ammo level?" Lieutenant Ross asked.

"Nominal," Berg replied. "We're still all in the green. One suit mobility damaged."

"Third will remain in support," Lieutenant Ross said.

"Second platoon will assault forward into the room. Move it out, Two-Gun."

"*Chither*," Berg said, sliding to the floor of the immense cavern, then popping back up to look around. He couldn't exactly stop for sight-seeing but it looked much like the other crystal caves, just immensely larger and with much larger crystals.

The crystals were the problem, as it was apparent the remaining Dreen were using them for cover. He could see a mass of fungus towards the rear of the compartment but between the Marines and the fungus a horde of Dreen thorn-throwers darted in and out from the pillars, laying down a wall of fire.

The only cover was the one difference between this compartment and the others, besides the size, a low wall that had an opening by the corridor but stretched in a semicircle around the compartment, truncating by both side walls. However, there was a fifty-meter open area between the wall and the crystals the Dreen were using for cover.

"I'm hit!" Shingleton screamed. "*Grapp*, I'm hit!"

"Stay frosty, Kelly," Sergeant Bae said. "How bad is it . . . ?"

"We need to clear those pillars," Lieutenant Bergstresser said. "Somebody needs to flank them!"

"Then *you* do it, sir!" Champion snarled. The sergeant had crawled forward on his belly and barely made it to cover behind the wall. But he was up and firing over it. Just as the last words left his mouth, though, he let out an "unk" and fell back, blood pouring out of his suit.

Berg was sorely tempted to do just that, but he also knew it wasn't his job.

Bae was down a man. With Champs gone that left . . .

"Staff Sergeant Carr," Berg said. "You will move your team to the right, using the wall for cover. When you reach the end of the wall, report in. We will provide cover fire for your movement to the pillars. Take the Dreen force in the flank and drive them out."

"Aye, aye, sir," the staff sergeant replied. "Dupe, Rucker, on me."

21

"We lost Sergeant Champion and Lance Corporal Rucker, KIA," Eric reported tonelessly. "Corporal Shingleton was injured by a thorn and we've been unable to stop the bleeding. He needs to be evacuated to the base. There appears to be a final defensive point beyond the fungus. When Staff Sergeant Carr's team attempted to approach from beyond the last crystal pillar, they took plasma fire. He stated that it was white in color, not green."

"Nitch," First Sergeant Powell said. "Maybe Mreee. Both of them use blasters and the plasma is white."

"That was where we lost Rucker," Carr said. "It tracked in on him. Right around the cover of the crystals."

"Yeah, that's one of those Mreee/Nitch blasters," Powell said. "They'll do that."

"We couldn't even get a good look at who was firing," Carr said. "There's a bunch of spread-fungus down there, too. I'd rather not get into that if we can avoid it."

"We need to clear this compartment, Staff Sergeant," Bill said. "But I'll admit we need something to clear the fungus so we can." He thought about that for a second and then snapped his fingers, the claws of his suit trying to follow suit. "Miriam."

"Miriam can clear the compartment?" Lieutenant Ross said, surprised. "How, sir?"

"Let's get your wounded and KIA back to the camp, Lieutenant," Bill said. "I need to talk to Miss Moon."

"Well, of course, I brought some with me," Miriam said. "I'm not done studying them. I'll admit, this isn't the best environment . . ."

The camp had been moved to one of the larger crystal caves and even the conversation of the camp tended to trigger the crystals. The whole area was lit by effulgent light from the glittering pillars.

"Well, here's an experiment for you," Bill said. "We can't clear that forward compartment until we get rid of the fungus in the way; that stuff will infest a Wyvern suit like nobody's business. Can your spiders clear it?"

"I've only got the two," Miriam said. "But they're parthenogenic. I don't actually know what their rate of reproduction would be in an optimal environment . . ."

"Would an optimal environment be a pile of dead Dreen?" Bill asked. "We've got that."

"I'm not sure," Miriam said. "I've never been able to experiment with Class Four biologies. The best I can suggest is we can try."

"It looks dead," Eric said, examining the space spider through the glass of the box.

"I evacuated the air," Miriam said. "They go into hibernation in vacuum."

She twisted the valve on the inlet, letting air into the box, and the spider immediately began to move.

"Okay," she said, opening it up and dropping the spider onto one of the dead dog-demons. "Here goes nothing."

The arachnoid appeared to be surprised to be awake, spinning in place in confusion, then began wandering across the dead Dreen, its antenna waving. When it found the exit wound from the .50 caliber that had killed the Dreen it paused for a moment then dove into the hole.

"I wonder what it's—" Eric started to say, then there were crunching sounds from inside the Dreen. "Yuck."

"Interesting," Miriam said. "No reaction to the increased oxygen that I can determine." She sat down with her back to the bulkhead and pulled out a lab book. "Time is . . . fourteen twenty-three. Now to see what happens . . ."

"That didn't take long," Eric said, trying not to retch as small arachnoids streamed out of the collapsing carcass of the Dreen. It had been less than two hours and starting with one of the space spiders the dog-demon was now almost totally consumed.

"Their rate of propagation in the presence of food resources from a Class Four biology is amazing," Miriam said. "Can you grab a couple of them so I can observe rate of growth? I'd love to get a count on them but I think that's going to be hard. Two thousand, you think?"

"I cannot listen to that anymore!" Sergeant Bae screamed, his Wyvern's claws up against his sensor pod. "Okay, external audio is *off*!"

"That shouldn't happen to . . . a Dreen," Eakins said, turning his sensors away from the pile of Dreen bodies.

When the wave of arachnoids from the first dead dog-demon hit the pile of Dreen by the entrance, they exploded, reproducing in enormous numbers. It had taken two hours to reduce the first Dreen to bones. It took about the same to do it to a hundred.

"They're moving," Staff Sergeant Carr said.

The, by then, hundreds of thousands of spiders had moved into the compartment, spreading out in a quest for more sustenance. They found it first in the scattered bodies of thorn-throwers, but that satiated them for barely five minutes. Then they hit the fungus.

"Now that's . . ."

". . . A hell of a thing," Berg said. He had used the cover of the pillars to move forward where he could observe the effect of the spiders on the Dreen fungus. Miriam had wanted to do it, but he'd forced her to wait in the corridor and monitor his video.

The spiders weren't having it all their own way. He saw dozens, hundreds, of them being captured by pseudopods thrown out by the fungus. The same thing had happened to humans during the Dreen war and even after. It had especially happened to the armies and mujahideen militias in the Middle East who had thrown themselves into the Dreen "crusaders" much as the arachnoids were doing.

But this was a small patch of fungus and *a lot* of spiders. While one might get captured by the fungus, a dozen other of the creatures swarmed over the pseudopod, eating it as fast as it could digest its captured prey.

Sometimes captured spiders even survived, breaking out to attack the fungus in their own turn. Some were partially absorbed, leaving shredded corpses behind. Perhaps the fungus gained some sustenance from them, but it was being eaten too fast to do anything with it.

As Eric watched, one of the most dreaded things in the galaxy shriveled and fell to the cute little spiders, who munched their way across, unheeding of losses, chewing it up, reproducing even as they moved, leaving little spiders behind which caught at the shreds, moved onward . . .

"Thirty-two minutes to ingest one hundred and sixty-four square meters of spread-fungus," Miriam said. "Not bad. Full time to clear the compartment, from one spider, was approximately four hours forty-nine minutes. Lieutenant Bergstresser, your compartment is now clear of fungus as far as I can see."

"Right," Berg said. "Gunny Juda, move teams forward by fire and maneuver to clear the compartment of remaining threats . . ."

"Sir, this is Bae! You need to see this, sir!"

"This" was a Nitch, a much larger arachnoid than the ones that had cleared the compartment, standing nearly eight feet at the shoulders. The Nitch were one of two Dreen slave races the humans had encountered in the Dreen War, the other being the felinoid Mreee. While the Mreee were a relatively recent addition to the Dreen empire, having been conquered within the lifetime of one of the survivors of the war, the Nitch had been slaves since time immemorial.

The spiderlike Nitch had silvery bodies that reflected oddly in any sort of complex background and actually acted as natural camouflage. But this one was easy enough to see, rolled onto its back, its blaster lying more then ten feet away as if tossed and its legs pulled up in contortions. It was also, quite clearly, dead.

"What's this?" Bae asked, squatting down next to the giant spider. "It's leaking fluid from holes on its sides."

"It was the sentient controller," Berg said, staying well back. He did not particularly like spiders and Nitch gave him the willies. The space spiders were just different enough from true spider forms he found them okay, but Nitch . . . "They're generally hooked into the fungus through tubes that feed them and I guess that they use to control the rest of the Dreen. If there was Dreen stuff *in* them . . ."

A juvenile space spider fell out through one of the holes, walked a few feet and then stopped, its legs pulling in and its carapace wrapping around it in hibernation mode.

This end of the compartment was littered with the hibernating space spiders, so many that it was impossible not to step on them. With the food supply exhausted, they'd apparently shut down in hopes that something would turn up. Space spiders appeared to be nothing if not patient.

"Well, let's get him back to base," Eric said, turning to leave and treading on another of the spider bodies. "And we'll need to get the compartment swept up. I figure Captain Weaver will be up here with his guitar in about . . ."

"We got a way to get these things cleaned up,

Lieutenant?" Weaver asked, walking up, guitar in hand. "I'm afraid the crunching will interfere with the acoustics . . ."

"We must watch the Tree closely for any change," Colonel Che-chee said over the comm. Nine of the dragonflies were parked outside the field of the Tree, hiding in its shade, while the tenth was waiting by the space dock. "In the event we observe any change, Cha-shah will immediately enter the space dock and report. My chronometer says that Captain Weaver will be starting at any time. Observe closely, males! *Any* change in the light patterns, even the slightest! *Any* change in the particle emiss . . . Oh My *GOD!*"

"CAPTAIN WEAVER!" the communicator screamed. "Colonel Che-chee requests that you cease playing immediately!"

"Why?" Weaver bellowed. "Anna Gadda Da Vida . . . !"

"Sir . . . sir . . ." the communications tech stuttered. "JUST *STOP!*"

"That's a hell of a thing," Weaver said, watching the video from Colonel Che-chee's helmet camera.

On the dot of the time-stamp of his starting to play, the entire Tree jumped about five times in luminosity. But that wasn't the really strange part. It began collapsing upwards, the base expanding in size at the same time, the higher points sliding in line with lower and stretching out. He'd stopped before the full transformation could take effect.

"And there was no apparent effect from inside?" Bill asked. "I was up front, so the change never got to me."

"Not that anyone could tell, sir," Captain Zanella said. "Until we got the transmission from Colonel Che-chee, we had no idea there had been a change."

"That's not all, sir," Figueredo said. The astronomy tech had been sent along to assist in investigations. While the exploration of the interior of the Tree had been uninteresting, the readings that he got from the Cheerick suits . . . "Admittedly, they were shielded by the Tree. But there was a sharp change in stellar emissions. They actually *dropped*."

"Run that one by me again," Bill said. "Define."

"Local heat output dropped by ten percent," the astronomy tech replied. "Solar wind dropped by *thirty* percent. Cosmic ray scatter dropped by nine. Those are near orders, sir, but probably close to accurate. Whatever this thing was doing, it was affecting the *star*, sir."

"Okay," Bill said, looking at the Cheerick. "Colonel, I want you to refuel your dragonflies then move out to at least two AU and observe the effects. But not all of them. Send two males."

"You think there may be hazard?" the colonel asked.

"I have no *grapping* clue, Colonel," Bill admitted. "But I'd rather not lose the flight commander."

"'Freebird'?" Weaver muttered to himself. "Too slow. 'Smoke on the Water'? Too bass. 'Jungle Love'? Too campy . . . Ah!"

He hummed to himself for a moment, then started slamming the guitar strings, his eyes closed and grooving to the music. When he finished the intro, he just had to open his mouth. The hell with these crystals and not liking his singing . . .

"*When the sun comes up on a sleepy little town,*" he screamed over the guitar, "*Down around San Antone, And the folks are risin' for another day . . . round about their homes . . .*"

"Sir!" Eric shouted. "Sir! Open your eyes!"

Weaver looked up and the guitar twanged a loud, flat C chord as it slid to a stop. Because he could see what he was doing.

He couldn't see what was happening to the Tree, but he could see the effects. The walls of the room had become transparent and all four of the Jovians were in view. Something was causing the massive planets to fluoresce in different colors. The only thing that would do that, Weaver knew, was massive energy input. Offhand, the amount of joules just wouldn't register. Actually, for a moment they did, then his brain locked up trying to count the zeros. Pretty close to the *total* output of Earth's sun was the best he could figure. For each Jovian. The energetic gas was flashing in all the colors of the rainbow and as the Jovians moved it streamed out behind.

"Don't stop!" Eric shouted again. "It's just started!"

Weaver caught up the melody again, grooving on the music and playing for all he was worth. But this time he kept his eyes open. *This* show was just too good to miss.

"Well, the secret of the Tum-Tum Tree is finally explained," Captain Zanella said, shaking his head.

"It's a concert venue," Weaver finished, grinning. "It's a *grapping* interstellar *concert venue*."

While Weaver was playing in the control compartment, the wall of the compartment the camp had been moved to became transparent as well. As the Tree spun on its axis, the Jovians could be seen fluorescing while the music was transmitted to the entire crew. After a few minutes of playing, the "beams" that the Tree was shooting out began collecting the gases, drawing them towards the Tree and fluorescing them along their entire length. The whole solar system was lit up with cascading waves of lambent color, reds, blues, greens, purples, every color of the rainbow as the gases reacted to the massive power of the Tum-Tum Tree and formed a huge spiral of shining, rippling light.

"Apparently an open one, too," Miriam said. "The caves are now explained. Besides being sort of stellar sky-boxes, they're rooms for bands getting ready to play to warm up. And they have automatic visual feedback if you're not up to par. No offense, Captain."

"None taken," Bill said dryly. "I think the main venue must have filtered out the vocal component."

"It is even more remarkable from space," Colonel Che-chee said. "But we nearly lost a dragonfly. Cha-shah came close to one of the beams and reported that if it had not been for his shield he would now be dead. And he was not even in the beam itself, more than a hundred meters away."

The video shots from the dragonflies showed that the tree opened up into a hemisphere, stretching somehow to engulf the upper *tenth* of the star then *entirely* wrapping it in some sort of absorption field. The incredibly hot, bright, star faded to insignifance, becoming almost black, keeping the light from the star from overwelming the show and feeding the masses of raw power into the beams that created it.

If anything, the most spectacular sight was the Tum-Tum Tree, which must have been using a good quarter of the star's energy itself. It blazed along with the music, visible only from space. But from the right place it would be magnificent.

"Time to full warm up was right at nine minutes," Figueredo said. "At that point, stellar output was less than three percent of normal and the power of the beams was blasting the Jovians so hard they've probably lost a good ten percent of their mass."

"Yeah, but it's gas," Weaver pointed out. "Most of it remained in the orbits. They'll collect it back over time. When this thing was in full use, though, I wonder how they kept them supplied?"

"With these guys, sir, who knows, sir?" Figueredo said. "They could have teleported it through gates from other Jovians. Especially if they could expand the size of the gates."

"Planet-sized gates?" Bill mused. "Heck, just set up a gate to move a smaller Jovian. Put one gate in the way of the incoming Jovian and the other by the one you're refueling."

"That is scary," Miriam said. "That's . . . too big."

"These guys used the *full output* of a blue-white star, twenty thousand *times* the power of Sol, as a *laser-light show*," Bill pointed out. "Throwing around Jovians would be comparatively trivial."

"The males did report something that troubles me," Colonel Che-chee said, her nose twitching. "They say that they could hear the music. Not over the radio, mind you. They could hear it as if they were present. They, in fact, complained about how loud it was."

"Impossible, Colonel," Captain Zanella said. "Noise does not propagate through vacuum, no matter *how* loud it is."

"I told them this," the colonel said. "They still insist that they heard the music."

"Was it in time with the pulsing of the planets?" Bill asked.

"I believe they said it was," the colonel replied.

"There's a way that you could do it," Weaver said musingly. "If you knew the make-up of the receiving ship, or suit in this case, you could tune a gravitational beam to cause harmonics in the receiving ship. But, my God, the computational requirements! You'd have to figure for light-speed lag, the materials you were encountering, location of the target referential to the Jovians and the Tree . . ." He shook his head in wonder. "And all this for an *entertainment* device?!"

"You know, in about eight years this star's going to start blinking from the standpoint of the nearest G class star," Bill said, watching as Red moved out of place and Gants stepped up. The Tree would hold in "playing" position for up to fifteen minutes, apparently to let bands change places. And it reacted to any music, even badly sung or played. It was best with better quality and reacted the most effectively to pure sonic mass, the more decibels the more the planets fluoresced. But it would even cause some reaction from a badly sung nursery tune, as Captain Zanella had demonstrated to everyone's dismay.

"Since there are ruins there, you have to figure that the race that built this thing had this star blinking on and off all the time," Bill continued. "You can just see it: *Those damned kids are at it again!*" He looked less excited than he sounded.

"I'm glad we found this," Miriam replied softly. "It's nice to find that at least one race could pour this much effort into something of beauty, that has no other use than to bring joy." She looked at him for a moment and then snorted. "Penny and some dehydrated fruit for your thoughts?" she added, holding out a bag of dehydrated apples.

"Is it that obvious?" Bill asked.

"Not to get too Star Trekkish," Miriam said. "But I'm also an empath. To me, yeah."

"I'm wondering whether I'm doing the right thing," he said, shrugging. "This is more my cup of tea than personnel records or wheedling clerks. Yes, I chose to be a Naval officer but I'm a scientist at heart. Astro was fun, exciting, challenging in a way that I found . . . useful and interesting. XO . . ."

"Sucks," Miriam said.

"In a nutshell," he replied. "And God only knows how long I'm gonna be stuck as one."

"And you don't get along with Captain Prael," Miriam said. "Not that I blame you."

"We're getting along *better*," he said. "But I'll admit I've been comforting myself with the thought: 'He's not going to be here long.' That said, what do I get next? Somebody more like Spectre? More like Prael? Worse?"

"What are you going to do?" Miriam asked.

"I'm not good at turning down a challenge," Bill said. "And I've gotten better at the paperwork. It's not the sort of paperwork I prefer, and I think it's really limiting my scope, but I'm getting better at it. Being XO has taught me stuff. And if I'm ever going to command the *Blade*, it's stuff I need to know."

"You want to command the *Blade*?" Miriam asked.

"Oh, hell," Bill said, snorting. "I want to *own* the *Blade*. I want to go off looking at what I want to look at. But the closest I'll ever come is commanding it. So, yes. And to do that, I need to be XO. No matter how much it sucks."

"So you're not going to bunk off to something else?" Miriam asked.

"Nope. I'll stick it as long as it takes for the Navy to trust me to command."

"Good," Miriam said. "In that case, I'll stick around too."

"I wonder what Gants is going to sing?"

"No idea," Miriam said. "But it couldn't be worse than Captain Zanella's rendition of 'Mary Had a Little Lamb.'"

Sub Dude stepped into the middle of the crystals and cleared his throat. Sticking his right hand into his blouse, he straightened from his habitual slouch, opened his mouth and proceeded to "sing":

"I am the very model of a modern Major-General,
I've information vegetable, animal, and mineral,

I know the kings of England, and I quote the
*   fights historical*
From Marathon to Waterloo, in order categorical . . ."

"Okay," Miriam said, laughing so hard tears were coming out of her eyes, "I was wrong."

22

"What we need is a band," Weaver said, rubbing his hands together.

"Sir, with all due respect, I think you're taking this too far," Captain Zanella said, smiling.

"I'm not sure he is." Miriam looked at her notes. "There are different effects for the guitar and singing. A band would have that much more effect. Actually, a symphony would be about right or a full opera . . ."

"Anybody else got any instruments?" Weaver asked. "Keyboard? Drums? A flute even?"

"I've got a keyboard," Miriam admitted.

"Really?" Berg said. "I've never heard you play it."

"*I* use headphones," Miriam said. "And I *don't* play '70s rock."

"God, not that Goth stuff," Weaver moaned. "There's hardly a guitar part in it."

"I play classical," Miriam said.

"Well, *that's* not gonna work."

"I dunno," Captain Zanella said. "Be interesting to see how it reacts to 'Toccata and Fugue in D Minor.'"

385

"Got any idea how hard that is to play on a guitar?"

"My point, which I'm making badly, sir," Captain Zanella said, "is that our mission was to investigate and explore this facility and determine *if* we could find its purpose and potentially activate it. *Not* to use it as a concert venue."

"Because we still don't understand its full abilities," Bill pointed out. "We've determined that it can distinguish between recorded music and live and reacts better to live . . ."

"Good thing Ashley Simpson doesn't have to use it, then," Berg quipped.

"That right there is something to investigate," Weaver finished, ignoring the lieutenant. "I see no reason, given that we've determined its purpose, not to fully explore that purpose. I want a survey of all of the sailors and Marines to determine if anyone has any instruments with them and their level of playing ability. I intend to *fully* explore the abilities of this facility."

"A one and a two . . ."

It turned out that there was more musical talent, for want of a better word, on the ship than had been realized. One of Colonel Che-chee's dragonfly pilots had a Cheerick reed-flute with him. The device looked like a super-recorder, played more like a bassoon and had the sound quality of a Peruvian flute. The LPO of the mess section had brought an Adar drum-set, a full collection of drums that could be folded down to the size of an alarm clock. When extended it wasn't much more than thin membranes and floor triggers but it had all the sound of a full drum-set.

With Weaver's guitar and Miriam's keyboard there was a minimal band. Heck, with just Miriam's keyboard there was a minimal band. Her keyboard was just as advanced as Weaver's guitar set-up but with a much broader range of abilities, capable of mixing or replicating a full orchestra.

After a brief wrangle, it was agreed that Miriam was lead singer. And since she was also unwilling to play the *wide* variety of suggestions from Weaver, from Lynyrd Skynyrd to .38 Special to the Allman Brothers, she had also picked the music.

Weaver still, ostensibly, led the band.

"*How can you see into my eyes, like open doors . . .*" Miriam sang as Weaver rolled his eyes. He didn't get to come in with some serious guitar until a third of the way into the song. What kind of rock and roll did you call *that*?

"Def Leppard even," Weaver said.

"Too '80s," Miriam replied, looking over the music that she had with her.

"But it's got big, big sound!" Weaver pointed out. "Big sound is good with this place. Blue Öyster Cult?"

"Ugh!"

"But it was the *original* Goth band," Weaver explained. "What else do you call 'Don't Fear the Reaper'?"

"Discordant noise. And you just want to play 'Smoke on the Water.'"

"That was Deep Purple."

"What*ever*!"

"But it's got a GREAT bass riff! I can set the guitar to bass . . ."

"Oh, here, Crüxshadows! You'll like them."

"*Who*? What the *grapp* is a Crew-shadows?"

"You don't look so good, sir," Captain Zanella said as Weaver slumped into their shared tent.

"The band is experiencing creative differences," Weaver said loftily. "I managed to get Ke-cha on my side with Jethro Tull, since there's actually a flute part, but Miriam's insisting on a bunch of Goth and Industrial bands nobody's heard of. One of them she wanted to replace the fiddle portion with flute and when Ke-cha tried to play it, well, let's just say that he's an okay flute player but he's not up to that person's fiddling. I pointed out that not only was I in command of this expedition, the speakers were mine and *she* suggested that I sounded like a vulture squabbling over carrion when I sang back-up and . . . Well, we're having creative differences."

"Command is a lonely thing, sir," Captain Zanella said, trying not to grin. "But to put it in nautical terms, sir, sometimes you just can't fight the tide."

"Your input is duly noted, Captain."

"*A choice profound is bittersweet,*" Miriam sang. "*No one hears Cassandra cry . . .*"

"That actually wasn't all that bad," Weaver said, plucking at the strings of his guitar and working over a riff he'd flubbed.

"Planets seemed to like it," PO Carpenter said. "But you could tell it was written for a drum machine."

"Well," Miriam said, sighing. "I think that there's a band that you and Captain Weaver would prefer. I *suppose* we could try Manowar."

"Mano . . . who?"

"Their blood is upon my steel!" Weaver screamed, head bobbing as he slammed the guitar, *"Their blood is upon my steel . . ."*

"That wasn't entirely awful," Miriam said, taking her earplugs out. "You should consider getting into death-metal. You've actually got the voice for it."

"Was that a compliment on my singing voice?" Weaver asked, amazed.

"Not really," Miriam said. "I was thinking of something like Rob Zombie. You just sort of growl the lyrics. I'll point out that the lead singer of *this* band has a rendition of 'Nessun Dorma' on one of their albums that's good enough for the Met. But you didn't do *too* badly."

"Like the drum part," PO Carpenter said, tapping the snare drum. "Really got the argon planet flashing in the middle there."

"I wonder how much mass we've blown off," Weaver said, looking at the system. Even with the pause in the music, the tendrils of gas between the planets were still fluorescing from unexpended energy. They'd been playing, off and on, for long enough that there was now a solid band of gasses joining the Jovians.

Ke-cha had returned to his duties as a dragonfly pilot. They'd tried to work in the flute playing, but it really didn't work. The Cheerick was just as glad. After the first session he'd taken to wearing his flight-armor since it cut down on the decibels.

"I wonder what would blow the *most* off," Carpenter said.

"Dragonforce," Miriam admitted. "But we don't have four guitar players who can also sing. Or one for that matter . . ."

"So what do we have down so far?" Weaver asked, ignoring the jibe.

"I don't think we have any of it *down*," Miriam pointed out. "Unless you consider a band playing at a high-school prom as having the music *down*. I suppose we could just play 'Cocaine' over and over again and it would be fine by *you*."

"Perfectionist."

"Neophyte . . ."

"Creative differences again?"

"We were just getting the sound right, you know . . . ?" Weaver felt more relaxed than he had in months.

"Okay, no arguing this time," Weaver said, holding his hand up and lifting his chin. "We have six songs we all agree upon, more or less. We'll just practice those. That's enough for one set. Then we'll see what we can get this system to do. Miriam, just one question. Are there *any* of the '80s stadium band songs you can stand? Because that's big sound and we need big sound."

"'Final Countdown,'" Miriam muttered under her breath.

"What was that?" Weaver asked.

"'Final Countdown,'" Miriam muttered, somewhat louder.

"Spectre's Anthem?" Carpenter said, laughing. The former CO of the *Blade*, back when it was a submarine that snuck off planet by outrunning *Akulas*, would use the song, blasting at full power of the sonar system, to warn the Russian submarines he was coming through and they needed to get out of the way. Or whales for that matter.

"I like it," Miriam said angrily. "Okay? Is that enough? I admit it! I've got the sound effects programmed already. I've also got a Whitesnake's Greatest Hits CD! Satisfied?"

"Just when you think you know somebody," Weaver said. "Okay, let's try that . . ."

"Whoa . . ." Weaver muttered, watching the Jovians rippling in after-effect. "It *really* likes 'Fight For Freedom.'"

"And it's got a great guitar riff," Miriam pointed out.

"And piano," Carpenter said.

"Lots of drum."

"It's a winner."

"No more creative differences?" Captain Zanella asked, looking over the patrol reports.

"I've got to admit, some of this newer stuff isn't bad," Weaver said.

"Manowar's been around since the early '80s," the Marine said, not looking up. "I had one of their albums in *high school*."

"Really?" Weaver said. "Go figure. Thought there was a reason they were good . . ."

"This is boring," Cha-shah said, looking at the starscape.

"Be glad you're out here and not listening to what

humans call music," Ke-cha replied. "It is awful stuff, the worst caterwauling you've ever heard."

"I heard some of it. It is *very* bad," the Cheerick acknowledged. "How can they listen to that horrible stuff."

"I don't think they have ears like we do," Ke-cha said. "In fact . . ."

"Why is this light blinking so hard all of a sudden?" Cha-shah asked.

"I do . . . not know," Ke-cha said, slowly. "It is a red light. That is bad. You have one as well?"

"Yes . . ." the Cheerick male said, puzzling out the words under the flashing light. "Dreen . . . emissions . . . indicator . . ."

"Captain Weaver! We have Dreen emergence in-system!"

"Damn," Weaver muttered, leaning his guitar on a crystal pillar. "I thought we were getting that last riff together, too . . ."

23

Weaver looked at the combined sensor data from the dragonflies and tried not to flinch.

The good news was that the unreality node the Dreen were using was well out from the star and the Tree. Given Dreen known accelerations, it was going to be at least eighteen hours before the main body of the unit arrived.

The bad news was, he now knew what a Dreen *fleet* looked like in sensor data.

Useful information, but there was no way in hell they were going to be able to show it to anyone. Not with over *sixty* Dreen warships in the system. Seven of the emissions were higher than any previous recorded; one of them was so immense he had to wonder if the Dreen used planetoids. It wasn't a patch on the output of the Tree even when quiescent, but it was a huge *grapping* emission for a ship. And it was definitely moving, albeit slowly. Change that estimate to about an Earth day. But about thirty minutes after they arrived, every human on the space station would be dead.

One mega*grapper* ship. Six uberdreadnoughts. Nine Dreen production dreadnoughts. Three capital ships, emission type unknown, probably converts. *Seven grapping* carriers. Seven. That meant upwards of *four hundred* Dreen fighters. The rest were what were identified by humans and Hexosehr as cruisers, destroyers and frigates. Of course, a half dozen destroyers were considered a fair match for the *Blade II*. This was . . .

"Well, that's a hell of a thing," he said, nodding calmly. "Captain Zanella, kindly ask Colonel Che-chee to join us in our quarters."

System change over seven percent. Analysis.

<Energy has been transferred to gas giants creating out-gassing. Method and reason unknown. Emissions from small units detected. Tentatively identified as space fighters or shuttles. Species unknown. Anomaly has changed configuration: Correlation?>

Correlation data preliminary. Analysis of energy spectra indicates inability of species to have effected change. More data must be gathered. Establish communications with Sentient 754-839-847-239. Send small-unit task group to anomaly. Possibility anomaly has fallen into new species' hands. Attach ground combat task-group.

<We are loyal.>

"A smaller unit has broken off the main fleet," Captain Zanella said. "Smaller being a relative term. Six destroyers and three fast units about the same size whose signature we've never seen before. And they're headed here. Estimate one day away."

"Not much else in the system to head to," Weaver pointed out. "Are you getting that puckering feeling in your bottom that I am?"

"Fast personnel carriers?" Captain Zanella said. "A boarding party?"

"They're probably detecting the dragonflies and the changes in the system are going to be really evident," Weaver said, shaking his head. "Maybe playing the music was a bad idea, but it's too late to worry about that. Colonel Che-chee."

"Yes, Captain," the Cheerick said. "We are prepared to fight in space or on the ground."

"Yeah," Weaver said. "But are you prepared to run away?"

"Where are we to run to?" the colonel asked.

"Back side of the sun from them," Weaver said. "By the Jovian on that side. The *Blade*'s estimated to return in no more than four days. Could be as little as two, God help them. Your mission is to load up on consumables, pick up your drop tanks and get out into the deep system and hide. Make contact with the *Blade* when she returns and tell her what this thing is."

"I would remain by your side, Captain Bill," the Cheerick said, using the only name they could say before having the Hexosehr translators.

"That's nice and all that," Bill said. "But there's really no reason for you to die, too. *We* don't have a way to escape and *somebody's* got to be around to explain how this all went wrong. You just drew the short straw, Colonel."

※　　※　　※

"Rotator guns here and here," Captain Zanella said, pointing to two of the intersections. "That closes off the last two approaches to the control cavern. First and Third Platoon will engage the enemy forward, degrading their action capability and determining their action plan. Second Platoon will remain in positional defense, holding the control cavern. Smart mines set to rhino output along all the corridors. Thirty percent on the final two corridors. If the rest bypass them, it means we'll be able to take out up to thirty rhino-tanks at the cost of not engaging any of the dogs or throwers. Commander's intent is to hold this position long enough for the *Blade* to arrive. If it gets here before the main fleet, it may be able to extract noncombat personnel and wounded. Are these orders clear?"

"Clear, sir," Berg said. The other two lieutenants just nodded.

"Camerone, sir," First Sergeant Powell said, grinning. "Guess you got me the wrong sign, Two-Gun."

"I'm planning on seeing the fields, First Sergeant," Berg said. "We've been in worse predicaments before."

"Name *one*."

"That *has* to be a Dreen brain-ship," Bill said, looking at the sensor data.

Three of the Cheerick pilots had remained, rotating out from the docking cavern to give the units inside information on the approaching Dreen. Bill sometimes wondered if it wouldn't be better to just not know.

But he was getting a better and better look at the approaching storm. What had to be a Dreen brain-ship was an immense organic construction, nearly as long as the Tum-Tum Tree and actually massing *more*. It wasn't a planetoid, but something made entirely of organic materials. The firepower was going to be immense. Enough to destroy the Tree? Well, it probably wouldn't have to.

They'd taken a look at Dreen destroyers, or the leftover bits anyway, after the battle at Orion. If you stripped out the weapons systems and just left the engines and life-support, you'd be able to pack quite a few Dreen combat units in one. How many? Well, a lot more than the Marines were going to be able to stop, that was for sure. And the whole task-force, which was less than twelve hours away, would be able to enter the space dock. That meant cover fire from the destroyers for the landing phase.

"The *Blade*'s not going to be able to engage that force, sir," Lieutenant Ross said. He'd been acting as the away mission XO and was examining the sensor data trying to find any way out of the trap the team found itself in. "Even if they arrive while it's still in system. Just the fighters are enough to keep them back."

The *Blade* attacked by slashing in at superluminal speeds, dropping out of warp for a brief moment and firing its broadside. Based on the results from Orion, when they'd only had one of the chaos guns, it should work well on a Dreen destroyer and even on the cruisers. It would require a large number of attacks to take out one of the dreadnoughts. It might be impossible to destroy the brain-ship. And each time it dropped out of warp, it was vulnerable to fire. It was only vulnerable for a brief window, but that was generally enough time for the Dreen targeting systems to get some licks in.

But its real weakness was the fighters. They could rarely hit the *Blade*, but by the same token the *Blade*'s targeting was designed for getting in close and hitting a *big* target. Coming in at plus the speed of light meant it had, actually, pretty poor targeting. Sticking around to get a better shot usually meant getting holes blown all the *way* through it. It was a PT boat up against battleships; stick and move was the only way to survive.

Dreen fighters were too small and too nimble for the *Blade* to effectively target. And there were going to be a lot of fighters. By itself, there was no way that the *Blade* was going to be able to do a damned thing about this fleet.

"We need to figure out a way to stop them," Bill said. "Destroy at least some of them."

"Well, sir," Ross said slowly, "I don't see us being able to slip any Marines on the brain-ship this time."

"Neither do I," Bill replied. "But there's got to be something we can do . . ."

He looked at the sensor data, then pulled up the solar system map, plugging the information into a navigational program.

"Hmmm . . ."

"The thing is, we can either engage the main fleet or the approaching boarders," Weaver said, bringing up the scenarios. "Both are going to cross the beam going to the xenon gas giant. If we engage the main fleet, we're probably only going to get part of it; most of it is going to be off the elliptic. Ditto the boarders. But we can at least cut either one down."

"We're playing for time," Captain Zanella said. "I

recommend taking out the approaching boarders. Of course, that means some of my Marines might actually survive."

"There would be a time window when we could all survive," Bill said. "If we get most of the boarding group and the *Blade* gets here before the main fleet . . . Okay, that's what we'll do. Time to get the band together."

"This is flipping nuts, sir, you know that," Carpenter said, tapping his drum set.

"Yep," Bill said, looking at the laptop propped in front of him. It had the estimated approach vector of the boarding task force on it and a projection of the beam that would fluoresce the xenon gas giant. The trick was going to be to get the beam to intersect the task force, before it realized it was in trouble. "But that's what we're gonna do."

"'Warriors of the World'" Carpenter asked.

"'Winterborn'" Miriam suggested.

"My calculations, based on spectral data from the fluorescing planets, is that the optimum tonality is soprano vocals in the key of C," Bill said. "Damnit."

"And that would be . . ." Miriam said, grinning.

Change in emission from artifact. Change in shape of artifact. Change in solar output.
Send warning to boarding force, prepare for attack.

"*I can see when you stay low nothing happens does it feel right?*" Miriam sang, soft and slow to a quiet piano and muted drums.

❅ ❅ ❅

*"Late at night
things I thought I put behind me
haunt my mind."*

Long enough for the system to warm up. Long enough for the shield to stretch out, covering the star and absorbing its full energy. Then the power increased . . .

*"I just know there's no escape
now once it sets its eyes on you
but I won't run, have to stare it in the eye . . ."*

Bill looked at the readouts then over his shoulder. "Two . . . three . . . four!"
"*STAND MY GROUND, I WON'T GIVE IN!*" she sang, putting every ounce of vocal energy she could into the powerful chorus as guitar screamed and drums thundered.

*"NO MORE DENYING, I GOT TO FACE IT.
WON'T CLOSE MY EYES AND HIDE THE
    TRUTH INSIDE.
IF I DON'T MAKE IT, SOMEONE ELSE
    WILL . . .
stand my ground . . ."*

The window had opened up as usual but something else was happening. All of the ships in the system were now highlighted and as the beam shot out from the powerful system, one by one outlines of the oncoming fast-movers blinked and blazed, then vanished. The defenders were watching the effect of the station on the ships even as Miriam shifted back to verse:

> *"It's all around*
> *getting stronger, coming closer*
> *into my world*
>
> *I can feel*
> *that it's time for me to face it*
> *can I take it?*
>
> *Though this might just be the ending*
> *of the life I held so dear*
> *but I won't run, there's no turning back from here*
>
> *STAND MY GROUND I WON'T GIVE IN . . . !"*

"We got four of the destroyers, one of the possible troop-carriers and a piece of one of the other destroyers," Bill said jubilantly. "And all through the power of music!"

"If anybody says anything about Muadib, I'm going to strangle them," Miriam said.

"What?"

"Sorry, obscure sci-fi reference."

"Okay, sir," Captain Zanella said. "I appreciate you making my job a little easier. But I've got a question."

"Go."

"What are you going to do for an encore?"

"Oh," Bill groaned. "Captain, put yourself up for punishment."

"That was just *weak*, sir. You shouldn't try to get into a pun fight a cappella."

"Speaking of weak! At least I'm in harmony with the group."

"I think you're sounding a discordant note, sir."

"Stop! Stop!" Miriam screamed. "You're making me want to pitch you both off the station . . . Oh my God. Now *I'm* doing it . . ."

<*Power beams used to cause excitation of gasses in the gas-giants. Task Group encountered one of the beams, either through probability error or intent, causality unclear at this time. Purpose of excitation phenomenon not understood. Unknown species probable cause of structural change and excitation phenomenon. Sentient 475-829-467-821 destroyed. Orders?*>

Order fleet to maneuver out of elliptic to avoid beam. Order non-sentients to assault station and destroy enemy infestation. Sonic anomaly analysis?

<*Gravitational waves induced sonic response in hulls of ships. Reason unknown.*>

Danger?

<*Nominal. Gravitational level too low to effect damage.*>

"Everything has a harmonic," Bill said, gesturing at the station. "Even this thing does. If you get just the right harmonic, you can shake it apart."

"And this means what?" Carpenter asked, tapping his cymbal.

"So do ships," Bill said, gesturing at the opaque wall of the cavern. "One of Che-chee's pilots reported that he heard sounds when they were in space. I don't see this thing being only for the people inside. The best view is going to be from in space. But you're going to want to *hear* the concert. Space doesn't propagate sound."

"The gravitational beams you were talking about," Miriam said. "You think we can use those to shake the ships apart?"

"It's worth a try," Bill said. "And, at the very least, I don't think they probably have our taste in music. Maybe if we annoy them enough they'll go away."

"'Those damned kids . . .'"

"Exactly. It worked on a neighbor when I was in high school . . ."

"Captain Weaver has something he thinks may take out some of the other ships," Captain Zanella said. "But that's not our problem for now."

"Our problem is an unknown quantity of Dreen that are about to board this station," Lieutenant Ross said.

"Exactly," Zanella continued with a chuckle. "But with the captain taking out some of their ships, I figure we've got a fighting chance. They're maneuvering to dock at the moment. Last minute suggestions are accepted."

"Where'd we put those hibernating spiders?" Berg said, after none of the other officers spoke up.

"Like that one. *Just* like that one."

"These things give me the creeps," Lance Corporal Moorehead said.

The Marines had gathered up the hundreds of thousands of mostly quiescent space spiders in every available container and First and Third Platoons had carried them forward, scattering them along the approach corridors. Nobody knew if they'd attack live Dreen or not, but it was worth a shot. And they were great for cleaning up the battlefield.

"Just keep scattering," Staff Sergeant Robbins growled. "And be glad it's not with your hands."

Alpha First was the most forward team, scattering the spiders along the corridors that had been first explored, right down by the landing platform the *Blade* had used. Most of the teams were much farther back, in the corridors that were certain to be used to approach the control cavern. But enough gear had been left scattered on the platform that the Dreen might use it for entry so it was decided to leave a few presents behind.

"I'm just saying," Moorehead replied, tossing spiders as he walked along. "These things are creepy."

"And I'm just saying scatter them and shut your gob," Robbins said. He was about fifty meters from the platform, in view of it in other words, when a shadow swept over the crystalline structure. "Scatter faster! Scatter faster!"

"Alpha First reports Dreen landing on the same platform we used," Captain Zanella reported. "Numbers unknown. I've left sensor pods behind to try to get a count, but none on the platform."

"Go to it, Captain," Weaver said, looking up from his equations. "I don't think we're going to be able to anticipate the harmonics; we're just going to have to jam. I hope your troops can fight and listen to music at the same time."

"You'd be surprised how often they do just that, sir," Zanella said with a sigh.

"Now that Captain Weaver's given up singing, it's really not all that bad," Lance Corporal Strait said. He was crouched at an intersection, peeking around the corner looking for the foe.

"Kinda strange hearing 'Winterborn' sung by a girl, though," Corporal Hamilton pointed out.

"I miss the violin," Sergeant Lyle said. "The synthetic just isn't the same."

"Face it, nobody does 'Winterborn' like—DREEN."

"I didn't think the Dreen played music," Lyle said, triggering a burst of fire into an oncoming dog-demon. "I've never heard them play at all . . ."

"Third Platoon falling to secondary positions," Captain Zanella said. "Prepare to pass them through your lines, Lieutenant."

"Aye, aye, sir," Berg replied. "*I will not run, this is my place to stand . . .*" he whispered. "Platoon, prepare to pass Third through the lines! *And in the fury of this darkest hour . . .*"

<Report from non-sentient boarders. Moving forward in face of resistance from units identified as Species 27264. Ten percent casualties in boarding units. Ground Combat Level Four units entering combat. Organism 8139 detected on station. Per standard procedure, ten percent of combat units deployed to prevent infestation of ships. At least ten k units of 8139 detected. Organism

has begun replication processes in unrecovered combat units. Organism infesting active combat units.>

Dreen sentient units did not get angry. They were created without true emotions. They could, however, get frustrated. The presence of Organism 8139 would mean that the entire station would have to be laboriously swept to eliminate them before any analysis of the station could be performed. Even leaving *one* of the little rat-bastards on-board meant the possibility of the entire station force becoming infested. And as for Species 27264, they had caused more damage to Dreen main worlds than any *four* species that had been assimilated over the last ten thousand years. Finding their home planets and wiping the pestiferous race from the face of the galaxy was a Dreen priority right up there with finding the last space spider in the galaxy and crunching it underfoot.

Sonic anomalies?

Even a dispassionate Dreen intelligence could place first priority on something annoying rather than vital.

<Projections from station. Unable to intercept short of capturing station and halting projection.>

Order all ground combat units to assault positions of Species 27264. Ship units return and rendezvous with fleet to load ground combat units. Primary mission: Eliminate sonic anomaly.

And make a mistake when it got too annoyed by those damned kids and their caterwauling.

The space spider, Organism 8139, a biological combat unit crafted by the long defeated Nitch *specifically* to attack and eliminate Dreen, had been happy enough to just find the body of a dead dog-demon. The metal suit locked in final throes with the Dreen was less appealing. Only with Dreen did the space spider live to eat, only with Dreen metabolics did it get the space spider equivalent of a sugar rush. Everything else, even from Biology Four, was just survival sustenance and the organism was genetically programmed to avoid consuming anything *but* Dreen organics in all but starvation environments. However, when its young burst out of the creature, they found a veritable smorgasbord.

The dog-demon, per standard procedure, had been carried back to the troop carrier for processing. Its organics would eventually be used to create still more of the living combat robots.

Which meant that over a thousand units of Organism 8139 had just infected the Dreen troop carrier, a semi-sentient Dreen organism itself, from the point-of-view of a baby space spider just chock *full* of juicy goodness.

"Rotator gun nine down," Gunnery Sergeant Juda reported. "Dreen at final junction two. First Platoon falling back to third positions. Multiple casualties."

The problem with the corridors was that they had exactly *no* cover. The Marines had been soaking up fire in direct line of sight to the Dreen. Without the ability to stack and overwhelm the aliens in the corridors, they'd also been soaking up casualties. Total Dreen numbers were unclear; they'd been destroying the sensor boxes as soon as they found them. But it was upwards of three hundred and that was just too many for the Marines to hold.

"This is where we *draw the line*," Berg said over the platoon frequency. "They *do not pass us*, Second."

"Dreen!" Sergeant Bae called. And then all hell broke loose.

Second, unlike the other platoons, did have cover. They had the low wall the platoon had sheltered behind on the assault on this same room. So they could pour fire into the mass of Dreen with minimal risk.

Minimal did not mean none. The Dreen were leading with thorn-throwers, dispensing with the dog-demons who had no long-ranged weapon. They also were throwing themselves into the Marine fire profligately, but that was working. Mass has a quality of its own, and the Dreen were using that quality to simply overwelm the fire of the Marines.

Berg's indicators showed Wyverns dropping off the screen one by one, each one a soldier it was his duty to love, cherish and in the end use as a human shield if necessary.

"Gunny, bring up Alpha team," Berg said calmly. The threesome had been held in reserve. It was often said that the last person to use his reserve won the battle. Berg knew damned well that he'd just lost this one. "Captain Zanella, I have three KIA, two suit-kills. I have sent in my reserve."

"I'm on the line," First Sergeant Powell said. "They're not going anywhere, Two-Gun."

As if in answer, there was a bellowing roar from down the corridor.

"*These* guys again," Berg muttered.

The bellow could only have come from a rhino-tank—a

rhinoceros sized and generally shaped organic tank capable of firing a plasma blast that could destroy a main battle tank. Its frontal armor was proof against any portable weapon the Marines had at their disposal and there were *very* few ways to get around that.

"Lieutenant," the first sergeant said, "if you'd like a suggestion on how to take one out . . ."

"Been there, done that, First Sergeant," Berg snarled. "This is not the time!"

Rhino-tanks were invulnerable on their front; even their eyes were deep-set in armored sockets smaller than the diameter of most bullets. But just after they fired their plasma balls, they tended to roar in what sounded to human ears like triumph.

If a suit could survive the plasma, a rare situation, a Marine could get one shot at the rhino. *If* he could recover fast enough from being in the near blast radius of the plasma. *If* he could effectively target a still small spot with all the damage his armor was going to have taken, including overload of all systems from EMP at the very least. *If* he wasn't baked to a crisp.

Berg had done it. Once. But it had taken using pistols, since his machine-gun ammunition had chain-exploded from the heat of the plasma. And it had very nearly killed him. And he didn't have his pistols.

But there were a couple of other ways to kill one. None of them particularly safe, mind you, but . . .

"Slap a limpet on?" Berg asked.

The rhino's primary armoring was to the front. If a Marine could get a sufficiently powerful explosive onto the rear of its abdomen, it would take one out.

The problem was getting to the rear of its abdomen.

"Can we get somebody up to the door?" Powell asked seriously. Clearly the junior officer was not in the mood for humor. "Get it as it comes through?"

"Maybe," Berg said, looking at the layout of the remaining platoon. As he watched, Dupras's suit went offline. "If I've got anybody *left*!"

"Lurch, Corwin, on me," the first sergeant said. "You keep their heads down, Lieutenant. I'll take care of that rhino. My turn, Two-Gun."

"Good luck, Top."

The fire from the thorn-throwers had started to slack off. That wasn't a good sign. It meant they were getting out of the way for the rhino-tank.

"For what we are about to receive," Berg muttered over the platoon freq.

"Say again, sir?" Staff Sergeant Carr asked.

"An old prayer, Staff Sergeant," the lieutenant replied as the snout of the tank came around the last corner. It wasn't moving fast. The term that came to mind was "ominous." "An *old* prayer, the Marine's Prayer. You've never heard it?"

"No, sir," the senior NCO said. He had many more years than Bergstresser in the Corps, despite Berg being prior service, so he was a little surprised the most junior lieutenant knew a Marine prayer he didn't.

"It's pretty simple, really," Berg said, staying on the platoon frequency as the rhino-tank got lined up, spotted the enemy and started to charge its plasma horns. "It goes: For what we are about to receive, may we truly be thankful. Platoon, DOWN!"

❊ ❊ ❊

The plasma blast filled the compartment with over-welming sound and heat. The wall had an opening, the same width as the corridor leading to it, directly in front of the corridor. The rhino-tank had targeted the starboard corner of the wall, where it had detected enemies sheltering.

Normally, the powerful plasma bolt would have blasted a wall to smithereens and destroyed anything behind it or around it.

In this case, the plasma released its titanic energy mostly in the immediate area, the wall effortlessly resisting its immense thermal and quantum power and shrugging off the blast.

That didn't mean the Marines were safe. The plasma bolt was simply too powerful for that. Staff Sergeant Carr and Sergeant Bae were holding down the two corners of the wall. The plasma opened up Staff Sergeant Carr's armor like a firecracker in a tin can, vaporizing the Marine senior NCO's body. The blast only penetrated Bae's armor, but the rush of stripped atoms turned him to a blackened hulk in a bare nanosecond.

Even Marines farther away weren't safe. Ducksworth's interior temperature rose to an astonishing two thousand degrees, giving the lance corporal just enough time to howl in agony before he began burning to death in his own personal crematorium. Lance Corporal Antti-Juhani Kaijanaho, Dancer, Prancer, Donner or Vixen, take your pick, was struck by the machine-gun from Sergeant Bae's suit, which punched through his armor, fortunately killing him before the heat could really register.

※　※　※

Lieutenant Bergstresser shook his head to clear it and immediately checked his readouts. His suit was functional, incredibly enough.

But he no longer had a platoon.

The only suits reading as functional were Eakins's and Gunnery Sergeant Juda's. Eakins's vitals indicated that he was out; unconscious, in a coma, it wasn't clear.

"Gunny?" Berg croaked.

"Here," Juda replied. "Here, sir. *Grapp*."

"Well, you know the *Blade* motto," Berg said. "'It's just us.'"

"Yes, sir," Gunny Juda said, more forcefully. "Two items: Third Platoon now reports a rhino on the other corridor. And ours is advancing. Orders?"

"Yeah," Berg croaked. "Keep your head down and hope Top can take it out."

First Sergeant Powell had positioned his team well clear of the door. They'd been outside the blast radius of the plasma ball, but their armor was still hot as Hades.

"When it emerges, we're going to have to move like lightning," Powell said. "You can stop these things from moving with a couple of Wyverns if you give it your all. You two make sure it can't turn this way. I'll slap on the limpet."

He waited for the beast to emerge, sure in his heart that they were all going to die. But the noncombat personnel were sheltering at the far end of the compartment, the same place the Nitch commander had made his last stand. If the rhino-tanks got through, there was no way in hell that they'd survive. And the entire battle would be for nothing.

He waited, patiently, then impatiently, then in annoyance.

"Top?" Lurch asked. "You'd usually hear them by now."

"I know," the first sergeant said. "Damnit. Where *is* the damned thing?"

"Third Platoon reports theirs has stopped," Corwin said. "It just sat down."

"That doesn't sound right . . ."

Eric was tired of waiting, too. He didn't want to give the rhino-tank another target, but he also was wondering what the Dreen were up to.

He finally popped up a sensor to get a look. Hopefully the rhino wouldn't even notice the hair-thin wand.

The tank was stopped halfway between the last fork and compartment. It was trying to drag itself forward with its front claws, but since its rear was down it wasn't getting very far. It tried to fire its plasma-horns again but the green glow faded and then popped out of existence.

As Berg watched, wondering what could have happened to it, it lay down completely and rolled over on its side.

Then he could see the malfunction; the rear of the rhino was a mass of purple spiders.

The spiders had found an opening where humans hadn't, one that virtually every major organism possessed, and infested the body of the tank. Berg shook his head as the massive fighting-machine shuddered in agony and blood began pouring out of its beaklike maw. Finally, the thing gave a heaving sigh and was still. Mostly still. The body continued to ripple as the space spiders fought over every last edible scrap.

In the end, a wave of spiders spilled out, hunting back down the passage and leaving only the less palatable armor draped over a skeleton.

"Turns out there were more than two rhino-tanks," Captain Zanella reported. "The smart mines killed some, or at least wounded them enough that they were easy meat for the spiders. We don't have a hard count, but there were over forty."

"That's an ugly number," Bill said. He'd fought rhino-tanks before.

"Yes, sir," Zanella replied. "But corridors are clear all the way back to the dock at this point. Well, they will be once we clear up the skeletons and all the new spiders. You can't walk for stepping on them. Places you can't walk for stepping on Dreen skeletons, either. And some of them are places we didn't even hit them."

"The Dreen ships?" Weaver asked.

"Gone," the Marine reported. "Don't know if they were fleeing us or the spiders or heading back for reinforcements. But they're gone."

"Casualties?" Bill asked, wincing.

"Eighteen KIA, four WIA," the captain said tonelessly. "And thank you for not saying something like 'butcher's bill,' sir."

"You're welcome," Bill replied. "But that's not many Marines left to hold off the Dreen."

"The increase in spiders may make that moot, sir," Captain Zanella pointed out. "As I reported, they're now packing most of the corridors from bulkhead to bulkhead."

"We have to assume that the Dreen fleet has a way of eliminating them," Bill said. "They might have been surprised by this incident, but when the main fleet arrives, they're going to clear the corridors. And with your handful of Marines, I don't see a way to stop them."

"Then the fleet has to be stopped, sir," Zanella said. "And that would be up to you."

"Oh, thanks so much," Weaver replied. "Now everybody *likes* my guitar playing! Damnit, where in the *hell* is the *Blade*?"

"Damnit, we could have been back there two days ago," Captain Prael swore. "I want to know what's happening back at the anomaly!"

"The Hexosehr were adamant that we wait, sir," the TACO pointed out unnecessarily.

"We could have picked up a group of scientists and been there by now," the CO said. "Another six hours. The hell with this. Head for the Tree. Who *knows* what could be happening with Weaver in charge. . . ."

24

"*I'm a freee-eee bird, yeah!*" Weaver sang, then started in on the seemingly unending guitar solo.

"Sir," Carpenter said, setting down his drumsticks. "Sir, it's not working!"

The thing about harmonics is that they aren't nearly as easy as some people make them out to be. Otherwise stadiums would fall down every time there was a rock concert. The harmonic of one material is not the same as the harmonic of another material. Two materials in juncture tend to damp the harmonic effect unless there is a chord that has the destructive harmonic for both. With more materials, the harmonics become more complex.

Shattering a wineglass is easy. Shattering a wooden bridge given a small unit of marchers isn't that tough. Shattering a space ship, especially an organic one, is much, much harder.

"This station has so much power, there *has* to be a way to stop these bastards," Weaver shouted, tearing off his guitar and preparing to sling it across the room.

"Maybe we're going at this the wrong way," Miriam said, holding up her hand placatingly. "If you promise to never subject me to 'Freebird' again, I'll explain."

"Go ahead," Bill replied. "But after four straight hours of that Goth and heavy metal *chither*, I needed some *real* music."

"Promise?"

"Promise."

"I should make you add the entire repertoire of Lynyrd Skynyrd, The Allman Brothers, The Doobie Brothers, .38 Special and Crosby, Stills, Nash and Young, most of whom I had *never heard of* before today and hope to never hear of again," Miriam said. "But I'll hold it at 'Freebird.'"

"Is there a point to all of this?" Weaver asked.

"Do you really think that somebody went to all the trouble of making something that could fluoresce gas giants and that's all it does?" Miriam asked, waving at the window. The space beyond was now a mass of gaseous particles that could hardly be called vacuum. Oh, even if a being breathed hydrogen, argon or methane it wasn't going to be breathable. But it was thick enough to see without the fluorescence and stretched vertically across five degrees of view. "There are over a thousand points on this Tree. The dragonflies reported that the power was coming from the points. So you think it only fires at the gas giants and only from four of them? Chosen at random?"

"Chosen from whichever is pointed at the Jovians," Weaver said. "But go on."

"There's a wall of gas out there," Miriam said. "If you could hit it with other beams, it's going to improve the show, yes or no?"

"Yes," Weaver said. "But the only beams . . ."

"Because we haven't figured out how to *get the rest to fire*," Miriam interrupted.

"That Dreen fleet is headed this way while you're talking," Bill said, waving at the transparent walls and the icons of the Dreen ships. "Could you get to the point?"

"That's the point," Miriam said. "There has to be a way to get the other beams to work."

"They could have used any control method, ma'am," PO Carpenter pointed out. "If somebody from, say, 1950 tried to use most of the stuff in my apartment they wouldn't be able to. They'd need the implant stuck in my head or one like it."

"Implants are a transitional technology," Miriam said. "Do you use an implant to run a grav-board? Do the Cheerick use an implant to fly their dragonflies?"

"You're saying this thing could work by telepathy?" Bill asked. "Why would it work for us? We're not the race that built it."

"We're not the race that built the boards," Miriam pointed out. "I frankly doubt that only one race used this system. It's worth a shot."

"Okay," Weaver said, plucking a chord on his guitar. "Let's all think about invisible energy beams destroying those ships. 'Mountain High, Valley Low'?"

"Is that Lynyrd Skynyrd?" Miriam asked dangerously.

"Actually, it was a joke," Bill said. "Your idea. You lead."

"Conn, CIC."

"Go, CIC," Prael said, watching the blue star swell on the main viewer. More than two light-days away it was still a dot, but at the speed of the *Blade* they were going to be on it in . . . What the hell?

"We're getting strange emissions from the star, Conn," CIC reported. "Changes in stellar output . . . Uh . . ."

"CIC, if you'll look on your viewers you'll see that the star just winked . . . What the . . . ?"

The star had simply disappeared on the viewer for a few seconds, then reappeared. It couldn't have been the viewer; stars in the background were still rock solid.

"All stop," Prael said as the star winked out again. "Damnit. What the hell is going on?"

"Conn, we're getting lots of strange readings from that solar system," CIC said, almost plaintively. "Frankly, we can't make anything out of it. One of our systems is saying that the star is in preliminary nova stage, sir. Another disagrees and says that it's simply ceased fusing, reasons unknown."

"Damn," the CO said. "There's only one way to find out. Pilot."

"Sir?"

"If that thing goes nova, get us the hell out of here *before* I order it."

"Yes, sir."

"Engage."

"Conn, CIC."

"Go, CIC."

"Uh . . . Sir, you'd better come down here."

"I can see what you're seeing from up here," the CO said with a sigh. "What is causing the gas giants to flash on and off like lightbulbs?"

"Conn . . . CO to CIC, please . . ."

"Beams of what?"

"Lots of secondary output, sir," the TACO said, pointing to the particle sensors. The CO noticed that it was his erstwhile canary manning the board. "They appear to be beams of energy high in the EM spectrum. The effect is to transfer energy to the gasses in the Jovians causing them to fluoresce. I'm not sure of the reason, sir. . . ."

"Well, among other things it's pretty," the CO said dryly. "What happened to the star?"

"We're less sure what's going on there, sir," White admitted. "But the current theory . . ."

"Dreen emission detected," the sensor tech said calmly. "Multiple Dreen unreality translations. We're getting them in rapid sequence because of our approach, sir, but the count is over sixty Dreen warships . . . Numbers and types coming up on the screen now, sir."

The CO was glad that the need for seamen to laboriously write in the details of ships on clear glass screens was a thing of the past. Because he'd have to get half the crew in here, give them classes . . .

"Well . . . That's a hell of a thing."

"Sierras One through Eight are things we've never seen before," the TACO said musingly. People reacted differently to disasters. Some panicked. Some became very calm. The tactical officer's reaction was clearly to become severely academic, not the worst of reactions for that sort of position. "The Hexosehr had, though. Sierra One is a Dreen brain-ship. Ten kilometers long, heavy weapons to size. They're considered worthy of a small fleet of Chaos ships on their own; their plasma guns and mass drivers can take out a Chaos ship at beyond even capital ship's range. Figure with us they'll be an increasing threat from five light-seconds out. Worse as we get closer, of course. The next seven are superdreadnoughts . . ."

The CO listened to it all but on another level he was drowning it out. There was no way for the *Blade* to take on even a fraction of this force. They mounted popguns compared to even the medium class ships in the Dreen fleet. Their most effective technique, dropping mines on the unreality node, was already moot. The Dreen were in the system.

". . . Maneuvering to avoid the beams . . ."

"Run that one by me again," the CO said.

"The beams from the Tree apparently took out part of the putative boarding force, sir," the TACO said, gesturing to that part of the replay. "That was before they'd boarded. The fleet, however, is now maneuvering to avoid the beams."

"Accident?" the CO asked.

"Since we don't know what is causing the effect, sir, that would be my first guess," the TACO said.

"Somebody," the CO said, "and I'll give you two guesses who it was, toss a coin, pressed the wrong button."

"Or the right button, depending on your point of view, sir," the TACO said diffidently. "The Tree did manage to take out some of the Dreen ships."

"Point."

"We have sufficient time to reach the Tree and extract any survivors. That assumes the Dreen have not taken the entire station and that the survivors can reach the ship. We may not even be able to contact them. However, in its current configuration, approach will be . . . interesting."

"How much time?" the CO asked.

"Assuming that there is not another speed run by the boarding ships, six hours," the TACO said. "That is the point at which the Dreen, assuming deceleration time, will be within six light-seconds of the Tree. We'll have to maneuver to avoid them, in real space, as they approach. There is a danger from fighters . . ."

"That's enough time," Prael snapped. "I'll be on the Conn. Contact me if there are any changes."

"Aye, aye, sir."

"'And if the paths that I have followed have tread against the flow,'" Miriam sang, "'there is no need for sorrow I am coming home . . . ' There! There!"

"What?" Weaver asked, placing his hands on the strings of the guitar. "Where?"

"I saw it," Carpenter said. "Like a figure eight between Xenon and Helium."

"Yes!" Miriam said. "Let's try that again. From the top . . ."

"Wait," Weaver said, looking at the screens. "There's a new ship inbound . . . Fast. *Blade's* here."

"'I have tasted the wisdom of divinity and the horrors of its sting . . .'" Berg whispered.

"Sir, the XO reports that the *Blade* is on its way in," Gunny Juda said. His armor was blackened from the plasma fire but if it bothered him it wasn't obvious.

"Acknowledged," Berg said. Lieutenant Mendel had been lost in the running battle in the corridors when the Dreen had gotten a force around his platoon. The remainder of the platoon had fought its way out, with other casualties, so the CO had reconfigured the platoons. Berg now led the reconsolidated Second Platoon, consisting of the survivors from First and Second, while Greg Morris still had Third. Gunny Brunswick, the Third Platoon sergeant, had also been lost, so Gunny Vankleuren from First had taken the slot.

"Second," Captain Zanella said. "Prepare for extraction. Third is going to cover the noncombatants; your job is to make sure the corridors are clear and make contact with the ship."

"I'll try to find a broom, sir," Berg replied.

"What the hell?" Prael said as the *Blade* screamed in at almost four thousand times the speed of light. "What in the hell is that noise?"

"That would be the song 'Return' by the band Crüxshadows, sir," the COB said. "A Goth band based in Tallahassee, Florida, it first hit the major charts with the song 'Sophia' in—"

"Okay, COB, if you're so smart," the CO snapped. "Explain to me how we're hearing it in *space*!"

"Got me there, sir."

"Approaching warp-denial field," the pilot said.

"Slow to normal space drive," the CO said. "Flank speed to the shield. Damn . . . This means . . ."

"We've managed to get secondary output from the

system, Captain Prael," Weaver said, taking a puff off of his pipe. "We really *should* try to hold the Tree. (Puff, puff) It's a major resource, both technically and militarily. Fascinating. Really . . ." (Puff.)

With the *Blade* back in the field of the Tree, the "anime zone" had reestablished. It looked to be a permanent issue.

"Mr. Weaver!" the CO barked. "There Are! Sixty! Dreen warships! Approaching! This *Space* station!"

"Fifty-eight," (puff, puff). "Sixty-one originally. We got three. And with the secondary output system working, well . . . we can get more."

"You are Basing this On Fantasy!" the CO shouted, looming over the XO. "This Is My Decision! We Are! Evacuating! Then we shall DESTROY this installation," he added, rubbing his hands together. "The Dreen Will Never Have It! I Swear On the Blood Of Our Fathers!"

"Not so sure (puff, puff) that's possible. Bits of it have been hit by Dreen plasma, you know? (Puff . . . ponder . . . puff.) Not sure a nuke (puff) would so much as *scratch* it. And if the Dreen capture it, well . . . (puff, puff, grin, puff) Wouldn't want to be the feller explaining that one, by God I wouldn't." (Puff, grin, puff.)

"Do you think that SpaceCom would be upset?" the CO said, shrinking to normal size and suddenly wearing glasses. He'd also developed a stoop and was rubbing his hands together like a squirrel. "Really?"

"Did . . . (puff, puff) Did Spruance run at Midway?"

"No!" the CO said, swelling back to his monstrous size and placing his hand on his chest.

"Did Dewey (puff . . . puff) turn away from the Spanish Fleet?"

"He wasn't outnumbered a *thousand to one*," Prael said, suddenly nearly normal in appearance. "The brain-ship *alone* outmasses us by more than that."

"Still," Weaver said, puffing away and filling the compartment with smoke. "Fight the effect, Captain, but think . . . (Puff, puff, point stem at the CO) This station is a monumental victory (puff, puff) or an enormous defeat. Holding it could (puff) turn the tide of the war. Losing it (puff, puff . . . ponder) If the Dreen can learn to control *stars*?"

"We Cannot Defeat That Fleet!" the CO said, back in anime form.

"The Tree (puff, puff) *can*. Blood of my fathers and all that. Just (puff . . . ponder . . . puff) keep the boarders off if you can, would you be a dear?"

"If It! Is Falling! It Must! Be Destroyed!"

"Oh, I rather think, yes," Weaver said, setting his pipe down. "Special munition?"

"The Largest We Have!" the CO said, nodding and holding out his hand. "The Megadestroyer Bomb! That Will Destroy A Star! We will evacuate the noncombatants. Good luck, Mr. Weaver!"

"Oh, one 'noncombatant' (puff, puff) will have to stay."

"Who?!"

"Sou da ne bokura atarashii jidai wo!" Miriam shrilled, boucing in front of her keyboard. *"Mukaete mitai ne kisekiteki ka mo ne!"*

"Nooo!" the chimpanzee behind the drum set screamed, nonetheless banging away for all he was worth. "Not *J-pop*!"

❦   ❦   ❦

"Load Mine Tubes!" the CO barked as the *Blade* made its way around the Tree and into the shadows. "Deploy All Mines As We Clear The Field!"

"Deploy All Mines!" the COB shouted. "Arrrrrh! We'll blow them to smithereens so we will! We shall sail under the Black Flag and space shall be our *empire*, shiver me bones!"

"Not *Until* We Clear The Field! You Imbecile!"

"You hurts me with those words, Cap'n . . ."

"Put Yourself! On Report!"

"Am I still supposed to put myself on report, CO?" the COB asked.

"No, but we're still dropping mines. Just as soon as we modify them a little."

"It'll be okay," Weaver said, uncomfortably patting the linguist on the shoulder. "Seriously. Nobody will know."

"You could hear it through the *entire solar system!*" Miriam screamed. "And the *Blade* records EVERYTHING! Oh My God. My reputation is *so* ruined. I'm going to have . . . *otaku!*"

"Hey, *I* was a chimpanzee for God's sake," Carpenter said. "And what are . . . Oh-ta- . . . whatever."

"Anime fans," Bill said darkly.

"Oh. Them."

"She was playing J-pop!" Gants said, bouncing on the deck and waving his arms over his head like a monkey. Some people took longer to get over the effects of the field than others. "*Sou da ne bokura atarashii jidai wo!*"

"Jesus, man," Red snapped. "Get ahold of yourself. You're embarassing me."

25

<Drive systems failures in Units 57,035,837 and 8,808,992. Infestation at seventeen percent in Unit 779,877. Cleaner Systems Class One through Three production initiated in all units.>

Ensure uninfected conditions in Units 125,867 and 7,507,434. Dispatch to anomaly. Escort: three Class Fourteen Space Combat Units, one Class Nine. Escorts are not to enter anomaly docking bay. Begin construction of Class One and Two cleaners, enroute. Launch fighters. Twenty percent to escort boarding parties.

With the infection of the primary ground unit construction ship, Unit 779,877 which the *Blade* had identified as a cruiser, the entire mission to explore the anomaly and retrieve its scientific and technical data was in jeopardy. If the infestation could be brought under control, though, in time the fleet could be completely reconstructed. Well, except for . . .

<Units 57,035,837 and 8,808,992 entering retrograde orbit.>

Destroy them.

There was a pause from the secondary entity that handled communications within the massive brain-ship.

Since Dreen sentients occasionally fissioned—breaking off a lower-level sentient for colonization or to create a new brain-ship—explanations were apparently in order.

When Organism 8139 consumes all functional material in the units, the organism will break out, spilling into space. The units will be on our direct course to the anomaly. Destroy them now, maximum *firepower. Ensure all units of Organism 8139 eliminated.*

<Order sent.>

"Sir, we've got two interesting things going on here," the TACO said. The *Blade* had reached the edge of the warp-denial field and was shadowing the massive Dreen fleet, hoping against hope that Weaver and Miriam could figure out how to use the Tree to defeat it.

"Go," Prael said, looking over at the boards. A number of ships had broken away from the Dreen fleet. Six of them seemed to be accelerating towards the Tree while the other two . . .

"We've got a Dreen task group, consisting of one cruiser, Sierra 31, two troop carriers, Sierras 38 and 42 and three destroyers, Sierras 48, 50 and 53, accelerating towards the tree. The group has been designated CruRon One."

"We need to set up to intercept that task group," the CO said. "Get Astro started on a course."

"Yes, sir," the TACO said. "Message already sent to

Astro, sir. The odd thing, though, is this other task group. I'm not even sure that's the right thing to call it. The Dreen fleet is in deceleration to match orbit with the Tree at this time. Two ships have stopped deceleration. That means that they will arrive near the Tree before the rest of the Dreen fleet."

"Another attack group?" the CO asked.

"I don't think so," the TACO said. "They simply stopped deceleration. The cruisers and destroyers have enough legs they can accelerate from their current position and still decelerate later. Not much accel, but it will get them there faster. This group is just . . . drifting if you will, sir. And on their current course they're on a retrograde orbit. Unless they get under power soon, they're going to miss the Tree and slam into the star. They are, however, pulling away from the rest of the fleet."

"Bomb ships?" the CO asked. "A suicide run? Can the Dreen get the star to go nova or something?"

"Possible, sir," the TACO replied. "But then why not accelerate? I think they're just . . . broken, sir. Looks like drive system failure to me."

"Well, let's hope so," the CO said.

"Whoa," the sensor tech said. "The Dreen are firing."

"On what?" the TACO said. "We're not in range."

"Those two disabled ships," the sensor tech replied. "Every ship is firing that has line-of-sight. Sierras 41 and 46 are *gone*, sir. They're just gas. And they're still pumping plasma into the area."

"Wow," the CO said. "The Dreen have a hell of a penalty for having a bad Eng. I need to point it out to ours. How's the modification of the missiles going?"

"Queasily, sir," the TACO said. "But we'll have at least one spread converted in twenty minutes or so. It was a nontrivial exercise."

"That pretty much describes everything we do, Lieutenant."

"So how did you get the beams to work?" Weaver asked when the linguist had finally calmed down.

"It was just a method of thought," Miriam said, standing up and taking her place at the keyboard. She looked at it distastefully but powered it on. "I've had so much poking around my brain, I've sort of learned to poke in odd spots myself. I'll see if I can do it again."

"Okay," Weaver said. "What do you want to play?"

"Anything but J-pop . . ."

"Colonel, are your dragonflies prepared?"

"Now that they've been resupplied, Captain Prael," Colonel Che-chee replied. "I even have calmed my males. They very much did not care for waiting in space with no way home."

"Glad to hear they're okay," the CO said distantly. "It's important that you stay close to the ship. Our maneuvers will be minimal on the firing end, but we will be maneuvering. Especially on the second jump."

"Understood, Captain," the colonel replied. "Are we going to do this or not?"

"Dreen fighters redeploying in our direction, sir," the TACO said.

"We'll do a multidirectional jump, then," the CO replied. "Set it up. I want to jump into the boarding group, out to a point triangulated between them and the main fleet then into the main fleet and back out."

·"Into the main fleet, sir?" the TACO said.

"Yes," Prael said.

The *Blade* exited warp at whatever velocity and vector she had had prior to entry. This meant that each time she entered a star system, she had to adjust to the local vectors. More importantly, it meant that to attack a ship, she first had to match course and speed, then flash in, drop out of warp, fire, and flash out.

Her approach was superluminal, making locking onto her nearly impossible. But for the brief seconds she was exposed at the firing end, she was vulnerable. And Dreen destroyers and cruisers had excellent targeting software.

"Sierra 31 is releasing vapor," the TACO reported. "We got in some hits at least. No change in delta V."

"CIC, Damage Control," the Eng reported. "Hull breach in Section Forty-Two. Two KIA, one WIA."

"They got in some licks, too," Prael said. "Colonel, lock your Flies to the hull for this one. Maximum spread."

"Acknowledged," Colonel Che-chee said. "Must report one dragonfly and rider destroyed."

"You have my condolences, Colonel," the CO replied. "Now lock down. We're going to be maneuvering on this one. TACO, set mines for release on approach of Dreen emissions. Launch all tubes, minimum ejection, hold in field. Set course for the middle of the fleet. Go for one of the heavies. On exit from warp, maneuver in normal space, vector one-one-four mark zero."

"Attack orders set," the TACO said. "Target Sierra

Five, superdreadnought. Mines deployed and holding inside field."

"Engage."

The *Blade* flashed in again, this time to the middle of the oncoming Dreen fleet. On exiting warp, she fired all twenty Chaos guns on either side, the starboard targeted on the three-kilometer-long superdreadnought barely ten thousand kilometers away.

All but three of the Chaos balls hit, smashing meter-square holes into the side of the superdreadnought.

But the massive ship barely seemed to notice the damage, responding with deadly accurate plasma and mass driver fire. The *Blade* had a Hexosehr plasma screen, but under the hammer of the gigawatt plasma guns it flared and died in a nanosecond and the stripped atoms tore at the skin of the ship, punching huge holes into the hull and ravaging the interior.

More fire poured from the ship's sisters that were massed around the brain-ship, creating an impenetrable wall. The area around the *Blade* for a moment became a blaze to rival the output of the Tree. And then she was gone . . .

"Damage report!" Captain Prael said over the communicator. At the first pop in his ears he'd slammed down his helmet and he could tell by the shadows the compartment was now completely in vacuum. Given that there were at least a dozen air-tight doors between CIC and the hull, that was a *bad* sign.

"Multiple hull breaches," the Eng replied. "Nine chaos guns down portside, four starboard. Rear torpedo room out of action. Forward reports two tubes damaged. Hits went deep into the ship. Casualty reports still coming in."

"CIC, Dragonflight," Colonel Che-chee said. "Four dragonflies destroyed by fire. Are we going to do that again?"

"I sure hope not, Colonel," the CO replied, sighing. "Colonel, your people are getting slaughtered by this. Grab some drop-tanks and stay out here. Cover us if any of the fighters get close. If we're destroyed, you can still make it back to the Tree. TACO, did any of the mines survive?"

"We got feedback reports from two out of the ten, sir," the tactical officer reported. "I don't know if the Dreen detected them or not."

"Well, if they did, we just took all that damage for nothing. . . ."

When the smart warhead on the SM-11 space-torp detected Dreen emissions in range it didn't fire its engines. That would have been far too much signature. It simply fired the exploding bolts holding the terminal stage to the main torp. With everything that was still popping and sparking in space around it, including the ravaged shells of eight of its brethren, the release of the bolts was hardly noticeable.

The warhead didn't use its powerful radar nor its laser range finder. It didn't engage its targeting engine. It simply drifted, just another bit of space debris. With its electronics heavily shielded and running on the simplest of battery systems, it appeared as nothing more than a rock. Just a rock. Nothing to endanger a Dreen warship.

That was, until it came within a thousand meters. Then, again, it did a very minor thing, jets of air puffing off a plastic shroud.

And releasing two thousand space spiders into the vacuum.

But space is vast. A bare three hundred actually impacted on the hull of the Dreen superdreadnought. Of those, most were killed by kinetic energy. Others bounced off. A few though, a bare handful, woke up in time to grab on. They paused there, drawing on their last shreds of food energy to produce enzymes capable of converting the Dreen armor into more food energy. And, as an important byproduct, drilling into the hull.

"Matched on course and speed of Sierra 31," Conn reported.

The Dreen knew what was important in the boarding task force. The Dreen destroyers and cruiser had surrounded the troop carriers in a tight shield that required taking out one or more before the *Blade* could attack the vulnerable transports.

Perhaps he should have targeted one of the more vulnerable destroyers to start. But the Navy doctrine was always the same: Go for the Heavies.

"Damage control?"

"We got one more gun up on the port side," the Eng replied. "The rest aren't going to get repaired short of a Hexosehr space dock. Well, and possibly a few months of fabber time."

"Understood," the CO replied. "Conn, adjust vector to come in on our starboard side." That one had taken the lesser pounding when they'd made the run on the fleet.

"Vector adjusted, CIC."

"Engage attack system."

Analysis.

<Enemy Space Combat Unit uses a previously unreported superluminal drive. Primary weapon system: Species 27314 instability generator. Signals analysis indicate unit controlled by Species 27264. Instability Generators previously unreported type, seventy percent smaller than previous units. Effect estimated minimal on Class One through Four Space Combat Units. Multiple hits on Unit 30,440. Reports minimal damage. Effect increases as units decrease. Effect on Class Three Ground Combat Carrier rated high.>

Ensure security of Combat Carrier Units. Dispatch additional Class Fourteen escorts.

"Dreen cruiser is still decelerating," the tactical officer said. "But it's trailing vapor like mad. We're hitting it hard. Fire level was down at least twenty percent on that last run. But the fleet just dispatched reinforcements; nine more destroyers. With their drives, they'll be up to the troopships before they enter the warp-denial zone. Fighters are also deploying forward and opening up their spread. I think they're trying to figure where we'll come out to intercept us."

"CIC, Damage control. Two chaos guns down starboard side. Hull breaches in Sections Forty-Nine, Seventeen and Sixy-Three. Three KIA, one WIA."

"At this rate we'll take it out just in time for it to take us out," the CO said sourly. "But set up another run. Get in close and pound her. What's that line from Nelson?"

"'I could not tread these perilous paths in safety, if I did not keep a saving sense of humor'" the TACO said.

"No," the CO said.

"'Desperate affairs require desperate measures.'"

"No. But close."

"'If I had been censured every time I have run my ship, or fleets under my command, into great danger, I should have long ago been out of the Service and never in the House of Peers.'"

"NO! Something about running your ship alongside the enemy. Trafalgar, I think."

"Hmmm . . ."

"CIC, Damage Control. Hull breaches in Section Forty-Two, Section Nineteen, Section Twenty-Three . . ."

"'First gain the victory and then make the best use of it you can.'"

"No."

"'There is no way of dealing with the Frenchman but to knock him down—to be civil to them is to be laughed at.'"

"No, but I like that one . . ."

"CIC, Damage control . . ."

"'Gentlemen, when the enemy is committed to a mistake we must not interrupt him too soon.'"

"No. God, the guy could talk, couldn't he?"

✖   ✖   ✖

"'Firstly you must always implicitly obey orders, without attempting to form any opinion of your own regarding their propriety. Secondly, you must consider every man your enemy who speaks ill of your king; and thirdly you must hate a Frenchman as you hate the devil'"

"No, but another one I like. It was something about get in close . . ."

"Oh!" the TACO said. "That wasn't a quote. It was a signal. 'Engage the enemy more closely.' First signal at Trafalgar, even before they were engaged."

"That's it," the CO said.

"CIC, Damage Control. Compartments Eleven, Twelve and Ninety-Six breached. Six KIA, two WIA. Forward Torpedo Room out of action. Laser Two deadline. That's a cut in the power system, we might have it repaired in about thirty minutes. Down to six guns starboard. Most of them are unrepairable and I just lost one of the gun teams in the last run."

"Damage Control, CIC. Get the laser back up; fighters coming in," the CO said. "What's the status on our friend?"

"Bleeding air and various other components," the TACO said. "In the case of Dreen ships, it's not a metaphor, if you know what I mean. They really bleed. Still under power, though, so we can't get through to the troopship."

"Come in from our port," the CO said. "We've got more guns left on that side and the starboard damage control teams need a break. But keep hitting their starboard. We're going to get to the guts sooner or later."

"'If a man consults whether he is to fight, when he has

the power in his own hands, it is certain that his opinion is against fighting.'"

"You can stop now, TACO."

"Sorry, sir."

"Hey," the CO said, looking around. Something that had been nearly constant, so much so that it had become background, had stopped. "What happened to the music?"

26

"*And I will write her name and cast it to the sky,*" Miriam sang, drifting shining beams across the wall of gas. The formed silhouettes of light, a circle, a swirl that resolved into a dragonfly. "*Silhouettes recede into a mother's tearful eyes . . .*" Her eyes were wide and staring into the distance, lost in a world of music.

"Miriam, bring it down and to the right," Bill said. "Miriam . . ."

"I think she's out of it, sir," Carpenter said over the officer's implant.

"It's not much good if she's not going to target it," Weaver responded. "I don't want to break her concentration, though. Come on, girl, down and to the right . . ."

As if his will drove it, the image of the dragonfly dove, swooping into the Dreen fleet, and appeared to grasp one of the destroyers protecting the upper side of the fleet. The destroyer, under the power of a dozen Earth suns, flashed in fire and disappeared in an instant, simply adding some constituent molecules to the gases filling the system.

"I felt that," Miriam said, shaking her head as the

beams of light collapsed, the dragonfly left as a glowing image for a moment and then fading. She grabbed her head and squeezed. "There was feedback. I don't understand the feedback. But I could *feel* the ship dying."

"You're going to have to take it," Bill said. "You've got to get into the brain-ship and take it out."

"I know," Miriam said, wincing. "I'll try. I need something more soothing for now."

"Yes!" the TACO shouted as the Dreen cruiser erupted in fire. It stopped decelerating and drifted away from the formation, trailing air and water then detonating in a flash of white. "Sierra 31 is *toast*!"

"We're not much better," Captain Prael said, looking at the damage report. "And if we don't get one of the troopships in the next five minutes, we're going to have nine more destroyers to deal with."

"We got some accidental hits on Sierra 50, sir," the TACO said, still jubilant. His job was killing other ships, *other* officers had to deal with the damage to this one. "Recommend next run be on Sierra 50."

"Sir," one of the tracking technicians said. "Sierra 41 just detonated."

"Blue on Blue again?" the TACO asked.

"No, sir," the technician replied. "I'm not sure why . . ."

"Sir," the sensor tech interrupted. "The Tree has been making some odd emissions. I thought they were random, but a series of them just tracked across the position of Sierra 41. Emission levels were approximately six hundred *exajoules* of energy in the area of Sierra 41. I repeat. Six. Hundred. Exa. Joules."

"Holy Hanna, our biggest nukes are less than a *thousandth* of that," the TACO said. "That makes taking out that cruiser a pretty minor accomplishment."

"Not really," the CO said. "So far, that's the only hit that the Tree's gotten in. And if somebody doesn't stop this task force from taking the Tree, then they're not going to get many more. Set up an attack run on Sierra 50."

"Already laid in, sir," the TACO said.

"Make it so," Prael replied. "But I'm glad that Miss Moon is back singing. Lovely voice, I'll admit. Hearing her sing 'I Stand Alone' is a bit odd, though. What's next? Ozzie?"

"Sierra 50 terminated, sir," the TACO said as the destroyer broke apart. No secondaries, but it was in pieces and drifting which was good enough.

"Was it my imagination or was the fire much less effective that time?" the CO asked.

"No, sir, it wasn't your imagination," the TACO said. "Return fire rate was lower and less interlocked. Don't know why. But we took a lot less damage. And there's a hole we can fire through to one of the troop carriers."

"No, take out one more destroyer, first," the CO said. "That will ensure we can get through. Sierra . . . 48. Set that up."

"Ready, sir," the TACO said a moment later.

"Engage."

Status of boarding force.
<Units 1,336,788 and 25,463,785 destroyed. Enemy combat unit damaged, 70% reduction in fire, significant air and water loss. Enemy combat unit preparing new

attack run. Estimate loss of one Ground Combat Carrier prior to arrival of secondary escort group. Arrival at space station in point four turns.>

"Dreen fighters redeployed around the boarding group," the TACO said. "Boarding group entering warp-denial field."

The CIC was more than just evacuated at this point. Despite being deep in the interior of the ship, light could be seen coming in.

On the other hand, they'd managed to destroy six Dreen destroyers, one of the troop carriers and the cruiser. Not a bad haul, even if they *had* gotten the ship blown to ribbons.

"That's all we can do here," Captain Prael said. "Let's go pick up our dragonflies and see if we can get the old girl patched up. The rest is up to Commander Weaver. If he can get it together."

"Look, the brain works in strange ways, okay?" Miriam said defiantly. "Mine especially. I've tried just about every song you two can't mangle too badly. I've thought about beams of light, lightning, hammers, everything I can think of. Nothing seems to work. 'Dragonfly' worked once. I just can't get it to work again. But there's *something* there, I know it. I can *feel* it."

"You know, it actually *was* the dragonfly," Carpenter said. "I mean, that was the attack method. A big, glowing, green and yellow dragonfly. Does that help?"

"Yeah," Bill said. "I mean, what *hit* the ship was the beams, but the thing that *attacked* them was a dragonfly."

"I made a dragonfly?" Miriam asked, blinking. "Cool."

"Well, it was like a laser light-show dragonfly," Bill pointed out. "It was about as insubstantial as mist."

"That just makes it cooler," Miriam said. "A mist dragonfly is cooler than a real one."

"But that's what did it," the petty officer said. "That big mist dragonfly . . . ate the destroyer. Does that help?"

"Sort of," Miriam said, staring into the distance. "Avatars."

"And that means . . . ?" Weaver said.

"An avatar is, in Hindu mythology, the descent of a deity in carnate form," Carpenter said. "In computer terms—"

"I know what an avatar is, PO," Bill said. "I meant, what does it mean in this context?"

"It means I have to have an image of something to form," Miriam said, still staring into the distance. "Songs with avatars. 'Dragonfly' . . . I'm blanking."

"'Black Unicorn'" Carpenter said then shrugged at their expressions. "Sue me. I'm a Heather Alexander fan. I can set this thing to bodran."

"Got some music?"

Analysis of gaseous phenomenon.
<Phenomenon generated by combination of gravitational beams and coherent energy beams interacting with gaseous particles. Phenomenon nonhazardous. Intersection of combat units with coherent energy beams transfers six hundred exajoules of energy to combat unit resulting in termination. Secondary effect of gravitational beams irrelevant.>

Defense?

<None. Power levels are equivalent to multiple main sequence stars. Only defense is capture of station.>

There was a pause as the Dreen fleet-mind considered this new weapon the hell-spawned thing Species 27264 had created.

Why is it black? And why is it just . . . hovering?

"*If you ever meet me standing there, you'll wish that you were never born,*" Miriam sang. "*I'll seize your soul and strip it bare, I am the Black Unicorn.*"

"Come on," Weaver whispered, mostly to himself. "You've formed it, now use it!"

A black unicorn with bat-wings out of nightmare was crossing the system, galloping through glowing clouds of mist. Just as insubstantial as mist, it was, nonetheless, impressive. Especially given that it was bigger than all four of the Jovians put together and using about ten percent of the output of the blue-white star to generate.

It had formed slowly, most of the way across the system from the Dreen fleet. Now it closed on the Dreen, seemingly moving in slow motion. The actual speed was very close to that of light, but from their position it seemed ominously slow.

If the Dreen had anything similar to emotions, it was going to seem *agonizingly* slow.

As the music crescendoed, the monster from the deeps of space lowered its horn and drove it into the Dreen fleet.

The fleet was gathered in an egg-shaped formation around the brain-ship. As the horn hit the lead ships, dozens flared and died under the enormous power of the Tree. The entire vanguard of the fleet was ripped asunder.

Miriam gasped in response, but maintained the image and continued to sing. The unicorn, though, only circled the fleet as the music continued. It only seemed to attack on the instrumental portions, diving in again to slash its horn through the fleet, ripping dreadnoughts, superdreadnoughts and destroyers apart as if *they* were the insubstantial mist.

As the song drew to a close, the unicorn turned and began trotting away, fading into the stars as the last chord died, the only sign of it a flash as from a silver hoof.

"Damn," Bill muttered, looking at the Dreen fleet. It was redeploying, fast, and seemed to be putting most of its combat power forward, as if to shield the brain-ship.

"And I will stand here at the gates," Miriam sang, *"and face the onslaught, fighting . . ."*

Again, the avatar had formed slowly, fading into view from the mist that now filled the system. A Greek hoplite in full armor, spear extended, shield up and helmet down. Smaller than the unicorn, he drifted into reality between the station and the approaching fleet, then began striding forward.

All units, engage the anomaly.
<Anomaly gaseous in nature. Engagement futile.>
Obey.

Beams of plasma, massive chunks of heavy metal driven to relativistic speeds, the full output of the remaining fleet flashed out at the warrior. He paused and raised his shield, shedding the fire as if it were so many Persian arrows. As strikes got through to his armor, though, it was penetrated, red blood running unheeded down his chest.

A stab of the planet-sized spear and a destroyer flared into nothingness. Another and a superdreadnought was cut in half. A cut of the spearhead and a dreadnought exploded in actinic fire.

But as the song reached its end, the avatar faded away, raising his spear in a final tribute.

"No stopping this time," Weaver said. "'Fight For Freedom'. . ."

"Now that there is something to see," the CO said, watching the screen. The major interior holes in the ship had been patched and while the atmosphere in CIC wasn't exactly thick, it was at least breathable.

"Sir, with respect," the TACO said, "I'm glad Captain Weaver talked you into letting him go back to try to get the system working."

"Duly noted, TACO," Prael said. "Duly noted."

All combat units, shield retreat. Maximum deceleration. Exit by nearest warp point.

"*Where The Eagles Fly I Will Soon Be There*," Miriam sang.

> *If You Want To Come Along With Me My Friend*
> *Say The Words And You'll Be Free*
> *From The Mountains To The Sea*
> *We'll Fight For Freedom Again . . .*

※ ※ ※

A bald eagle, its wings as wide as planetary orbits, stooped through the fleet. Where its wings passed, dreadnoughts shuddered and faltered, destroyers flared white-hot and exploded, frigates ceased to exist. The fighters trying to provide cover lasted no longer than gnats caught in an oxyacetylene torch. Where its talons closed, superdreadnoughts burst apart, their refractory armor as insubstantial as tissue paper.

The Dreen fleet had changed vector, heading off for points unknown. The brain-ship was in the lead of the retreat, showing an unexpected turn-of-speed for such a large vessel. The eagle disdained to engage the enemy commander, as if letting it flee to tell of the power of the rulers of this patch of space. Ships had fallen out of the retreat, untouched by the power of the station they simply ceased to accelerate. Some of them, those that were fully Dreen, exploded or came apart like overripe fruit. Converts simply coasted, leaking air and water for reasons unknown. The eagle disdained these carrion of the battle as well, concentrating on the ships that tried to avoid the battle.

As the song closed the eagle didn't fade. It simply took up a proprietary position between the fleet and the station, a bundle of arrows appearing out of the mist for it to perch upon.

"Can you hold that?" Weaver asked.

"Easily," Miriam said, her eyes closed. "Now that I know what I'm doing. In fact . . . There," she continued, opening her eyes. "It's set, now. Until I tell it to go away or we shut down the station. Easy, really."

"For you," Weaver said. "You sure you can't get the brain-ship?"

"There seems to be a range limiter," Miriam admitted. "I can't get out much beyond the gas cloud. They're already past that."

"We really shouldn't let them get away," Weaver said with a frown. "We're going to have to fight them again some time."

"Like, right now, sir," Captain Zanella said. "The Dreen boarding force just entered the docking bay."

"Damn," Weaver said. "I *knew* I'd forgotten something important."

"Interesting," Berg said, watching the new monitors in the docking bay. "It's not landing."

"Would *you*, sir?" Gunny Juda said.

The docking platform was covered in space spiders, to the point where it was solidly purple in spots. The spiders had also sensed the approach of the Dreen and were up and awake, scurrying around in groups trying to get to the hovering ship.

What the Dreen apparently didn't realize, was that there were spiders on the upper levels as well. Berg could see them cascading off the upper platforms in a broken river. Many of them were killed by the impact on the hull of the Dreen ship, others missed and plummeted into the depths. But quite a few were landing on it.

The Dreen ship, unheeding of the parasites, opened up a hatch on the underside and dropped out seven of the oddest things Berg had ever seen. They seemed to be sea anemones, with thousands of tentacle legs.

As they hit the platform, the legs flashed out, scooping up the spiders. Nearly as many orifices opened on the side and the spiders were flipped in to be crushed by what looked like large molars.

The cleaner systems probably would have worked if there hadn't been so many of the space spiders. Unfortunately, as fast as they ate spiders, more and more came on. The cleaners were actually increasing in size from all the sustenance, bulging from the mass of the spiders they were consuming. But the spiders were getting through the flickering tentacles, climbing up onto the bodies of the things, cutting with their claws and looking for a way in that didn't have teeth.

The ship dropped two more of the cleaners but it was fruitless; the station had become packed with the Dreen-eating spiders. And just as the hatch was opening, the ship suddenly gave a massive twitch as if it were a dog bitten on a nerve by a flea. It spun in place and headed for the airlock. It was already beginning to shudder as it exited the Tree.

"*God*, I love those things," Eric said, grinning. "Captain Zanella . . . ?"

"Okay, we've got about seven destroyers by the door," Bill said. "I'm not sure how we're going to get rid of them; the system won't shoot under the station. Maybe the *Blade* can drive them off. But as long as they stay inside the field . . . I don't think the *Blade* can get them. And there's a few hundred fighters left. We can't even see them with this system, so they're going to be a pest until they run out of fuel . . ."

"Or into a space spider," Miriam said. "I told you they were cute."

"Very," Weaver said. "And we've got the brain-ship headed out of the system. But we're sort of stuck here."

"We are, aren't we," Miriam said, frowning. "It's the destroyers by the door that are the problem."

"I wonder how they'd react to an airlock opening," Berg said.

"Why?" Weaver asked.

"Well, sir, in space once momentum is imparted to something it maintains it," the lieutenant said. "And we've got all these damned spiders just sitting here . . ."

"I can't believe we're down to throwing rocks," Day said.

"Just get ready to hand me spiders," Lurch replied. "Opening airlock."

When there was no immediate reaction he stepped right up to the edge and looked out.

Two Dreen destroyers were "down" from his perch. He couldn't tell how far away but it didn't really matter. Once velocity was imparted to an object in zero gravity . . .

"Take *that* you interstellar menaces," Sergeant Lyle shouted, throwing one of the baseball-sized ovoids. "Eat space spiders you . . . you . . ."

"People-eating morons?" Day suggested.

"Jerks," Lyle said, continuing to throw the spiders. "I think one just . . . Yep, we have spiders on-board."

"Why are you throwing, anyway?" Day asked.

"Were *you* the pitcher of your school's baseball team?" Lurch asked. "No? Then hand me some more balls. I wonder if they'd fire if we did a space walk? The others have to be inside the shield somewhere . . ."

<Organism 8139 infestation in quadrant three.>
Source?
<Unknown. With degree of gravitational disturbance in system and reported numbers of infected units, random source high probability.>
Degradation?
<Five percent failure in forward armaments and shielding. And increasing.>
Divert all available resources to Cleaner Unit generation.

"What's our status, Eng?"

"Sickbay is overflowing," Commander Oldfield said. "We've got Laser Two back up and three of the damaged ball guns on the port side. Starboard is trashed, though. We've used up all our molycirc getting the port back up and we'll have to find some more osmium before we can do anything on the starboard. And, frankly, sir, most of the guns are beyond local repair. The fabber isn't big enough to make some of the components."

"That gives us, what? Seven guns on port and two on starboard?" the CO asked.

"Yes, sir."

"Good," Prael said. "That's enough. Conn, set course for the brain-ship."

"Sir, are you insane?" the Eng snarled. "We're going to get our ass handed to us! We've done enough!"

"TACO?" the CO said. "What was that about all the times I've busted up my ship?"

"'If I had been censured every time I have run my ship, or fleets under my command, into great danger, I should have long ago been out of the Service and never in the House of Peers,'" the TACO said automatically.

"With your shield or on it, Eng," Prael said. "With your shield or on it."

"CIC, Conn. Two minutes to intercept."

"I miss the music," the CO said. "What do we have in the way of tunes?"

"About a billion MP3s, sir," the TACO replied.

"What to play, what to play?" the CO said, accessing the entertainment server. "I'm getting a bit tired of rock, heavy metal and Goth. Hmmm . . . Ah. There we go . . ."

The TACO looked up as orchestral music started to pour from the 1MC and tapped his foot.

"I don't think I've ever heard this before, sir," the TACO said. "Catchy tune, though."

"That's because you were forced to attend that wimpy liberal school in Annapolis, Lieutenant," the CO said. "If you were an Aggie, you'd have learned the words by heart.

Yes, we'll rally round the flag, boys, we'll rally once again,
Shouting the battle cry of freedom!
We will rally from the hillside, we'll gather from the plain,
Shouting the battle cry of freedom!"

"Yes, sir, very nice," the TACO said, wincing. Like the XO, the CO really should let others sing. "But we've got an emergence at the warp-point."

"What?" the CO asked, standing up and walking over to the sensor operator. "What class?"

"It looks like a Dreen convert," the sensor tech said. "Dreadnought class. Pretty much like that one we captured in the Orion battle. But the readings are off enough I'm not sure. Accel is way up, total energy output is up about ten percent. So . . . I'm not sure, sir."

"Just one more Dreen to engage," the CO said, sighing. "Sound the battlecry, men, we're going—"

"CIC, Communications. Incoming transmission, SpacCom codes. Visual and audio."

"Put it on," the CO said, resuming his seat.

"Captain Prael, Admiral Blankemeier, Alliance Flagship *Thermopylae*," Spectre said, grinning evilly. "I see you've managed to make hash of my ship. Again. Congratulations, glad to see the tradition has been upheld. But we've got this one, you can back off."

27

"That is a bold statement, Captain Spectre," Ship Master Korcan said. "However, a Dreen brain-ship outclasses this vessel by nearly ten to one. Our odds of survival . . ."

The two were viewing the battle from the *Thermopylae*'s CIC, a massive room that looked like an auditorium with a two-story screen on the far wall.

Humans and Hexosehr didn't, frankly, know much about the race that had built the *Thermopylae*. The Mrreee sentient which had commanded it called them the Karchava. The massive dreadnought had been captured from the Dreen and converted to Human and Hexosehr use. This, however, would be its first taste of combat with a regular crew. And most of the crew was playing catch-up figuring out the systems. So it looked to be a trial by fire.

"*Never* tell me the odds," Spectre said, leaning back in his command chair and interlacing his fingers behind his head. Technically, he had another similar compartment next door from which to command a fleet. And technically he shouldn't be sitting next to the commander of the ship, looking over his shoulder. But the Hexosehr didn't seem to mind about that sort of thing and the Karchava had installed a control point right next to the commander for some reason. With the massive Karchava chair replaced by a human control position, he figured he might as well use it. Korcan had been a corvette commander previously. A highly decorated one, but only the commander of a corvette. Stepping up to temporary command of the *Thermopylae* was a *big* step. Sometimes two brains could be better than one. And it gave him a chance to have this conversation more or less face to face, given that the Hexosehr didn't have eyes. "Did the *Caurorgorngoth* turn away in the Battle of Orion?"

"No," the Hexosehr commander replied. "But the *Caurorgorngoth* was dying and far from outclassed even then. We are a brand new ship. Perhaps letting this one flee would be the wiser choice?"

"Okay, call it a human thing," Spectre said, regarding the blinking red icon of the Dreen flagship calmly. The Hexosehr had managed to comprehend the Karchava systems well enough to change the color of the icons and the information readouts next to them. Fortunately, the rest worked really well. If humans ever met the Karchava, Spectre suspected they'd be people to get drunk with. "If so much as one ship escapes this system, the Dreen will know what happened. If not even their brain-ship returns, they will have only dread. I'm not the commander of this ship, Korcan, but I am your senior officer. And as your senior officer, my orders are to engage more closely. . . ."

�֎   ✖   ✖

<Karchava dreadnought, identified as lost Unit 24801, approaching on course for warp point. Signals analysis indicates control by Species 27264.>

Engage all weapons.

<Forward systems inoperable due to Organism 8139 infestation.>

Recall all fighter systems. Engage enemy combat unit.

<Dispatched.>

"It is not deviating," Ship Leader Korcan said.

"It's trying to escape the system," Spectre said.

"And we must prevent this," Korcan said. "Entering our maximum engagement range. We should have been taking fire from the brain-ship before this. Their range is greater than ours."

"Be thankful for small favors," Spectre replied.

"Permission to open fire?" Korcan asked.

"Your ship, Ship Master," Blankemeier replied. "I'm just along for the ride."

"Very well," Korcan said. "Main Gun Control."

"Aye, sir," the gunnery officer replied.

"Target the brain-ship. Open fire."

"Dude, we need, like, those cool Death Star uniforms," Gunnery Petty Officer Third Class Sherman Zouks said. He had the helmet of his ship-suit latched up and was looking at the gun board dyspeptically. "You know, black, shiny?" He dropped the helmet and hummed some ominous music. "Doom, doom, doom . . ."

"Man, you would bitch about anything," Gunnery PO Second Class Santos Braham said. He'd latched down his helmet and had his feet up on the gun board. "Here we are running the biggest fricking gun in creation and you're all 'it's not the Death Star!' Puhleeeaze. Just hope like hell these suits are good enough to—"

"Mass Driver Control, Gunnery."

"Mass Driver Control, aye," Braham said, his feet slamming to the floor.

"Initiate Main Gun Fire Procedure."

"Main Gun Fire Procedure, aye," Braham said, looking over at Zouks. "You got the book?"

"Got it memorized," Zouks said, pulling down the gun fire manual and opening it to a marked page. "Main Gun Fire Procedure Step One: Warm Capacitor Banks One Through Fourteen."

"Warm Capacitor Banks One Through Fourteen, aye," Braham said, pressing the series of buttons. "Warming capacitors."

"Step Two: Ensure Capacitor Warm State by verifying indicators One Through Fourteen colored purple."

"Ensure Capacitor Warm State by verifying indicators One through Fourteen colored purple, aye," Braham said. "Capacitor seven orange."

"Crap," Zouks said, flipping to another page. "Contact faulty capacitor crew and determine status of capacitor . . ."

"Come on, work you son of a bitch!" Gunnery Petty Officer Second Class Salomon Shick shouted, hammering the carbon-fiber casing with a wrench.

"Cut it, Razor," Gunnery Petty Officer First Class Colton Shafer said, grabbing the wrench. "Cracking the case would definitely put this thing off-line. Grab the manual."

"It's always something," Shick said, pulling down a thick tome. "I just fricking *ran* a diagnostic on this fucker."

"Then we'll run one again. . . ."

"CIC, Gunnery."

"Gunnery, CIC."

"Main gun is temporarily off-line."

"Main gun temporarily off-line, aye."

"Oh, how truly good," Korcan said. "I apologize for this lapse, Admiral."

"Don't sweat it," Spectre said. "Unless I'm reading this board wrong there's a passel of bandits headed this way, too."

"Fighter control."

"Fighter control, aye."

"Determine optimum launch time for counter-fighter mission. Tell the dragonflies to get ready."

"Why is my gun not *working*, PO?"

Gunnery Master Chief Daniel Todd strode into Capacitor Seven's compartment like rolling thunder. Master Chief Todd was the chief in charge of the Main Gun. As such, by both historical custom and lawful regulation he "owned" the gun and was responsible for ensuring it was good to go at any moment. Since it was the *Thermopylae*'s main weapon, the chief took that responsibility very seriously. He was less than enthusiastic that at the precise moment when *his* gun was needed

most, *his* gun was kaput. There were questions of man-
hood involved!

"Diagnostic is good on our end, Master Chief," Shafer
said, flipping through the manual. "The capacitor is
warmed and ready to discharge. But main gun section is
getting a fault."

"Found it," Schick said, sliding out from under the
capacitor. "Communications relay is screwed."

"And do you *have* a replacement communications
relay, Petty Officer?" Todd asked, taking a sip of coffee.

"It's stored in Compartment Nine-Nine-Two dash One
compartment inventory, Master Chief," Shafer said, looking
at the computerized inventory.

"Engineering, Guns," the master chief said, tapping his
internal communicator.

"Go, Guns."

"I need a comm relay, standby number."

"Ready."

"Two-One-Six-Niner-Foah-Two-Fahv-Three-Six-One-
Two Dash Alpha. Compartment Niner-Niner-Two Dash
One inventory."

"Two-One-Six-Nine-Four-Two-Five-Three-Six-One-
Two Dash Alpha, aye. Compartment Niner-Niner-Two
Dash One inventory, aye."

"And I need it A mother*grappin'* SAP."

Spectre took a sip of coffee and regarded the discussion going on at the base of the CIC auditorium with
interest. Three beings were involved: an Adar, standing
nearly nine feet tall and wearing spandex shorts and a
Hawaiian shirt; a Hexosehr, a race that looked a bit like a

blind otter and disdained clothing; and a human, the lieutenant commander in charge of the Gunnery section. The three-way conference looked like it was about to become an argument.

"Do you think I should intervene?" Korcan asked.

"Your ship," Spectre said.

"Not until they come to some consensus, then," Korcan replied. "I would know what they are discussing, however."

"And I think we're about to," Blankemeier·said as the threesome made its way up to the commander's position.

"Sir," Guns said, looking at his Hexosehr commander and trying to pointedly ignore the human admiral sitting beside him. "The fault in the main gun has been detected. Capacitor Seven is functional, but it's in bad communication with the main gun control. All it is is a comm relay. Local controls indicate that it is in full preparation for discharge. I wish to fire before repairs are completed on the relay."

"And there is disagreement," Korcan said. "Ship Technician Caethau?"

"The personnel making the judgment that the capacitor is ready to fire are undertrained," the Hexosehr engineer replied. "I have Hexosehr personnel on the way to verify the fault."

"Time?" Korcan asked.

"No more than seven treek," the Hexosehr replied.

"Human terms, Caethau," Korcan reproved. "This is a human ship. Fifteen minutes. If the fault is as determined, time to repair?"

"Another two treek," Caethau replied.

"Adar . . . Monthut?" Korcan said.

"Fire," the Adar said. "This is a battle. If you wait for everything to be perfect, you'll never fight it."

Korcan thought about it for a moment.

"Concur," the Hexosehr commander said. "Lieutenant Commander Painter, you have my permission to fire."

"Permission to fire, aye," the human said. He turned and looked down at the guns position and made a gesture. "Firing, sir."

"Override on Step Two, aye," PO Braham said. "Override on Step Two."

"Guess we're going to have to fire without seven, then," Zouks said. "Step Three: Pre-energize power runs."

"Pre-energize power runs, aye," Braham said, pressing the controls. The room began to hum as if filled by a billion bees. "I hope like hell this step works. Got purple on all power runs."

"Report main gun prepared to fire."

"Report main gun prepared to fire, aye . . ."

"ALL HANDS, ALL HANDS. STAND BY FOR MAIN GUN FIRE."

In the end it was as easy as pressing a button. And the dreadnought, as wide as a human supercarrier was long and nearly a kilometer in length, a construction beyond any human endeavor save the Great Wall of China . . . shuddered. Seemed to almost stop in space . . .

"Yeah!" Shick shouted from under the capacitor. The discharge, despite heavy shielding, would have fried everyone in the compartment if they hadn't closed up their armor. It especially would have fried the technician fumbling around underneath it. "That's what *I'm* talking about!"

"Capacitor recharge nominal," Shafer said.

"And this baby is *still* up! Charge you bastard, *charge*!"

The penetrator was not just a chunk of random metal. The optimum design had been found on the Karchava engineering database and slavishly copied. At the core was a long, pointed, chunk of heavy metal, in the case of this penetrator depleted uranium. Of all heavy and hard metals it was the most available to humans since it was made from reactor waste that had been reworked to remove all trace of radioactive particles.

Out from that it was simple steel. A lot of steel. Enough steel to make a World War Two destroyer.

The outer layer was a thin sheaf of carbon monomolecule. It was there to prevent significant damage from micrometorite hits. Like a diamond, the penetrator was hard but fragile. Even a very small pebble could, potentially, crack the penetrator before it hit its target. And that would be sad.

Accelerated to a small fraction of light-speed, the titanic dart gained a boost of energy from Einstein's famous equation, raising its potential kinetic energy to right at the output of every nuclear weapon on Earth at the height of the Cold War—several exajoules of energy.

When it hit, a significant fraction of that astronomical energy was transferred to the Dreen brain-ship.

The penetrator hit on the nose of the brain-ship,

slightly to starboard. Most of its mass converted to plasma immediately, the inertia of the impact carrying the blazing ball of hell deep into the vitals of the ship. Bulkhead after bulkhead was vaporized as the gaseous fire burned through everything in its path. The plasma ripped through seventy percent of the weapons controls on the starboard side, devastated starboard fighter systems, which had yet to launch, and tore apart thirty percent of the ship's environmental systems.

But at its core, in a way worse, was the massive dart of depleted uranium. The impact mostly vaporized the steel around it and, due to simple physics, the plasma front could outstrip the speed of even the relativistic dart. But the harder, stronger, heavier metal remained intact for a few moments, blazing at the heart of the plasma ball.

That is, until the plasma expended its last joule of energy. Leaving the dart to fly ahead of its wavefront and smash *further* into the interior.

Depleted uranium is very strong but it is also, again, fragile. As soon as it hit a major obstacle, a primary support beam for the ship, it broke apart into a thousand pieces. And like flint and steel, when uranium hits even itself hard enough, it sparks. Then, like magnesium, it *burns*.

Thousands of chunks of white-hot uranium crashed into the depths of the brain-ship like a flaming shotgun blast.

<*Mass driver impact. Significant damage to environmental, starboard fighter support, starboard fighter bays . . .* >

The sentient didn't need its child to tell it that the damage was *significant*. It could sense the ship screaming.

It was tied into the depths of its creation, as much the brain of the ship as the brain of the task force. The ship's pain was *its* pain, and it had just had the equivalent of a flamethrower hit it on the shoulder.

But the hit had missed the heart and the brain.

Close to range for secondary weapons. Roll to engage from port when in range. Launch all remaining fighters.

"Oooh, that's gotta *hurt*," Spectre said. He was looking at the long-range viewer repeater on his own console. The Karchava apparently didn't have *Star Trek* viewers, either. The system was a near twin of the one on the *Blade*, the only difference being even better jitter controls and the fact that with the circumference of the dreadnought and the larger individual telescopes it hosted, it was the largest telescope ever built. The resolution was just *awesome*. And he'd never seen a better image to resolve than the one of a Dreen brain-ship spouting fire.

"Reports indicate serious damage," Korcan said. "The brain-ship is streaming air and liquids."

"You just blew out its whole starboard *side*," Spectre said. "Serious is a bit of an understatement. I mean, it gushed plasma along a third of its length. I'm surprised it's still operating at *all*. That gun is bad news."

"Alas, it takes time to charge."

"Commander, reaching optimum engagement range for fighter launch."

"Launch fighters."

"Tallyho!"
The midsection of the *Thermopylae* hosted thirty fighter

bays, fifteen to a side. When it was captured, the Karchava fighters were long gone, replaced by Dreen organic fighters.

Now it hosted a new version of organic fighter, the Cheerick dragonflies.

Perhaps it had been some constraint that was still unknown to the Alliance or perhaps it had been simple oversight. But the Dreen had maintained one fighter in each bay.

When the dragonflies were boarded it became immediately apparent that the Alliance need not be so sparse in their allocation of resources. Dragonflies could maintain themselves for quite some time on minimal resources and there was more than enough room to pack them into the hangar bay. They could, in fact, be stacked on top of each other.

Thus, when the fighter bays opened up they opened all the *way* up, not only opening their hatches but their internal clamshells and evacuating the hangar bays. Instead of thirty fighters the ship could disgorge *eighty-six* shielded, laser-eyed, giant-chinchilla crewed dragonflies.

Colonel She-kah knew that she could not, however, control them. From reports they had already gotten from Che-chee she knew there was a way to train other than by flying in space. But up until they reached this system, all she could do was occasionally train her males when the ship rested or was moving from one node to another.

Thus, they were not the crackest cavalry in the galaxy. But they were eager.

"Follow your icons, males," the Cheerick Mother said. "As soon as you see the enemy, though, you are on your own. Teams stay together. Fight well. Re-ka, you shall stay on *my* tail and not leave it. Do you understand?"

"Yes, Colonel," the young cavalryman said.

"Let us do battle."

"We're taking long-range fire from the Dreen fighter group," the defensive systems officer reported. There had been a faint shudder through the ship, barely noticeable in CIC. "Permission to open fire."

"Fighter control, time to dragonfly engagement range."

"Colonel She-kah has ordered her fighters to hold their fire until they are closer," Fighter Control relayed. "They're planning their initial sweep at under a light-second. Fighters have been vectored up and away of direct path. Most of them followed the vector. About fifteen seem to be totally lost."

"We'll collect them later," Korcan said. "Defensive Systems, open fire."

"Open fire, aye."

The angle of retreat and the fact that the brain-ship had only been able to launch from its port side meant that the majority of the Dreen fighters were to starboard of the *Thermopylae*.

All along the starboard side, plasma cannons, lasers and mass drivers swiveled forward and began to belch incandescent hell at the oncoming Dreen assault.

"Colonel!" Re-ka shouted. "The ship is on fire!"

"They have opened fire against the Dreen fighters," She-kah replied over the full circuit, trying not to sigh.

Males were always so excitable. "You can see the fighters firing at the ship as well."

"The icons are moving around . . ." Re-ka replied. "I cannot really follow them."

"They are evasively maneuvering," She-kah said. "Which is why we are waiting to fire."

"Twelve bandits destroyed," Defensive Control reported. "Continuing to engage."

"Discontinue engagement when the dragonflies make their pass," Korcan said.

"Discontinue for dragonfly pass, aye."

"Minor damage to the starboard forequarter," Damage Control reported. "Mass drivers nine and six out of action. No casualties."

"Tough ship," Spectre said. "That much fire from fighters would have made a hash of the *Blade*."

"She is a tough ship," Korcan said. "And another species lost her to the Dreen. And then the Dreen lost her to the *Blade*. Any ship can be defeated."

"Point."

"Colonel She-kah, formation approaching one light-second from the forward portion of the Dreen fighter group."

"Roger," She-kah said, squinting. The icons she was watching were still jiggling around, indicating that the Dreen fighters were maneuvering. But she could not for the life of her see them, yet. She knew that the cavalry-men could not engage simply on the basis of the icons. They were going to have to *see* their enemy. She had not realized that a light-second was so far. "We are going to continue to close before firing."

"Main gun charged," gunnery control reported.
"Fire as you bear," Korcan said.

"Main Gun Fire Procedures."
"Main Gun Fire Procedures, aye."

While the Dreen fighters were still invisible, only appearing as icons or the occasional flash of plasma guns, Colonel She-kah could clearly see the massive Dreen brain-ship. The monstrosity, ten times the size of the *Thermopylae*, seemed as large as a planet and they were starting to take fire from it.

The fire became momentarily wide and sporadic as the massive ship gouted fire from every port in the forward section. Chunks, still burning, broke off and drifted away into space. But the massive dreadnought continued forward, still apparently under power.

"Colonel . . . I see . . ."

Colonel She-kah had also not considered the speed with which something very hard to see could suddenly become *much* more visible and much *much* closer at astronomical speeds.

"All dragonflies open fire!" she shouted as her helmet suddenly became a mass of red icons.

The only thing that permitted the dragonflies to get any hits in at the closing speeds was the fact that it was a target rich environment. Over two hundred Dreen fighters remained from the battles deeper in the solar system and they had been joined by another eighty from the survivors of the first hit on the brain-ship. Nearly three hundred fighters were approaching the *Thermopylae* in a, for space, very small formation. Which Colonel She-kah had piloted her functional fighters right into the middle of.

The only thing that was statistically improbable was a mid-space collision, but Cavalryman Tre-trak managed even that, impacting his dragonfly directly on the nose of a Dreen fighter, despite its best attempts to dodge the idiot.

Everyone in the interpenetrated formations was dodging wildly, with the relatively small space so filled with plasma and laser bolts it momentarily gained something resembling an atmosphere. Both fighters could maneuver in three dimensions with rapid axis change, something that Colonel She-kah had not really realized until necessity taught her very *very* fast.

From She-kah's perspective, the encounter was a confusion of spinning stars, fleeting shots and *way* more plasma than she ever wanted to see again in her life. She was unsure if she'd hit anything but as the dragonfly formation passed the Dreen formation, both groups turning and sending Parthian shots at the other, she could see drifting and smashed Dreen fighters. Along with far too many dragonflies.

She could also see the enemy headed towards their ride at a very fast clip.

"Follow them!" she shouted. "Section leaders, report casualties."

❈   ❈   ❈

"Permission to reengage Dreen fighters," Defensive Control asked.

"As long as you don't hit the dragonflies," Korcan replied. "Fighter Control?"

"I would not use the term 'control,' sir," said the lieutenant commander, a former FA-18 pilot who was itching to get these medieval idiots to learn real air-to-air tactics. "Dragonflies appear to have taken out eighteen Dreen fighters for a loss of seven. One of those may have been a mid-space; the encounter was too confusing for our computers to really keep track of. Definitely don't know who got what. Some of the Dreen losses may have been blue-on-blue and ditto for the dragonflies."

"Clearly we must get this simulator Che-chee has developed," Korcan said. "Order the dragonflies to decelerate and pursue."

"Colonel She-kah's on it."

"Why are we still not catching up?" She-kah snarled, then waited impatiently for the response. This thing about "light-speed lag" was still confusing. It seemed to her as if the controller on the other end was dawdling.

"Colonel, you had a high relative vector to the Dreen formation," the combat controller said, trying not to sigh. "They're decelerating to engage us but you're still not even headed *back* to us, yet. Your velocity was too high for your accel to get you going in the right direction, yet. You have to keep decelerating for a while. I'd recommend random maneuvering as well. You're well into the engagement basket of the brain-ship."

"I noticed," She-kah snapped.

"*Maneuver,* you young idiot," She-kah said as a plasma bolt from the brain-ship passed by.

"I'm trying, Colonel," Re-ka replied. "But I'm getting very confused."

Everyone in the formation was. The best they could do was try to figure out which way the various icons were pointed and try to follow them, not an inherent Cheerick skill. The only thing in view from their perspective was the brain-ship and the torrent of fire pouring out from its midsection. The dragonflies had gotten so scattered on the pass through the Dreen fighter group many of them were out of sight of each other.

"Fighter control, can you turn off all the icons but one?" She-kah asked.

"Aye, aye," the controller replied a few seconds later. Damn this lag thing! "Which one, Colonel?"

"Mine. I need to rally my force. Wave the banner high, Fighter Control."

As the Dreen fighters approached the *Thermopylae* its fire became more accurate, taking out more and more of the fighters.

However, the Dreen fighters had a functional engagement range of nearly two light-seconds, nearly twice the distance from Earth to the moon, and they were *highly* maneuverable. It was impossible for the guns to track on them and ensure a hit at that range.

But the *Thermopylae* had *a lot* of anti-fighter guns. The belching battlewagon simply filled the space the fighters were passing through with lasers, plasma and chunks of iron.

It didn't mean the ship wasn't taking damage of her own, though.

"Gunnery Control, Plasma Nineteen," Petty Officer First Class Malcolm Charles shouted over the internal communications circuit. "Nineteen is toast. Compartment is evacuated. Gun's total slag. Dockyard job."

"Roger, Nineteen," Gunnery Control replied. "Initiate Damage Control shut-down procedures and evacuate the compartment. Casualties?"

"Negative," Charles replied. "Blow-out panel initiated and shielded us. If I ever meet a Karchava I'm gonna kiss him right on his bulgey forehead. Initiate shut-down procedures, aye."

"Roger, Nineteen. Gunnery Control, out."

"Okay, Colonel, you're headed back for us," the combat controller said patiently. "Looks like your formation is getting in good tune, too."

"Where are the Dreen?" She-kah asked. "Give me icons back."

"Single icon for the near center of the formation, Colonel," the controller said. The lag was much less this time for some reason. "You got it?"

"Up and to my left," She-kah said. "When we have to . . . slow down, whatever the word you use is, give me the order. Keep only my icon on my other fighters. Let them follow me this time."

"Roger, Colonel, will do."

✖   ✖   ✖

However, while the Dreen fighters had good "space legs," a range of over seven hundred million kilometers or nearly five times the distance from Earth to the sun, the initial battle had taken place deep within the system. They had been dispatched, initially, to try to screen the ground combat assault force and got to within an AU of the local star.

Now, with their carriers dust, they had to push their way back out to cover the brain-ship. And while they had high accelerations, they had to decelerate to slow to the velocity of the human flagship. All of that took fuel.

By the time the majority of the fighters approached the *Thermopylae* they were, in human terms, "bingo."

That didn't mean they were useless. The power system for the plasma guns was independent of the drive. It did mean they were relegated to either keeping up with the still accelerating battlewagon or maneuvering.

Being Dreen, they chose following the battlewagon, eventually most of them settling into a nice predictable straight line.

"Majority of the Dreen fighters have stopped maneuvering," Defensive Control said. "They're just following like they're on a string."

"I take it you've used that to our benefit?" Korcan asked, looking at the damage report. "If you can."

Spectre sighed, winced and leaned sideways.

"Rotate the ship," he whispered.

Korcan let loose a stream of quiet clicks, the first sign

of emotion he had given in the entire battle and far too quiet to be noticed in the CIC.

"Conn, CIC."

"Go CIC."

"Rotate the ship to engage fighters with upper and port batteries."

"Rotate ship, aye."

"Should have done that earlier," Korcan said.

"We're all learning," Spectre said.

"I have *been* a ship commander before," Korcan said. "Not one as large as this, but a commander nonetheless. You should not have to tell me."

"You were in stasis for a long time," Spectre replied. "It's not quite like riding a bicycle."

The Dreen fighters dispatched from the brain-ship still had fuel and were maneuvering wildly through the incoming fire from the Karchava battlewagon. With most of their brethren toast, they were the only remaining attackers pounding fire into the now rotating *Thermopylae*. But they, too, were following the dreadnought like beads, jinking around, yes, but nonetheless following a mostly predictable path.

A path that lead directly to the dragonflies, which were now closing at their maximum of one *thousand* gravities of acceleration.

"Colonel, begin deceleration," the combat controller said. "They're headed for you, now, and you're going really fast at them again."

"Roger," She-kah said, thinking "slow down" at the

dragonfly. She could see the *Thermopylae* now and by looking where the fire was headed and the icon she could figure out more or less where the enemy was. But she still couldn't judge distance. "All dragonflies slow. Form box formation around my position. We will charge them as cavalry should."

The last fighter battle was, in direct contrast to the first, the slowest space battle in the history of the galaxy. And extremely one sided.

The Dreen continued to pour fire into the *Thermopylae* even as the decelerating dragonflies closed. The dragonflies began firing as soon as they came in view of the Dreen, continuing to slow until their relative speed was barely faster than humanity's Space Shuttle, in astronomical terms the walking speed of a very old and decrepit man. The dragonfly lasers were strong enough to penetrate and destroy a Dreen fighter with one blast and, inaccurate as they were, they had time to fire multiple blasts into the fighter formation before they passed.

One by one, in pairs and in groups, the Dreen fighters came apart under the hammer of the dragonflies. There were thirteen left, though, as the dragonfly formation passed. This time, Colonel She-kah didn't even need control to handle the reassembly. She reformed her fighters, accelerated back to the Dreen formation and closed on them at what was, even at normal air-breathing fighter speeds, dead-slow.

Closing at the speed of a World War One biplane, at ranges that were not much more than those paper-air-planes fought from, the Cheerick fighters simply could not miss.

As nine dragonflies concentrated their fire on the last remaining Dreen, Colonel She-kah let out a yell of triumph.

"Fighter Control, Dragonflight. All fighters terminated as far as I can tell."

"Roger, Dragonflight. You should be good on fuel for a bit. Stay out there. Conditions are going to get a bit frosty around here."

"Okay, I thought the *Thermo* was tough," Spectre said, shaking his head.

The Dreen brain-ship had taken four solid hits from the mass driver and still it headed for the unreality node. It wasn't going to make it, unless Spectre was much mistaken, and even if it could it was unlikely to be able to go into unreal space. But it was still plowing along. It had started to decelerate but apparently there had been some damage to engines because at its current rate it was going to overshoot the node.

But it was still coming.

"If we continue on our current course and speed we're going to practically ram it," Korcan said. "Conn, prepare to yaw the ship to maintain fire by main gun on the target. Yaw will be to port to engage their port side."

"Prepare to yaw port, aye."

Yaw the ship to engage with starboard batteries. Fire all guns as they bear.

The two battlewagons, one massive and one monstrous,

began to twist in space, slowly, oh so slowly. Like the Karchava dreadnought, the brain-ship's main guns were forward, four massive meson cannons each with more power than the *Thermopylae*'s single mass driver. Those, however, had been taken out early by the space spider infestation. While they had been mostly crisped by the mass driver impacts, the damage was done. The main arsenal of the brain-ship had not been a factor in the battle at all.

But arrayed along her sides were weapons nearly as powerful. Multiple hundreds of terawatt class directed weapons, plasma cannons to dwarf anything made by humans or Hexosehr, mass drivers nearly as large as the *Thermopylae*'s.

Crippled as she was, the brain-ship was still Goliath to the *Thermopylae*'s David. But as with Goliath and David, the *Thermopylae* had one thing going for her; she was more maneuverable.

"Main gun charged."

"Wait to fire until we bear," Korcan said. "The brain-ship is maneuvering. We do not want to take too much fire from her secondaries. But I want a shot right . . . here . . ." he said, marking a spot two thirds of the way back on the massive dreadnought and centerline. "This is the best guess we have for the location of the sentient. It is the location of the controller on other Dreen ships. If we can fire a round that penetrates to the controller . . ."

"Worth the shot," Spectre said. "But for what we are about to receive . . ."

"Target maneuvering counter to our maneuver,"

Combat Control reported. "They're trying to get their starboard side to bear. We're trying to fire into their port."

"We're slightly out of plane from them," Korcan said. "Conn, maneuver downwards as we skew. Continue rotation."

"Dreen secondaries firing," Defensive Control reported, just as there was a shudder through the ship.

"Damage control's going to be busy."

The two ships continued to close, the *Thermopylae* circling the bull like a matador. But bulls don't have plasma cannons.

"Can the mass driver take this?" Spectre asked as the ship rang like a tocsin to a Dreen mass driver strike.

"That is why there are mostly acceleration rings forward," Korcan said placidly. "And most of the fire is hitting our flanks. Serious damage, but the mass driver still has over ninety percent operability. Good design."

"Hope there are some Karchava left somewhere," Spectre said. "I want to shake their hands. Or claws or tentacles or whatever."

"I think I have a firing solution," Main Gun Control reported. "Should hit the location you designated."

"Fire."

It was like pithing a frog. The enormous mass of the projectile hit the armor of the brain-ship low on its port side, penetrating upwards through the refractory material to blow all the way *through* the massive battlewagon.

And it missed the brain.

However, there are three necessities to any ship. A brain, the control section of a human, Hexosehr or Adar vessel, or the sentient controller of a Dreen battlewagon, which *always* has a redundant backup; the lungs, the environmental section that all spaceships need, and the heart, the engine room that all ships, space or otherwise, require.

It missed the brain. But it hit the heart. Most hearts don't explode. Unless they happen to be already over-loaded fusion cooling systems.

"Whoa," Spectre said as fire began to gush out of the ship from every hatch along its entire length. "Nice secondar— " He closed his eyes at the flash on his monitor and blinked. "What did you *hit*?"

"I think we just found out where the engine room is on a brain-ship, Admiral," Korcan said. "Ops. Discontinue combat action. Divert all personnel to damage control. Recall the dragonflies. Our work is done."

EPLOGUE

"As soon as gates are installed we're going to be heading home," Captain Zanella said. "The *Blade* will be heading back as soon as she's repaired. There are plenty of Marines on the *Thermopylae* to ensure station security."

"And then there's the spiders," Berg said, nodding. "Orders?"

"Get some rest," the CO said. "We'll be here a couple more days, max."

"I've got some stuff I still need to do, sir," Berg replied.

"Up to you," the CO said. "If part of it's catching up on mail, your evaluation's in your inbox."

"Thank you, sir," Berg said.

"In case I have to tell you, you did a damned fine job. Get some rest. You've earned it."

Berg nodded to the CO as he left, then brought up his eval. He looked at it carefully but really couldn't find anywhere that the CO could have written it more glowingly. It was said that any evaluation that didn't make an officer sound like the next Napoleon was a guaranteed career killer. Berg's first evaluation as an officer made *Napoleon* sound like a piker.

The lieutenant nodded again and closed the file. That was one of hundreds if he stayed in. Each of which would be just as important to his career.

That was the past. In the meantime, he had work to do.

"Dear Mrs. Kaijahano, It was my honor to be your son's platoon leader during the mission where he lost his life. In all my time as a Marine, I have never known a finer . . ."

"That was why the Hexosehr told us to wait," Prael said, shaking his head. "That's a damned nice ship you've got there, Admiral. Even as beat up as it is at the moment. What I don't get is how you got out here so fast."

"The Hexosehr completed the conversion while in orbit around one of the gate stars," the admiral said. "I'd known it was going to come on-line soon, but not exactly when. I'd just come out with the advance party when we got the news about the Tree. So I jumped out immediately with the tech reps still aboard. Bit of a surprise for them, but waste not a minute, as Nelson would say."

"Did you have the same TACO I had, sir?" Prael said. "The real question is: Don't admirals usually command *fleets*?"

"I'll have one soon enough," Blankemeier said, grinning. "Especially with you holding onto this facility. Right now I've got a temporary Hexosehr commander, Ship Master Korcan, good guy. He's got his ship under construction, now, though, a Chaos destroyer. The *Thermopylae* is, according to agreement, an American flagged Alliance spaceship, just like the *Vorpal Blade*. Which means she needs an *American* CO."

"Frankly, sir," Prael said, looking around at the assembled officers. "If you want a suggestion, Captain Wea—"

"I was told that if everything looked right, the commanding officer had already been decided, Captain," Spectre said, cutting him off. "Given the actions in this system, the *Thermopylae* is yours. She'll remain in this system to help the Hexosehr convert the Tree to an advanced base for the Alliance and as local defense. The Karchava did a fine job, but the Hexosehr had a few fillips on fusion and drive tech they didn't, so she's about ten percent faster and twenty percent more powerful than the original. She also has new hull plating, so she'll take a pounding and keep coming. I think she just proved that last one."

"Thank you, sir," Prael said. "But I really think . . ."

"Decision's final," Blankemeier said. "Besides, Weaver's going to be busy fixing the *Blade* and training a *new* captain."

"It's my lot in life," Weaver said, sighing.

"Once the Hexosehr are up and running, we'll seed the whole system, and especially the jump points, with spider mines," Spectre said, rubbing his hands together. "Between that and the Tree, this solar system is going to be well nigh impregnable. And with the space dock already constructed, the Hexosehr can get to work on ships right away. Then there are the captured converts, three more dreadnoughts. As I said, I'll have a fleet soon enough. Just one thing. Miss Moon?"

"I do not want to be stuck on a space station for the rest of my life," Miriam said.

"Can you train someone else to use the system?" Spectre asked kindly. "Pretty please?"

"You'll need someone trained as a singer," Miriam said. "And a back-up band. And they'll have to be . . . Actually, I don't know."

"We'll hold auditions," Spectre said, nodding. "Shuttle people out here to test them out. We'll find somebody. You're too valuable to leave here, even *with* the importance of this system."

"Thank you," Miriam said, dimpling.

"There are a thousand issues with this plan, sir," Bill said. "Personnel?"

"Put gates in orbit," the admiral said. "Not direct to Earth, obviously, but we can bounce them through a couple of planets and mine those. Personnel and comestibles can be transferred through those and shuttled in with Hexosehr shuttles."

"And the station can't stop the Dreen from approaching Earth," Bill continued.

"It will be a hell of a thorn in their side," Spectre said. "We can build fleets right here, fill them with personnel gated in from Earth and Adar. Even if the Dreen come through, we'll be hitting their supply lines the whole time. And they won't be able to hit ours. And if the Hexosehr can crack some of this technology, well . . ."

"I see you've given this some thought, Admiral," Bill said, grinning. "Last two: Are the Hexosehr planning on repairing the *Blade*? Again?"

"Yes," the admiral said. "We've got the better part of a factory ship onboard the *Thermopylae*. They'll be starting as soon as they get their fabbers and bots set up."

"Then I would suggest they do so in space rather than in the Tree, sir," Bill said. "Really seriously suggest."

"Noted," Spectre said, frowning quizzically but not asking for clarification. "Last item, Captain?"

"*No* J-pop."

The Following is an excerpt from:

The Sorceress of Karres

Eric Flint
Dave Freer

Available from Baen Books
January 2010
hardcover

Chapter 1

Threbus looked more than a little alarmed at the sudden appearance of the slitty little silver-eyed vatches all around them. "I suppose . . . these are the kind that can't be handled by your mother?" he asked of Goth, his middle daughter. The tone was faintly hopeful. The expression was not.

His daughter shook her head. "I reckon not. Captain, how about you? You're a real wizard with vatches."

Pausert considered the problem. It seemed clear enough that the little fragments of otherwhere, pieces of impossible whirling blackness called vatches, had appeared because of Pausert. Pausert was a vatch-handler, a vatch negotiator, he who had done the impossible, and made friends with the creatures who were normally puppeteers playing with humans for a sort of dreamlike amusement. It would seem that there was such a thing as too much success.

Eventually, he shook his head. "If I tried and failed—

even on one, it'd be pretty fatal. I think we're going to have to learn to co-operate with them, Threbus."

"How?"

"Rather like one deals with the Leewit," said Pausert.

Threbus groaned. "One does not deal with my youngest daughter, Pausert. One merely tries to limit the damage and then distract her."

Captain Pausert, who had had plenty of experience of the Leewit, grinned at his great-uncle. "Yes. That's it, I think."

Threbus took a deep breath. "Pausert, you have repaid us for what we did to you."

Because of the Karres witches, Captain Pausert had been though more near-death experiences than he cared to think about at any one sitting. He patted his great-uncle—and future father-in-law, if Goth had her way—on the shoulder. "I hope so. It was a bit rough at first. But I wouldn't have missed it for all the worlds in the Empire."

"More to the point the Empire wouldn't have survived, without you getting through it," said Threbus.

Pausert nodded. "I understand that . . . now. And I wonder if the vatches are not doing the same thing for Karres."

Threbus looked thoughtful. "You can hardly have spoken to the precog teams, Pausert. It's because of what they're seeing that we're glad you came back here so quickly. They've been giving us worrying and confused views of the future. Not all good, either. I wonder if this is another klatha talent starting to manifest in you?"

"Nope," said Pausert. He'd been through enough of the otherworldly klatha development phases to recognize that feeling. "Just common sense. Karres has faced two terrible dangers. Been all that stood between man and Manaret, and between the Empire and the nanite plague."

"Could be," said Goth slowly, "that Karres, just by existing, draws trouble."

Captain Pausert felt an eerie prickle at the back of his skull. Some kind of klatha force was at work here.

It was plain that Threbus felt it too. "We can't exactly stop existing. We've always operated, if not in secret, at least not obtrusively. We could hide back in time or something . . ."

Goth shook her head, her high forehead wrinkled in concentration. "It wouldn't make any difference. Whatever causes this is like Big Windy the vatch. I reckon it's not limited to space or time as we know them. Not even this dimension. Manaret and Moander were pulled from somewhere else. Another dimension, thousands of complicated dimensions away . . . they *thought* it was by accident. But what if it wasn't?"

"I'd say we're in trouble. Again," said Captain Pausert, shrugging. "We're getting quite good at that."

"Clumping right," said the Leewit, arriving suddenly in their midst. "What are all these stinkin' little vatches doing here? Where is Little-bit? She's okay. I didn't invite all these other ones."

"Perhaps she's here, somewhere. It's a bit confusing," said Pausert.

"Well, go away, you lot," said the Leewit to the vatch-swarm. "Or I'll whistle at you. I don't know if it'll bust you up. You want to find out, huh? Anyway, Pa, I came to tell you Maleen is here at the palace."

Threbus brightened perceptibly. He was a fair man, Pausert knew. He never played favorites among his daughters. But he plainly had a soft spot for Maleen, his oldest child. "If they won't go away," he said, looking at the vatches, "I suppose that we could."

The Leewit looked warily at her father. "Not the Egger route . . ."

There was a boom as air rushed in to fill the space. The vatches flickered and rippled around where the four Karres witches had been moments before. They'd find them again of course. They had their flavor.

Chapter 2

"I didn't know that it was possible to teleport that sort of mass," said Captain Pausert, impressed.

Goth squeezed her father's hand. "Oh, yes. So long as you've got a hot witch doing it, it works pretty well."

Threbus wiped his brow. "If the range is not particularly great, I can manage large amounts of mass. But I'm pretty well limited to a few hundred yards. A group of us can manage a few miles."

"Still a pretty hot witch," said Goth. "I can only do a couple of pounds."

Threbus smiled. "You've got the range on me though. And you're young yet. When I was your age I had just started to discover a few klatha powers but they were so slight that I didn't actually believe they were real."

"That must have been just as well on Nikkeldepain," said Captain Pausert, thinking of his home planet. It was a very conservative and traditional place. Quite stuffy in a lot of ways. Karres witch tricks would not be happily received there.

The thought made him chuckle a little. Most of the people of Nikkeldepain would be horrified by the company he was now keeping. It had not been the easiest place to grow up in, in some ways. Not if one was just a little bit out of the ordinary. Captain Pausert could see now that might easily have been the start of his own klatha manifestations. But it had given him enough trouble at school, and later in the Nikkeldepain space navy.

That, and the infamy of his great-uncle Threbus, the very man who had just teleported them. It had been difficult growing up in the shadow of the stories about great-uncle Threbus. Harder because he'd never known quite where to stand on it all. His mother had always stood up for her strange uncle, in spite of what people said. Pausert had had a few bitter fights about it at school. He'd always held out that the stories had to be exaggerated. Now he had to wonder whether it had not been Nikkeldepain that had been the victim, not his eccentric great uncle.

They were joined by Maleen, who was with a young man Pausert didn't know. Pausert hadn't seen much of Maleen since the day that he had left the three witches of Karres back on their home planet after rescuing them from slavery on the Empire world of Porlumma. He'd always been a little suspicious about that. The witches were certainly capable of rescuing themselves from most situations. Maleen was a precognitive Karres witch— which gave him enough ground for extreme suspicion.

Precog was not an exact science. But it was good enough for her to have prepared a tray of drinks for them. Tall green Lepti liquor for Captain Pausert and her father, and a pale frothy brew for her two sisters. When Pausert had last seen her, Maleen had been a pretty blonde teenage girl. It made him sharply aware of the passage of years to see that she was now definitely a young woman.

"Captain," she said proudly, taking the young man's hand possessively, "this is Neldo. My husband."

Pausert extended his hand. "Pleased to meet you." Well, she had said that she would be of marriageable age in two years, Karres time. Pausert was still not too sure just how long a Karres month was. But he, together with Goth and little sister, the Leewit, had been on quite a number of adventures since then. Come to think of it, he wasn't entirely sure how many months it had all taken.

Neldo shook his hand warmly. "I've heard a lot about you." Then he turned to his father-in-law. "Maleen has got some great news."

"We're going to have a baby!" said Maleen excitedly.

Threbus beamed and hugged both of them. "Would it be too much to expect for a precog to have some idea what sex it's going to be?"

Maleen blushed. "You know we're not supposed to do that kind of thing."

"So you got Kerris, or one of the others, to do it for you," said Goth, grinning.

Maleen and Neldo smiled at each other. "You might be right. We might even know what we've decided to call her."

The Leewit stood in front of them, her arms folded. "There is only one 'the Leewit.'"

Maleen laughed. "We know that. And it still didn't put us off having children. Her name will be Vala."

"Why?" asked Goth.

"We don't know," answered Maleen. "It's not a name that either of us had ever heard before."

Captain Pausert was a little taken aback by the name. It brought back a flood of memories which he had thought were gone for ever. "I knew a Vala once, back on Nikkeldepain."

Goth looked suspiciously at him. "You said that . . . sort of funny. Who was this Vala?"

"Just a girl I knew when I was growing up." Pausert had a bad feeling his ears were starting to grow slightly red.

"I bet she was your sweetheart, Captain," Maleen sniggered. "Hope she was better than that insipid girl, what was her name, Illyla."

"She wasn't a bit like Illyla," said Captain Pausert reminiscently. "Actually, if anything she was more like Goth. Except that she had red hair and was a bit older. She got me into a fair amount of trouble, but I don't remember that I minded too much. Like the lattice ship that came to Nikkeldepain at about that time. She was one of those people that you never really forget. Oh well, it was long ago. It's a beautiful name. I'm glad you chose it."

"Huh!" said Goth, looking at Pausert from under her dark brows. "Anyway, I've never had much time for babies, not until they grow up a bit."

Toll came in. "And then they turn into something like

the Leewit," she said, looking at her youngest daughter and smiling.

The Leewit shrugged. "Babies are no fun anyway. I have decided that I'm going to stay with the captain for the next while. Things happen around him. And he takes pretty good care of us. Makes us wash behind our ears even."

That last was plainly something that she felt was a little unnatural. Pausert had to smile to himself. The Leewit was a handful to deal with, but at least he felt that he was dealing with a child, even if he knew very little about how to do so. With Goth he was less certain. She was growing up. Fast.

According to the Karres precogs this was going to be a very important year for Goth. The year had started with their departure from the Governor's palace on Green Galaine, on a life or death mission to escort the Nartheby Sprite Hantis and her Grik-dog Pul to the Imperial Palace. Of course no one had seen fit to tell him that the trip was going to be quite as risky as it had turned out to be. It had been a period during which the captain's own klatha skills had grown immeasurably. But although Goth had matured, he could honestly not say that it had been that much of an important year for her development. Except . . . . they still had a couple of months to go. Pausert could not help but be a bit nervous as to what they might bring her.

A little later, when Goth had gone off with her sisters, Pausert broached the subject of his next mission with Toll and Threbus. His relationship with the Witches of Karres was an interesting one. At least in theory, Captain Pausert was just an independent trader, with a fast armed merchant ship. But in practice he was part of the community of Karres. That was more about a willingness to do what was needed, than merely a reference to your citizenship or place of birth. And if Karres needed him, he was willing.

"The Chaladoor," said Threbus, referring to a dangerous and mysterious region of space, the lair of pirates, the Megair Cannibals . . . at one time of Manaret and the Nuri globes lurking within the Tark Nembi cluster of dead suns and interstellar dust and debris.

"Oh?" said Captain Pausert warily. He'd survived one crossing of Chaladoor. Admittedly, he'd been in more danger from those inside his ship—spies and the notorious Agandar—than from forces outside it.

"There is something going on in that area of space. Since Manaret was destroyed, quite a few ships have risked the crossing. And none of them have made it. The Daal of Uldune has also thought to expand his power in that direction . . . And he has been repulsed."

Pausert raised his eyebrows. He knew the hexaperson that was the cloned and telepathic ruler of the one-time pirate world rather well. Sedmon the Sixth was not a trivial foe. The Empire still trod warily around him, and the forces at his command. Whatever the danger was that lurked in the Chaladoor, it was something serious. "You . . . want me to do what, exactly?"

"You will be a kind of bait, to be honest, Pausert," said Threbus. "All we want you to do is encounter the problem, and then run away as fast as you and the Sheewash drive can manage. The Chaladoor is a large, complex region.

Karres could hunt for some years without encountering whatever the problem is. Problems tend to avoid whole worlds which are also spacecraft."

He looked at his grand nephew with a twinkle. "And we do really mean 'run', Pausert. You've proved yourself far more than just capable with problems. And you've taken good care of my daughters in the process. But not with something that was big enough to deal with eight of the Daal's cruisers and a battle wagon. They barely had time to say they were under attack on sub-radio, before being destroyed. Whatever it is, it is no easy foe to deal with."

Threbus cleared his throat and continued. "You have a ship which is very nearly the equal of a single cruiser anyway, as far as speed and detection equipment is concerned. We'll have it refitted with some more of the very latest equipment, at our expense. Your armaments are not quite to the same standard, but they are certainly up to holding off an enemy until you can engage the Sheewash drive. Now that you have also mastered the drive, and with Goth and the Leewit to help you in emergencies, we think you should be able to deal with running away. Leave us to the clean up!"

"You wouldn't take unnecessary risks with the girls anyway," said Toll, smiling. "My daughter has already made her plans for you. And you wouldn't be foolish enough to try and spoil them now, would you?"

Goth's plans were to marry the captain as soon as she was of marriageable age. At first the captain had not taken her terribly seriously—just as Threbus had apparently not taken Toll's similar plan too seriously. And see where it had got Threbus! As time had gone on and Pausert and Goth had shared adventure and danger together, Pausert had come to realize that he was very fond of her too. But he was a normal man, and she wasn't yet properly grown up.

Yet . . . the witches did have some other avenues open to them. He knew that Threbus must be at least eighty years old by now. Yet he looked to be no more than in his mid-thirties. He also knew from what they had learned on Uldune that Toll too could change her age at will. As they turned to leave, Pausert cleared his throat and braced himself to ask, "Er. Toll. About age shifts . . ."

Toll turned back and raised one eyebrow at him, with a quizzical half-amused, half-dangerous expression on her face. "What?" she said, in a way that would have made most men say "oh nothing. Nothing at all." But Pausert was quite brave. Or quite stupid. He was not too sure which of he two he was being right now.

"I was wondering," he said, "about, well, the age shift thing."

Toll smiled. "Oddly enough, Goth's been raising the same subject lately. The answer is 'no,' Captain Pausert. Compared to Nikkeldepain our way of raising children may seem a little strange to you. Karres children are very independent. They have to be. But, captain, they are still children, and need to go through stages of development, just like any other child. There are a number of important formative experiences Goth still has to go through. We did not let our children go with you lightly, Captain Pausert. We have ways of knowing that you are absolutely trustworthy. And anyway, because of the parent-pattern in their heads, we're around in a way, even when we're not."

Captain Pausert had encountered the Toll pattern in Goth. He'd wished that he too could have a resident instructor and mentor, sometimes. But Karres had decided that he was best left to learn on his own. "I've always done my best for them all," he said. "And if you think that is best for Goth, then we will just have to let it all happen at its own speed."

Toll patted his shoulder. "And it will. Take a step back from it, if you can. Age shift is one of the things we don't teach the young witches. Every single child among them wants to be grown up instantly. What child doesn't? Well, we found that although they can cope very easily with the physical changes in their bodies, it's not the same with their minds. Only time seems to achieve that properly." She cocked her head slightly and smiled. "See, it wouldn't just be an older Goth . . . my middle daughter is quite an old soul in a young body sometimes. But can you imagine what it would be like if the Leewit could suddenly choose to be grown up, or at least have a grown-up body?"

That was quite a thought! "Could make applying a piece of tinklewood fishing rod adapted to be a switch very interesting," said the captain. "I think I see your point. I don't think the galaxy is quite ready for that yet."

"Goth, you're being a dope," said the Leewit. "Isn't she, Maleen?"

"Shut up," said Goth. "It's more complicated than you understand, you little bollem."

Maleen, looking down on her younger sisters with the

vast tolerance of an older, and now married woman, smiled. "Don't you like the captain any more, the Leewit?"

The Leewit looked affronted. "He's not a bad old dope. Okay. He's not even so old. And he's not really a dope. I like him quite a lot, actually. He's good to have around especially when things go wrong. But I don't see what Goth's all upset about." She sniffed. "And don't tell me that she's not, because she is."

Goth gave her a look that would have sent sensible wildlife running. "It's your baby's fault," she said to Maleen.

"I didn't tell you everything Kerris and the other precogs said about her."

"Don't know if I want to hear," said Goth crossly.

Maleen put a hand on Goth's shoulder and pushed her down into a chair. "Well, you should. Because it is important. I need to talk to Toll and Threbus about it too, but I couldn't with Captain Pausert there."

"Why? What did they say?"

"Pausert's going on a mission to Chaladoor."

"I know that. We leave . . ."

"Except that you're not going to be with him," said Maleen.

Goth shook her head. "He needs me around. He doesn't have a pattern in his mind to guide him through the klatha stuff. And he . . . experiments. Look what happened with the Egger route. We ended up back in time. He'll get hurt or killed, for sure, if I am not there."

Goth knew full well that Captain Pausert had actually done all right a couple of times without her. But a girl had keep an eye on her man. And she was double uncertain right now. That episode was well back in his past, but she was not ignorant and naive enough not to know that the captain had given his heart to this Vala. Also, his tone said that she'd meant something very different to him than his former fiancÈe Illyla.

Illyla, Goth could deal with, just like she'd dealt with Sunnat. This Vala . . .

Goth hadn't liked his reverent tone. And she didn't like the fact that, in a way, the girl couldn't have been much older than Goth was now, when she got her claws into the captain. Well. He wouldn't have been a captain then. But still.

"You know what precog is like, Goth. No one ever sees the whole picture, but they do see what they see, right? And this is what Kerris said. You—Goth, nobody else— have got to do this or else he's not just going to get killed. It'd be like he never was. It's got something to do with what is going on in the Chaladoor."

Goth took a deep breath. "You tell me all that you know right now, Maleen." This was much more serious than some old girlfriend he'd never got over.

"Well, you know precogs measure might-be's. They predicted Vala's name. We both heard it and loved it . . . and they said that it was really important that she be called that. And they said that some power from the Chaladoor was going to murder Captain Pausert."

"What!" Goth leapt to her feet. "We could dismind him, like Olimy. Or he could put himself in a cocoon like he put the Leewit and me in . . ."

"And it happened when he was fifteen," said Maleen.

"There is a ninety eight point probability that he died before he ever left Nikkeldepain. Maybe some enemy figured out then it was a good idea to get rid of him before he developed any klatha powers. Before he had Goth and Karres to protect him."

Goth said several words that even shocked the Leewit.

"The captain will wash your mouth out with soap!" said the youngest witch, primly, as if she herself did not delight in using terms that would make a docker blush. Although she was usually careful to do so in a language that Captain Pausert could not understand. Her klatha gifts ran to the ability to translate and speak any language.

"Not unless you tell him, he won't. And I'll make you swim back to Karres on the Egger route if you do," said Goth. "You're going to have to look after him in the Chaladoor, little sister. I'm going to have to go and deal with this."

The Leewit nodded, wide eyed, looking at her sister. It was going to be quite a task. But that was pure Karres. If something needed doing, you did it. Karres people weren't much good at waiting for someone else to take the responsibility. "How are you going to get there?" she asked.

Goth gritted her teeth. "The Egger route. And there's not going to be anyone else to help me at the other end either."

That could be nasty. Really nasty. But by the look on Goth's face that wasn't going to stop her for an instant.

"I think you'd better talk it over with Toll and Threbus first," said Maleen. "And this may not be the perfect time."

Goth took a deep breath. "I am not going to be able to sleep unless . . . isn't this a paradox? Like, he must have survived or we wouldn't have met him?"

Maleen bit her lip. "You'd think so. But all precog could give us was that somehow they avoided the time paradox."

"Time is too complicated to play around with lightly," said the voice of Goth's Toll pattern, issuing from her lips. "Dimensionality comes into it."

They went to find Threbus and Toll. And, not surprisingly found them in consultation with several of the senior precogs. "You know the prediction that it was important that you spent the next year with my grand nephew Pausert?" said her father. "We've got a little more clarity on that."

"We're trying to establish the precise dates right now," said Toll. "But you will be leaving on the *Venture* with him, and then we think you're going to have to jump to the past, via the Egger route."

"I worked that out," said Goth, gruffly. "Been talking to Maleen. But why can't I just go now?"

"Because the flight schedules have been published and we are still trying to establish exactly when you have to go to, Goth. We have established you do . . . or did go back to Nikkeldepain. We have only one other insight, Goth. A lattice ship."

The Leewit bounced. "Yay! I want to go too! I want go too! I love the circus!"

"Well, you can't," said Goth firmly. "I need you to keep an eye on the captain. Anyway, you're the only one beside him that seems to be able to do anything with those little vatches."

Threbus grunted. "We need them to clean out nannite-infected people. But the follow-up on that has been a bit chaotic. It seems that they only do things because they like Pausert. We don't really have any way of motivating them."

"Little-bit likes me too," said the Leewit cheerfully. "I got used to her."

As if the vatch had known she was being spoken about, the tiny fleck of blackness with the hint of silver eyes appeared, flickering around the room. **Hello big ones. I have taken the others to watch a play. They like them nearly as much as I do.**

Goth chuckled. "I guess you've got your motivation."

Threbus nodded thoughtfully. "There are going to be a lot of traveling players visiting the outlying provinces of the Empire in the next while."

"On an imperial cultural uplift programme," said Toll smiling. "I'll have some words with Dame Ethy and Sir Richard."

"Should be pretty interesting with that sort of audience! They'd better not let the shows get stale or the little things will liven 'em up," said Goth. "But it could work."

Threbus nodded. "I like it. It gives us something the vatches want. The other issue with the nannites is that we've had the imperial scientists working non-stop on the material—dead material so far. They haven't given us anything to use to combat the plague, other than a possible repellant. But they have said that they're absolutely sure that the plague is an artificial creation.

The nannites were engineered. Made. They were programmed to do what they did."

There was a moment of silence. "That's a pretty powerful enemy."

Threbus nodded. "And one that has been around for a very long time. Working on records from the Sprites of Nartheby, the plague came from somewhere toward the galactic center. We, of course, probably weren't the targets. But it could be that something in there knows that their plague has been defeated."

"So they might be getting the next attack ready."

Threbus rubbed his jaw. "It's also, in a way, why humanity were able to expand off old Yarthe with such ease. We found so many habitable planets with traces of old alien civilizations on them, but no other existent aliens, except for the Sprites on Nartheby. But we have to face the possibility that the nannite plague might just have been the alien equivalent of a pest-exterminator, cleaning up before the new occupants got there. And the nannite problem won't just go away. It's with us for the foreseeable future. Even if we track down and destroy every nannite in the Empire, they could still be hidden away some-where—inside or outside the Empire, in the smallest colony, and could burst out again. We're going to have to be vigilant. And get people used to having Grik-dogs to smell out the nannite exudates being something they must have."

"Well, at least I like Grik-dogs," said Goth. "And I guess keeping an eye out for nannites will also mean that we're ready for other problems."

Threbus nodded. "We're going to be stretched pretty

thin though, for the next few years. We'll have to keep Karres people undercover, scattered around. And Karres itself will probably keep a low profile. We will have to find ourselves a new sun to orbit, because the planet will be top of their target list."

"I reckon," said Goth. "And we like the old place."

Chapter 3

Pausert was not prepared for Goth to sniff loudly and retreat, when he made a joke about his lousy take-off, instead of teasing him. The captain was almost sure she was in tears. But he couldn't leave the navigation controls just then to follow her and find out what was wrong. When she came back, her face looking recently washed, he started to ask. But she waved the question away.

She remained taciturn for the rest of the day—and all of the next, and the next. By then, Pausert was really starting to worry.

He tried to pry the Leewit, to see if she knew anything. But the little witch seemed to be in one of her non-cooperative moods.

By then, they were approaching the Chaladoor, and Pausert had something else to worry about.

❈ ❈ ❈

Neldo stopped vibrating after a while, and started breathing. "Touch-talk," he gasped, just as soon he had enough breath. "The things I do for love. Maleen couldn't come because of the baby. And I've had a team of witches damping the klatha output. We hope that Pausert is unaware of this, but I need to be quick."

Goth put her hands against him, and made contact with Maleen. "What have you got for me?" she demanded.

"Quite a lot. We tracked back the date a lattice ship last landed on Nikkeldepain. And discovered that a girl called Vala, the daughter of Sutherb and Lotl, was a student at the Nikkeldepain Academy for the Sons and Daughters of Gentlemen and Officers, for six months in the same year. Got a picture of her from a yearbook. It's you, all right. But your hair is curled and red. I've sent curling tongs and the dye that mother thought best match, with Neldo. You'll have to light-shift it a bit longer at first, but long term it's easier not to have to do light shift all the time. Oh, and here's a safe set of co-ordinates for you to go to— an impression of a place on Nikkeldepain. Father supplied that."

The image flooded into her mind. "Suberth and . . .?"

"Mother and father, you dope," said the Leewit. Complex codes were obvious to her. Mere anagrams were a joke.

"Oh. Yeah."

"The Leewit. You need to know seeing as Goth isn't going to be here. Someone is spending huge amounts of money on finding the *Venture* 7333. Offering a small fortune for her flight times and schedules. Whatever is happening in Chaladoor has fingers in crime in the rest of the Empire. We're digging for whoever has put up the money. But, even by Karres standards, they've been spending it like water. And the odd thing is they have a description of someone who looks a lot like mother, that they're also looking for."

"What's so odd about that?"

"The person has wavy red hair, and her name is Vala."

Goth put on as many layers as she could. The Egger route was tough on the body. The captain thought that he had some way to stop the vibration, but she couldn't ask him about it now. Anyway, his klatha skills were very powerful . . . and a bit scary and off the wall.

The Leewit was oddly silent during the whole process. A little wide-eyed and apprehensive. The Leewit *really* did not like the Egger route. Actually, Goth didn't like it much herself.

"Well," she said, taking a deep breath and fixing the touch-talk mental co-ordinates in her mind, "Here goes. Look after the captain for me, Leewit. And don't forget to wash behind your ears."

"I won't," said the Leewit, not arguing for once in her life, her voice a little small.